The Alien Club

When everything is your first, you're an alien.

9-30

Dear Sharon,

As a tree falling in the woods does not exist if it falls on deaf ears, a self-evident truth does not exist if we choose to turn a blind eye.

Great art creates a portal to the soul that overwhelms the senses, flooding the subconscious, thus provoking pure, naked thought into e

ISBN # 978-0-9971513-1-2

The Alien Club

Written by Trel W. Sidoruk

Illustrated by Aleksandra Klepacka

Edited by Lauren Sidoruk

Assistant Editors
Isabella Rose Sidoruk
&
Andrea Torrillo

Dedication

I have many to thank for whom I've become, but it's my beautiful wife, who is also my best friend and editor, as well as my three amazing children, Isabella Rose, Madison Joy, and Logan Trel, who make me want to be more than I am. For them and myself I wrote this book.

Though I wrote it for them, this book would not have been possible without my first family, all of whom have since left our planet for the greater journey. I never could have been the father, friend, and husband I am today without their love and unfiltered humor.

Libra, my Wonder Twin and greatest loss, the irony of your nickname, Sister Soul, would become painfully apparent once a piece of my soul died along with you. I have never accepted your death, which I've been told is paramount to the healing process, but in my defense, my fear is that I won't be able to keep you alive in what's left of me until I die. Thank you for always watching my back, lifting me up, and through your death, solidifying a truth I long since had suspected to be true —

'Tis better to have loved and lost than never to have loved at all. -
Alfred Lord Tennyson

Table of Contents

Prologue
Summer Sizzle

The summer of 1979 didn't go down as the hottest summer in history, most likely because the east coast didn't have sweeping blackouts or the accompanying riots that usually ensue in the inner cities. Nor did the summer break any records of major significance. And come to think of it, Long Island, which is where I'm from, didn't even have a summer that extended well into October, or a drought that destroyed the potato and corn crops.

Matter of fact, the summer of '79 was a tale of two summers. And though the first part of the summer didn't break records for heat or rain, it did have the highest 'miserable' index anyone could remember. An oppressively hot and steam-sauna humid affair that drained the soul of all living things, including the sun, which knelt to the horizon in a pool of its own blood each evening, eagerly awaiting the perpetually tardy moon to relieve it for the upcoming night shift.

Resources were tapped on a statewide level, from police and firefighters, to the actual water table itself, which in turn, meant local authorities had kept nonessential water services to a minimum, thus the yards of my neighborhood never looked so bleak. Cars were so dirty, many looked abandoned; once lush lawns were now brown, flowers wilted, and vegetable gardens were left fallow, no longer even weeded. The resulting water and enthusiasm shortages made the properties look even sadder than the humans they housed.

Our house was especially downtrodden in the first half of summer, for it wasn't until '84 that our next door neighbors, the

Kreagans, purchased central air, meaning we'd have to wait five more years before we inherited their old window unit. Thus, the only reprieve from the heat happened twice a day. Once in the morning and once before bedtime, my father would turn on our house's massive attic fan and suck in as much air as his cheap ass would allow for the maximum allotted time of fifteen minutes, effectively making the outside ambient temperature our thermostat.

Therefore, if the outside temperature was 92 degrees, that's all you could hope for, which was markedly better than the current inside temperature that usually hovered well above 102 degrees. In preparation for the "Big Suck" as my father so affectionately referred to it, we'd open every window and door in the house and allow the powerful fan to blow-dry the sweat and stank off every square inch of our electrolyte depleted flesh vessels.

On the most soul-wilting of days, my mother would line the kitchen windows with various frozen goods in hopes of lowering the incoming temperature by one or two degrees. Whether one stood in the kitchen, and bravely inhaled the damp, wafting cocktail of frozen pea soup and concentrated orange juice, or stood on the cold tile floor of a bathroom, all stood and faced a window with arms and heads raised, making sure maximum body and clothing surfaces were dried in the short reprieve. With eyes closed to keep the powerful winds from drying them out, one couldn't help but meditate. I remember on more than one occasion envisioning what an inmate must endure during the waning moments of his one break a day outside his cell. *Return to the bed you made and lie in it. Lights out!* As fleeting as the fifteen minutes of sweatlessness was, the time between seemed like an eternity. No one rode their bikes, or played sports or games. Instead, with shoulders slumped, foreheads scanned feet shuffling to and fro places of shade, displaying the decisiveness of leaves blowing in the wind.

Then the rains came—three solid days of it. Pounding rains from a tropical storm that forged its way up the coast. It had made it to the Island with such force and determination that it was exhausted by the third day and needed three additional days of rest before it could mosey its way up to Vermont. And as God rested on the seventh day and looked lovingly on his beautiful creation, the seventh day of our Island's rebirth was the most beautiful day not officially on record, and still is to this day.

The week of August 10th was a time for celebrations and backyard barbeques. Every get-together, party, function and game that had been put on indefinite hold was crammed into that week. At the center of my world was the one pool in the neighborhood. The Pelagatti's had an above-ground oval, ten feet by twenty-five feet, which managed to sap what was left of the sun's summer fury.

Hot, wet and salty was a visceral affair one experienced when seven Kool-Aid-logged children shared a large tub for a day's refresher. Salty was the result of a hard day's sweat and wasn't much harder to swallow than the over-chlorinated cocktail that kept the human feces at bay. An occasional super-heated jet stream emanating from the same corner your best friend was comatose in, only intensified the pointless games and frenetic frolics. Being that Christian Pelagatti, aka Kring - short for Kris Kringle - was one of my two best friends, life was good, for once we left his lavish bathing facilities, we were afforded ice cold drinks in his house, which was kept at an FDA-approved temperature for storing meats.

Our neighborhood was a thriving metropolis, packed with parents, parties, pets, and politics. Once the weather changed for the good, the social explosion was clear as day, even throughout the night. So was the exodus of youth to all places outdoors. Kids flocked to the streets and backyards, playing whatever game or sport that could be organized the quickest. I played like a gambler on a hot streak using his wedding ring as collateral. Whatever was available was my game, and I planned on winning or not going home. I wasn't alone of course, and just like the casino, the House always won—meaning playing in a neutral territory was always preferred.

Being that territories were now being explored at a rate not seen since the discovery of America, Wilder's Woods had become the Wild West. Wilder's was a twenty-seven acre wooded lot, which was purchased by the man who created 3D film and left to his widow upon his death, sometime in the last century. It abutted our street, La Rue (which is French for *The Road)* and several other streets around us. Thus, Wilder's became a small city, like the gold-rush towns in the West that connected various settlements throughout the foothills of the Rockies. Wilder's was even wilder than the name would connote. A trading post where all forms of debauchery were shined upon, from drinking and smoking to pornography and thievery.

As was the case in the Wild West, posses were the only true form of justice in Wilder's, thus safety in numbers was paramount to one's enjoyment of all that The Woods afforded a well-heeled, outdoor enthusiast. Thus, kids, like the gambling that had erupted in The Woods, were a numbers game, and since greater numbers delineated greater freedom, safety and power, clubs had become the political lay of the land. Power was at a premium as it always is when new lands meet new people. There must be a top rung to every ladder, a point to every pyramid, an alpha male for every pack.

I, just like all the kids on the block, had visions of grandeur, but unlike the average snot-sucking sissy sizing me up, I had the brains and charisma to actualize those dreams. I also had the ear of the little person portion of our neighborhood. I carried their hopes and dreams like a covered wagon heading west—a true representative of the people.

It was all going smashing well until Jim Kreagan, my other best friend, quashed my latest attempt at unifying the belts, when he unceremoniously cut me from the band that I had started and lead-sang for before my voice cracked. Though painful, the timing couldn't have been more propitious, for I was done playing second fiddle to Jim, who'd become corrupted by his newfound power, like the kings who wore Sauron's rings.

Chapter 1
From Outrage to Center Stage

I had charisma in spades and a sharp intellect, to boot. And though my witty, self-deprecating, cavalier personality would one day win me my fair share of friends and females, starting out in white suburbia with a black man's name, Trel, was not helped by the fact that I had a massive orange afro. Though my name and nappy hair were as black as you got, my blotchy, butt-white, freckled skin, wrapped over a frail, baby fat body composition, and subpar athletic skills, were anything but.

My superior intellect and sizable height advantage over the average ten-year-old fooled many adults into believing I was in my early teens. I wasn't a teenager of course, but that didn't stop me from hanging out with them every chance I got. And being one of the younglings meant I was continually fighting an uphill battle for a say in the day's events. Therefore, it meant the world to me not to be picked last for a game, sport or club, and thus I was willing and able to do anything asked of me in order to make and stay on the team. After years of teasing, taunting, and tribulations triggered by the chasm in age, I knew that the team I needed to stay on and lead was Team Trel, which meant I needed to create a fan base fast.

The problem was, my immediate neighborhood was comprised mostly of kids much older than me, therefore I needed to figure out a way to brainwash them into accepting me as their supreme leader. After years of deliberating my dilemma, I came to the conclusion that war was the great unifier. When the threat of war is imminent, people oddly enough begin to expect more of each other and less of their leaders—less brains, experience, morals, ethics, vision, etc.... Really, less is more in some regards for some apparent reason when a new leader is selected, thus my lesser age seemed to plausibly paint the picture of a powerful President, presiding over the expansion of Wilder's Woods.

Regardless of who you're going to war with or against, if you're going, it can't hurt to have a face that can launch a thousand ships. And while neither Jim nor I would ever be the best-looking guy in the room, we did possess a face that instilled both dreams and nightmares in enemy and ally alike with a simple glance. The Alien doll from the epic science fiction tour de force movie of the century, *The Alien*, was an eighteen-inch-tall, 1/5 scale, perfect replica of the Alien. What's more? The Alien doll came equipped with a slick lever that protruded from its back. When pressed, the Alien's mouth would open, and its second mouth would lunge forward and snap, accompanied by a sickly scream that silenced a room faster than nails on a chalkboard.

The doll served several functions within our club, from a recruitment tool, to the equivalent of the Conch Shell from *The Lord of the Flies*, whereas only the bearer, how temporary that may have been, was afforded the floor to speak or preach whatever was on his mind, while the second mouth was extended. The doll was also pivotal in our propaganda machine, for when alliances are forged, no one wants to be latched to a loser, so the image of awesome is always paramount to a thriving social hierarchy.

Though naming the club was a byproduct of my brilliance, ownership is nine tenths the law, and since Jim owned the doll, he'd taken control of the club rather quickly by demanding his toy back anytime he wanted to speak or to silence an opposing opinion. After a while, the only thing that interrupted his daily rants, were the orders he barked. I had enough one day, and found myself on the outside looking in, after a one-way argument, which had spiraled out of control from yet another one of Jim's lectures on an insignificant historical footnote in a land that I'd never heard of, became grounds for my unceremonious dismissal.

Forced to leave Jim's garage attic, stripped of my rank and dignity, I was dejected, embarrassed and extremely angry by the bed I'd made, but luckily, not alone, for I still had Kring—and when your best friend's got your back, you can face whatever's before you, and what lay ahead of me was the herculean challenge of once again building an empire from pawn one.

"I can't believe you were kicked out of the club!" Kring exclaimed.

"I resigned," I assured my good friend with the proper levels of disdain in both my voice and stance that would illustrate the nobility of my actions.

"No, no, I know..." Kring's voice purposely faded, along with his interest in pressing me for additional information.

Where I was tall, white, and hairy for a ten-year-old, Kring was short, tan, and hairless for nine. A good mix of Austrian and Southern Italian, Kring was blessed with a disarming cuteness, which he used to get what little he'd have to ask for. Though spoiled, Kring's demeanor kept him from being a brat, which was fortunate for me, since anytime we were in an argument, I was cut off from my toys. Though rarely enraged, Kring had little patience for anything other than success, whether that was conquering a video game, or a political foe; and being my current complaint smelled of failure to him, his interest was waning quickly.

But I was amped and yearned for an audience! "Besides everyone was stealing all my good ideas and saying they were their own."

"That's stone cold wrong," Kring willingly agreed.

"I was the one who said we should use the old shipwreck chest for the main secretary's spot. Jim said it was a dumb idea, and then pulled his, "Oh well whose house are we in? Whose chest is it?" Whatever! Then the very next day Franky says we should make it a desk. And Jim goes to him, right in front of me, mind you-almost looking right at me! "Nice. Put it right up front." Franky asks why and the scumbag tells him so we can have it for a receptionist's desk."

"You have got to be kidding me!?!?!" Kring shouted.

"Totally serious!" I confirmed with fury.

"You said something... I hope," Kring's voice feigning doubt.

"Hell yes I said something!" I assured him. "But he's never wrong!"

"Should of just laid him out," Kring stewed. "You would slaughter him!" He added after some thought.

"I know!" I agreed. And then added, "Oh, so after he tells Franky to move the desk there, he has the balls to order me to help him."

Kring was beside himself, "Come on!"

I once again confirmed the worst, "Seriously!" Then I paused, stiffening my stance and lowering my voice to project the desired effect, "So I just look him the eyes... And then I lost it."

Kring shot up, punching his palm, "Smack down?"

"I was like, 'yesterday I wanted to make this the receptionist's desk', and before I could get out the rest, he called me a crybaby."

Squinting his eyes as if the sun's rays had finally blazed a path through the weathered shingles of the dilapidated shed Kring's father had reconstituted into a treehouse, Kring inquired, "Were you crying?"

I erupted to such wildly outrageous speculation, "Please! I'd never give that bastard the satisfaction. But I was beyond pissed. And I'll admit, I didn't know whether my throat was going to crack before my chest exploded, 'cause I've never wanted to kill someone more than him, at that moment." I paced the perimeter of the 8 x 10 room as I relived the scene.

"But you did nothing..." Kring confirmed more to himself as he checked his laces.

Ignoring Kring's comment, I quickened my pace, while firing off egregious acts and disparaging facts, as if I were reading them from plaques on the walls of a museum. "Constantly pulling the rank thing! He's the president because we're using his parent's garage! It's not even attached to his house! A non-insulated attic above a rundown garage, and he treats it like it's waterfront property, with central AC!"

Eureka tickled Kring and he smiled wide-eyed in return. "We should start our own club," he said simply.

"Yeah, but who'd be in it? You and me?" I offered with little fanfare.

"I guess..." Kring seemed to instantly deflate as the daunting task set before us became painfully apparent.

But then the pawns began to assemble in parade formation and silently beg me for betterment. "Kenny would join. Kenny would be in a sec," I added with a twinkle in my eye.

Kring exclaimed, "We could get Roy to join too!" Quickly visualizing himself in a club with a member who failed to gain membership to a club in thirty-two consecutive initiation tests, made him add with shrugging shoulders, "If you wanted him in, of course."

Roy was your prototypical portly peon in the political landscape. Far larger than the vast majority of kids in the fifth grade, Roy was also painfully fat and suffered from a self-esteem that was crushed under his own weight. The only thing that saved Roy from being bullied by kids half his size on a daily basis, outside of the continuous use of his horrible nickname, "Fat Boy Roy", was his older brother, Bishop, who was ironically the neighborhood bully, and sadly the person most responsible for Roy's complete lack of confidence, other than his drunken and disorderly white-trash of a father, Herman Culver. To add insult to injury, Roy was forced to don a wardrobe of clothes inherited from a second cousin who was two years younger, three-inches shorter and forty pounds lighter, making all of his ensembles borderline child abuse, and thus chum for the school sharks.

"Not yet. I would like to see the outcome of our initial membership drive," I answered as nicely as possible, for Kring and I were brainstorming at this point, and to shun another's idea was to put a halt to the acceptance of all ideas, no matter how great the next idea was—even though Fat Albert had a better chance of hazing the KKK, than Roy Culver had of making any club I was running.

And make no mistake, I was going to run this show, and not just run it, rule it... Rule it with an iron fist!

While taking a mental bathroom break from the epic film, *Visions of Grandeur*, which I personally wrote, directed and starred in, I noticed Kring staring off to the side, cringing, as if knowing the inevitable answer to his poorly perceived proposition, as does a dog begging at a table. "What about Dave?" was all Kring's stored breath could muster before his shoulders collapsed into his lungs. David, Kring's kid brother, was of course far too young, and therefore could not be trusted with such sensitive information as the start of a new secret club.

So when I responded with a decisive, "Done," Kring's face switched expressions as fast as a runaway train switched tracks. Though he still looked off into the distance, it was quite obvious the visions were not of David's hurt feelings, nor the arguments Kring would have to endure on a daily basis convincing his sibling to leave us to our plottings. Instead, Kring's distant stare was filled with the camaraderie induced by epic victories, and the lavish spoils afforded to the conquerors.

"He'll be psyched!" Kring proclaimed. "Plus, we can get away with a lot more, since he'll cover for me, instead of squealing like a pig every time I do something. Plus, he'll help me get much needed supplies."

I knew Kring was happy, but worried I was going to change my mind, therefore he was listing David's positives like a real-estate listing in the Sunday paper. I needed to refocus him and myself, so I cut him off by summarizing David's central role, as well as adding another youngling, which would finally put his worries behind him. "Dave working on the inside? Sounds like a plan. We could get

Karen to help too, and I know my sister will do her part as well. Which means we're at six people and almost as big as the Alien Club before we even open the doors." I clapped my hands hard at the outlook.

Shaking his head, Kring wondered aloud, "The Alien Club... Who thought of that retarded name?" Finishing his sentence, he casually looked to me for my customary comedic response, only to find my lip being swallowed by my mouth's vortex.

"What?" he asked.

"I thought of that name," I said slowly. "But it wasn't stupid when I thought of it," I assured him with more doubt than I hoped.

Searching for an out no doubt, Kring questioned my last statement, "I thought Jim came up with the name?"

Raising my hands as if giving up another argument, "Oh sure, the second time. Once again, spitting my ideas out after the fact, and screwing them up in the process."

"Wait? The name wasn't stupid the first time?" Kring asked in all seriousness.

It was painfully apparent I needed to educate my good friend on not only the origins of the club, but the secret order and the subsequent use of abbreviations that I had brilliantly created, only to have Jim destroy it by trying to make it his own. Kring didn't seem to be as impressed as I thought he should be, and after a good hour of delving into the details, Kring still couldn't piece together why a club without phones needed a receptionist. Truth be told, I didn't want to take too much time discussing what I did, for it kept me from discussing what I was going to do next, and besides, I was done with Jim—for now at least.

"I already have a good name for the club," I said cheerfully to suppress the dankness of spilled milk.

Kring cut me off, "How about NAMBLA?"

"What's that?" I asked somewhat impressed.

Kring shrugged his shoulders, "I don't know, Jim said last week that a bunch of us were NAMBLA material, and they were recruiting or something... Maybe we could be a local chapter? I thought you knew who they were."

"No idea, but I'm sure it's some stupid government organization that does nothing but push paper and raise my dad's taxes."

"What's the name?" Kring asked.

After some thought I decided to hold my Ace, "Nah, it's stupid. Can you think of anything?"

Kring offered, "We could name it after something in D&D?"

"That would work," I inclined, and then added, "Nothing with 'dragon' in it, though."

"Why?" Kring asked.

"Bishop and Roy have that weird club in Wilder's Woods, and either the name or their logo has something do with a dragon."

"When did they change the name?" Kring asked with great interest.

I stopped my pacing once again and considered the brevity of my next statement, "Weird things have been going on in those woods, ever since Bishop started to hang with the kids from the other side."

"Hey what's up with that anyhow?"

"Don't know," I said with a shrug. "We were going to run reconnaissance missions up in Wilder's to find out, but since the fallout, I'm sure those plans, as with all my others... were shelved until Jim can reinstate them as his own later in the week."

"You were going to spy on them?" Kring asked somewhat surprised.

"Actually, I was going to lead a team with you and Kenny," I said sheepishly.

"When were you going to tell me about this?" Kring asked annoyed.

I raised a palm to lower his temperature, "It was top secret."

"Top secret?" Kring mocked.

"Nothing personal, Homeslice," I tried to ensure him to no avail.

"I think it is," Kring answered as he played the scenario back in his head.

"We have a snitch. Correction: they have a snitch. But yeah, there's a snitch in the club, that's for sure."

"Who do you think it is? Wait, you thought it was me?" Kring's voice rose as he feverishly fingered his chest.

"No! No way Bro. Never. Franky or Kurt is my guess, since they both hang with Bishop in The Woods."

"Kurt," Kring said with disdain.

"Most likely. But Jim and I couldn't agree on who not to tell, so we agreed not to tell anyone about it."

Looking to me with a broad smile, "We should go."

Smiling back, "We should."

"Dude, I have an awesome pair of binoculars!"

I raised an eyebrow with a thought, "Spy club?"

Kring's grin was all the approval I needed, so when he added an elongated "Niiiiiice," to my suggestion, I knew we were flying high.

An epiphany had turned all the lights on in the stadium for me while I stood smiling in appreciation of Kring's affirmation. The Alien Club in all its glory could never lead a man to battle, for it had no goals to achieve, nor beliefs to defend, thus it could never justify a means to an end. In essence, The Alien Club was merely a series of tasks we performed to keep ourselves occupied. Our spy club, on the other hand, could actually do real world things, for real people. We could be hired out by the various clubs in Wilder's Woods to spy on the other clubs, or run booty to and from the various camps for a piece of the pie, like Han Solo in *Star Wars*! We could forge new paths and alliances, becoming an integral part of the economic ecosystem and the warring political factions of The Woods, rivaling Great Britain at the turn of the 1700's.

"We could execute the mission directives even if Kenny isn't a member in time to come," Kring added, as if reading my thoughts before I finished them.

I paused my pacing and stretched my arms behind my back, "Well we're good on the first mission, the club's initial members, and of course the type of club that it will be. Now we just need a name, and a place to put it."

"I don't know about the name, but we can run the club from my treehouse, and in the basement."

"Sweet!" I sang.

"We could store all our valuable club secrets in the security of my house, and base our operations out of here," Kring added.

I began to pace again, "Now we're cooking!"

"Of course, we better keep this under wraps for a while. Secrecy is our best ally. If Jim finds out about this, he'll try to destroy it by convincing everyone not to join," Kring sternly stated.

I added, "We also wouldn't want to alert the Culvers to our club."

"Especially that it's a spy club," Kring added excitedly.

"Totally Top Secret," I agreed.

"Agreed," Kring finalized.

With where and what we'd do, along with who we could trust and not trust, which apparently was no one, it was now time to talk strategy and end game, which, as with all great leaders, happened to be my forte. "If we make an alliance with the Dragon, we could control three-quarters of this block," I said with a knowing smile.

"The Woods would be a perfect staging area for the final assault on Upper La Rue," Kring added.

"That was never the plan! Never on the table!" I snapped as if Kring was a lowly corporal speaking out of turn during the planning of D-day.

And as poorly as I had checked my unwarranted and unexpected emotional response at the door, my utter failure to properly praise Kring's pragmatic plans was even more alarming, and to a lesser degree, damaging, since it was clear Kring didn't consider himself a corporal, nor I, an emperor. "U.L. is always on the table! Besides, an empire must grow, must expend the resources to conquer more. Keep the peasants occupied with grander ideas than those that form in their own puny, malnutritioned minds."

Though he was technically correct, his rhetoric was out of turn and thus had to be mocked, "OK Caesar dressing."

Not understanding that I had no choice but to dismiss his idea as folly due to the poorly timed presentation of it, Kring sounded dejected as he crossed his arms, "Once again my greatness is lost on you."

"Whatever you say, Napoleon dessert."

Kring rose from his milk crate to ascend his metaphoric soap box, tapping his chest in a rapid, physical cadence, "I understand the reasoning behind the alliance. I know the benefits."

"Forget the benefits!" I snapped. "If we don't make an alliance with the Dragon, someone else will."

Kring addressed the 900-pound gorilla in the room, "What if they want us to join them? What then?"

"We'd simply say, "No thank you.""

"No thank you? Like we're being offered an extra piece of cake at a birthday party?"

Overtly ignoring his sarcasm, I responded with a purposefully placed, "Pretty much."

Kring's tone conveyed he believed I was winging this with as little foresight as a two-year-old springing a Jack in the box, "What if we say no, and Jim says yes?"

"Jim would have to dissolve the Alien Club," I answered coolly.

Kring had to consider the possibility. "He's an opportunist. I wouldn't put it past him."

Knowing neither of us could see Jim seceding to the Union, I added, "We both know his ego is even more powerful than his desire to conform." *Even bigger than mine and I was a future emperor by all accounts.*

"True."

"Besides, the Alien Club marks the first time in his pathetic existence that he's fit in. If he goes to The Woods, he'd be left to the wolves once again."

"You don't think he'd negotiate terms?" Kring asked.

"Jim's no dummy. He may be a poor politician, but he's an astute historian. No one knows better than Jim Kreagan that terms are pointless if the deal has no chance of being honored," I said, much to my chagrin.

Pushing his lip and nodding, "I guess after what he did to you, he sees the writing on the wall."

"What comes around, goes around," I said with a wry smile.

"Does that mean your mom could give me AIDS again?!?!?

"Stay on point!" I snapped.

"Sorry Bro. Old habits..." Kring said as he grabbed his crotch and sat back on the milk crate that had been topped by an accent cushion, from an old cream colored leather couch.

Resting a hand on the massive branch that protruded through the center of the fort, which doubled as a support beam and pullup station, I mused, "The Culvers and The Woods are most definitely wild cards."

Speaking with a face reserved for sour grapes, Kring muttered, "I don't trust the Culvers, especially since they changed their friends and their club's name."

I tried for levity, "You really liked the name, The Legion of Doom?"

But Kring would have none of it, "Get serious fool! A, we don't know these other guys, and B, we don't know who the snitch is. What if Bishop slips it to the snitch and then the snitch slips it to Jim!"

I needed to taper his zeal, "What if I slip it in your mother? Besides, Bishop won't let the info get back to Jim."

It worked, Kring breathed and repositioned himself on the seat, producing a quick double clap, "Continue loyal subject."

"It wouldn't take a rocket scientist to figure out that the person who delivered the info would either be the snitch or know who the snitch was, meaning Jim would know who the snitch was pretty quickly."

"And?"

"And... Jim and I already knew Bishop has a high-ranking mole deep within the Alien Club, and I don't think Bishop would be too keen on losing the crown jewel in his spy network. Besides, we have an ace in the hole, regardless of what Jim finds out."

"You're beginning to babble," Kring said.

"Sorry. I'll slow it down for you Cletus. For starters, if Jim does find out who the snitch is, it will eat him alive until he confronts the snitch. This will create a vacuum in the Alien Club when that person leaves, or is eventually kicked out."

Kring asked, "You think he'll confront the snitch, knowing his power is already depleted with your departure? Another vacuum would surely bring the club to its knees."

"You said it yourself; his ego rules his decision-making process."

"I know, but that seems to be cutting off your nose to spite your face."

"You know the difference between someone who's hungry for power and mad with power?" I inquired smugly.

"Not really... Do you?" Kring asked mockingly.

Ignoring his mock, I resumed my pacing with my hands locked at the base of my spine, "Both desire the same amount of power in the end, which in the end, is all of it. The difference is their appetite. Someone who's hungry can be satiated, someone who's mad, cannot."

Rolling his eyes and his head back, "Your point being?"

"My point, which is a brilliant one by the way, is our Ace in the hole."

"Go on," Kring said.

"Bishop smacked Jim around a month ago pretty badly."

Kring agreed, "That's an understatement."

"Those scars are still fresh in Jim's mind. He was embarrassed by Bishop and then in return, Sean bitch-slapped Bishop on his own front lawn. Hell, the only reason Jim agreed to run the recon missions into The Woods was to determine where the new base was, and if it was vulnerable to an attack. Jim hates Bishop and Bishop isn't too fond of Jim."

Shaking his head in astonishment, "I know Sean gave it to Bishop just as hard as Bishop gave it to Jim."

I stopped and pivoted, "Harder. It looked like a hooker and her pimp."

And just like a hooker knows she's going to get bitch-slapped by her pimp for not bringing back the night's minimum, Bishop knew once he beat up Jim, that Jim's older brother, Sean, who was also the starting nose-tackle for the Huntington Blue Devil's Varsity football team, was going to exact revenge. For he knew the Kreagans as the classic Irish-Italian family that they were. Meaning, though they'd had more than their fair share of family brawls, they also had the propensity to punish outsiders for past aggressions.

And just like any public punishment from yester yore, this one had the entire neighborhood in attendance on a large centrally located village green—i.e., the Culver's front lawn. Perfectly situated on the border of Upper and Lower La Rue, the Culver's front yard soon became a social scene for the entire neighborhood as they congregated to witness Bishop's come-up-ins. To Bishop's credit, he saw the far larger Sean and the hungry crowd gathered on his front yard, and made the long walk to his executioner with as much dignity as his wobbly knees could afford him.

Furthermore, being a bully himself, Bishop knew Sean would not only announce his crimes and subsequent punishment to the public, but would deliver the justice with a ferocious flair intended to instill fear in those unlucky enough to witness the sentencing. Kring being nine and me being ten, made the first-time viewing of someone being beaten until their eyes closed, as their body went limp, far more horrific than the Kung Fu movies we'd watched to prep us for such an event, had led us to believe it to be.

Kring sprang to his feet once more, standing less than a foot from me, "So what are we waiting for? Jim and Bishop won't team up until the wounds of war heal, and in this case, it could take years!"

I retreated to the corner, where my trusty barstool awaited, "We need to make sure those guys from the other side are not bad."

Kring looked out the lone window, "Drugs and stuff?"

"Exactly. You never know. Jim said they're pot heads and the guy I saw on the minibike was donning a heavy metal T-shirt and a mustache."

"A mustache? You think it could be the same kids that killed that kid in Smithtown back in the spring?" Kring questioned quaveringly.

On April 21st, 1979, John Pius Jr., a thirteen-year-old boy, was found dead in woods similar to Wilder's Woods, no more than fifteen miles away, in Smithtown, NY. The newspapers had a field day, panning the public with horrific satanic sensationalism, since they'd found the boy near a school, buried under a pile of logs and leaves, with dirt, debris and six rocks lodged in his throat. And though the police had not formally accused anyone as of yet, rumor had it that it was in fact a couple of local boys of similar age who'd killed him, and not some random psychopath passing through town. The heightened parental guidance was bordering on a police state, though daily excursions into The Woods were still permitted, as long as one had verifiable buddy-backup.

Embarking on his pacing of the room, Kring asked, "How do we approach this?"

"We perform a recon mission deep into The Woods, but the mission parameters change. Instead of looking for the base and a way to destroy it, we find out who and what comprises this so-called Black Dragon. Once we determine that, we work Roy over the course of a week or so and bleed the pig."

Abruptly stopping in his tracks, Kring pivoted to me, "Think we got a week? Things could change quickly, as you well know, especially in Wilder's. We could be on the outside looking in."

"True," I acknowledged.

The tree fort was close quarters and the exposed rusty nails used in its hobo chic remodel made Kring's attempt at a leisurely walk and talk preposterous at best. So when he began to resume his strutting stroll with his eyes closed, I winced.

"I say seventy-two hours is more than enough time," he offered.

"Seventy-two hours?" I blurted.

Still sleepwalking mere inches from objects that could land him in the ER in need of a massive Tetanus shot, Kring surmised, "We could run three recon missions in that time period."

"And Roy?" I asked.

Kring didn't waver in his walk, "Roy could be fit in."

I had the fist to the chin, signaling deep thought and righteousness, "We need to invite him over, feed him, go to his house at least once, and play something."

Kring stopped in his tracks and warmly opened his eyes, admiring the inner sanctum of our newly formed center of government, "Why don't we bring Mohammed to the mountain?"

"Sweet! We show him the fort—all the cool stuff. The benefits afforded him via a true alliance."

"Exactly," Kring agreed and raised a finger to make a point, "But we don't tell him he's standing right in the middle of our new club and at the epicenter of awesomeness."

I smiled a sheepish grin, "Just an outpost, with some perks."

"Be ultra-secretive as if we're hiding something more," Kring said as he began his awkward attempt at pacing a nail studded, walk-in coffin.

I was rather impressed with our plan and couldn't help but think out loud, "It will add to the mystique."

Turning to me with his hands locked behind his back, Kring slyly stated, "He'll be drooling for more."

I jumped up to my feet, "He'll run, not walk to tell his big bro Bishop of our little enterprise."

Extending his hand, Kring proudly predicted, "Bishop will invite us up there to show us his new digs in no time flat."

I extended mine with a winning smile and shook Kring's long and deep, "The final scouting mission won't even have to be covert."

Not letting go to symbolize our interwoven fates, Kring returned the bravado, "We'll be invited to spy like James Bond!"

"Sounds like a plan," I exclaimed as my hand retreated to the windowsill.

"Flawless," Kring added under his breath, as he reminisced over victories not yet fought.

Looking back to my comrade in arms, "If you want flawless, this plan of ours has got to go by the numbers, which means we must first get an overview of this situation, especially before we go walking into the lion's den."

"No doubt," Kring agreed.

I turned and stood before my little lithe accomplice, transformed from a mere boy of above-average height and below-average muscle tone. I was now a hardened commander addressing Seal Team Six before a raid. "'By the numbers' means the recon missions must be scheduled at different times during the day. No sense in repetition with such a short timeframe. No surprises is essential to the success of our first official meeting."

Kring closed in on the shed's corner with the unlit candle, offering me a view of his shivering back, which betrayed his calm voice, "Would you do a night mission?"

"Would you?" I countered.

"I asked you first."

I paused "Maybe..."

"Maybe I'm your father!" Kring quickly followed with forced ferocity.

I blew off his bait with a "whatever," and immediately began to deliberate the end game of such a brazen operation. I'd been to the edge of The Woods at night, like a crazy man scanning the abyss of insanity, but never jumped in for the same reason—the fear of no return...

The Woods were a wondrous place during the day, but equally dark and disturbing at night, since no one knew for sure who had moved in with Mrs. Wilder in the last couple of years. And though the reports of shadowy figures and strange events were more likely than not fanciful fabrications of a youth's unbounded imagination, the murder less than fifteen miles away in the spring, left a taint of evil on all things unknown. And make no mistake, once you walked into the deep ancient forest, with a canopy so thick not even a harvest moon could show you the way home, you might as well have been on another planet.

"I would if I were packing heat," Kring tossed to see if I'd chew.

"You definitely have the fire power," I surmised.

Kring turned to me, squatting underneath the corner shelf that held the rooms only light, "How would we smuggle them out?"

That was a no brainer. "During the day we would move them stealth-style to the tree fort and then move out at night fully loaded."

"What if someone sees us? There's nowhere to run! Not with a rifle!"

"Who would see us?" I asked.

"My dad for starters. He's always walking the street at night, smoking a butt in his freaking bathing suit."

"I thought that was your mom."

"My mom quit last summer."

"But doesn't she still walk the streets at night half naked?"

"Okay—DICK! Seriously, though—we can't take the main road with rifles. We would wind up having to ditch them when we took cover."

"Around the bend would be difficult," I mused.

"Around that bend a car's headlights would only give you seconds to react, and I'm no deer," Kring bluntly stated.

"No escape route for the first leg on either side," I offered.

Kring was beside himself, "The first leg? Try nowhere to run for the first 250 yards."

"It's a crap shoot," I agreed.

"Then how?"

I lowered my voice like an old sage sitting humbly around a hunting party's campfire, not wanting to wake the evil spirits, while telling a story of a horrible tragedy that awaited the unsuspecting travelers. "Across the salt flats," I offered.

Kring shot to his feet, "Screw that!"

Taken back somewhat, I became intense in my defense, "You said it yourself! The middle is shot! And you can forget the right, right now. Three sets of dogs for starters. Mr. Collins has spotlights on motion detectors, not to mention the seven-foot rusty metal fence with pricker bushes separating the Brush's from Old Lady Wick's."

Kring exhaled as he scanned the accidental skylights that littered the ceiling, "That's a lot, I'll give you that."

"A lot? It's a freaking meat grinder! Dogs, motion detectors, spotlights, metal barbed-wire fences?!?! Hansel and Gretel had an easier time navigating the woods."

A brief painful smile was all that showcased Kring's many disastrous forays into the very lands we spoke of, "True. But no obstacle in plan A scares me more than a gun. Plus, we would have to go behind the Culver's house where Mr. Culver is always in the backyard drinking and smoking."

I worked over the math, "Yeah, and he's always in his swim trunks, as well. Is there some kind of correlation between cigarettes and getting into your swim trunks?"

Kring peered at the tip of his nose as if noticing it for the first time, "Maybe... Come to think of it, the Culvers don't even have a pool."

I feigned awkward, "Maybe your dad and Mr. Culver— "

"Screw off," he retorted halfhearted as he once again took a seat on his trusty milk crate.

I laid it out, "So, up the left side through Brady's, across Menten's, then the salt flats, then the Smith's, finishing with the Culver's in the side."

Kring nodded with each name given and then asked the rhetorical question on both our minds, "When was the last time you were up there at night?"

"Never," I said quicker than I wanted.

"Me neither..."

"We'll do just fine," I replied as I absently closed my hands in silent prayer.

"I sure hope so."

"Only dopes hope."

Chapter 2
My Enemy's Enemy is My Ally

As with any organization, a secret club needs a strong base. In our case, we had possibly the greatest base of operations in the history of spying. Raised fifteen feet above the ground, wedged atop three massive oak branches, each having a diameter of no less than two and half feet and a structural load capacity that could support a freight train, was an 8 x 10 oak plank toolshed that Kring's father had raised to its lofty perch via an industrial construction crane supplied by one of his largest clients.

Kring's father was in the big business and whenever a home improvement project could go big, Kring's father, Leo, would go for gold. Not only did the ten-man crew secure the shed to the tree with enough high strength steel to withstand a 150 mile per hour Class 5 hurricane, they installed all the over the top extras Kring had on his last-minute wish list—the coolest of which was the hand-winch operated elevator with a 400-pound load capacity that came through the middle of the shed via a hide-away trap door. The handcrafted fold away bamboo ladder wasn't as cool, but was still highly useful, as was the 100% not-to-code outlet that was installed as an afterthought. The impetus for the impromptu tree fort was Mr. Pelagatti's desire to have a larger, newer, better shed, thus he needed something to do with old shed. And since the old shed wasn't really that old, he couldn't live with tossing good money to the curb, so he hired a construction crew, crane operator and master electrician to save a small fortune.

Kring was bestowed one job—to paint it. If completed, it would act as a token of his appreciation and justification for Leo on the big expense, since he could tell people that Kring was learning what hard work was really all about—and one couldn't put a price on that at this age... I of course had agreed to assist my good friend in this endeavor, since we both knew I'd be enjoying the fruits of his father's labor as much as Kring. We, of course, had failed to do a single thing since taking residency three summers ago, including cleaning it to any real degree. So needless to say, the place had begun to age rapidly. Several of the roof shingles were severely damaged in the move and were never fixed, making water damage a continuing issue that had further exasperated the aging wood's decay.

Decaying wood in a highly shaded environment becomes an incubator for mold and carpenter ant colonies. Branches had grown through many of the wood side planks and into some of the roof shingles; moss had covered the remainder of the roof and mold crept up the corners. The constant critter traffic, from squirrels to giant furry spiders with lips—yes lips—made the treehouse seem magically alive, and since we lived in an age when boys played fantasy-adventure board games, where they had to act out scenes in character, having a structure that looked to be erected by tree elves was simply awesome.

The fact that more than two-thirds of the block had no idea what the inside of the fort looked like added to its mystique. In three years, Roy had never even whiffed the inside of the fort, and since the fort was well hidden behind thick evergreens from three sides, allowing only a partial view from deeper within Kring's backyard, Roy had only seen it from afar a half-dozen times.

Knowing the anticipation that a first-time walkthrough generated in one of our contemporaries, made Roy's speedy acceptance and arrival to Kring's random phone call invitation all too predictable.

"This place is the tits!" squealed Roy.

"Thanks," Kring replied.

"It took a long time," I added.

"Is that a trap door?" Roy asked excitedly.

Pointing casually with one finger, Kring casually responded, "Check up."

"What's that? A pully?"

"That's right," Kring said with a sly smile.

My pride couldn't be contained, "Open the trap door and we can hoist packages without the hassle of the ladder."

Raising a paused finger, Kring added, "Forget the packages, if we got two up here, we can pull a third up."

"You couldn't lift me," Roy replied with a forced smile.

I did my best to make the obvious less uncomfortable, "Hey, you look like you lost some."

Kring added some much needed emotional support, "Yeah, don't knock yourself."

"You're big-boned," I chimed.

Kring nodded as he slowly sized Roy up, "If you worked out, you'd be diesel."

I added my raised eyebrow of approval, "You would definitely be a force."

Looking down at the hole and then slapping his massive belly, which was currently exposed below the navel by a stained white t-shirt that was too small for him even in the maternity ward, Roy admitted, "Well, I know I'm not fitting through that hole."

Kring attempted in vain to calm the leviathan, "We could expand the—"

I quickly cut Kring off with a subtle air-pat of my hand before the hairs on the back of Roy's fivefold neck began to raise. I went friendly, but formal, "We want this to one day be the main outpost for the entire lower La Rue territory."

Roy looked up from his massive belly with wide eyes, "You want to see an outpost? You gotta see the fort in Wilder's."

Kring looked to me, then back to Roy, "Sweet?"

"Sweet? It's become a small town!"

That was a revelation that left me a little slack-jawed, "Town?"

Roy, sensing my bewilderment, smiled as he listed the criteria for his boastful claim, "There's a sheriff, bar, trading, religion, and bank."

Kring cut in, "Bank?"

"Bishop runs it."

Half to myself, "Bank Bishop..."

"He's the mayor, too," Roy said with outward pride.

"Mayor?" Kring repeated incredulously.

"Who's the sheriff?" I asked.

"Derek."

In unison Kring and I gasped, "DEREK?"

Looking around as if the answer was written somewhere within the treehouse, rather than indelibly marked in his memories, Roy's voice and demeanor softened, as if he was explaining the story to his father instead of his peers. "Derek's from the other side..."

Kring's head rolled back and gently tapped the wall, as he breathlessly uttered, "Wow."

Sounding more nervous, Roy betrayed cool by desperately trying to portray it, "It's cool."

"I'm sure," I said slowly and sarcastically.

Trying to win back a losing cause, Roy went into campaign overdrive, "No, really! The Woods have become a real exciting place. Yesterday, these girls were there. One was wearing sneakers, Daisy Dukes, and a bandana across her perkies."

That was too much for me, "Come on!"

"Her face..." Roy began to dream aloud, until I severed the cord.

"Did you talk to her?"

"For a sec."

"What'd ya say?" Kring asked while staring at me with an eyebrow arched.

"What's up?"

"That's it?" I asked.

"She was older."

"How old?" I prodded.

"Can't say. Think she was about your sister's age, maybe a year younger."

"Where'd she come from?" Kring questioned quicker than he'd liked.

"The other side."

I got up from the bar stool and put a hand on Roy's shoulder, making sure eye contact was firmly established before asking, "How many were there?"

"Four."

Kring was now on his feet as well, "Girls? Or four total?"

"Four girls," Roy said feverishly without looking away.

I slowed down further, "How many guys?"

Roy finally broke eye contact and began to scan the room, as if the answers were encrypted on the dust particles that uncloaked while subjected to rays of sunlight slicing through the weathered planks. "Five, maybe six."

Kring staggered back and barked, "Holy crap!" as if he'd just stumbled upon the unlikely and unfortunate viewing of his grandparents bumping bones.

"They're cool," Roy quickly reiterated.

I gripped his too-fat-to-be-real shoulder, "They're from the other side!"

"They're alright. Trust me. You got to."

Kring had finally caught himself in his disbelieving freefall and was now leaning casually against a wall, as if he was scouting for digits at a bar, "No problems at all?"

"Well, there's been some tension as of late."

I released my grip and wiped our combined sweats on my shorts, "What kind of tension?"

"Nothing crazy. Most of it was settled when the power was split between Bishop and Derek."

Throwing up his hands in utter disgust and despair, Kring raised his head back, and closes his eyes, in order to blow out the statement, "We've lost The Woods."

"Split power for now," Roy protested.

"For now..." I said, as my worst fears began to occupy territory held fast by outrage. *Power can never be split, capped, nor checked, regardless of what our founding fathers fancied.*

Sensing our appreciation for the gravity of the situation that Roy and his brother found themselves in, Roy began to babble like a brook. "It got out of control so quickly with upper La Rue coming."

I cut him off, "Upper La Rue's in there too?"

"Last week, but some of the older kids chased them out."

Still leaning against the wall and staring at the ceiling, Kring asked, "How old are these kids?"

"8th, 9th, 10th."

"Holy crap cakes!" I blurted like Robin to Batman.

Roy fumbled as he painfully failed at pulling his sweat soaked t-shirt closer to his unbuttoned army shorts, "I think one or two may be in 11th, possibly 12th."

Still looking at the ceiling, Kring dropped, "Maybe?"

I turned from Roy and walked to the window, "Well, there's no maybe in losing total control over Wilder's."

"We never had it!" Roy cried.

I turned, "Never had it?"

Kring finally looked down to Roy, "We ruled those Woods like storm troopers."

"That's what you think. Besides, we're not what we once were."

Kring took an angry step to Roy, "I'm bigger. And as for you—"

I stepped forward to intervene, "Hey, easy partner."

With more sadness than animosity, Roy stated an undeniable fact, "We had a strong La Rue until the splits."

Kring dialed down his presence, but not his rhetoric, "Whose fault is that?"

"Not mine," Roy responded with a tap to his chest.

"Well it's definitely not mine," Kring answered.

To them both, I raised a hand in symbolic truce, "Not now. We need to focus."

Roy, now an emotional mess, was suddenly filled with anger, due to the plain-as-day-picture of his family's role in the loss of such a strategic and historic sanctuary. "We couldn't hold The Woods alone!"

Sensing his spin, I tried to tether him, "It's cool my brother. We're good. That said, you should have said something."

Roy's vocal sarcasm was only outshone by his facial expression, "Said something to who? To you? With you leading recon missions on our camp?"

I feigned oblivious, "What are you babbling about?"

"Oh, please."

"Please what?" I pressed.

"Building Yankee stadium was more covert."

Kring still two feet from Roy, squared up to the far larger boy, "Who told you?"

"Admit it," Roy said without looking to Kring.

Looking back to Roy, I couldn't fight the curiosity, "Who told you?"

"Admit it. Then I'll tell you."

I gave a politician's answer, "We didn't run one mission."

"You were going to."

"True," I responded despite myself.

"Yo—!" Kring barked in utter disbelief.

"Liars," Roy hissed.

I took a step towards Roy, "I told you the truth."

Still holding my stare, Roy chewed his cheek, "You were going to lie."

"It's a covert operation; what do you expect?" I asked.

Kring locked his hands behind his back, "Yeah, we have to maintain secrecy at all costs."

I positioned myself in front of Roy, "You're lucky we're letting you leave alive." And with that, we all couldn't help but smile.

Kring took another step closer and was now less than a foot to Roy's left. "Who told?"

"That's top secret."

I pumped my right fist while taking hold of Roy's sweat-drenched shirt with my left. "Don't screw with us. You made a deal."

Kring looked at Roy as if he'd just caught him trying to hide gum under his favorite chair, "Have you no honor? Or did you sell it all at the Wilder's Mall along with the rest of your Momma's More 100's?"

Shooting Kring a hurt glance, "Basically everyone knew—and my mother smokes Newports now."

"Who's everyone?" Kring demanded.

"Franky, Freddy, Kurt, and Tom."

"How?" I asked in utter disbelief. *How could I have been so blindsided? What was I blind to now? Blinded by the tree... I can smell the forest burning, but can't see the flames!*

Shrugging his shoulders, "Don't know. I think Jim told one of them."

Then it hit, and it was my turn to throw my hands up in the air, "Oh my God!"

Kring turned on a dime, "What?"

The picture was too painful to peruse any longer, for I'd been had. "It's not one snitch, it's the whole freakin' club!"

"I didn't say that," Roy stuttered.

"Yes, you did," I snapped back.

"No I didn't."

Correcting him, I confirmed the obvious, "Not outright, but you said it without meaning to."

Kring once again walked away from Roy shaking his head, "Smooth move Tubby."

I explained my theory to Roy, "If you know who knows, that means you talked about it with them, or they talked to each other at some point in front of you."

Kring threw out, "Jim might have told them."

"All of them? And at the same time?" I questioned. *No, they've known.*

"Maybe he wanted to set us up?" Kring thought out loud.

"Maybe?" I mused.

Kring had taken to his seat and began whittling away at an old walking stick he'd long since perfected, "You think he's that diabolical?"

"Not sure. Sometimes he just can't keep a secret. Throw in, he could tell everyone he gave me an order, versus the truth, which was that the idea was mine and I volunteered."

Finally looking to Roy, Kring pointed to me with his thumb, "Trel left the Alien Club."

Still standing at attention in the middle of the room on top of a small puddle of his own sweat, Roy responded with a curt, "I know."

Much to my chagrin I acknowledged, "News travels fast."

"Faster than you think."

Not taking Roy's bait I casually created conversation, "You know, me leaving will mean the end for that club."

Kring chimed in, "I'm out, too. So is Kenny."

"I know," Roy said as he stood smugly savoring the morsels of his superior spy ring.

Astonished, I found myself smiling, "You're chock full of knowledge, aren't you?"

Even stiffer than before, Roy's formal and painfully uncomfortable stance was now accompanied by a jawline that looked tired from chewing an old piece of gum, "You guys would love to know how I know, wouldn't you?"

I didn't want to know, but needed confirmation nonetheless, "It's obvious Butt Breath."

"It is?" Roy asked astonished.

Kring cracked, "At least from here it is; you should put some toothpaste on that brush tonight."

"You should."

Kring laughed Roy off, "You should work on your rank backs, because, 'you should' is really weak."

As Kring and Roy went back and forth on who was lamer, the truth finally had time to metastasize in my mind. *I was the lamest of them all, for I was so busy being "The Man", and so consumed with Jim trying to take away my power, that I had been blinded to the fact that I never had any real power in the first place. I didn't lose rank before I resigned, for there had never been anyone below me to outrank. I was a general without an army—a paper tiger in a book no one cared to read. I was no Caesar. How could I have been so vain as to occupy my time with visions of the Ides of*

March? Caesar had an army. Men feared and respected Caesar. No one feared or respected me. Certainly not enough to take the time to plot my demise, for they probably spent the entire time behind my back mocking me.

"They all hang in The Woods. The whole lot of them. They were never loyal to the Alien Club," I said it like I read it in *The Bible.*

"And why would they be loyal to you?" Roy asked angrily.

I was stunned by his simple question, "Why?"

Looking to Kring and then back to me, Roy began to chop away at the house of cards. "Your club was run totally out of control. Jim was Hitler, and Kurt was his S.S. officer."

I interrupted him, "That was changing." *Or was it I who was changing?*

But Roy would have none of it, "Your club had paperwork; who needs paperwork? My dad gets paid to do that."

Half kidding, Kring added, "Jim got a receptionist."

"You don't even have phones, do you?"

"No," I answered absently. *And if we did, who would call us other than the prank callers who were comprised of our constituents anyway?*

"If you thought paperwork was stupid, why did you want two secretaries?"

"Because I could..." *He even knew about positions in the club that weren't even filled yet! He probably knew our secret handshake, and mocked it while he imitated Jim and me giving one of our pompous-ass motivational speeches on how to be a better pledge.* I began to cram any available space not stockpiled with embarrassment, self-pity, and shame, with white-hot anger.

Roy droned on while I shook with fury, "The Woods are free. Smoke, drink, guns."

With my teeth grinding, and jaw locked like a Pitbull I spat, "It was always free, Roy. You haven't changed anything for the better. The only significant change is the balance of power."

Kring had noticed my drastic change in mood and adjusted his. "You let the only thing that shouldn't change, change."

Looking up to Roy, I growled, "You let it change hands."

From defiant to defensive, Roy was now more nervous than a prize pig the day after the fair, "It's a democracy."

"A democracy?" I mocked. "You have your brother, Bishop, a self-elected official, which in the adult world is referred to as a dictator, keeping the "peace" via a foreign militia being paid in sex and drugs."

"They were elected."

"An uneasy peace at best," Kring added as he dropped his walking stick in disgust.

I quizzed our nitwitted neighbor, "And how does your new population see it?"

Chin held high, Roy responded, "The citizens are quite content, thank you very much."

Kring looked at me somewhat astonished, "Really?"

Still silently enraged, I kept my sarcasm as my hate's gatekeeper, "Well, you're a regular Ellis Island aren't you?"

"We accommodate the needs of the masses."

Kring shook his head, looking from the floor to Roy's massive roll farm of a belly, "The masses are asses, and in your case, large asses at that."

I was more discerning in my dress-down. "A dictator, a conquering army, and now unloyal subjects."

On his feet once again, Kring walked by Roy and addressed me directly, "The Woods will be burning down in no time."

Peering over Kring's shoulder I asked, "How many citizens do you have?" while air-quoting citizens with dramatic flair.

"Over ten," Roy proclaimed with his chest protruding so far with pride that it eclipsed his belly.

"Including chicks?" Kring asked more excitedly than he surely intended.

"Yeah."

Trying to wrap my head around the unthinkable, "You said you had trade..."

"Yes."

"Trade is good," I acknowledged. "I wanted to implement that for a long time."

"Why didn't you?"

Sensing a dialogue that could lead somewhere other than a circle, "We needed the muscle, and a place to store the goods."

"We got muscle," Roy proudly proclaimed as he pounded his chest, only to cringe when the noise of goulashes galloping through mud puddles ensued when his sausage strapped palm slapped his sweat soaked T-shirt.

"And your house doubles as the warehouse I gather?"

"Correct."

"I would imagine your bottomless supply of cigarettes and porn have made the two of you extremely rich and powerful," Kring stated.

With his chin even more pronounced than the smile he could no longer contain, "Times have been very good indeed."

"Indeed," Kring whispered, looking to me as if the word was a clue.

I saved the snapshot and asked Roy, "What does the outside world use?"

Shrugging his shoulders, "The same. The older ones exchange booze and pot, instead of mags and toys, while cigarettes are still the gold standard."

"You got plenty of booze and cigarettes," Kring chimed in to keep Roy singing his song.

"No, not really. My dad marks the bottles and only keeps a six in the house at all times and ever since the state raised the taxes on butts, my parents are counting the drags."

"I got booze," I tossed out to see if anyone would pick it up.

Kring did, but with a joke, "Your parents could buy The Woods with their booze."

The truth can hurt more than a heavy weight punch, especially when it blindsides you. "I know…" I uttered with a downcast gaze.

Roy finally looked to relax from his toy soldier stance. "We could always use more partners in trade."

Pleasantly surprised at the new upside, I added, "Well then, we need to discuss trade and territories."

Kring stood next to me, facing Roy, "You allowed to speak for your community?" Kring made sure to use his fingers in making the mocking quote symbols on community.

Roy thought about it a second, then shook his head, "I think Bishop would want to handle this one."

Not wanting to sound too eager, I made myself sound available without sounding desperate. "We're open to negotiation, but I should put the cards on the table and let you know there have been several tender offers made already."

Roy brushed my bravado aside, "I think we all know that an alliance with us is your only option."

Kring snapped at Roy with a frustrated filled fact, "We know nothing, except for what you've told us!"

Kring was right and I needed to capitalize on that, "For all we know you could have been sent here by Bishop to find out more information about our outpost, and you made all that stuff up about The Woods."

Kring, who was now fully turned around, stood to my right with his arms crossed as he dressed Roy down, "Come to think of it, Daisy Duke running around The Woods with Roy Culver?"

"Which one of you is Bo?" I chimed, "'Cause you don't look like a Luke."

Kring feigned disdain, "We've been had. Nice job, Jelly Belly."

With each speculation acting as an emotional smackyoulation, Roy quickly began to melt under the intense scrutiny, "I'm telling the truth! You'll see for yourself!" The sentence was said and the path had been laid. There was no turning back now.

Kring looked Roy up and down once again before asking, "You have permission to show us the inner wall to your Jade City?"

"I could, but I think Bishop would want to set up the time. Besides I'm sure the council would want to approve any outside forces before they enter the inner sanctum."

I'd had enough and needed to play on my emotions before they betrayed me, "Jade City? Inner Sanctum? It's Wilder's freak'en Woods, and it's free to all those who travel it. You tell Bishop we'll meet with him, but let him know right off the bat, that I'm not too happy with him having to persuade a bunch of thugs, from the other side mind you, that it's cool for his friends to stop by."

Kring had wanted to slap Roy around the moment he stressed the pegs on the ladder, "Yeah, we're your neighbors and longtime friends. Bishop might have a new club, but we're old friends. You tell Bishop if they give him crap about meeting us, it's a knock on him, and you for that matter."

"They don't tell Bishop what to do, They discuss it with him."

Kring cocked his head back slightly and arched his brow, "Do they discuss it over tea?"

I didn't like the road Kring's line of questioning was taking us, so I blazed a new path, "Bishop's cock diesel; he should be discussing the future of that club with his fists, and you can tell him I said that."

"I'll tell him."

Luckily, Kring was good with directions and made a U-ee "Let him know he's got a brother who's solid too, and one he should be using to watch his back."

Roy's eyes seem to go glassy and he needed to swallow hard before saying, "I tell him that every day. He knows I got his back."

I knew we had struck a nerve and now it was time to dull the pain with a quick sedative, so the patient would highly recommend us. "Hopefully we can work this out, and improve all of our standings, as well as solidify the wellbeing of this block and all those we proudly call friends."

Roy exhaled with a heavy-hearted, "I would like that."

Kring added much to Roy's delight, "Besides, the three of us could hang out more, like old times."

Roy's voice and eyes perked up, "I would like that."

With that I knew we could go no further. Anything more that would be said would only jeopardize our hard work and amazing mind-altering propaganda. I got up from my stool, extended my hand, and looked Roy in the eye, "Good luck in your travels, old friend. May the force be with you."

Extending his lamb leg, Roy sternly replied, "And with you."

Roy turned to Kring, to find Kring's hand extended. "May the force be with you," Kring said, with more sincerity than I had hoped for.

Roy took and shook it with great formality, "And with you."

As Roy made his slow descent down the over-stressed bamboo ladder, I walked to the edge of the door and gave him one last ego boost, which surely would make Roy our biggest proponent, and the future facilitator of our most scrutinized visit. "Do yourself a favor, and The Woods a favor for that matter."

Looking up from halfway down, "What's that?"

"You tell Bishop that not only does he have the right guy watching his back, he's got the right guy negotiating the terms." It was hard to tell if Roy actually blushed, since his face hadn't come down from beet red since his ascent, but I could tell he was quite taken by my measure.

"You know I will." With that Roy made it down the rest of the ladder, stumbled through the wall of overgrown bushes, and got on his bike.

As we watched Roy pedal just fast enough to maintain his center of gravity, Kring found it difficult to look at me as he tried to swallow his smirk. "The only thing you could have done gayer than that last statement was to swallow his meatstick."

"Please! I was flawless."

Squeezing his hands to his heart he twirled as he squeaked out a mocking, "You tell Bishop that if I was going to have someone pump me like a flat tire, it would be you big boy."

"I was in character!" I snapped without conviction.

"Oh yeah? What character were you in? Super-gay-man?"

"I had to add a little relish on top towards the end, mostly just to compensate for your subpar performance."

"Worry about yourself."

"I was. Besides, that last statement was for his ego. He'll want us to succeed for nothing less than himself succeeding. We work out, he works out. He's the bastard step child in that club."

"You think?"

I looked at Kring in utter amazement, "You think he has any say whatsoever? His job is probably no more relevant than one we'd give to your brother."

Kring nodded with a knowing smirk, "I bet they don't even let him talk to his brother any longer."

"They don't? Please. You think Bishop is paying attention to Roy and his fat boy titties, when there're real ones bouncing around all over the place?"

Kring picked up his trusty walking stick and tapped the windowsill, "So you believe him?"

I shrugged, "Sure, why not."

"What if he's lying? Then what?"

I walked to the windowsill trying to find Kring's eye, "About all of it? Too much. If he lied half as much as he ate, he couldn't come up with that much. Most of it's true, I'm sure of it."

Still looking off in the distance Kring opined, "Then the question is, how much was the total truth, and what was him just exaggerating?"

"Well, the girl was real, but his conversation with her was most likely fabricated, or at a minimum, greatly embellished."

Kring nudged his jaw in acceptance, and then added, "I'd say the stuff on the number of people were true, but the roles of those people may have been lessened."

"I agree. He was doing his best to downplay the truth about what's really taken place in The Woods."

Kring stopped his tapping, "Agreed... What do you think's happened?"

I rested my hands on the sill and leaned close, "I think Bishop is on the verge of being disposed of."

"So do you think we'll still receive the invite then?"

"Even more so now. By tomorrow the latest."

Kring looked my way, "That early?"

"Heck, I wouldn't be surprised if Bishop sent Roy back here after dinner."

Looking somewhat perplexed at my predicted speed of future events unfolding, Kring turned from the sill and asked, "You think they'll have a council meeting just for us?"

"No. Actually, I think Bishop will invite us without informing the others. I think he's been looking for an opportunity to establish himself over these immigrants, and this is his golden opportunity. Make himself more powerful with trade, get some familiar faces around him, and at the same time, send a stern message to everyone that he answers to no one. Roy will drive that home when he sees him later today, for he's got visions of us getting his back in those woods."

Kring began to use his walking stick as a fencing sword and air parried as he spoke, "Speaking of backs, Bishop's back has surely been against the wall, with only butterball there to protect it... I'm a genius."

Ignoring his boast, I kept us on point, "We'd better start making plans for tomorrow. This has really moved faster than I would have liked."

Kring stopped mid-swing, "Morning mission?"

I turned to Kring, resting my back against the sill, "As I see it, we really don't have a choice. We could have Roy over here by midday inviting us over, and then any time delay on our part would not only be an insult to Bishop, but a nick in his armor, if in fact, the council was informed of his formal invitation to us."

"How about some gamesmanship?"

"If we stall Bishop, we hurt Bishop, and therefore hurt our own chances at making this work."

Kring resumed his sword practice, "So a morning mission it is."

"Agreed. Early."

"How early?" Kring asked as he lunged for the kill against his invisible foe.

"Crack of your ass early."

Kring parried his adversary, "Could you leave the crack of my ass out of your morning please."

"Put your joke book back on the shelf for now; we have to plan. This has got to go by the numbers."

Kring stopped mid-swing, "Roger."

We sat down and began discussing what rations and equipment we'd need. Better to go light and fast. Crack of dawn meant leaving before our fathers went to work, which meant questions. We decided to tell our parents that we had planned a scientific expedition into The Woods for the collection of various species of frogs. We both regularly received monthly *Mr. Wizard* periodicals, and I remembered that the last month's issue had an expos`e on starting your own frog farm. Parents loved to watch a child's mind expand through nature. Little would they know what we planned to observe was unnatural.

Chapter 3
Where There's Smoke, There's Fire

The smell of a campfire in the morning is one of those smells, which sears your subconscious. As a kid, we associate a campfire with friends, family, and vacation. We never think of a campfire used for anything but good times. Heck, the only thing you cooked over the fire was a marshmallow or two, and if you were really lucky, a frank. To think that ancient man depended on the open flame for the vast majority of his meals, as well as for heat and protection, was just as far from a child's mind as man using fire as a weapon, or the men who died everyday putting fires out.

But this morning would be different. As we stalked the overgrown gravel driveway, the tall, thick, ancient oaks and maples made a canopy so dense, sunlight was scarcer then the brave few who would enter this forbidding forest alone. A football field in, with the road no longer visible, birds and cicadas replaced cars and kids. What normally would be a breath of fresh air, was replaced by smoldering timbers and burnt plastic of all things. Other smells assaulted my nasal passage: pungent odors that reminded me of the glasses left in the sink by my parents from the night before, and the dark, wet clothes left in a gym bag for a week. With the high humidity caused by the morning dew's rapid evaporation, every breath became labored, every sniff tainted. Smell is an alarming sense, and the smells that were emanating from this campground screamed, "Run! Don't walk!"

Before the camp came into view, I knew I wouldn't like what I saw. Three hundred yards in and another hundred off, the smoldering remains of the site's fire pit came into view. Kring fanned out to my right, dipping out of sight below a brush line some thirty feet away, while I crept directly towards the main clearing of the site. The massive fire pit took center stage and my absolute full attention, since the size, scope, and tattered condition of the entire site quickly became overwhelming to my visual senses. I noticed right away that the main fire had been hastily put out by the tell-tale signs of stamping feet, flying dirt and a poorly thrown bucket of water. *Why so fast? Grown-ups?* I quickly scanned for signs of grown-ups. Surely, the four-foot circumference of the fire and half-burnt logs piled two-feet high made it a lighthouse on a cliff perch, and thus visible from all four corners of The Woods. *Fools!* No firewalls were used to block the direct views of the blaze from the neighbors, which meant this could not be Bishop's work. Not only was this not Bishop's work, Bishop was most likely not even invited to the festivities, for he would have at a minimum, blocked the view from his own yard by propping up a section of old stockade fence, which was abundant throughout the western portion of The Woods. Besides, Bishop would never allow a fire to burn this bright or rage this long, with such little use of precautions, for Bishop knew that if The Woods went down in a ball of flames, so would he... *No way in Hell Bishop was here last night—that was for sure. Who was? Was the question...*

A silent scream from twenty yards away woke The Woods, "Tire tracks!"

"Quiet!" I hushed.

Kring apparently didn't hear me, since humans weren't meant to verbally communicate from twenty yards away without raising their voices, "Trel, Trel—tire marks!"

I placed a finger to my tightly puckered mouth as I silently stalked to his side, "Shhhhh!"

Kring pointed feverishly like a hunting dog would at a fallen duck. I did not have to run over to the treads to know the distinct tracks of a cop car. *Fools. Grown-ups and now cops. Fools!*

The Woods were changing and not for the better. Regardless of whether or not they were cop treads, the mere thought of getting caught by a cop on private property, especially in the middle of the aftermath of a murderous satanic ritual in a nearby town, made my heart race. On my way to Kring, I didn't just have to navigate over and around branches, but also beer bottles, which were strewn everywhere, as were cigarette butts, half-burned toys and sparklers. *Where did they get those? Fireworks on top of booze and porn? How in the last month had my Woods turned into Vegas?* Any more debauchery and I thought I was going to trip over the cold, dead corpse of a slaughtered virgin.

I let out a perfectly mimicked owl call, "Ka-wa-ha-hah-wah-wah!"

Kring immediately turned, eyes instantly focused on my hands and the impending call sign. I made the fist into palm, which meant *converge on to my position—immediately.*

Kring moved as quickly as the fallen branches would allow him. Brittle branches that were strewn across The Woods' floor were like individual laser trip-wires that were attached to mini alarms; a crack made by one stick could be heard for three acres. If one got startled, he would pick up the pace, trying to distance himself from the origin of the noise, which surely had woken the dead! But doing so in such a flustered fashion usually resulted in yet another snapped twig on the very next step, causing the individual to panic even further. The self-fulling prophecy ended in a limb flailing, full-fledged sprint, which sounded more like someone towing a cineplex-sized popcorn maker through an open warehouse, rather than a silently speedy getaway. Kring made the forty-foot journey quite nicely. He stepped on only one branch, but followed stealth procedures perfectly, which of course was to crouch in position and face down for forty-five seconds. I did as well, for there is no reason to look around. If someone is coming, you'll hear them long before you see them. *Grown-ups know nothing of the way of the ninja...*

When Kring finally descended onto my position, his eyes opened so wide that I couldn't tell he still had lids.

A silent yell of "My God!" was all Kring could say as he desperately tried to take in the scene.

"Devastation," I decreed.

Kring turned to me with primordial fear in his eyes, "Devil worshipers?"

"Hard to tell..."

A creaking of a branch was heard by us both, and we immediately crouched, this time scanning the far-off terrain for unwanted guests.

"Rabbit," whispered Kring.

"Maybe." We stayed crouched as we turned our attention back to the scene.

Regaining his composure quicker than his fear would have liked, Kring trembled as he stated the obvious, "It went down last night."

"Whatever happened, wasn't good," I concurred.

"You going to make a sketch?" Kring's voice cracked.

"I got to make the sketch last time, so it's up to you."

Kring and I both liked to draw, so we made a point to allow one another to take turns, while the other made a detailed list of events and inventory. This drawing was worth seven regular maps, for this was no fake treasure map in my backyard; this was a detailed schematic of an enemy camp, and perhaps a legitimate crime scene, which is why I was floored when Kring told me to draw it. I didn't question his decision and gladly swapped pads, before he changed his mind.

As I surveyed the scene, what jumped out at me right off the bat, was how much beer these guys drank. They had consumed an entire case. *These kids were full-blown alcoholics.*

"Trel—Trel! Qua, qua—"

I turned to see Kring fifteen feet away, motioning me to come to his position with as much zeal as a third-base coach would use when motioning a runner to steal home in the bottom of the ninth, during game seven of the World Series. I quickly put my palms out and made the chill motion. This stopped Kring's frantic motioning for approximately one second, when he then began to point so hard at the ground that if I did not make it to him lickety-split, his finger had a high probability of going right through the center of the earth and up a Chinaman's ass who was sitting innocently enough on the crapper. I hurtled a couple of logs and a stack of branches, most likely collected to fuel the fire. Kring was crouching on a rather large pad of moss, measuring six to seven feet at its widest and meandering twenty feet from tip to tail. But he was not pointing at the bed's natural soft green velvet mattress that Mother Nature had taken such careful time preparing for the squirrels' siesta, but rather what lay upon it.

"A fucking bra!" Kring silently shouted. Light pink and lacy, with cups large enough to hold peaches. *Someone went to second base last night.*

"Should we take it?" Kring asked.

"Huh?"

How long I was staring at that bra, I'll never know. I do know one thing—if Kring hadn't have said something, I would have stared a little longer. When I came back to The Woods, I thought out loud, "What if she comes back for it?"

"Right."

"But then again, she wouldn't think that we took it," I reasoned.

"Right."

I followed the train of thought, striking a decisive blow in my single player chest match, "Plus, maybe by taking it, she'll think it was one of the guys from the other side and a fight will ensue, forging a schism, severely weakening their group."

"Genius."

"As always, my friend. As always," I boasted.

Kring looked to me, then to the bra, then back to me, affording me the same level of cordialness one would offer a guest when deciding the fate of the last braised shrimp, "You want to pick it up?"

"Do you?"

Kring offered a noncommittal, "Not if you want it."

I left the door open, "I don't want it; I just want to collect it for evidence."

Kring was on it like a cheap suit, "I have my backpack; we can store it in that."

I knew it wouldn't be the last time I'd see it, so when Kring snatched it from the ground, like he was shoplifting tampons in a department store, I couldn't help but giggle, "You touched it."

"I'll wash my hands when I get home," Kring said without looking up.

"Yeah, you'll wash them in baby oil," I chided.

Kring was more offended than the jest warranted, and a scolding, "Fuck you!" just added fuel to the fire.

"Just don't say that to me when I come over to your house tomorrow and you're wearing it."

"Dick. You want to hold it?"

"Just screwing with you. Besides worst case scenario, you could give it to your mom. She goes through bras and panties faster than the Hulk goes through jeans."

Kring was no longer taking the bait and fishing bored me, "You think this belongs to the girl Roy talked to?" Kring asked.

I hadn't put a face to the bra, since I'd spent the last minute putting boobies to it, "Maybe."

Kring looked off into the distance, as if he'd heard something I hadn't, "Screw the late day mission, we need to find out what goes on here at night."

I felt his fire and fanned the flames, "These are our woods!"

But Kring did not follow suit, for he was deep in thought; thus we studied the surroundings for a little longer in complete silence before hightailing it home. No need to lollygag looking for lucky pennies when you've already found the pot of gold. Certain things I did remember to write down, such as the angle the camp seemed to face and how many people I believed could have been there. *The second fire pit was odd... What did they use that for, and why did they take the time to dig that hole so deep and take such time in making it so symmetrical?*

Chapter 4
Down the Rabbit Hole

Since leaving The Woods, Kring and I had spent the remainder of the morning in the tree house, going over the why, when, how and who. Tensions and sugar levels were through the roof, due in part to the heralding adventure, but more so from the consumption of a dozen carrot cupcakes, 2 liters of Coke, a half-box of ginger snap cookies, along with an entire bag of trail mix. For in our current state of paranoia, we thought getting rid of all the evidence of our whereabouts of the last two hours, including the rations, was a prudent decision. Oddly enough, the bra hadn't been discarded as hastily as the binoculars.

As both of us stood like generals in a war room, surveying the tokens of a scaled battlefield, I wanted to address our new found enemy's might, "From the size of the camp, I'd say there could have been ten people there last night."

"Try fifteen."

"Fifteen? That might be stretching it."

"Four massive logs around the main fireplace—that's seating for eight minimum. The old chair, the ground near the main fire, what's that? Eleven, maybe twelve, and that's not even counting the people manning that other fire pit people, or the ones humping on the moss."

Though Kring's assessment was rather well reasoned, I found folly in assuming every show was performed to a packed house, "That's to say every seat was taken."

"What's saying different?"

"For starters, I didn't see a lot of footprints."

Kring didn't so much dismiss my observation, as summarize his own observations, "I saw a lot of empty beer cans."

Though intelligent for nine, Kring was naive for ten, and some real-world education was in order. "Four guys could drink that much beer."

Immediately dismissing my fact for sensationalism, Kring waved me off as if I'd just told him the world was flat, "Six beers a piece? They'd be dead."

I didn't want to explain to him that I'd personally seen my father drink a twelve-pack on more nights than I cared to remember, only to stare out a window of a speeding car on the way home from a family get-together, "Maybe."

Annoyed with my cavalier noncommittal comment, Kring fired out wild speculation to keep the dialogue dancing, "We'd surely see some vomit; no one can drink that much and walk out unharmed!"

I couldn't get the girl I had created around the bra out of my mind, "Maybe the girl was..." I trailed off, realizing I had gone back to her for the four hundredth time.

Kring shook his head and rolled his eyes in silent protest to my mental masturbation, "What?"

"Who says she wanted to go to second?"

"What are you saying?"

I looked to the window, "Maybe she was the one that drank too much. Maybe they planned it."

"Dude—it would be in the papers by now and cops would be all over the place."

I had to agree, "True... What I can't figure out is that second fire pit."

Kring shivered, despite the warm summer breeze that was currently refreshing the stale quarters, "I know, kind of eerie, ain't it?"

Finding a ray of light, I squinted, "More than just eerie—out of place."

"Yeah, it looked like a robot honed it from a block of clay, while the rest of the camp was hastily erected by a bunch of hobos."

How they made it was less fascinating than why, but before I could revisit the inner thoughts of people I didn't have a mental image of as of yet, the sound of a dirt bike, needing chain grease, interrupted my budding logic tree.

Kring quickly raised a hand as if I would object, "Hard, slow crank."

I concurred, "Roy."

Soon the bike stopped on the other side of the fence from the fort and the whining brakes and no skid-out confirmed the rider.

Immediately I pointed to the knapsack, "Lose it."

"Roger."

Kring quickly crammed the knapsack in the secret compartment that was located atop the doublewide false ceiling joist.

As he scurried to perform one last site check, I casually stuck my head out the window, cascading casual confidence, "Yo—what's up?"

With a big wave and smile, Roy yelled up, "Hey guys, want to play?"

From behind me Kring snapped, "We are; what do you want?"

Roy either didn't hear Kring's comment, or pretended not to, "I want to come up."

"Fine." Kring exhaled.

As Roy parked his bike against the wall, I turned to Kring for reassurance.

Knowing me better than myself, as best friends often do, Kring peevishly answered the unasked, "I'm cool; worry about yourself."

"I am."

Roy was now at the base of the ladder and Kring was growing impatient with what he knew was Roy planning the climb, as if the ladder was Everest, "What are you waiting for?"

"I'm coming," Roy moaned as he lumbered up the ladder. When his head cleared the fort floor, Roy made a face more bizarre than our morning.

"And I thought his mama was ugly," Kring's petulance punctuated his continuing clear lack of patience for Roy's attempts at physical humor.

Roy took exception, "What's up your ass?"

Kring shrugged as if his annual checkup had revealed high cholesterol, "Feel great."

I, of course, felt Roy's pain and didn't want to lose our prize tuna before we could haul it in the boat. I extended my hand, as I rolled my eyes, "He's just screwing with you, Bro."

Roy took my hand, but before using it as much needed leverage for his final ascent, he made sure I was tethered, "So, what ya guys doing?"

We both answered simultaneously with an innocent, "Nothing." I continued doing nothing as I observed Roy with my peripheral vision. Roy seemed oddly preoccupied for someone so eager to start something new.

"You guys eat lunch yet?"

Kring snapped, "Can you stop thinking of chow for once? My God!"

Roy was taken back by Kring's sting, but he did not reply in kind, "I was going to invite you guys over for lunch; my mom just made some iced tea and we have a ton of sandwich meat."

The Culvers' iced tea was urban legend. Crafted over two days, three days in the spring and fall, with a fourth day added in the winter, each pitcher of sundrenched herbal love was infused with honey, brown sugar, lemons, oranges and fresh mint from Mrs. Culver's garden. Over the years, many mothers, including my own, had unsuccessfully tried to imitate the Culver's tasty brew. I gently declined his offer and Roy accepted my decision without the usual high-pressure sales gimmicks that made his daily overtures painful at best.

Kring sneeringly scanned Roy for sweat and food stains, "What did you do today?"

Roy pulled his too tight for primetime shirt down below his belly while scanning the floor for crumbs, "Nothing really. Bishop was being really mean earlier, so I just left."

Kring cocked a smile, "Troubles with the natives?"

"Not really. Just Bishop being Bishop."

I offered my condolences, "Sorry you got to deal with that." And before I knew it, without ever even discussing it, Kring and I had assumed the roles of good cop, bad cop.

Roy appreciated my empathy, "Thanks."

Assuming his bad cop role, Kring ate and shat sympathy, like a meal worm in carrion. "So, is your problem with your brother going to affect your position in the 'pecking order'?" Kring made the standard quote signs with his fingers as if his dramatic, sarcastic tone wasn't enough to give away his opinion as to the validity of The Woods' current regime and Roy's chances of pledging any club not named Weight Watchers.

Briefly closing his eyes to change the channel, Roy muttered under his breath, "Most likely not, since I never had one."

I needed more from him, "You kidding me? That's bullshit."

Kring jumped from his milk crate, "You're such a sucker!"

I put an arm out, "Those woods are more yours than anyone else's."

Over my shoulder I could feel Kring's desire to cross the room, "Your brother's the mayor of that little podunk town and couldn't land you a cushy office job?"

I didn't need Roy defending what he couldn't control, "Who got the other posts?"

"Kurt got one and the rest were filled out by the other kids."

Thoughtfully I asked, "What about Franky and Freddy?"

"They wanted to... Franky and Freddy decided not to join."

From over my shoulder, Kring grilled him, "I thought you said they were up there all the time?"

"Not as much lately, but they were never really a part of the other stuff."

"What stuff?" Kring pressed.

"That's secret—sorry."

"Then leave!" Kring ordered.

I knew I needed to take the reigns, "Hold on, Bro. If Roy has to keep a secret, he has to keep a secret."

Roy finally felt Kring's flagrant firing of questioning, "Yeah—where's your code of honor?"

"Where's your neck?"

Roy clearly had enough, "I'm gone."

And Kring was going to ride him like a donkey to his front doorstep, "You wear a thong?"

I grabbed the turning Roy with one hand and silenced Kring with the other, "Enough! Roy's been through more than his fair share today."

Realizing the final straw was about to break the camel's back, Kring relented, "Alright, you can stay."

Looking to me, Roy paused before accepting the halfhearted appeasement, "Fine."

I took my hand and warmly placed it on Roy's shoulder as I guided him from the ladder to an old couch cushion on the floor, since my stool lacked the structural rigidity needed to support his girth. "Sorry about you being left out like that. You must be furious."

Easing himself to the floor, Roy winced, as if he'd carried his bike over, instead of riding it, "Yeah, well, what you gonna do? Most of them are older."

I did my best to assure him of our loyalty, "If we were there, that wouldn't have gone down like that."

Kring added with conviction, "That's for damn sure."

I did my best to match Kring's bravado, "No way would they have pushed you aside like—"

But Kring assumed his role, meaning he cut off mine, "Treat you like a bitch, did they?"

"No."

Taking Kring's lead, I resumed mine, "Hey, us younger kids have to stick together. Kring or I would have been screwed over just as hard."

Kring slapped my statement to the side, "Speak for yourself."

Roy wouldn't concede contrite, "You can talk tough now, but you'd be crying like a bitch if you were there last night."

Kring and I heard the lock on Pandora's Box click open ever so gently. There was still a latch to move, and the next question would either blow the top wide open like a porch door in a storm, or slam it shut with the same ferocity. And though the next question was paramount in determining the proper direction of the wind, pausing for too long might give Roy the chance to reflect on his last statement, and hide in the storm cellar 'til the coast was clear.

Kring was staring at Roy like a new toy in a Christmas window, most likely envisioning himself and the bra's owner fornicating on the soft moss, while people covered in white ash danced hypnotically around the fire, chanting reverse Latin.

I stepped forward with, "What happened?" *What happened? What an amateur move!* And Kring knew it for the egg it was, for he stared startled, of course after he checked his shorts to see if Sergeant Salami had pitched a tent in front of the campfire between his legs that began to blaze while he was busy daydreaming about the girl he'd never met.

Distant and somber, Roy offered vague, "Crazy things."

"Like what?" Kring asked intently.

Shaking his head in a vain attempt to snap himself out of whatever held him, Roy offered more of the same, "Just crazy."

Before Kring could jump up and strangle Roy, I squatted next to Roy and rested my hand on his shoulder once again, "Crazy? What's considered crazy these days?"

"Crazy is something a sane person would never imagine."

It was quite clear that Roy was not bragging at this point, for he was donning a mile-long stare and not his habitually pinched smile and anxious body movements. No, Roy had seen things last night that were reserved for grownups' eyes only and as a consequence, something was not right with Roy today. Something had definitely been stolen from him, other than the cliché of innocence lost. Of course I didn't make that connection right then and there, but I did make the connection between the happenings from the night before, and the current condition of my demoralized neighbor.

I spoke only to pull him away from the pain, "So you don't want to talk about it?"

"Huh? Oh no... Not really. It's not that I don't trust you guys, it's just that... well I think we should not talk about our respective affiliations when we hang out as friends."

I nodded, "I can appreciate that." Looking to Kring, "How 'bout you buddy?"

Kring had since taken a knee to mask his new appendage and looked up with a contorted cocktail of embarrassment, anger, and guilt. "You bet. Silence is a virtue."

Roy now seemed sad, masked in deep troubled thought, surely mulling over the visions and decisions that haunted him from the previous night. "I'm actually not feeling that great."

A mother's empathy erupted from deep within me and I spoke accordingly, "You want something to eat? Maybe you're just hungry?"

"No, I think I just need a nap... I was going to nap at my house earlier, but I knew my dad wanted me to do yard work, so I took off before he could ask."

Finally, Kring's voice carried some genuine concern. "So where you gonna go?"

Blinking away the cobwebs in a shuddered soul, Roy appeared not to care where the winds blew him, "Don't know really... I think I'm just gonna try to sneak into the basement, and sleep on the couch."

The pain was too powerful for me to ignore, "Wow, you're really hurting."

Roy began to rise to his feet in slow motion, "Yeah, well it's been a rough couple of days."

Now that Kring's bloodthirsty brain was finally being allocated some much needed nourishment, Kring sounded more like a doctor than a friend, "You better take it easy for the next day or two. When you feel better, come on over and go in the pool."

As Roy finally stood straight, he smiled slightly, though he maintained his distant stare, "That would be great. Thanks guys. I needed to talk with some friends."

I did my best to drive home his hopes, "Hey, we're always in your corner, Bro."

Kring followed suit, "Yeah, someone's got beef with you, they got beef with us."

"That means a lot." And with that, Roy made his way to the ladder, sighing a labored breath with each step. Though he was grossly overweight, his normally overtaxed aeration system was accompanied by small moans of pain, which meant Roy's muscles were aching. Though carrying his weight around would fatigue even Hercules, Roy was in obvious pain due to external influences, meaning something had not only damaged his mental state, but ravaged his body as well. *What was so crazy that a sane person couldn't even imagine? Why was he so afraid he couldn't even talk to his brother about what they'd both witnessed, or sleep in his own home? What was he hiding, and why? What in God's name had happened there last night?*

Chapter 5
Logistics and Planning

With the last labored crank of Roy's ungreased chain fading in the distance, I began to place all the cards on the table, "You think he's holding back?"

"Certainly not at the buffet line."

"You were a bit hard on him."

"Not any more than he deserved."

"Who are we to judge?"

"We are gods."

I wished Kring was correct and that we were gods, for I could simply smite those who had desecrated our most holy of places. But we weren't gods, and apparently Roy was even less almighty than us. "I think he knows less than I originally thought."

Kring smirked, "Got sent home before the festivities were underway."

I turned toward Kring, but focused on a large fly that was having trouble finding the exit, "Actually, I think he left on his own accord."

Kring rubbed his temples, "Fat and weak is a sad combo."

"We need to find out what the hell is going on, and tonight's the only opportunity we have."

Kring exhaled hard, "Tell me something I don't know."

"You know shit from Shynola, boy!"

"I know your breath don't smell like Shynola."

I smiled, despite myself, "You're pretty quick, kid. Pretty quick."

"That I am..." Kring said as he perched his outstretched legs on the window sill.

"Let's hope you're just as quick on your feet tonight as you are with your mouth."

"You sound just like your mom."

I had to hand it to the kid, "Pretty quick, indeed..."

Kring was bothered by something other than the fly that continually dive-bombed the doorway, "I think we should start getting ready, ASAP."

The day was taxing to say the least, and I needed a second wind and something to eat before I collapsed, "I agree. What time you got?"

"3:30."

"Shit, where'd the day go?"

Kring seemed lost in thought as he scanned the ground, "Who knows, but I bet Culver ate up a lot of it... ALONG WITH OUR CAKE!"

Oh my God... how? When? Roy had mauled Kring's favorite meal of all time—Entenmann's coffee cake, with the deceptive dexterity of a cat burglar.

"Can you believe him?!" Kring screamed in vain, as he dramatically flailed to and fro the walls, like a madman in an insane asylum awaiting his noontime sedative.

"How? When?" I was truly at a loss.

Now yelling at the ceiling Kring paced, "Right under our noses!"

I tried to piece the puzzle together, but to no avail, "I thought he had one piece!"

Kring looked at me with disdain, "Yeah, the left side!"

"I didn't even see him eat. I thought when he sat down it was to take a load off…"

Kring seemed hurt by my gullibility, "Take a load off? Oh, he'll take a load alright. Tomorrow, in the bathroom, he'll take a huge load when he craps my cake!"

I became flustered fast, "I only offered it because he was— "

"You offered Entenmann's cake to a food processor! Hide the knapsack? We could have suspended the knapsack from the ceiling with the bra like it was a freaking wind chime, and he wouldn't have been the wiser."

"Easy, Tex. There's still some left."

Kring grabbed the box in disgust and tossed it out the window. "All gone."

I recoiled, "Are you crazy? There was good cake left!"

Kring slapped his hands hard, signifying satisfaction, "On the contrary. The food was tainted; I saved you."

"You're crazy."

"Perfectly sane."

I scanned the floor for crumbs, "Now what are we gonna eat?"

"Not that disease-ridden cake, that's for damn sure," Kring snapped as he kicked his walking stick.

I was on edge of enervation, "Then what? It's at least an hour until you have dinner, so there is no way you're going to get anything out of your house, and if you did, it would most likely be a freakin' rice cake with honey on it!"

Looking amused at my predicament, "Why don't you go home and get something?"

"I'm in once, and out. I'll make my stop when you eat dinner."

With that we refocused on the task at hand, shaping our intertwining alibies, for as it turned out a bit of good fortune had landed in our laps; Kring's parents were off to a party at the Rocco's, which meant they'd be getting home sometime before sunrise. In their stead, they'd hired the legendary Miss Mary—a woman so old, she had personally met everyone on Mount Rushmore. Not only was she ancient, she had actually legally died once before, only to have her family force the doctors to bring her back, due to some technicality on her driver's license. While on life support, in intensive care for well over a year, Miss Mary had begun to literally rot. Parts of her body began to severely sag, while swaths of skin began to peel away like bark on a birch, forcing her children, who were senior citizens in their own right, to send her upstate during the hottest of months, in hopes of slowing the decomposition. Luckily for us, the weather had cooled.

Over the next hour, Kring and I weathered the painful stabs of hunger until the Pelagatti's dinner bell rang. By then we knew what we would need to pull the job off, when we were going to make our move, and how we were going to hit the target area. The only nagging question still needing answering was why. Why were we going to risk our necks? The simple answer was answers...

For a question that no one has a desire to have answered is no more relevant than that of the sound a falling tree makes in the woods when no one is to be found to hear it. If the questions we had about the happenings in Wilder's Woods were falling trees, they would be Redwoods falling on churches, come Sunday morning.

Chapter 6
Dinner and a Show

Dinner was cordial at best. My thoughts elsewhere made the mundane dinner conversation, which was comprised of problems with the aging house's plumbing, to being over-taxed on our property, go from boring bitch-babblings to background blips.

"What's wrong, baby?"

Still using my plate as a portal into my impending mission, my mother's sweet prodding went unheard and therefore, unanswered.

My father's voice, though, shattered the viewing lens, leaving only the cold, half-eaten meal before me. "Hey!"

"Sorry."

"Is everything okay?" My mom inquired.

Before I could lie, my father probed me, "You feeling right?"

My only sibling and most powerful of all big sisters, Libra, exuded less empathy, "Freak."

I offered her a steely-eyed, healthy helping of silence.

To that, Libra covered her mouth and mocked an "Oooh."

I couldn't afford an escalation, so I did not respond in kind, "I'm not feeling that great."

My mom, who was one of the most caring people to ever walk the planet, was always one complaint away from turning the dining room table into a triage station, "Stomach? Fever?"

My father, on the other hand, had the bedside manners of a mortician, "You got the shits?"

"Walter!" Mother scolded.

"I don't want to waste his food if he's just going to squirt dirt in five minutes."

"WALTER!"

"Boy, you going to go number three? For all those who are not familiar with number three, it's number one, out the number two hole.

Libra loved the new line of questioning and did her darndest to facilitate more dialogue, "Butt juice on the loose!"

"LIBRA!" My mother screamed.

Libra loved goading my mother by harassing me, "Mom, Trel's sick. Oh, Little Brother, I hope you don't die in your sleep tonight, making wetties in the beddies."

"Have no fear, Sis. If I'm gonna die, I plan on taking you with me."

"Trel!" My mother shot.

My father looked at me strangely, said nothing for a minute, and then dropped some Parenting 101 on the table, "If anyone is going to kill your sister, it will be me."

"Walter!"

Libra turned to my dad, feigning shock, "Oh my God, I hate you!

Dad rolled his eyes, "Oh, I was just kidding!"

Libra loved the drama, "Murdering your daughter? Oh my God, I am so done with dinner!"

"Honey please! I made a blueberry pie just for you!" *Wait, blueberries were my favorite. What in God's name was going on here?*

And Libra knew it, for she looked at me as she tenderly cupped her heart with both hands, "Blueberry pie? For mwaa?"

"Yes, sweetie—blueberry pie."

Libra turned her affections back to me, "You know, if you eat it, you'll have blueberries pouring out your pie hole!"

"Libra! Be nice," my mom scolded Libra with little ardor.

Libra was on fire and I thanked my lucky stars! For little did she know her little side show was laying the groundwork for my alibi. *A pawn in my plot. Nothing more than bad dinner entertainment.*

I gently touched my stomach and lowered my voice to a lethargic level, "You know what? I think I'll be fine. I was supposed to sleep over Kring's tonight, but I might not."

"You're not sleeping anywhere," my dad barked.

"Walter," was all my mom could muster in my defense, which meant she knew it was more pontification than policy.

I needed to play the victim card quick, "You want me to stay up all night? So be it," I sniveled as I rubbed my temples.

"Don't get smart with me, boy; I'll stop that mudslide in your pants with my fucking foot!"

"Walter!"

Realizing he had gone too far by physically threatening one of her children and cursing to boot, my father relented and pointed to me with his thumb as he went back to eating his meal, making sure to avoid contact with a fork-wielding wife, "He's a wise ass."

Libra, of course, was in her glory; a dessert made especially for her that her brother loved, but could not eat added fuel to her fire, "He's got an ass alright. One that's gonna kill the bathroom tonight."

"Libra!"

My sister looked at my mother with puppy eyes, "What?"

Trying her best not to smile, she pointed her fork first at Libra, and then at my dad, "You have a terrible mouth! And Walter, you're encouraging her!"

After fifteen years of marriage, my dad knew the tightrope he could tiptoe, "Can you fault me for giving a crap about the crap my son will take?"

Sensing the situation was getting out of hand, I took the initiative for peace and extended the olive branch to my sister. "I hope Leebs is wrong, for I really wanted to play over Kring's tonight. If this does get bad, I'm going to have to come home."

"You'd better," my mom said.

"You'll be fine," Libra said in an oddly out of place, compassionate tone.

My dad showed less compassion in his projectile predictions, "If you shit your pants—"

"Walter, enough!" my mother yelled.

I had to reposition my hands from my temples to my mouth in order to conceal the smile that I could no longer hold back, for I had gained permission to sleep over Kring's without ever asking, nor implying that Mr. or Mrs. Pelagatti had given their blessing. What's more? Covering my mouth, doubled as a non-verbal sign that I was not in fact feeling well. I was learning how to master the human psyche at an astonishing rate. A warm summer breeze blew through the wide open windows and all at the table basked in the brief reprieve like caribou on the Serengeti. I craned my neck as the droplets of sweat cooled behind my ears. My father blinked his eyes and began to slowly shovel food in his mouth, while my sister stared at the huge wall painting above my mother's head that looked like a TurDuckEn, making love to a melting igloo.

My mom was the first to brush off the benevolent beauty of the breeze, "Honey, why don't you just get ready and I'll clean up."

I looked to my sister and dad, both of whom looked like goats grazing, "Thank you, Mommy."

I got up while the getting was good and held my speed in check as I made a beeline for my bedroom. I had already packed all my equipment and rations for the evening and tossed the knapsack that contained them out my bedroom window and into the pachysandra patch. Since I was already donning my entire uniform under my civilian fatigues, I would be out the door before they finished the dishes.

My room was a box by today's standards, not any bigger than Kring's treehouse. It was designed and used by the original family as a home office. Barely large enough for a single bed, dresser and desk, the room afforded me zero room to leave things out of place, which meant my room was in a constant state of disarray. Cheap toys are two things: poorly made and big, giving the guilty parent some level of satisfaction at least until the wrapping is ripped from the box. My floor was littered with the remains of every toy too cheap to be built in China, such as my knockoff of a knockoff of Optimus Prime that was made in North Korea out of spare parts from AK-47 assault rifle stockpiles, left over from the Korean War.

The most ostentatious example of piracy gone luncacy was of course my Transformer, or as the box read, TrainsPerformer, since my Optimus Prime, who was actually named Prime Time, transformed into the locomotive of a circus train, with all the other TrainsPerformers comprising the remainder of the "Train". The pipeline of product was eventually shut down by border patrol before their arch enemy could be launched on American soil the following Christmas. The DeceitfulExCons, which were nothing more than robotic hobos, sourced from WWII T-34 Russian tank treads, followed the train from town to town, disrupting their traveling menagerie. Obviously, the storyline of the DeceitfulExCons continually arriving to the one horse town the day prior to the TrainsPerformers because they were privy to the train's predetermined track and schedule, got old quick.

Matter of fact, all cheap toys get old quick, making the purchase of newer, cheaper toys inevitable. Thus the graveyard of misfit toys which littered my floor and shelves made it impossible to scan the room for last minute supplies. Though frustrating on several levels, it wasn't worthy of worry, for the moment of silence before the storm was what I truly needed. I sat on my bed Indian style and closed my eyes, doing my best to breathe like a man who knew what he was about, when an inaudible argument erupted from the kitchen signaling it was time to shine. I got up, made the quick two-step to the door and swung it wide. My sister stood smack in the middle, blocking my passage.

"Oh Brother, you live!" And with that Libra wrapped her arms around me and squeezed me like a ripe grapefruit. I didn't move, partly due to keeping in character and partly due to the fact that regardless of my current crisis with Libra, Libra's hugs always felt the best—even better than Mom's, which was saying a lot. Libra hugged me like an old Italian man during the holidays; her strength of body, mind and soul recharged me whenever I was fortunate enough to have my personal space violated by her. She knew it too, and it was the one thing she never joked about, for it was just as precious to her as it was to me, especially since as of late our hugs had become less frequent and somewhat uncomfortable, (at least for me) due to Libra's breasts quadrupling in size since the winter. The greatest moments are fleeting and the hug came to an abrupt end when Libra pulled back and looked to the kitchen through the dining room wall.

"You better mosey before Dad has another drink and picks apart your story."

"What story?" I said too quickly to feign innocence.

"Move it or lose it kid. I'll give you what I can, but that window's shorter than you." And with that, she kissed me on my forehead and strutted to the kitchen for some after dinner theater. Knowing my sister was spot on, I followed five paces behind. My father was in the kitchen doorway arguing a point over the Middle East and blind hatred. Libra stopped short of him, as my mother hastily cleaned some pots in the sink that had already been cleaned before we sat down for dinner.

My father saw me and swung around, pointing to me with his half emptied red wine glass, "Stop right there."

The inertia threw fluid from my father's glass, and Libra noticed the splatter, and was quick to offer assistance, "I'll get that, Pops."

Looking down at the spill, my father tried to measure the amount of the spill in ounces and divide that amount into the cost of the bottle, in hopes of figuring out his total loss.

I spoke before he could regroup, "Since Miss Mary is watching us until the Pelagatti's get back from dinner and the movies, do you think it's possible I can bring a flashlight?"

Micro-managing Libra's labor, my father answered absently, "Make sure you bring it back."

"Yes, Father."

Now I was really rolling! I had just killed two birds with one stone, thus completing my equipment list with the only item I couldn't take prior without potentially raising questions, while stopping my mother from calling the Pelagatti's at the same time. Bottom line, the only person that my mother dreaded talking to more than a drunk Walter, was an undead Miss Mary. As I walked out the front door, I had an alibi, rations, equipment, and an unexpected ally for the evening's outing.

I dropped a kiss in stride without turning, muttering, "Love you guys—Peace out Leebs." Quickly opening and exiting the door before receiving the proper partings, I immediately exited right, and trotted to the front corner of my house to take stock of my situation underneath a massive weeping willow. Before turning on my flashlight, I wrapped a piece of tracing paper around it that I had previously colored with a purple magic marker. Once around the flashlight, I secured the paper with a thick rubber band. Making sure it was pointed toward the ground in front of me, I turned it on and began to scan the immediate area. With just enough light to afford me both depth perception and basic shape recognition, such as bushes and stumps, I located my backpack within seconds. After locating the pack and performing a quality control check on the straps and pockets, I sheathed the flashlight in a hastily made holster from an old gym sock and string. With the pack and light secured, I proceeded straight out to the front of my driveway at a brisk pace, taking to the street's shadows, verses cutting across Jim's well-lit yard.

I quickly closed in on the sparsely pruned, thirty-foot-high wall of overgrown arborvitae bushes that acted as the Great Wall of China, separating Jim's and Kring's yards. Near the front of the yard, a passage had been carved over time, but one had to have mastered the slight left juke in order to avoid impaling themselves face-first onto the "eye-popping" branch, which jutted out directly in the middle of the path, purposely putting first-time explorers and rushing invading armies in harm's way. I knew the path well, but at this point, any use of my new, high-tech visual aid was welcomed. For starters, I needed to get the holster-pull down pat before I was in The Woods. Last thing I needed was to be caught off-guard, fumbling for my flashlight while the enemy was closing in on our position. *Besides, having the ability to whip this bad boy out like Clint Eastwood would a 44 Magnum in a Dirty Harry flick for the first time in front of Kring would be priceless.* Precisely four steps before the evergreen wall, I seamlessly pulled the flashlight from the side sock holster and extended my other arm to shield me from errant branches. This time, instead of sidestepping the wooden lance of death, I did a quasi-spin move in slow motion, since I was more comfortable between the bushes than Barry Sanders between the tackles.

With the treehouse before me, I decided to ascend via the trap door, instead of climbing the ladder. Though it meant an additional step of removing my knapsack and hoisting it up with the pulley system prior, my ascent was now fully enclosed within the vast array of the tree's inner branch network, which meant I was no longer subjected to the possibility of being spotted by anyone who was more than fifteen feet away from the tree's base. Once inside, I quickly closed the door below me and grabbed the knapsack from the suspended wench, which was positioned on the highest rafter above the opening.

"Nice work."

I turned quicker than a gecko changes its colors.

Kring's smile was bigger than the moon that lit it, "I hope you're more aware of your surroundings when we're in the middle of the action."

Fumbling for my pack, I countered, "Worry about yourself."

"I am."

I stopped and tapped my heavily taped-up and weighted sock, "Don't worry about me tripping you up; I'm feeling it tonight."

"Sound just like your momma."

"Glad your spirits are high."

"What's in the bag, Bitch?"

"Rations and equipment. Why?"

"Got any extra room?"

"Some. How much you need?"

Sitting Indian-style against the far wall, Kring leisurely grabbed a box of pellets from behind his back and slid them to me across the floor, "Enough for these?"

I looked at them before I grabbed them, "What's up?"

Closing his eyes, "A little insurance policy, that's all."

"Live ammo? You're crazy."

Kring opened his eyes, "Perfectly sane."

I was beside myself, "You think stepping on a dried twig makes noise? This will be the shot heard 'round the world!"

"We're not taking my hand pistol."

"Your pump-action rifle?"

Kring smiled once again, "That's right."

I had to put an end to his over-packing, "It takes ten pumps to barely have enough juice to penetrate paper. It's useless."

"You're useless," Kring retorted.

I didn't need a fight; I needed solidarity, "Seriously Bro, not only is the gun a chore to load, but it's too cumbersome to carry."

Shrugging off the obvious, Kring replied, "I agree."

"What am I missing? Your fake M-16?"

"Finally..." Kring dramatically exhaled.

"Though it's a one-pumper with a magazine, it's twice as heavy and ten times as bulky as your rifle."

Kring reached behind him and proudly pulled out a sawed-off M-16 replica pellet gun. "Not anymore." Holding it briefly with both hands, he then extended it to me. "Go ahead. Hold it. How bulky is it now?"

I took it slowly from his grasp as if it were dynamite. "How and when?"

"About an hour ago with my dad's metal saw." Not only was the handle sawed off, but Kring had taped his Mini-Maglite on top. The Mag Lite had a red saran wrap finish.

I had to hand it to the kid, he was good. "Nice." I turned the light on and aimed it at the wall.

"Point and shoot."

"Point and shoot," I repeated.

Kring's voice carried skepticism, "What did you bring?"

"Wrist rocket."

"How prehistoric..." Kring drawled.

I quickly added, "I also have a box of smoke-grenades, a mega-stink bomb, an M-80, a shoulder-fired bottle rocket launcher with twelve rockets, and six Roman candles... Plus some extra special goodies in case it all goes to crap."

"Great. All we need now are balloons and a cake, and I can invite my cousins over."

I reminded my comrade that desperate times called for desperate measures, only to have Kring counter that it was a little strange for a guy who was questioning the decibel signature of a pellet gun, to bring enough T.N.T. to the campsite to strip-mine it. I assured him that the Roman candles and bottle rockets were only in play if things went south in a hurry, and the M-80 was for the outside chance of total Armageddon. As I handed him the Doomsday device, Kring inquired on the fuses duration.

"Maybe four minutes."

"Sweet. How far do you think we'll get from Ground Zero before this puppy goes nuclear?"

"If we lit it at camp's edge, we could theoretically high-tail it halfway across the salt flats before the big bang."

Kring canned my conclusion with contempt, "Never."

"Why?"

"Too far."

I knew what I knew, "We could make it."

But so did Kring, "We could also be caught behind the Culver's, waiting for Mr. Culver to finish his More 100 and Whiskey Sour."

"Point taken," I agreed, much to my chagrin.

Kring rolled the ordinance back to me across the floor, "So, 86 the M-80."

I snatched it up like I was playing jacks, "Can't do that, Bro."

"Why?"

"We have to send a message."

Kring was adamant, "Send them a singing telegram for all I care, but not that though. It's too risky."

"And that's why it must be this! They have to know right off the bat that we're no joke. They need to know the stakes. No games. If they come back tomorrow, we'll know."

"Know what?" Kring asked, somewhat unsure of where I was going.

I composed myself before continuing, "We'll know if they're for real. They come back and we all know where we all stand. No sense in dragging this out and wondering how far the other side is willing to go. Let's find out tonight."

"What if we just piss them off? What then, Captain Courageous?"

"Then the next time we go in with twelve M-80s, circle the place, take up strategic positions, and lay waste to the place with Roman candle mortars, Yellow Jackets launched via arm slings, and five dozen shoulder-fired bottle rocket packs. That's what we do. Those are our woods, and tonight is the first night in a long campaign to take them back. If you know of another reason for us going into Wilder's freakin' Woods, strapped to the hilt without our parents' permission, you let me know now."

Kring was taken back by my bravado, "I was just asking."

I did another equipment check, signaling the end to our debate, "Get pumped. We're going in."

Chapter 7
Night Mission Bravo

I slid down the rope that dangled precariously from the top rafter of the fort to the ground with little drama, and immediately looked up with arms extended. The knapsack was first, followed by Kring's shoulder sling and then his gun. Kring came next and descended too quickly, partially landing on my shoulder before I could sidestep. His flustered freefall aggravated me more than it hurt me and my uncoordinated countermeasure added insult to injury. Once on the ground, we crouched, refocused, and synchronized our watches.

"What time you got?" I whispered.

"9:42 pm."

"I got 9:40 pm."

"Even your watch is slow."

"Hold on," I grumbled.

After some fumbling, I managed to move my watch up two minutes. I looked Kring in the face. The use of our mothers' respective foundations and blush for camouflage made this closeness somewhat strange, for we surely looked like the two baddest men on the block, but smelled like rather sophisticated women. Hopefully the rest of the night would not have the long-term effects on our psyche, as did this moment.

My heart was pumping hard, and when I thought about how hard it was pumping, it pumped even harder. My throat doubled as a tourniquet, tightening with each beat of blood, stemming the flow in order to keep my head from exploding like a birthday balloon filled with tomato sauce. I had to go and go now. There was no calm to be found on a night when the cicada bugs were singing a song that sounded like a thousand whistles whistling in which the base-thumping cadence of our beating-heart drums and the machine-like precision of the neighbors' sprinklers played bass and treble respectively. The symphony of insanity made any background noise, whether that noise was our enemy, a neighbor walking his dog, or in the worst case scenario, a random cop car, next to impossible to detect, thus our sentences had to be formed to fit the breath.

Looking to Kring I confirmed his level of commitment, "By the book."

"Cover to cover."

"My lead, five paces. Meet at the Brady's side of the yard divide."

"Safe base?"

I nodded, "Eleven pm. After that on the fifteens."

Kring adjusted something on his utility belt, "By midnight, whosoever left crawls in and up."

"Which window?"

"Backside. It's open."

I took a moment to visualize, asking for confirmation, "Inside?"

"Cake walk."

"Above the washer, dryer?"

"Roger that. Set up night lights for visual."

I attempted to gain some level of emotional control by visualizing our way points and, more importantly, our potential escape routes. The plan was to rendezvous at the treehouse by

10:45pm if we got separated. If the other wasn't there by 11pm, the early bird was to hide behind Kring's pool only to crawl back along the bush line on the 15's to see if the other had made it back. At 12am, you were to go inside regardless of who showed, which still hadn't added up... *Who's hopping in bed and pretending to be asleep while their best friend just went missing on a night mission behind enemy lines? "Good morning Trel, have you seen Christian this morning?" "No Mrs. Pelagatti. I haven't seen him since 11ish... when we were laying waste to twenty enemy combatants and I subsequently crapped my pants and then figured I'd just come back here, change my undies and get a good night of sleep... What's for breakfast, or does my role in Kring's disappearance mean I should probably just get a muffin and OJ to go?"*

As that extremely uncomfortable scenario played in my head, I had to laugh out loud at the whole plan we'd hatched and my current physical condition. Forget losing Kring in the heat of battle, I was already panting, squatting absolutely still within the safety and serenity of Kring's stockade fenced yard. If I couldn't control my heat index here, what were my chances of controlling it after sprinting full speed through Wilder's, down La Rue, and into Kring's basement window, where I could only hope his parents weren't up to interrupt my stealthy ascent to his room on the second floor, where upon making it to the "safe base", I would have to change into my pj's, while discarding my fatigues, faster than Superman in a phone booth, while at the same time removing enough makeup for an entire car of clowns, only to jump into bed and pretend to be in a deep sleep.

There was no way in Hell that Kring's room was the final safe base, for there wasn't a safe base after tonight. There was no turning back at this point either, once we hit that camp. We were like long-range intercontinental ballistic bomber pilots. Sure our plane came with ejection seats and enough fuel for the return voyage, but we weren't expected back, and no one was going to miss us if we didn't make it home, for home would no longer be there either. Hell, no one even knew we were going in the first place. "Top Secret" was even more intense than I'd imagined it to be. Oddly enough, coming to grips with the worst case scenario for any mission ever, relaxed me somehow. *Is this what adults did in a time of crisis?* One thing for sure, concentration was now obtainable and I felt the onset of the 'zone'.

As Kring was describing the safe house accommodations, I smoothly whipped out my flashlight.

Kring gave it a quick, disapproving look, "Too much light."

"No, no. Check it." The cool purple light highlighted all the branches of the evergreen wall. And though our path through the wall was crystal clear, the light, which mimicked the wee moments of dawn, seemed to just die beyond the last of the leaves.

With his head nodding in approval, Kring whispered, "Sweet."

We crouched at the bushes' edge and surveyed the first leg. Though this was the least dangerous, it was by far the most visible. Timing and speed were everything, but nothing without some much needed luck. Running across the road was one thing, but diagonally across a total of three locations was another.

Practice makes perfect and lack thereof makes mistakes. Mistakes in judgment and timing are the most critical, of course. The time it takes to second-guess yourself is twice as long as it takes to expire all your options. Yes, we ran through the entire mission a thousand times. Diagrams, schematics, time-test trials, logic trees: if Mr. Culver sees us here, we go there. Over and over we scrutinized our plans, making corrections so minute that our plans would have rivaled the most intricate bank heists in history. At one point we argued over the color of the Brady's garage. Though neither side budged from the drawing table, the truce came in the form of "Who gives a crap? It's at night." But although our diagrams were so detailed that the shading of the bushes took almost an entire afternoon, the bushes were just that—drawings. They were not real, nor was the street, the Hammond's dog, or the wall of pricker bushes that separated the Neighborhood from the Forest.

In hindsight, the map was too detailed, if anything. We took too much time shading objects that were never going to come into play, too much time arguing over the square footage of each other's yards, and not enough time discussing the effects of the terrain. A map whether drawn by a pirate, or by AAA, makes a three-dimensional place, two-dimensional. The effect one experiences when running full force through a three-dimensional world after scrutinizing it in a two-dimensional format for such a long duration of time, creates a similar visual distortion as being star struck. You've seen this actor a million times throughout your life, you know his mannerisms, favorite car, designer, what his best role and line is, but it's when you experience him for the first time in real time, that you're awestruck. He may look taller or shorter, fatter and/or older, even less interesting than you'd envisioned. Regardless of his appearance, your subconscious is battling the strangeness of this familiarity, while your cerebral cortex is trying to come up with a witty sentence to capitalize on your one shot at making an impression on someone who has burned themselves into your memories and dreams. *Don't ask the wrong question. Don't make a false step. Whatever you do, stop looking like a slack-jawed yocal and ask the man for his autograph...*

But I could speak and quite succinctly, "Sixty paces to the wall. It's not home plate, so watch your slide."

The Brady's were notorious for watering their lawn at night. The state-imposed drought restrictions placed on households made it impossible to water your lawn on a daily basis. Many families began taking care of their lawns at night "in secrecy". Walking their property at night, checking on heads and dry spots, as if their grass was of the illegal kind. Everyone was guilty of this in our neighborhood, except my house of course, where my father relished the fact that he had finally been handed a legitimate excuse as to why he couldn't water the lawn. He had already saved mega bucks this year, not only in water, but in gas, for if your lawn is so dry that the fire department had to come and put out a grass fire, your lawnmower will certainly be getting less use as well. And when the fire trucks and News 12 finally left, my mother broke down and accused my father of being insane, only to have my father eloquently state the fact that the town said he couldn't water the lawn, so he had the town water the lawn for him. My mother should have packed her things right then and there.

Needless to say, the Brady's were using enough water to supply a theme park, and if I came in too fast, my feet would surely slide out from underneath me while my body propelled itself briskly along a path toward the prickers that were skirting the cold brick foundation of the house. The last thing I needed was to come into this first checkpoint like Steve Austin in the opening scene of the Six

Million Dollar Man. Besides, my father would be too cheap to rebuild me, forget about sporting the extra cash for the fast legs and the right hook. *"Boy—who the hell needs a set of million-dollar bionic eyes when you can get a pair of binoculars for less than twenty dollars? And good binoculars at that!"*

My watch hit 9:45pm – Go Time. I sprang into action, getting to three quarters speed by the end of the road and maintained it for another twenty feet. I broke speed at the large elm that bordered the Brady's property with the Hammond's, fifteen feet from the pricker bush. Good thing, for I slid somewhat, but corrected my balance before I needed an open palm on the ground for stabilization. I pivoted flawlessly and crouched like a monkey, relaxed in my setting, but aware nonetheless. I focused in on Kring's position across the street under the bush line, pulled my purple beacon from my knapsack and hit the light twice. Two things struck me when I finally made Kring out from across the way; across the way was farther than we both had calculated and there was less room for a second tornado to come whirling in. I knew at this point a third flash would be necessary while Kring was in transit, for there was no sense in having him rush to an area that was smaller and slipperier than a snail's track.

Kring shot across somewhat unsure, looking to both sides as if he was crossing 5th on 43rd in Manhattan. Forty. Thirty. Twenty. Fifteen feet. I gave a quick jolt of the flashlight. Kring tripped midair. He hadn't been able to focus on where he was going, because he was too busy scanning the terrain while in full gallop. Fear and lack of field time had caused Kring's eyes to move from the checkpoint where I had positioned myself, to a thousand other places. And while he made brief visual contacts with the Jansen's cat running across the street, a neighbors' darkened window that mysteriously turned bright yellow, and a blurred place in the distance where a barking dog could be heard, Kring had lost focus on the one place he needed to be the most—the place where he was going. By the time I had flicked the flashlight on, Kring's mind had already passed me, with his focus now somewhere near the Brady's pool. In hindsight, I should have let him dive headfirst into the pool, for when he finally saw the light, processed what it was, and where he was in relation to the landing zone, Kring was in midair and the switch of direction and speed could only be processed by one leg, the left, which caused it to cross over the right, making his landing a rough one. Thump.

"Aww—shit."

"You alright?"

"Oh my God. Fuck. Fuck. Fuck." Kring rolled over and over, like Tarzan wrestling an alligator.

"Speak," I whispered.

"I'm fucked."

"Where does it hurt?"

"Fuck you."

"Keep it down," I whispered angrily.

"I'll be dead before they come."

"Is anything broken?"

"Your face in a moment."

"Yo—just 'cause you run like—"

"What are you, a lighthouse?"

"You were coming in too fast and off course-"

"I was fine until you blinded me."

At this point it was clear that the only thing that was hurting was Kring's pride.

I relaxed my face and lowered my whisper, "Can you go on?"

"Worry about yourself," Kring spat between elongated exhales.

"I am," I assured him.

Kring took a moment to respond and offered a measured response, "I'll be fine."

"You look like you might have gotten the wind knocked—"

The creaking of a screen door from around the corner interrupted me. Kring and I stared at each other with our eyes and mouths open so wide we resembled fish on plaques. Panic began to seep in. *Should we move? Should we run back to the base? Should we remain frozen? Would the person come around, or did they not hear us?* Some relief was felt when the distinct sound of a metal garbage-can lid was removed and then slammed back on tight. Mr. Brady was taking out the trash. I made the hold sign with a strong fist and Kring nodded. The wait for the porch screen door to open seemed like an eternity, though the exact duration took no longer than for a bead of sweat, which had formed on my brow, to cascade down over my eye, jump to my cheek, and dive off my chin. When it hit my boot, the door opened. After the door finally closed, we held our awkward positions for a baited-breath moment, before we both slumped against the house's foundation with a mighty exhale.

"You think he heard something?" I asked.

"Don't know."

"He took his sweet ass time getting back," I commented.

"You think he sensed our presence?"

"Don't know."

"You think it's clear?" Kring asked while he massaged his shin.

I looked to the street, then up to see if a light had come on in the room above our heads. It hadn't. "I'll check. If it's good, I'll give the sign."

Kring looked to his leg, "Roger that."

"Once I give the sign, I'll do a silent twenty count and hit CP2."

Kring looked to his knee again and then added, "Do a silent one-minute launch on my call."

"Roger that."

I got down on all fours and slowly crawled to the corner of the house. I had to make this quick, for my visual exposure from the Hammond's den was crucial. The light illuminating from their windows meant they had no view of the outside, as long as it stayed dark outside of course. Above me now was Mr. and Mrs. Brady's bedroom. The T.V. was on, but the shutters were closed. *Perfect.* I could piss on their window and they wouldn't be the wiser. Turning my head around the corner, the Brady's simple cement staircase that lead to the back door was lit by a yellow 45-watt bulb. To the left was a four-foot high, black mesh metal fence, which surrounded the pool. To the right stood a one-story, two-car garage, which matched the materials and style of the house. The rear of the structure was half sunken into the slope of the terrain, making it possible for one to gain access to the roof via a makeshift hand crane from a buddy. Though I had no plans for Kring to hoist me up to the roof for additional reconnaissance, the left back corner of the garage was checkpoint two.

And though in the original plans I drew the line from CP1 to CP2 with a ruler, there would need to be a small deviation in my trajectory to compensate for the hill, hedge line, and soaked sod surface, in hopes of avoiding a massive spill. Visualizing the multiple traumatized locations resulting from my legs going from perpendicular to parallel with the ground wasn't what had me sweating bullets. Rather, being caught gasping for air in the Brady's backyard, dressed in black and carrying enough ammo to take over Rhode Island, made the simple maneuver, complicated.

Less talk, more walk, is the shiny side of the more balls, less brains coin. Looking to the checkpoint, I whispered, "I'm going. Wait for my signal for checkpoint change."

"Roger rendezvous signal. Timer set. One minute and counting."

I quickly scanned my person for any open pockets that would throw items in mid-sprint. *Good.* Tightening the straps to the backpack, I slowly descended into the "loaded" position. Digging my cleated soles into the packed soaked soil, I made sure to grab the grass as if it belonged to the mane of the bronco I was going to tame as soon as the gates went up at the rodeo. Like the quarter-mile in a car, the initial traction is what makes the run.

"T-minus 15. 12. 11. 10. 9. 8. 7. 6. 5. 4. 3. 2. 1. Fire! A slight slip and I was off, full-tilt with my scope on the corner of the garage. Halfway up the small incline, night turned to day. *Floodlights...*

While in mid stride, I created a split-second logic tree, which after evaluating everything from why the lights would have gone on, to the harrowing chase that would ensue leading to our inevitable capture and torture, led me to the only possible plan of action: *"Run!"*

I kept running up the hill as fast as I could. Whether Kring followed or fled back to base camp meant nothing to me at this point. My life was in grave danger and I needed to remove myself from the impending threat. "CP3! CP3!" I yelled.

Whether Kring would have the presence of mind to meet me at checkpoint 3, aka the corner bush line, before the salt flats, would remain to be seen. Whether the mission was scrapped depended on Kring and my courage showing up. I panicked and I knew it. I had run from my buddy. *Never again!* Suddenly, I heard a rustling in the bushes, followed by a hard thud.

Praying to the Gods for Kring and not Mr. Brady, I had enough internal fortitude to finally muster, "Yo!"

Kring's was breath was loud, but his voice was low, "Yo."

"You alright?"

Kring responded between breaths, "Yeah, you?"

"I'll live. Sorry."

"You see.... someone?"

"Just light."

Still gasping for air, Kring stated the obvious, "We should move."

"Roger." A loud bark from the Hammond's dog signaled danger.

"He's out!" Kring exclaimed.

"The fence is..." A second bark, this one markedly closer than the fenced divider between the Hammond's and Brady's yards both interrupted and finished my thought.

Kring eyes were whiter than fine china. "He's loose!"

"Run!" I screamed.

We took off full speed across the most dangerous stretch of the journey without a second thought. The terrain of the salt flats was actually some of the lushest lawn outside of the Caribbean. A perfectly symmetrical, pristinely landscaped, one-acre plot of land was protected with the vigilance of a leopard sanctuary in Southern Guinea by an 85-year old World War II vet, armed with a high pressure CO_2 rifle, loaded with hollow-tipped salt-filled pellets. Rumor had it, Old Mr. Willets was a sniper in the German SS, and was living under the alias of a retired stonemason from the Midwest. How he hadn't even registered a blip on the International War Tribunal's radar was rather astonishing, simply for the fact that not many people born in Columbus, Ohio spoke in a thick German dialect and garnished a firearm designed to terrorize children on their daily stroll to the mailbox. Ironically, his salt of choice was Kosher.

So though I never saw Old Man Willets in action, I knew that if half the stories of his legendary marksmanship, cold steel nerve, and what appeared to be a zero fear of the law were true, he was a worthy adversary. Therefore, whether Mr. Willets was a former SS officer, sociopath, or just a senile old man with an overzealous pest control plan for his property, bullets would surely fly before yard's end. Oh yeah, Willets had a dog too, and a mean one at that... A hundred-plus pound Doberman Pinscher named Blitzen. In hindsight, Willets could have dressed up in crotchless black leather fatigues and had his dog pull him up and down Main Street in a chariot on Sunday morning, while blasting Beethoven from a hand cranked phonograph, and no one would have been the wiser.

It was at the first tree line where everything happened at once... Unlike a true desert oasis where one takes several days to revitalize oneself before continuing the long hard journey, this patch of dense growth was simply a waypoint in the original plans—nothing more than a place to stop and reflect, gather information and courage. Irony, of course, would try its darndest to turn the stop we had earmarked for replenishing our internal fortitude, into our final resting place. As we descended on the black blur, which on our map was an ornate flowerbed with a weeping willow tree in the center codenamed CP4, the angry bark of the Hammond's dog pierced my soul. There was no time to stop and try to climb the tree, for the bark was quickly followed by Willet's dog's deep, angry howl, which in turn led to the most frightening of all sounds: a faint squeak off in the distance, signaling a porch door opening and the impending hissing of air being thrust aside by hollow tipped projectiles covering 700 feet per second.

If the field had mines, we would have been running for Check Point Charlie. I could hear Kring off to my left, more than a few paces behind. *Was he still even carrying his weapon? Would he drop soon due to fatigue? Would he panic and try to climb the weeping willow and be fish in a barrel for the Nazi sniper? Would I have the nerve to stop once the dogs began to circle his lifeless corpse like the Chuck Wagon?*

"Keep running!" I yelled.

"Stop!"

"Keep running!" I yelled again in vain for us both, for I knew Kring was just as exhausted as I.

Between panted breaths Kring mustered, "W-a-i-t."

Between burning gulps of air I muttered an exasperated, "Crap!" for I knew I couldn't abandon my comrade-in-arms twice in one mission.

"Pleeeassse sstoppp—" was Kring's final polite plea for help and it caused me to look over to my left and locate Kring with my peripheral vision, which of course occupied enough of my heightened mental and physical abilities to allow for a terrain guidance malfunction, AKA I tripped over a stump. The "in air" portion of the trip was quite lengthy, considering the hang time was long enough in duration for me to both extend my hands like Superman, and subsequently change my body's trajectory, thus altering my approach angle enough that a small roll at the end was achieved, as if I were rolling down a steeply graded hill. Though far less debilitating than the dreaded face plant, the down side of rolling was that even though you got to your feet quicker, you usually had no idea which way your feet were pointing. Too much spin and your head was not necessarily ready to stop once you were. When I finally planted my feet, I didn't know in which direction I was facing, only that I wasn't facing in the right one, for CP4 was no longer in sight. A bright green glowing light appeared to my right, and then flew away at fifty miles per hour, arcing at a good forty feet, before it began to descend in the distance.

Kring exclaimed, "Run!" with renewed confidence and energy as if he'd thrown his negative karma toward Willet's porch instead of the glow stick.

"Which way?" I babbled.

Kring grabbed and spun me like a dreidel, pointing me once again toward the black blur, "Run!"

The light stick was a good idea in theory, but so was a checkpoint in the middle of a war zone, for that matter. For though it would surely halt the advance of the Hammond's dog, the glow stick would also act as a signal flare for Willets' Pinscher and scope, giving them the much-needed coordinates to launch their blitzkrieg. Looking back on it, I'm surprised Old Man Willets didn't drop the glow rod like he was skeet shooting.

"Load your gun!" I yelled.

"Can't!"

"I'm lighting one!"

"Fool!"

"We won't make it," I wheezed.

"I can't see!" Kring cried.

"Your lighter! Now!" I reached for my pack of Jumping Jacks, which was taped to my right bicep, or at least the space allocated on my arm that one day would hopefully house a muscle referred to as the bicep, and yanked. But instead of snapping, the tape bunched together and formed a strong, thin cable-like wire around my arm. I pulled again in frustration only to rip off half the jacks instead. *My God, did I just yank all the fuses off?*

"Fire!" Kring yelled.

"You fire!"

"I can't see a thing!" Kring screamed.

On cue the dog appeared as a blackened shape crouched before us, fangs glistening in the moonlight. We were dead men regardless if we survived this vicious attack or not, for the real killer was surely lurking beyond the shadows now, waiting for both predator and prey to tire before launching his brutal display of force. *What now? Kring can surely see him as well as I, but I didn't hear his gun load, nor cock for that matter. Is Kring paralyzed with fear? Would he scream as the dogs tore apart his stomach and fought over his liver?* Though I could not make out the defined lines of the Hammond's large Labrador slash German Shepherd mixed mutt, I could make out the stance clear as day, which was the attack stance, signaling he wasn't there to scare us, but rather eat us. As it lowered its huge head below its massively muscular shoulders, the dog's growl intensified into a fevered frenzy. And though I could not see the saliva dripping from its fangs, I knew it was, as would our blood soon enough.

Kring must have had the presence of mind to notice my inaction, for he yelled 'fire' like it was coming from his house, "Fire!!"

I looked at my shoulder, looked at the lighter, and then once again to the dog. The calmness in my voice surprised not only me, but the dog, for when I began to speak, the dog stopped its vicious growl and tilted its head as it listened intently.

"Kring, I'm going to light the jacks that are taped to my arm now. They're not coming off, and therefore I'll light them on my arm. Once they begin to fire I'll run to Smith's fence, which is CP5 if you've forgotten." I took the lighter, put it to my arm and lit the jacks. "You'll stay with me, won't you Kring?"

An unintelligible answer came from Kring's mouth, a mumble that surely meant 'yes'.

I stared at the fuses, which were stuck to my arm like veins. Some fuses were longer than others and I knew I had to wait until at least one went off to see if it would scare the dog. No sense in running with the dog still chasing us. Before I was ready, the first went off and shot right next to my face. I snapped my head back like a turtle, avoiding major fire damage. The dog yelped and jumped back a considerable distance. Instincts proved right, for the second one went off, firing straight down to the ground between me and the dog. The dog leapt backwards a good ten feet and on the third jack's launch, the dog scampered away faster than it had pursued us.

With the same tempered tone in my voice as if offering Kring a piece of gum on the bus, I turned and said, "Run."

I ran as fast as I could, trying to keep my arm behind me angled enough so that I could potentially land a direct strike on my four-pawed pursuer, while at the same time tucking my head beneath my other arm, in hopes of avoiding an errant explosion from the jacks that were now flying one after another in every direction other than the one I wanted them to fly. The awkward exodus made me look more like Quasimodo running to ring the bell tower, than a frightened child running for a fence.

"Fire something!" I yelled.

"You have the lighter! Run!"

Pow! Bang! The jacks were now exploding in the air and on the ground. Another fired from my arm, and then another. The line of bushes that marked Smith's yard came into view. Though we would surely be chewed up by the four-foot wall of pricker bushes that lined the base of the six-foot stockade fence, the thorns were not fangs and scrapes were not gashes. Though gladly swapping a migraine for a headache, our plan was a mess, regardless. The original plan for CP5 had me holding my hands together and forming a human hoist for Kring. Once over, he would stand on the top support beam and help me over with a hand and rope. There was now no time for that maneuver, for we would need to scale the fence like Spiderman in order to avoid the impending thrashing. I scanned the event horizon for another form of egress.

Kring obviously had the same thought, for he yelled at that exact moment. "Follow me to the tree!"

There was in fact a tree off in the distance farther back toward the corner of Smith's yard. We did not incorporate the use of the tree in our original plans for it led to the backyard of a property that was from another block, which of course was uncharted territory. An old apple tree that had slumped to one side over the years, formed an almost perfect sky-bridge over the fence. Though easily scalable, it would be one soldier at a time and since Kring had found it first, I'd have to wait for him to get up to at least the first set of branches.

"Go, go, go!" I yelled behind him.

Kring jumped to the first branch, swung for a quick second, moved his arms out away from the trunk and then hoisted his legs around the large branch that he was hanging from. He then began to contort his body over the branch so he would be hugging it from the top, rather than from the bottom. Another tactical error was committed when Kring took his gun with him, instead of allowing me to take point while he climbed. I turned from Kring to see if the dogs had pursued and to my horror they both stood behind me no more than three feet away. *I never heard them breathe...* They were playing with their food before they ate it, like a cat pawing an injured bird.

I had the lighter in my hand but knew I'd never reach my fireworks in time. I stood there frozen. Then I heard the distinct sound of Kring's gun pump. A single pop rang from the barrel and shot the lighter in my hand, shattering it, leaving me with only the smell of propane in the air. The dogs hunched and showed glistening white fangs, as they let out guttural growls. Kring's gun pumped again, with a pellet firing within milliseconds, only to hit the tree branch next to my head. A shard of bark pierced my eye, causing my vision to waver, as the needed fluids flushed my retina. Kring's wildly inaccurate shots, which were a sheer sign of panic, only enraged the already angered animals. Tears began to roll down my face, as if my mind subconsciously decided to blur my vision in hopes of softening the atrocity I was about to witness. *Whoosh*—a small branch was blown off the tree by a powerful rifle round, setting the Hammond's dog in motion.

The dog leapt up and pinned me against the tree's trunk before the branch hit the ground. Growling deeply from within its diaphragm, four inches from my face—*whoosh*—the dog flew off of me, yelping as it hit the ground. It spun a 180, landing on all fours before I could squeal. Facing the Willet's Dobie and clearly believing it must have been the Dobie that attacked him, he lunged in retaliation. A horrific battle to the death ensued - howling, barking, yelping, and growling, with spit, fur and blood flying everywhere, affording me a fleeting moment to flee.

I hopped up to the nearest branch and performed the same maneuver that Kring did, though on a branch farther from the fence. I climbed another one up and then quickly moved safely behind the tree for protection from another round from the salt-slinging sniper rifle. *If Hammond's dog didn't jump me, Willet would have hit me dead on! The dog saved my life twice, first by taking a bullet and then by taking on Willet's hellhound. Dogs truly are man's best friend!*

When I looked over to Kring and found him sitting on a large slumping branch as if he was there picking apples for his Ma's baked-from-scratch apple pie, I was beside myself. "Get over the fence now!"

"I'm moving.'

"Willet is shooting; he almost killed me!"

"I'm here too..."

Kring took his sweet-ass time, and in hindsight, rightfully so, for if he fell, the dogs would have forgotten about their differences and bonded on his buttocks. As soon as Kring made it over, I barked my second command. "Get back up and shoot the dogs, or Willet's, or something! Don't hide Bitch!"

"Okay, okay," Kring bemoaned as another round smacked into the tree.

"Shoot at him!" I pleaded.

"Just come over!"

"Lay cover fire!" I begged.

"He'll hit me."

"He can't see you; that's why he keeps hitting the tree! He can only see the tree and me! Now shoot back so he stops for a second, so I can make it across!"

"Just come; he won't hit you."

"He won't hit me if he's ducking—now shoot your gun!"

Another bullet slammed into the trunk halfway between the dogs and me. I was safe at the moment, but if Willet were walking toward us, his aim and accuracy would become better with each step. Kring was not going to return-volley on a world-class sniper anytime soon, while being afforded absolute anonymity from behind the fence. I waited for the next shot as if the barrel rested on my breast. This time the whoosh of the bullet sounded more like an axe strike, slamming deep within the trunk, directly opposite from where I hung. He'd obviously somehow calculated my elevation within the tree and had compensated accordingly. *Astonishing...* I quickly made my way over to the branch that Kring had hung from and then over the fence I went. My belt caught on the top of one of the pickets as I went face first down the other side, leaving me hanging upside down and my legs exposed. "Unbuckle me!"

"Hold on."

"Quickly!"

"Bend your legs, so he can't see them."

"Unbuckle me!"

Kring did what he could, but the pressure on the belt was too great for him to pull back on.

"Yank me!" I screamed.

As Kring tugged with all his might in vain, the picket that I was suspended from exploded as a round made its way closer to its intended target. The near hit freed me. Landing to the ground on top of Kring, we quickly got to our hands and knees after some frantic fumbling.

Panting with pain and panic, I screamed, "He's here! Run!"

"Where?" Kring questioned quickly. Kring was right to be hesitant. We had no idea where we were. For all we knew the owner of this house could be a Rottweiler breeder and we were better off hopping the fence back to Auschwitz.

Pointing to a dilapidated shed at the far corner, "That way!"

I could have pointed to the moon, for we were off in the opposite direction of the guy with the gun, which meant I'd chosen wisely. We ran with renewed energy, across a lawn with a house in the near distance. With the lights on in the stranger's house, I felt strangely secure. Across a pachysandra patch, we came to the back of the shed, where an old fence leaned towards its grave. We scampered over it with ease and found ourselves in Wilder's. We needed to keep moving, for the dogs might still be following our scent and though I knew we were in The Woods, I didn't know where in the woods we were.

"Kring, you okay?"

"Think so; you hit or bit?"

"He shot me in the ass, but luckily the ten-pound turd I made moments before saved me."

Kring and I laughed between breaths.

"We made it," Kring touted triumphantly.

"We're not out of the woods yet."

"What?" Kring responded annoyed, thinking the plans had changed.

"Just an expression. We're good."

As the endorphins began to wear off, I began to feel the throbbing sensation of a major wound on my stomach. I pulled my shirt up and winced from the pain. Turning on my flashlight I could see even in the purple light, I had some major scrapes, bruises and several large splinters, but amazingly, no sign of blood from what I thought would definitely be a gaping wound.

"You need first aid?"

"I'll live."

"What now?"

"Either we climb a tree, or keep moving," I offered.

"I say we move."

"Agreed; let's move... My lead, three paces."

Looking behind us, Kring wanted a cushion between him and the wolf pack. "Screw that, I'm first!"

"Sure thing; just move then."

"Worry about yourself."

"I am."

We began to move as fast as we could without making noise. Concentration was paramount at this speed, for not only did you have to distinguish every minute item that lay before your feet in almost total darkness, but you had to keep a heads up for the terrain in front of you, watching for both low lying branches, as well as the enemy. We covered a football field worth of woods at sub- trot speed, pacing and spacing ourselves with the same level of exactitude as the Blue Angels flying over the Super Bowl.

Chapter 8
A View from Afar

Before we saw them, we smelled them, and before we smelled them, we heard them. Just as we walked, we stopped, crouched, and dropped our jaws in unison.

"My God, how big is that fire?" Kring asked bewildered.

I couldn't distinguish the size and scope of the blaze from our distance, nor the shapes moving around it, "Are they dancing around it, or is that my imagination?"

"I can't tell from here," Kring frustratedly muttered.

Scanning the nearby terrain, I made a suggestion, "We should reposition ourselves behind that fallen tree."

"We should get as close as we can."

"That's as close as I plan on getting right now," I notated.

"Pussy."

"Tough talk from a guy who just shot the lighter out of his partner's hand, while hiding—"

Kring quickly ended my rant with a curt, "Fine. You first. Three paces."

Before I turned to lead, I asked Kring, "How far can you see?"

"What?"

"Could you make out my signals from here if I make it to the tree?"

"You're not leaving me here!"

"Keep your voice down pussy," I leveled.

Unimpressed with my dress-down, Kring enthusiastically answered, "You're damn right!"

I couldn't blame him, "Fine. Three paces."

Kring still shaken asked, "Should we leave some gear behind?"

"No. Unless of course you're fine with leaving it behind for good."

"We'll get it on our way out, fool."

I was finding myself less patient of my good friend's frantic fussing, "You're the fool, if you think it's a given that we're just gonna stroll out of here, perusing for gear and mementos in the pitch black."

Unsure and unhappy with his clear lack of composure, Kring quipped, "You gonna get us caught?"

"Worry about yourself; I'll be sitting on one of those logs in five minutes roasting a fucking marshmallow. But if you snap another twig with your block feet, we could be running out of here full tilt in the next couple of minutes."

We were fracturing under the pressure and Kring's retort of, *'I'll snap your neck, before I snap a twig'*, was both out of character and off base, and I needed to set him straight before he drifted too far.

"Not 'a' twig Rambo, but another twig. You already snapped two since leaving the fort, not to mention almost taking a plunge in the Brady's pool, tripping me up midstream as I dodged flying bullets across the salt flats, and let's not forget almost shooting me in the eye, on your way to emptying an entire clip, as you blindly missed 280 lbs of attack dog from pointblank range."

Kring was quickly humbled by my assessment of his play so far and gave a halfhearted, "You'd be dead if it weren't for me."

I lightened the mood with a deftly delivered mother-joke, "You'd never be born if it weren't for me, Son."

"Screw you."

He was back and now I needed to lead him to victory, "Hey, you can redeem yourself with some deftly placed rounds."

Piquing his interest, Kring closed the gap, "What do you mean?"

I took a step closer as well and lowered my voice, "Sniper, and ground support."

Looking off to the distance momentarily, Kring returned with the campfire in his eyes, "Go on."

"You and I going in lack one thing."

"What?"

"Backup."

"Go on."

"I get close, check the scene, and give you a full report."

"That's bullshit!"

"Keep your voice down!" I scolded.

"Worry about yourself" Kring sneered.

"I am," I assured him.

Kring looked off into the distance once again, reevaluating our predicament, "We should stick to the plan."

I could tell he was contemplating our next course of action, so I laid out the end game, "Well, let me ask you this... What happens if they spot us from twenty feet out?"

Shrugging his shoulders in indifference, "We run or fight."

"Which one?" I pried.

"It don't matter to me at this point," Kring said with an exhale.

"Oh no? Well, it makes a world of difference to me, especially if I decide to stay and fight, and you decide to run."

Kring exhaled once again, while rolling his eyes and shaking his head, "Well, we can make the call together when the time comes. Besides, they're our only two options as I see it."

"Well, as I see it, both those options suck."

"You suck," Kring countered.

"You think we can run faster than those kids? How about fight?"

"Hello, we got these." Kring's arm jutted out quickly, with his fist clenched tight, holding the BB gun's pellet pack like an angler hoisting a world record. "My fists travel at 650 feet per second."

I had to hit below the belt, "You couldn't hit a dog three-feet away in plain sight; now you're gonna shoot over your back from twenty feet, through trees, at multiple targets, while running full steam ahead?"

The blow hurt, but he withstood it, "I'll stand my ground if you will."

"I know you would, but our ground won't mean a hill of beans. Half our arsenal is designed for long-range volleys and what is designed for close combat, just isn't enough at these odds. Heck your gun is a one-pump, and you could probably drop two of those guys with your skill, but the only way they'll even know you're shooting at them, is if you hit them. The ones you don't hit won't assume that their fallen comrades were hit with a round from your rifle, but rather a tree branch. They won't even know to be scared."

Kring responded, but before he did, I could see his eyes play the scenario out, "You got the firepower... I thought that's why you brought it to the party in the first place," pointing to my backpack, which cradled the stockpile.

"True, but from that distance, half my ordinance will take too long to detonate. I have a couple of things on short fuses, but for the most part, I have long fuses for an offensive sneak attack, or a long-distance defensive strike."

"What about your M-80 with the suicide fuse?"

Gently patting my utility belt without looking down, "I got it. What if it's a dud? Besides, you shot my lighter out of my hand and now we just have only the one lighter."

"True."

Sensing Kring knew I was making sense, I offered him a way out, "What about you going setting up shop near the old tires, by the Culver's hidden entrance, where you could get a clear view of the entire field of play, as well as have the ability to deliver a proper barrage on to the target area, if needed?

Looking into the far off distance, at the Culver's well-lit, but well-hidden house, Kring added, "Who makes that call?"

"Well, if I need you to hit them, I'll yell out 'attack'."

"Am I gonna even hear you from there, and what if I see something unfold?"

"Good points..."

We listened to the lawless for what seemed like an eternity, when Kring offered, "I can send up a signal-flare."

"Use a jumping jack with a short fuse." Then I quickly added, "Cut two, in case one's a dud. Make sure you throw them that way," pointing to the pitch black of The Woods. "That way when it goes off, their attention will focus away from your position."

"They may see the tracer caused by the fuse."

I had to admit, "They may…"

"What then?" Kring asked with baited breath.

I scrubbed my head, like I was shampooing mud from it, instead of sweat, "Set up two Roman candles with short fuses inside a pricker bush aimed directly at the camp. An M-80 with nothing less than a four-minute fuse. Light the M-80, then the candles, and then run." Before he could argue I added, "Trust me."

Kring was in the game now and surveyed the distant battlefield, "I'll also hook up a second Roman fifteen feet back on that tree with the V trunk. On my way out, if I got the time, I'll light that as well. They won't follow me; for they'll be too busy running for cover."

"While you're at it, lay a rocket pack on them."

A rocket pack consisted of six bottle rockets, with the fuses tied together, allowing them to be easily ignited by either the right or left. Since the fuses varied in both length and amount of gunpowder, the bottle rockets always launched in a linear volley, one after another, regardless of when and where you lit them from.

"Give me at least five minutes to setup before you go to the first checkpoint."

"Roger that," I confirmed.

"When I'm done, should I give a signal?"

I contemplated the use of a signal. "Use your gun light. One quick flick. I'll respond with one back if I'm ready, two if I'm not."

"Roger that."

"Reload your weapon, and your second clip."

"Roger that."

I pressed him, "Reload it now."

"I'll do it while you're on your way to the checkpoint," Kring snapped back.

"I may not make it to the checkpoint."

Kring let out a yearly doctor's checkup exhale, "Roger that."

Chapter 9
Dante's Inferno

As Kring reloaded his gun, I kept a vigilant lookout. We were roughly 175 feet from the fire, situated behind a large, thick, evergreen bush. At least this checkpoint had not changed since drawing up the plan. Behind us was a large patch of white birch. The trees afforded us sufficient cover from the backside, in case any of the Druid priests were to levitate by on their way to the ritual. As I peered from my prone position under the belly of the bush, I saw something that made every hair on my body stand at attention. There was a large person at 11 o'clock, standing approximately halfway between the camp and us, staring directly at us. He was so still that I hadn't noticed him until he struck a match to light his cigarette. *My God, had he seen us?*

I violently whispered, "Stop!"

Kring stopped immediately and didn't utter a sound, for he knew better than to ask why. He knew there was a reason, and right now, he didn't need the answer; he needed to know when the coast was clear, and if it wasn't going to get any better, when the hell he had to run.

I didn't softly whisper the news until he took his third drag, "There's a guy roughly thirty yards in front, and twenty feet left of the fire, staring right at us."

"Does he see us?"

"He can't see us now, but maybe he saw us get here."

"Options?"

I heard some scuffling coming from Kring, "Don't move a muscle."

"Leg cramping..."

"Don't move—statue."

"Got to sit back or fall."

"Hold pose."

"Can't..." Kring began to fall back in slow motion, like a bus tipping over a cliff. I couldn't see him fall, but heard the creaking of debris below his feet, which signaled the shift in weight. All I could do in that eternity was to hope that when his butt hit the ground, it did not land on a twig, but rather a soft fern, which would muffle his fall. My eyes were closed, and face muscles clenched, as if I had just knocked a baseball over my neighbor's fence and was awaiting the impending smash of a garage window. But no noise came, simply a thud. Kring had hit soft dirt!

I let out a deep exhale, "Jesus Christ."

But Kring's voice was far from relieved, "Got to straighten leg."

Whispering a yell, "Hold!"

"Can't-hurts..."

"Hold—"

"Can't." Kring extended his left leg straight, from being bent at a ninety-degree angle, and in the process, snapped his third twig of the night. Three being the charm that it is, this one sounded like Indiana Jones cracking his whip. The man clearly heard it, for he stopped his drag in mid-pull and fully adjusted his body to face us.

I muttered a silent, "Fuck."

A whistle, followed by a, "Yo!" was all I needed to confirm that he had heard something.

I muttered another Fuck.

Still sitting up, with his left leg extended, Kring asked hopeful, "Did he hear?"

"Yes."

"What now?" Kring asked frantically.

"He's calling for someone to come over, or he's calling us."

"He sees us?"

"Doubt it, but he definitely heard us."

Kring lowered his whisper to the point I could barely hear him, "You think he's coming over?"

"Maybe."

"Maybe he thinks we're an animal," Kring offered with guarded optimism.

"Maybe."

"What if he comes?"

"Get that gun trained on him."

"I'll have to move."

"Then move."

Kring carefully put his gun down, and slowly maneuvered his body from sitting to the prone position. Once on his stomach, he grabbed his gun and slowly wormed forward. As Kring got into position, another individual walked toward the large human. Once together, they would surely have enough courage to investigate the mysterious noise. Could Kring train his weapon on the two, and have enough balls to stay in position to hit the oncoming threats? I knew I had to act quickly if the shit hit the fan, for the majority of my ordinance was in my knapsack, which lay several feet behind me. The only thing I had on my person was the M-80 with the suicide fuse, and a belt of Ladyfingers, and Ladyfingers couldn't blow the balls off an ant, let alone the finger off a 300 lb killer.

"Got'em," Kring had gotten into position, and placed a bead on the shadowy figures faster than I thought possible, and I knew they didn't hear him, for I hadn't. But they knew something was out there, and what were they going to do about it? Suddenly the new figure crouched to the ground. He stayed there for a couple of seconds, then stood up again.

Kring's whisper was drenched in distress, "What's up with that?"

"Can't tell; maybe he tied his shoelace."

"In three seconds?"

"Maybe he was trying to get a better look—"

The new figure's body jolted forward maybe a foot, and it appeared that his arm did something, but from the distance I could not tell.

Kring let out a hushed, "What the—?"

Suddenly a crackling noise sounded in the distance between them and us. Then another a split second later much closer to us, then another, and another even closer yet, closer, louder, and then— thud. A rock slammed the tree to our immediate left. He had picked up, and threw a baseball sized rock at us. *Did he know we were here, or did he just know something was here? Maybe he was hoping to hear the scurrying of a fox, or raccoon. Should we make a noise? Should we just lay and wait?* I could hear Kring's heart pound, which was quite a feat, considering mine was deafening.

Kring squeaked, "Shit."

"Stay still."

"Say the word, and I'll drop the giant."

Kring was not being melodramatic, for the giant, was just that—giant. The new figure was dwarfed in his presence. It looked like a father and son. But this wasn't a father, son, or Cub Scout camp out, and at this point in time, I was more scared of that giant figure than I ever had been of my own father, which was of particular note, considering my father had once beaten me so badly that I had to go to the Emergency Room to have my eye put back into the socket.

I wanted so badly to look at Kring to see if he was still there, and if he was, to see if he was trembling or not. For if his hands were shaking like mine were, he surely couldn't hit the broad side of a barn, let alone a man forty yards away, regardless of his supernatural size.

I whispered an uneven, "You good?"

Kring's ready reply was uplifting, "Perfect."

"I'm only going to move slightly."

"Why?"

"I need some juice in case this goes down now."

"Roger that."

Luckily for me, of what little I was carrying of my weapons cache was easily accessible on my utility belt, with a slight body roll. I got out my M-80. No sense in giving a show with the Ladyfingers. If it came to me having to light something now, I was going to light the one thing that could be lights out for anyone within a twenty-foot perimeter. God knows I didn't want it to go down like this, for I knew the M80 wrapped in tacks wouldn't just scare somebody, but rather tear through bodies, which meant that if I got caught, which most likely I would, I would be in big, big, big trouble. This was about to go to from Defcon 4, to Defcon 5 in a flash.

Kring was almost too calm, "Anything?"

"Nothing," escaped with a short breath.

"Scan for others. I got my sights trained on the Giant."

"Roger that."

A branch snapped twenty feet behind us. I was frozen. Paralyzed with fear. *Crack—*

"Watch where you're going, you fucking jackoff!"

"You watch it, Bitch."

"You can watch me stab you in the fucking neck."

Crack. Now the walk was ten feet to our left. *My God...*

"Well, well. Look at this... "

"Two gay woodknolls."

"I say we kill them."

I rolled over slowly to make eye contact with my soon-to-be assassins.

From the distance a horse yell of, "Yo!" filled the night air.

"Yo yourself, you big bastard!"

From my half-turned overview, I could see Kring still lying face down in the weeds, and with half his body under the bush, he was almost invisible. Less than eight feet away stood two large boys, maybe six-foot apiece, lean, with long hair, sporting black T–shirts, and some of the whitest skin this side of Ireland—any whiter, and I would have thought The Woods were truly haunted.

But the only part of the two boys' appearance that was of any real significance to me, was that they appeared to both be facing the two other boys in the distance—meaning they had not seen us and had no idea we were laying right next to them. *My God, what was going through Kring's mind right now? Was he trembling with fear? Did he know from the call in the distance, and the response*

to his left that he was not in immediate harm? Or was he? Was I?
The two boys could glance to their right at any given moment, and
see us both laying there, and kill us.

"Yo, I got to take a leak."

Oh God, please not on me. Piss on Chris. Piss on Chris.
Please God, piss on Chris.

"I'll meet up."

"Make sure after your little jerk session, you bring some
wood back. Derek doesn't take kindly to those who show up to the
show without a ticket."

"Fuck Derek."

"Watch your tongue!"

"I'm done with his bullshit."

"You'll be done alright. You make your feelings known, and
you won't make the sunrise."

"I'm not afraid of him."

"You should be. Derek is straight up evil."

"Yeah, well I'm a pretty bad-ass motherfucker myself."

The one boy turned quickly and grabbed the other boy's shirt
right under the chin and pulled him close.

"Hey, get the fuck—"

"Derek is evil. You hear me! He's not just a very bad
individual; he's bad to the bone. You don't want him as an enemy."

"Alright, alright! Jesus, Kevin! Let go of my shirt!"

"I don't need you getting yourself killed."

"Don't you have my back?"

"Yes, and no."

"Well which is it? You gonna sit by and watch him kill your
best friend?"

"No, I didn't say that."

"Then what?"

"Just do yourself, and me a favor, and do your part."

"What is my part in all this, anyway?"

"For now, it's taking a leak and finding some fucking firewood. You think you can handle that?"

"I can handle that."

"Good. I'll see you at the show."

The boy now known as Kevin walked quickly to the others. Standing statue-still, the boy he left stared at the festivities until Kevin met up with the Giant and his child. "Firewood. Fuck all ya'll."

The familiar sound of a pair of jeans being unzipped conveyed to Kring and I that the boy at least for now had no idea we were lying right next to him. In the moonlight I saw the glistening rainbow of piss shoot out, quickly followed by the pseudo rain noise created by it hitting the leaf-covered ground. If he turned right now, the piss would need only a range of five feet in order to drench Kring, seven feet would mean my first golden shower. Swaying left to right, the boy began to urinate sprinkler style. On his last lazy turn, the boy made eye contact with me. The piss stopped, for his pipe was frozen like the rest of his body. Neither of us blinked. The stare was now in its second, second. Time crawled, vision chopped screen shots, as my racing heart exploded in my ears. In a millisecond, the view of the boy was replaced by Kring's black back. Kring had sprung from the ground to a full stance faster than a jack in the box. The boy had no idea that Kring was even there, for he'd been looking over Kring's prone body, in to the only white in the night – my eyes.

"You want to die bitch!"

I got up as fast as I could and stumbled to Kring's left. When I finally gained my balance and some of my composure, I noticed Kring had his gun barrel resting on the nose of the taller boy. The cool blue light from the gun light illuminated the boy's frightened face. Scruffy, dirty, definitely a dirt bag. The boy didn't dare to breathe, let alone attempt to put his dick back in his pants. Still holding it, he began to piss again, now on his pants rather than on Kring. Was Kring going to kill him? Why did he crack and give away our position?

Spitting out the words, as if the words were the boy's urine, "Piss on me you fucking dirt bag."

"I'm – "

"Get on your knees, dirt bag!"

Outside of the trembling caused by the fear, the boy did not move, nor breathe for that matter.

I tried in vain to take control of a situation that had gone sideways since sunrise, "Get on your knees, and don't say a word."

Kring spat odium, "On your knees, or die standing."

Without thinking, I walked over to the boy's right, put my hand on his shoulder, and thrust him to the ground. He went to the ground with surprising ease, most likely because his knees were already on the verge of buckling. And though taller than me by at least a half a foot, the boy was quite frail, and apparently not too coordinated, either, for he didn't just fall, he collapsed without even using a hand to brace himself, which in turn, meant his face took the brunt of the impact. And unlike Kring's fall, the boy hit a large jagged rock, not soft dirt. Kring immediately put his boot on the side of the boy's head that was facing up, and rested the barrel on his right eye lid. *Talk about being between a rock and a hard place...*

Kring moved his head close to the boy's, "Move and die." Turning his head slightly, "Get my tape, and the rope."

"Tape?" Asking for clarification.

"My left back side pocket. Rope's in the bag."

I grabbed the tape out of his pocket, and then glanced off to the distance. *Where were those boys? Had they seen this go down?*

Kring apparently was not too concerned with the others' whereabouts, and when he gave the order, "Do his hands," it didn't sound like this was his first rodeo... Kring not only sounded like someone with extensive experience in sequestering an individual, but also someone that had more than dabbled in eventually disposing of the body after questioning. I quickly went behind the boy, knelt beside him, and took both his hands. He began to resist on the second hand, but when Kring noticed it, he applied additional pressure with his boot, and shoved the barrel hard against the boy's eye socket, where the pain must have been extreme. Moving in close, Kring offered the boy some options, "Tie or die."

The boy became limp. Not even a breath could make it from his mouth now, let alone a cry for help. We were now in the shit up to our necks. There was no negotiating a truce; no begging for lenience based on our age; we were in it to win it, for our very lives now depended on it.

Kring approved of my work and gave further direction, "Nice... Good and tight. Do the legs next at the ankles."

I went about my business like a cowboy on a steer at the county fair rodeo. Within seconds, he was completely incapacitated. I looked up again to see where the others were.

Kring was on it, "I got watch. No one saw shit. I should kill you now, and be done with you."

I was kneeling, looking up at Kring; outside of his eyes, he was completely black. The smell of fresh urine assaulted the senses. The boy was lying in a pool of his own piss by now. I had not escaped unscathed and Kring was obviously not the driest person in The Woods, nor the sanest, for that matter.

Kring took his eyes off the distant fire and scanned our new hostage, "Do his mouth."

As I scurried up to the back of the boy's head, I took my right knee off the ground, and lodged it into the middle of his back. No sense in making this comfortable for him. If we got caught now, I was a dead man. I grabbed the back of his long greasy hair, and pulled his head back, slapped the tape to his forehead, and began to wrap it around his head like it was a cardboard box filled with books.

"Cover the eyes," Kring demanded.

As I did, I couldn't help but think how painful it would be for the boy when he'd have to remove the tape from his face and head. The kid would no doubt look like a cancer victim, after four months of chemo come the morning.

"Nice, nice," Kring's voice had changed, and I realized he had changed with it, as if he had just gone through puberty, while serving time in a penitentiary.

Kring grabbed my shoulder, "Hold up. We need to put something in there before you cover it. No sense in our friend talking in his sleep."

Kring had one of his father's black dress socks on his belt in which he kept a couple of things. Quickly removing the items from the sock directly into his right side pocket, he took the sock and forcibly shoved it into the boy's mouth. But before I could go about my business, Kring yanked the sock out of his mouth and violently rubbed it on the tree stump and surrounding ground, before ramming it back in to the boy's mouth. "How you like the taste, and smell of your own piss bitch?" Tapping me on the shoulder, "Tape the mouth."

As I began to finish around the mouth and nose, I noticed the boy was bleeding significantly from both orifices. He'd apparently fallen harder on the rock than I originally thought.

Kring either didn't notice, or didn't care much for our new guest's condition, "Get the rope. We'll move him behind this tree."

I moved quickly to Kring's knapsack and retrieved the rope. But before going back to Kring, I motioned him to me. Kring did not see my request for he was splitting his attention between the boy and the fire.

"Pssst.." I called.

Kring's head snapped like a bird's. I motioned him to me, with the fist. He scanned the boy, then the lay of the land, and then back to the boy, before removing his boot that he had repositioned on the boy's neck. Walking to me, he took his time, making sure he didn't step on any branches, while pausing more than once to observe the dark distance behind us, ensuring this situation did not occur again. Kring got to my position and took a knee, still holding the gun with his finger on the trigger.

Kring was all business, "What?"

"We going to drag him or pick him up?"

"What?" Kring asked vexed.

"To the tree... I gather you want to move him to the backside of this tree, and tie him up against it so he can't move, nor be seen."

"Correct," Kring confirmed.

"Two things. If we drag him over, which would be easiest, it will mean that we have to clear the ground between him and this tree, so we don't make more noise than the cans on the back of a newlywed's car. If we pick him up, we still have to clear the area where he is in case he begins to frantically flail his legs out of fear, or to possibly alert someone to his presence.

Kring contemplated the predicament, "Do we have enough rope to tie his legs to the tree?"

"Negative."

Kring now seemed more irritated than irate, "Fine. Clear the tree area, I'll clear the path, and we drag him by the arms."

"Roger that."

Looking at Kring walking back to the lifeless body of the teen made me wonder if he had gone over the edge. For some reason at that point I would have been less shocked to see Kring kick him in the ribs than I would have been to see Roy turn down seconds. I pulled out my Maglite and began to scan the ground for twigs. There were several, and the leaves had to be moved as well. I was sweating so much now that I had to wipe my eyes, more than a couple of times while I looked around, which was surprising considering I was wearing a do-rag to alleviate said sweat streams.

As I was sweeping the last of the leaves from the area with my forearm, Kring walked over to me, and took a knee. "How much longer?"

I did one last scan, "Ready."

"Let's do this."

"Roger that."

We walked quickly to the body, and Kring stepped over to the other side, grabbing underneath his left arm. I grabbed the right.

"On three," Kring clarified.

"One, two, three," we whispered in perfect unison.

We hoisted the boy to our waists, and dragged him to the tree with less trouble than I had anticipated. Kring's gun was slung over his back. A rowdy scream and chuckle could be heard in the distance as the celebrations were merrily on their way. No one missed this loser, and all three of us knew it. Once to the tree we parked his rear down rather hard, and I handed the rope to Kring. Without a word, Kring made a nose hole, and then wrapped the rope around our captive and the tree, tied it, and secured the rope in less than a minute.

I was already planning our next move when Kring demanded the M-80 with the suicide fuse. I looked at him as if he asked me for my underwear, "Why?"

Kring did not answer as he extended his hand and his menacing stare. I knew he was up to something bad, but acquiesced to keep us from becoming mired in a fluid situation.

"Roger," I put the M-80 in Kring's open hand, while gladly breaking eye contact with him.

When I looked back up, Kring had not looked away, nor most likely blinked for that matter, "Tape."

I hesitated for only a second, and then put the tape in his other hand, which was now open, "Roger."

Kring moved his head right next to the teen, and in a low, deep voice unleashed any and all fears that the boy had prior to being tied to the tree. "I'm going to tape this M-80 with these rusted tacks to your head. We call it a S.A.D., which stands for suicide and death; due to the explosive's short fuse, which one only uses when everything goes to shit, and nothing matters anymore, except the satisfaction that comes from mutual destruction."

The boy let out a sob. His nose was filled with blood, and the sock that was lodged in his mouth had cut off much of his breathing. His entire body trembled, as if he was suffering the effects of a high fever. I felt terrible for him, but I knew deep down inside that this was a necessary evil. For our enemy was evil, and one had to fight fire with fire. Besides, something was telling me that if the teen somehow escaped and alerted Derek, we would be sorry that we didn't kill him right there and then.

I got on board big time, "Position it next to the temple so it takes the medulla first."

Kring seemed to spunk up at my new found team spirit, "Roger that."

I knew fear would hold him even better than the tape and rope so I added some visual effects for his nightmare scenario, "It won't hurt as much for you, son, for you're at the center of the blast radius. By the time your eyes roll by your friends, you'll be long dead."

The teen let out a deep sob and fart. I felt his fear and pain tenfold this time, for I purposely produced those feelings within him and instantly felt shame for what I'd done, so I wasn't sure whether it was the stench emanating from his ass, or the stench emanating from my soul that had caused me to throw-up in my mouth. But I fought through the remorse for what I had become and swallowed the bitter bile, because I knew to my core that I'd rather be a living crappy version of me, than a really good dead version of me.

Kring apparently wasn't busy battling his inner demons, "Can you hear me Boy?" The boy did not move. "If you can hear me, move your head, or I'll move it for you." Still the boy showed no outward signs of cognition. Slowly and gracefully, Kring lowered himself cheek to cheek with the terrified youth and lowered his voice to a library level. "Tune in Tokyo... Come in Tokyo."

The boy moved his head fast, as much as he could for he was tied tightly, and his muscles were surely depleted of much of needed blood, due to the circulation restrictions. As Kring wrapped the tape around his head, he reassured the boy that cooperation was paramount to his head staying on his shoulders. "If we have to light this fuse, it's not because we want to, but because we have to. You see, it's a numbers game, and your number will come up if you alert anyone to our presence. Shake your head if you understand me."

The boy shook his head.

"Good boy," Kring said approvingly, as he gently stroked the sweat-soaked hair away from the boy's eyes, like a father to his own fever-stricken child. "It's not you we want... Understand? So if you play your cards right, you'll walk out of here in a couple of hours with nothing more than your pissed stained panties. But you try to play the hero, and your parents will be walking these woods come the morning trying to find enough of you to fill the coffin." Kring now held the boy's hair like a gym rope, pulling it back so hard I thought the kid's Adam's apple was going to pop out of his throat. "Blink bitch."

The boy blinked as if the sun, not Kring, was in his face. Something had fundamentally changed for the worse in my good friend... I didn't know at the time whether it was a case of innocence lost, or a dark side finally surfacing. What I did know beyond a shadow of a doubt, was that I genuinely feared for his soul. I was also equally afraid of him, as I was for him, for I remembered one of my mother's liberal rants on children turned into killers in the feuding countries of Africa, where innocent boys were brainwashed to become soldiers, carrying out brutal crimes against humanity, as our country stood by and watched, offering nothing more than lip service to stop the atrocities. I remember thinking at that point that the jungles of Africa had nothing on The Woods of La Rue. Kring was losing more than just his innocence, he was losing focus; I needed to act deliberately.

"Give me your gun and step back."

Kring handed me his gun. I took Kring's gun with both hands, raised it to the side of my body and smashed the kid in the side of the head.

"What did you do?!?!?" Kring reeled.

"I took control!"

"You could have hit the S.A.D. and killed us all."

"I saw it." *I didn't. I needed to get control.*

The brutal display of force seemed to snap Kring back to reality, "What if he needs a doctor? We got to get him some—"

"Time!" I demanded.

"Fuck time! This kid's running out of time!"

"Focus, or you'll be envying this kid's predicament."

Kring blinked and exhaled hard before squinting at his watch, "10:08."

"Not what time, but how long?" I barked.

"What?"

"How long did this take? The kid, how long did we spend?"

Five minutes? I don't know... We saw the boys..." Kring's voice trailed off as he tried to peer through the fog of war.

"I think his friends will begin to wonder of his whereabouts sooner than later."

"He's collecting firewood."

"I know, but his buddy was already concerned when he left and may think he's a deserter."

Kring's voice showed signs of sadness and skepticism, "You think his buddy will come back to check on his progress?"

"I wouldn't bet either way."

"What now?"

"Scrap the visual and leave the audio."

Regaining some of his bravado, "Bang, bang."

I took a long hard look at the roaring fire and my chances, "I'm going in."

Kring nodded, "I'll take position."

"If anything goes down, fire and forget."

Kring looked to the fire and then to me, "What about sniping?"

I shook my head as I played out the end game, "Too risky. Just stay until the first Roman goes."

Looking behind us, "What about the kid?"

"What about him?" I asked.

"I want justice."

"Justice?" I blurted incredulously. "You wrapped his head in duct tape until he resembled a freakin' mummy and then I pistol whipped him into a coma, where he now resides in a pool of his own blood and urine. And from the smell emanating from him now, I'd say he crapped his pants as well."

"So..." Kring acknowledged.

"So? So, if we have enough time on the way out, you can make him don a lobster bib, and force him to eat the crap out of his pants for all I care. But something tells me the only shit you should be concerned with right now, is the shit that's gonna hit the proverbial fan if we get caught here making plans, instead of executing them.

"Roger that."

"Set watches. Time?"

"11:10."

Looking one last time at the task at hand, I put the plan in to motion, "At 11:11 hit timer."

"Roger that."

I stared at my green-lit Timex watch as the seconds ticked. T minus, ten, nine, eight, seven, six, five, four, three, two, one.

In perfectly controlled monotone unison, "Set."

Chapter 10
A Course Correction

The campfire was blazing now, which meant two things –
One the party was getting wild and two, wood was in short supply.
Being the party's main supplier was incapacitated at the moment
meant someone would either look for him or for more wood,
meaning the probability of me being spotted entering the perimeter
of the camp just went up tenfold. I decided on a crouch pace, for a
crawl would take too long and with the multiple bathroom breaks
induced by the beers, someone would eventually see me
approaching if I was anything above hip-high.

*Kring... Is he set? You better have this jungle vaporized if
shit goes south... How did he get the remote control job and I'm
deep inside enemy territory? Whose idea was this? I'm so dead if I
get caught. Did that guy just see me?*

At about twenty-feet away the reality of the situation finally
slammed home and I almost passed out from panic. I was twenty-
feet from drunken teenagers—two had knives! Knives! Oh my
God... The one taller boy, with the dark, curly, long, greasy hair was
throwing his knife into a tree stump, while the other looked to be
whittling a spear or possibly a magic wand.

I'd never seen any of these boys before. Not in The Woods,
not riding my bike to school, or even downtown. *Wait, the kid with
the orange shirt and green bandana... He looked familiar. The
stock boy at Southdown Market! A face... Maybe if they captured
me, I could use that to my advantage. I bet he didn't want his
parents finding out about this anymore than I did. What if he*

didn't have parents? What if these kids were homeless and they all survived in The Woods on his lone salary? Maybe all the beer and cigarettes here were involuntarily supplied by Southdown. How would they feel if I told them that they were unwittingly sponsoring organized crime? Focus!

I tried breathing myself to a calmer state, but there would be no crouching tiger yoga pose for me; I was scared out of my mind, and for good reason. If I got caught here, I was going to be beaten like an egg. I'm sure our duct-taped Pharos would demand street justice on a grand scale after the boys had their fun. *Think... What do you need? Head count. One, two, three, four... five, six... For the love of God... who was that?*

Even though she was sitting, I could easily discern via the firelight that her legs were longer than a math final and her hair was almost as white as a unicorn's. *Her boobs were tremendous!* I was told that boobs that big were almost always fake, but there was no way a teenager could get fake boobs, especially if she was living off an eighth of a stock boy's salary. The only thing more out of proportion than her massive cannons were her lips, which looked like two Swedish fish. *Had she fallen recently?* I'd seen women in my dad's *National Geographic* magazines with lips that big, but they were all black and usually had huge hoops in their ears and noses. I couldn't tell if she had hoops in her ears, for her platinum thick mane covered her entire neck. And though she was sitting on a log in jeans, I knew sure as the sun would rise, that her ass was finer than a new set of throwing stars. She was well fed and groomed for sure, which meant she had a home she was going to a fro. *And speaking of bright... her eyes! Her eyes were... black?* I couldn't see the color, for they were mirrors to the flames. *Was she possessed? Don't be a fool; she's just smoking hot! Where was I? Oh—head count. One, two, three, four...*

"*Crack*," a fallen branch alerted me to their approach.

"Let's go."

"Slow down Derek."

"Hey, we need wood and I think so do you."

"Screw you, I'm not that type of girl."

"I'm sorry, did you say you wanted to screw me?"

"Get your hand off my ass!"

"Relax Gwen. I want your friend."

"You and everyone else."

"Yeah, well the difference is, I'm gonna have her, just like I had you."

"You're disgusting!"

"You didn't think so Friday..."

"I was wasted! You promised me nothing happened. Did you screw me?"

"Relax, I didn't do anything of the sort."

"I don't believe you. Where's my bra?"

"Don't know. Last I saw it you were flinging it into the woods while shaking that ass to Led Zeppelin."

"You're lying! I passed out and you felt me up!" Sobbing, "You raped me!"

"If I raped you, you'd feel it."

"Would I? I'm a virgin, how would I know what to feel?"

"Trust me baby, I'm the biggest in the grade."

"You're an animal and I'm going to tell on you if you don't give me back my bra."

Commotion, sticks cracking, leaves rustling. "Get off of me, you're hurting me."

"You're not telling anyone, anything bitch, cause what ya gonna tell them?"

"Stop!" *More rustling.*

"Stop what? Stop holding your arms down?"

"I swear I'll scream."

"To what end? You think Big Tits cares about you enough to run over here? And what if she did? You want her to get hurt on your behalf? For what? Besides, she looks about ready to take off her own bra and... wait... that's it, isn't it? You don't want anyone comparing your racks? I wouldn't want to be you either in that competition. But that's no reason to be a prude."

A staggering weep left her chest as the reality of her predicament sank in.

"Besides, what ya gonna tell Daddy? Daddy, I was partying in the woods again, against all your warnings and pleadings and I got so drunk I lost my bra. I'm not sure if I had sex or not, but the next day I decided to go back into the woods and hangout with the same guys again and that's when he raped me."

Gwen wept uncontrollably. Her sobbing seemed to fuel Derek's inner demons.

"Oh yeah, everyone is going to be talking about you! You think you look bad in Daddy's eyes now? Wait until the school finds out you had not one, but two gangbangs in one weekend."

"You can't... I came back for my bra... Please..."

"You came back at night? Why wouldn't you look for it the very next morning?"

"I did, but I couldn't find it... Please let me go..."

"Oh Daddy, please believe me! I couldn't see it in the bright sun, so I came back at night with every bad boy I could find and got drunk again, hoping the camp fire would illuminate it. HA!"

"I'm not drunk!"

"You were last night."

"Let me go!"

"Oh, I'll let you go, right after you apologize to me."

"For what?"

"For ruining my night."

"I just wanted to go home. You followed me!"

"I just wanted to bang your friend, but now she's feeling sorry for you and therefore won't give up the goods. You owe me."

"Owe you what?"

"Owe me the goods."

"Get off of me!"

"As soon as you get me off."

I could see their silhouettes move among the bramble as Gwen wrestled the Giant in vain. She was defending herself well, considering she started the match with her hands tied behind her back, against an opponent that outsized her by a hundred pounds and nine inches. But despite all her valiant efforts, in the end, she was no match for the beer muscles of the larger human. Derek scooped her up and body slammed her to the hard-packed ground, simultaneously dropping himself on top of her, doubling the impact. The air left her almost as fast as her spirit. She laid still not making a noise. *Was she unconscious???* Derek's heavy breathing sounded as if he'd just ran a marathon. *He must be crushing her over and over again under his heaving chest and she's not even conscious to compensate for the added weight. She could die right now!*

Between my stunned blinks, Derek had risen to his knees and was now straddling Gwen, pulling back his sweat drenched hair to expose his neck and shoulders to the air.

Derek seemed oddly exuberant, as he laughed and panted between a ragged smoker's cough. "Talk about playing hard to get!"

I was in shock. What could I do, but watch this nightmare unfold... *If I moved, Derek would hear the first pine needle under my foot snap, for I was too close to use stealth. Being the only witness meant I'd be a dead man walking, for if he'd rape a girl, he'd kill a boy.* I was frozen in fear. *At least Gwen had an excuse not to move. She fought to the end. I was just a pussy, peeing on itself.* I felt the first tear run down my right cheek and pause on my lip for a better look at the abyss, before it decided it'd rather leap in to the unknown, than hang with a chump. The irony of my tear having more internal fortitude than me, was not lost on me and the subsequent rage and hate for myself, rather than Derek, began to grow internally, feeding on my fears and inaction like a wild fire feeds on dried pinecones and bramble.

Then I saw it... Gwen's arm began to slowly raise. Derek didn't see it, for his eyes were half closed and his head was tilted back, as if he was basking in a summer rain. Her trembling hand slowly turned in to a shaking fist, and as if Gwen was a master puppeteer and I her marionette, I found my own hand raise in a tight grip around the 2-foot military grade Maglite that I had brought to illuminate the night. I froze with my hand held high like the Statue of Liberty, as Derek faced down on Gwen, with a chagrin of respect.

"Oh, looky here? Bitch got some fight left in her. Mad respect sweetie. I only wish you would have saved some of your energy for the good times, but..."

I was up and walking to Derek, like I knew him. I couldn't feel my left leg, for it had fallen asleep while in the prone position, so I limped to him like an old ship captain, determined and proud. Though the light levels of the crescent moon made definition hard to come by, Derek's shocked expression was not only apparent, but priceless, for I knew that just by me standing before him, I'd robbed him of his precious power. *Someone approached him without fear!* For once, he was on his knees before a terrifying stranger—and terrifying I was. I was dressed head to toe like an assassin and though I was just a child, playing games in The Woods, Derek had zero knowledge of why I was there, or who I was. I saw his fear emanate from his eyes and the rage that was now starving inside of me, due to the sudden lack of my internal readily-available supply of fear, yearned to dine on Derek's soul.

"Die Derek."

Chapter 11
Swing for the Fences

My father had played ball for the Yankees' farm team back before the Korean War, and was an amazing athlete. Six-foot five inches tall and topping 220 pounds on a frame with less than seven percent body fat, Walter Sidoruk was the dad who could kick the crap out of all dads. He loved sports and despised the fact that I was only average in them. On top of being of average athletic ability, I was a choker. I froze at the plate, dropped the pass in the end zone, and shot a free throw as if it cost an arm and a leg. My father finally gave up on me one day during batting practice.

He said, "You'll never hit the ball where you want, Boy. You think too much. Your body has enough trouble following what you're thinking, without you double-guessing yourself."

When he saw my shoulders slump and my head tilt to my feet, he hurt inside more than I knew at the time, for he'd given up on not just me, but himself as well. Our relationship was never the same after that day and neither was I. Nor were the weekends, for my dad stopped coming to the games and I stopped caring inside. I almost yearned for the days when he would hurl curses at me from the stands, while my mother wept in the parking lot on the shoulder of a complete stranger.

One day I was day dreaming in the outfield, far from the game and my natural position at short stop, when I noticed a tall figure leaning over the fence near a shade tree. *Father?* He waved and walked back to his car and drove off before we finished the inning. When the game, which couldn't end quickly enough, finally did, I raced to my mom who stood proudly next to the exit gate.

"Did you see Dad?"

"Yup."

"Where is he?"

"He went home to do yardwork."

"How long did he stay? Did he see me hit the homerun?"

"Yes!"

"Yes!"

"I'm so proud of you honey!"

"I can't believe I nailed that one clean out of the park!"

"The ball hit the car next to your father's. I can't believe it!"

"I can't believe I didn't see him out there..."

"He was sitting in the car when you hit it."

"Oh..."

"Oh honey, he's sooo proud, he can't contain himself."

"Really?"

"Really!"

"Why did he leave?"

"He didn't want to make you nervous. He watches most games from the parking lot."

"Really?"

"Really."

The drive home was the best drive of my life. I felt like I was meeting the president after winning the Super Bowl where I was just crowned MVP. As we approached the house, I saw my father sitting on the front steps with a beer in his hands. He never sat on the steps, due to his back... When the car pulled in, he sprang to his feet and strutted over to the car, holding the beer, as if he was meeting buddies at the bar.

"Wow!" was all he had to say when my mom put the car in park. And that was all the compliment I needed to hear, for his smile was the biggest I'd ever seen him wear. Add the beer in the middle of the day and it was crystal clear that a celebration of my amazing performance was underway.

"I had no idea you were watching me!"

"Neither did I."

"Walter!"

"Well..."

"Trel has been playing great this year!"

"OK. Relax. I meant to say, you swung at that pitch differently. You swung at it like you do at the end of Friday's practices'."

"You watch practice?"

"Sometimes..." my father sheepishly smiled.

"Your dad watches more than you think!"

"I've seen enough."

"I suck."

Before my dad could agree, my mom passionately interjected, "No you don't honey!"

Father looked her over and rolled his eyes as he took a deep swig of his Michelob. "You don't suck... You're just not the same athlete as your sister..."

"Walter!"

"Relax!" My father retorted, "Go inside, I'm trying to talk to the boy!"

"Screw you." And off she went storming into the house and slamming the door that had partially fallen off its hinges three years prior, due to my mother slamming the door, stating the exact same thing to my father over a fight no one could recall.

Before I could come down on myself further, my father put his hand up and took another swig. "You don't suck. You're actually an athlete, which is why I get so crazy when you play poorly." Taking a sizable sip, leaving his lips to hover over the bottle's mouth, "You see, you just choke. You're a choker..."

"I'm a choker? But I don't suck???"

"Correct."

"I'm an excellent choker?"

"You 'freeze' is a better term. You tense up and subsequently move like an old man."

"That can't be good..."

"During Friday's practice when the coach gives out a candy bar for who can hit the ball the farthest, you win the candy bar every week. And every week it's not even close! The other kids on your team have come to expect you'll win the bar and some don't even bother trying to hit the ball."

"Yeah, they call it the Trel Bar."

"Exactly!"

"What does practice have to do with it?"

"Everything!"

"It's not a game."

"It's all a game!" Looking off in to the distance, "A mental game..."

"So I'm an idiot."

"No!" Calming himself by taking yet another healthy dose of beer, my father's voice became somewhat scholarly. "You're my son, so you're far from stupid and since you have my genes, you're at a minimum, a better than average athlete."

"Better than average…"

"Well, your mom's freak show of a midget family tree took half your skill set to the circus."

Before my mouth could fully gape, "Say anything to your mom and you'll crap this bottle by the morning."

I blinked to acknowledge.

"You're not swinging and missing, or grounding out to first base because you suck, you're striking out, because you're afraid to screw up, thus you're screwing up. The self-fulfilling prophecy leaves you so psyched out that you can't even swing the bat. You tense, you cringe, you expect to strike out, so you don't even try to swing right in the end."

I caught myself shaking my head up and down slightly to acknowledge every point my father made, for I knew them as truths that I desperately hoped no one on my team would ever call me out on. My head actuation acted as the pump for my well of tears and the water level began to rise.

"Hey, don't cry," my farther warned.

"I'm not."

He closed the gap between us in one stride and tossed the bottle to the gravel driveway. Taking my head in his huge hands, he gripped tight on me, pulling me up to his chest like a baby would its favorite stuffed animal. I wept uncontrollably. I didn't care who walked or biked by, I was crying in my dad's chest. I shook violently, but he held tight. *Such love I hadn't felt in how long?* I felt his warmth, and not just because it was a hot summer day and he'd been doing yard work periodically throughout it, but real warmth. *Real love.* The smell of sweat, gas and freshly cut grass will forever bring me joy. After my initial surge of sadness passed, my father yanked my head back and held it firm. I suddenly felt small and helpless. He bent down and swiped his two giant thumbs across both cheeks, like windshield wipers. Releasing the pressure somewhat he bent closer and gently kissed me on my forehead. It was then I noticed the tears running down his own face.

"I never did anything with all my talent. I could throw a ball so fast, batters rarely even swung. A man who worked for the Yankees happened to be walking by the park one day and saw me and almost crapped his pants." Smiling off into the distance at what must have been an awesome memory, my father continued with zeal. "The next day I was given a contract to play minor league ball. I never even had to tryout! No one had ever been afforded such ascension to the greatest team in the history of sports as I! They knew what a talent I was from a mile away and they knew they had to snatch me up before word of my fastball got to the Dodgers." His voice slowed and lowered. "I should be in the Hall of Fame... I'm not of course... I never even saw the field for the real Yankees..."

"But you went to war! You're a patriot!"

"I took the easy way out. I could have made it."

"You threw your back out in the Army; everyone knows it."

"Everyone knows I played minor league ball for the Yankees and what they believe is that I wasn't good enough to go pro. It doesn't matter anymore, for I failed to give it everything I had and that in the end, is what it takes to be great... Everything and nothing."

"Everything and nothing?"

"Give everything you have and let nothing affect you."

"I try Dad! I do..."

He gripped tighter and made eye contact with both eyes from three inches away.

"You're your own worst enemy out there."

"Then I'm stupid?"

"Stop saying stupid things."

"OK?"

"When you swing in practice you swing for the fences. When you swing in the game, you swing for the fans, for your teammates, for me... You swing for everyone but you. Forget everyone, everything. Let nothing enter your head but you, and the image of you slamming that ball out of the park. It's all about you!"

"I should be greedy?"

"YES!" He shook my head harder than he wanted to and found himself gently kissing my forehead once again.

"Yes. Swing for yourself. Screw everyone! Be greedy! You get three to five bats a game and all should be for you, unless your coach tells you to bunt or hit a sacrifice fly. All other times, it's your time. Your time to shine."

"My time..."

"Your time." My father produced a ball that was oddly shaped. "You see this ball?"

I nodded once.

"You see that it's dented?"

I nodded once again.

"It was crushed today by an animal. A beast of a young man with a swing that would emasculate Paul Bunyan."

"Who?"

Laughing with his head back and eyes closed and he quickly refocused on me and looked me dead to rights. "You!"

"Me?"

"You!"

"I did that?"

"Yes!"

"No I didn't. No way!"

"Yes!"

"That's insane!"

"I haven't seen damage to a ball like this since I pitched to Joe DiMaggio."

"You pitched to Joe DiMaggio?"

"Yes."

"He hit a homerun on you..."

Holding his hand up to an observation made more times than of a rainbow, "It was my job to toss him balls he could hit during batting practice. If they would have let me, I would have fared quite well, I promise you that."

"Of course."

A knowing smile creased my father's face, making light of his furrowed brow.

"The point is Son, you can swing as hard as Joe DiMaggio."

"Really?"

"The proof is as plain as day Son. I'm a scientist by profession, and I'm holding scientific evidence. Furthermore, I witnessed that crushing blow firsthand and my observations were backed up by a stand-full of fans. You can swing with the best of them; that's irrefutable."

"So I suck, because I can't get out of my own way?"

"Yes."

"What can we do to fix it?"

"Nothing."

I was stunned, as if the family doctor just told me my sniffles were actually the onslaught of a rare and terminal disease with no cure. My father noticed my hurt face and quickly added, "There's nothing we can do about it from a baseball practice standpoint, for your swing is fundamentally sound." With a chagrin shrug, "It's your brain that needs rewiring."

"Oh..."

"That's a good thing."

"Yeah?"

"We can work on that over time, for it's all up there," piercing my skull with a hungry stare. "At least you have the tools Son. Few and far between are given such a set to work with. All you have to do is sharpen them and then learn how to use them."

"So how do we do it?"

"I'm not exactly sure, but I think you're going to be doing all the heavy lifting on this one kid."

"So... how long will I suck for?"

"Once again, you don't suck." Tilting his head, contemplating the validity of his last statement, "You're just a work in progress. How long will depend on who you become."

"I don't understand."

Slightly frustrated, "Let's keep it simple. You see this ball?"

"Yes."

"You see how hard you hit it?"

"Yes."

"Do you know how hard you hit it compared to the other balls you hit today?"

"I didn't hit any other balls, I struck out the other four at bats on twelve swings."

"Exactly! You failed to hit the ball trying to swing for the ball."

"But isn't that what I'm supposed to do?"

"Not you Son... No, you're different. From this day forward, don't swing for the ball, swing for the fences."

I stood before Derek holding the Maglite in both hands, thumbs locked, legs spread hip-width and bent at the knees... A cat ready to pounce on its wounded prey. Derek's voice no longer carried the arrogant air of unchecked power, but rather the soft whisper of an old hobo begging for a quarter and a sip of my coffee.

"Who??? Who are you?"

"I'm Joe DiMaggio's daddy." And with that I swung for the fences...

Chapter 12
First Contact

There are certain things one remembers of a traumatic event a week later, and there are things one remembers a lifetime later. The first indelible impression was at mid-swing. Derek's facial expression will forever be etched into my subconscious, a mix between true primal fear and genuine curiosity. If I had to bet on what was going through his mind before the earth shattering shockwave it would have been, *"Is he mad because I sold his son drugs, or his son's baseball card?"*

The second split second that will forever hold a place in everything I do, as well as one day dictate what I allow my own children to do, for that matter, was the impact, or more accurately stated, the corresponding devastating effects an impact of that magnitude would produce. Derek's face pre-swing could best be described as an 8th century Dracula, masquerading as a Duke of a mountainous region of Europe that exported smoked cheeses and dried meats only adults pretended to enjoy. A long, thin face with high, sharp cheekbones were literally overshadowed by a nose so long that it would emasculate Pinocchio.

The flashlight caught him between the nostrils and upper lip... My swing was true and the force was so fast and furious that his head could not snap back quickly enough and thus my swing carried me through his mouth and upper nasal passage.

The sensations of the impact would be the third freeze-frame that my less than picture-perfect memory would forever store in HD quality with multiple backups. The initial sound of the impact produced a deep bass and oddly enough, a wheezing sound, eerily similar to a harmonica solo in a blue grass band.

And though all I need to do to this day is close my eyes to hear that sad song, all I need to do to feel it, is open my hand and watch it twitch; for the sensation of connecting with Derek's skull with that Maglite, felt like I was crushing a ten-pound block of peanut brittle, suspended in Hawaiian Punch Jello, encased in Silly Putty, two-hundred yards with a sand wedge. The stimulus was a sensory overload for me, so powerful that to this day, makes playing any sport where I must at some point swing a stick with force next to impossible.

I should at some point see a sports therapist and address the fact that anytime I swing true and connect on the sweet spot of a ball or puck, I think of Derek's cartilage crunching, his bones splitting, and his teeth shattering like an ancient Ming vase. The "swing" affects more than just my ability to drive a ball, it affects my driving as well. Every time I'm on a highway and approach an overpass, I look for those yellow barrels of water that are setup at the base of the bridge's foundation that are designed to slow a speeding car's impact and immediately think of Derek's face. I sometimes subconsciously avoid the highways altogether and take the back roads in hopes of avoiding the modern art edifice of his face. If a passenger asks why we're taking the scenic route, I just tell them I hate traffic, when in fact I hate something far worse...

The fourth image that was magically tattooed to the inside of my eyelids, is the vision of my first crush... *actually my third crush—my first crush being the baseball, my second being Derek's face, making my third, Gwen.* The crystal clear image will forever be accompanied by primal raw emotions and vision quest revelations. I remember the only thing more apparent than her stunning beauty was her vulnerability. I also still feel ashamed for taking my time to take her in. But in my defense, there was so much to process... She was splayed on her back, physically and mentally exhausted, her assailant still half-lying on her, bleeding out like a pig being readied for process. She was covered head to toe in dirt, moss, and pine needles from violently rolling around on the forest floor; her face recently sprayed with a huge helping of Derek's blood.

How she had remained absolutely stunning in the moonlight, despite fighting for her life was truly remarkable. Why she remained completely still was rather obvious – she was staring at a bloodthirsty father, donned in black, packing a light saber. Derek's face had turned the switch on, illuminating me in a ghastly purple light, which I'm sure only added to my mystique. I extended my hand and uttered the least smooth pickup line ever vocalized in the history of pickup lines, since the first caveman blurted, "Ooooh, me likey your boobies."

"Come. Live. Now." Each word skydiving solo from my chest on the back of a shortened breath.

She quickly scanned me up and down, most likely wondering, "Where did this caveman learn to communicate?" Other than her twin pools of love laser beams locking me in, she remained statue-still. Against all protocol and common sense, the next thing I felt was my mask being ripped off my face by my own hand. *Stick to the plan, nothing can go sideways, don't panic, don't improvise, and whatever you do, don't let anyone know who you are.* I, of course, threw all of that away when I threw my mask to the ground.

The stupid act of compassion did its job though; Gwen's eyes became those of an owl and her hand a lobster, as she snatched mine with speed and strength that caught me off guard—so much so that I fell on top of her. Unsuccessfully trying to compensate for her unexpected physical attributes, made my descent to the forest floor all the clumsier. The painfully pathetic picture of me laying on top of Derek with my face buried in his chest, while I T-bagged Gwen's face, added insult to injury. If someone had walked up to us at that point in time, they might have just turned away and tried to forget the scene. Poor Gwen; her would-be assailant laid sprawled backwards on her legs and her only chance in Hell had the coordination of someone on an infomercial.

I quickly sprang to my feet and offered an uncomfortable apology, once again piercing the vail of secrecy, by using my real voice. "Oh my God! I'm so sorry. Are you OK?"

Gwen looked even more shocked. I hastily grabbed Derek's right arm and began pulling him off of her. The task was physically exhausting unto itself, for Derek was massive—at least twice my weight. If it weren't for Gwen using the force of her own legs to assist me in the endeavor, I would have never been able to budge him. That blaring fact rattled me to the core. *I'm in the big leagues now and I'm the smallest player on the field.* I grabbed her other hand and pulled her up. She was taller and closer to me than I was prepared for.

"This way!"

"No."

"Why?"

"I can't go."

"Why?"

"My bra..."

"I have your bra."

"You what?"

"It's at my friend's."

"You raped me?"

"No."

"How do you have it?"

"We found it this morning."

"I don't believe you."

"I just saved your life!"

"Where do you live?"

"I'm... I can't say. Come or die."

"Don't threaten me! You touch me and I'll scream."

"No, no. I won't harm you, but those guys are bad."

"They'll kill you, not me."

How did this spin so out of control? How could it get any worse? Gwen picked up my flashlight, "This is evidence. The police will want to see this."

The only thing this disaster was missing was—*boom!* A massive explosion no more than twenty-five feet away shook the forest. Then the balls came a blazing by...

The camp was pandemonium as people scattered faster than cockroaches in a newly lit ghetto kitchen.

"Aaahhhh!!!"

"Fire!!!"

"Duck!!!"

"I'm on fire!!!"

"My eyes!!!"

Kring had nearly hit us with a massive rocket attack, but the screams from the nearby camp told me he was hitting his target more often than not.

"I can't hear! Oh my God!" Gwen had dropped my flashlight and was cupping both hands over her ears. She looked completely horrified and was surely in a state of shock.

I grabbed the flashlight off the ground, slammed it in its holster and grabbed Gwen by the waist and began to run. Her state of shock allowed her to be moved, slowly at first, but she began to pick up her pace with each step. Her hands were still cupping her ears and her head was down as if expecting another blast at any moment. This made traveling through the woods arduous at best, for I had to not only watch for eye-popping branches for myself, but for my walking liability as well. I took a lot of body shots, until Gwen began to hit full-stride and use her hands to block the initial impact of the branches. She ran like a zombie—head straight, eyes wide open and hands straight-armed in front of her face, while she stumbled on every branch, rock, and bush within two-feet of her. *Maybe she had been partially blinded by the bursts of light...*

I did my best to keep one arm around her waist and use the other as a continuously swinging machete in hopes of at least warning my face of the incoming projectiles. Without my mask, I was feeling every single twig. Then it hit me - *My mask! I left my bra... A shred of evidence.* I careened over a two-foot-high boulder after I, of course, slammed my shin into it. Gwen had managed to put her hands on the boulder and was bent down. I rolled over and looked up at her. She stared at me as wild-eyed as ever, panting from the run.

"Your light!"

"It's mine!"

"It's on!"

"Oh crap!" I had left the light on when I picked it up and put it in the holster, which of course meant that anyone looking off into the distance could literally track us to right here! I had broken yet another law: don't panic. I fumbled for the light, for what seemed to be an hour and finally managed to turn it off.

Gwen turned towards the camp, "I don't think we were followed, but we better get going; the cops will be here any second."

The cops... My best friend just laid waste to The Woods and my victim laid waste right smack in the middle. I needed to get back to base camp ASAP. I rolled to my stomach and sprang up the best I could with a badly bruised leg.

"I've got to go."

"What?" Gwen looked at me like I had said it in the middle of our date.

"Home. Cops. Parents."

"What?"

I was clearly talking like a caveman again and Gwen was coming to the realization that her hero was a child and the only thing 'super' about him was that he was most likely in the middle of wetting his Super Man Underoos.

"You have to take me."

"I can't."

"You can and you will. You have my bra!" Gwen's voice was half mad, half hysterical. She didn't know who I was, why I was there, what I would do next or, of course, what had just happened. She was in shock, as was I, and thus even through the fog of war, I knew I had to do the right thing.

"Follow me." I didn't grab her hand this time, nor look back to see if she followed. She was either going to come, or not. I heard her right behind me as we approached a backyard. The lights were on, as they were on in several homes bordering The Woods, for everyone must have heard the noises, if not seen the display.

"We've got to find a yard with no lights on." I heard a couple yards down the distinct sound of an unoiled screen door swinging open. "Come this way. Watch the branches in front of you and more importantly below you, and whatever else you think might make a noise if you step on, or into it."

"I can't see a thing."

"You can feel everything."

"What?"

"Shorter, lighter steps. Try to focus on moving quietly, verses quickly." And with that we moved in unison from the exposed tree line near the curious neighbor. Gwen caught on quickly. We walked along The Wood's perimeter for a hundred yards until I saw that the Jefferson's were not home, or if they were home, were in deep sleep, for no lights were on. Also helpful was that the Blivens were their next-door neighbors, and even though there was a motion sensor light on in the backyard over the deck, it most likely was the result of a cat or raccoon, for the Blivens had gone away for an extended summer vacation. I knelt down at the beginning of the Jefferson's lawn and proceeded to give our next coordinates. Before I could utter a word, Gwen's arm rested on my shoulder. I froze.

"I need to catch my breath," she shouted exasperatedly.

"OK."

I was exhausted, so I was in no shape to argue. It also gave me a moment to reevaluate our position and more importantly, our predicament. A moment of clarity made me realize we were half-yelling the entire exodus, most likely due to our ears being permanently damaged from the mighty explosions.

I whispered, "We need to whisper."

Gwen whispered back, "OK."

She was good. Her whisper was great. *What was this?* My penis must have sensed something in The Woods that I failed to see or hear, for it began to grow and move, alerting me to imminent danger. *Or could it have responded to the frequency of Gwen's whisper like a dog whistle? Odd...* Regardless of why it began to grow, I realized that if it kept growing, Gwen would most likely not be impressed, but further traumatized, so I stayed in the crouched position and began to think of being arrested for not one, but two third-degree assault charges, illegal firearms, arson, and oh yeah, if all didn't go smashingly well with Gwen, rape. As if each charge was a dart, my burgeoning balloon deflated quickly.

I pointed to the Jefferson's shed. "We're going to run to that shed. From the shed, we'll run to the right back corner of their house. The people next door aren't home. When we get there, I'll see if there's a car in the driveway."

"How do you know they're not home?"

"I know." And with that I began to run. I over-crouched my run to show her true form, in hopes that she would follow suit. *Learning the ways of the ninja was not something someone learned in the first lesson.* As we approached the shed, something dawned on me that distracted my rapid approach to the shed, making my incoming speed and thus vector too high. I had to break abruptly and subsequently slid on some mud from the shed's leaky outdoor hose spicket, with the same grace as someone learning to ice skate three sheets to the wind. Ironically, what had distracted me, saved me. Gwen was holding my hand! Gwen lessened my fall by sliding back with me and when I landed on my butt with my legs sprawled before me, she wound up slammed against my back in a catcher's position, with her head resting on top of mine, which kept it from drilling into the ground. I froze.

"You OK?" Her whisper awoke my penis yet again. *Or was it the wet heat from her breath itself? Maybe my penis came equipped with a humidity detection system, which is why I never wanted to go to school on a rainy day...* Other obscure dealer-installed options were a motion detector, slash proximity alarm and a boom mic, which made it the Swiss Army knife of appendages, and thus earning its new battle-tested nickname, *Swissy*.

"Fine." My breath was ragged, due to the fact that I almost knocked the wind out of myself and the wheeze made my whisper sound as if I was possessed. I got to my feet as fast as humanly possible, and headed for the corner of the Jefferson's house at a more controlled speed. At the halfway mark, Gwen's hand had once again found mine. Her grip tightened on our final approach and I immediately slowed as if she was applying a hand brake. This time we didn't fall and remained in the crouch position with Gwen spooned over my back, still holding my hand.

I quickly separated from her with a whisper, "Shoe lace." Finding busy work that freed me from Gwen's grasp, which I now suspected was the hand pump to my penis, afforded me a position that hid my now growing appendage. Much to my chagrin, Gwen, who was still hunched over me, took both her hands and rested them on my shoulders.

Half giggle, half whisper, "Bunny ears."

"Where?" I responded quickly, for Gwen could be mistaking a neighbor's lap dog for a bunny, which meant we could have an eight-pound mobile alarm system going off and escorting us to the road.

"Your laces, Silly."

Oh my God! She knew I was a boy now for sure. All chances of seeing what was on the other side of that bra were eradicated by my social faux pas. I didn't think she'd see my actual tying technique in the moonlight. I thought she would spend that time surveying the landscape and assessing our situation in hopes of assisting me with our next course of action. The only feasible possibility was that Gwen must still be somewhat traumatized and therefore a little misdirection on my end, via a macho factoid could easily transport me back to the future, where I was still a man.

"Special forces exclusively uses the B.E. Style, for it affords the user total symmetry in the loops, versus the civilian half loop, which can lead to one loop being too long and thus an untied boot. And tripping on your laces is something that can't happen in combat."

"How did yours become untied?"

"Must have gotten caught on a branch..."

I could feel her smile penetrating my skull. I bet she looked beautiful smiling, but between the limited lighting and my inability to look up from the weight of my embarrassment, I was transfixed on my boot.

"What now?"

Her question snapped me from my funk. Luckily, her accidental emasculation of me had reversed the blood flow from my swollen body part and I now could resume with normal operating procedure.

"We're heading towards that big bush next to the fence. There's a small opening on the left, we'll be able to duck inside and not be seen, even by a search light."

"Are you sure it's right next to the road?"

"Sure as sugar."

"Is that a good thing?"

"It's just an expression." *Which I just made up in my stupid head! Sure as sugar... Did that last explosion jar loose an eighty-year-old granny from the south from deep within my Medulla Cortex?*

"We've used it before on recon missions. Go low." And with that I sprang to my feet and ran quicker than I intended. Right before I reached the hole in the massive holly bush, I dove face first with my hands extended forward. My belly slide was Olympic-worthy. Gwen was behind me in a flash and now laid next to me in the prone position looking low below the green canopy.

"It's huge in here. Are we really safe from lights?"

My whisper gone, "Oh yeah. This is an impenetrable fortress. When it snows, it becomes an igloo."

"Do you vacation here in the winter?"

Her jovial tone wasn't lost on me, but I was too embarrassed to admit that this was in fact the main snow fort for upper La Rue. The crown jewel in their entire defense system and thus a highly sought after piece of real estate.

Fully aware that boys who bantered got girls, "No." Was all my self-esteem could muster.

"Oh. Well it's cool. I've never seen anything like it."

Wait? She finds this cool? This is nothing compared to where I'm about to take you! Stay cool, don't drool. The real saying went, "Stay cool, don't drool a pool, like a fool in school." But anyone who was cool, knew that and didn't need to repeat it to themselves twenty times in order not to.

I felt compelled to carry on a dialogue, "You ever been in a real treehouse?"

"What?"

My question was so idiotic, she wasn't sure she heard me correctly. I'd blown it big time. I might as well have asked, "Have you ever spoken to a complete dweeb masquerading as a ninja?" That's right, I was worried what I'd said, even though I was keenly aware that I still donned my sister's leotard and my mom's makeup. *Wouldn't want to ruin her image of me anytime soon. It's not every day that someone so in touch with his feminine side can brutally slay a monster in cold blood...* Though acting nonchalantly would only exasperate my predicament, Pavlov's Dog began to salivate, for it starved for more self-destruction. "I really shouldn't talk about it, being that it's top secret..."

"What?"

"Shut up!" I yelled internally, until I could hear the echoes of follies' warning reverberate throughout the hallowed gourd propped atop my shoulders. And though I heard the warning, I did not heed it. "I'm taking you to our secret base to get your br—clothing accessory—question you and ensure your safe passage home."

"You're planning on questioning me? Why?"

"You know the others."

"The others? You mean Derek and his crew?"

Looking to every branch of the bush, "Yes..."

"What do you want to know?"

"I've got to ask you later."

"Why?"

"It's top sec..."

"Are you fucking with me?"

"No. No! I'm..."

"Wait... You know 'fucking with me' is an expression? Right?"

"Oh yeah... It's like "The" to me."

"What?"

"I use it all the time..."

"You curse a lot?"

"Not all the time."

"Do your parents know you curse a lot?"

"I don't curse a lot," sounding more insecure than I wanted.

"I won't tell."

"Nothing to tell."

"Nothing?"

"It's your word verses mine."

How I went from insecure, to defensive was completely beyond me. What wasn't lost on me, was the loss of control I'd allowed to be yanked from me by my prisoner over the situation. *Was Gwen my prisoner or my responsibility??? Would it matter that I could now add kidnapping to my professional criminal resume?* Either way she was a burgeoning liability, rapidly expanding her potential collateral damage blast zone by the breath.

"I think we went over this. I'm an eye witness to you beating a man to death."

"You have no idea he's dead!" My whisper screamed for blood.

Formally crossing her arms underneath her stomach with an aristocrat's grace, "You have no idea if he's alive, because you fled the scene of your brutal attack," Gwen opined with a stately heir.

"I fled because I was trying to save your life!" I answered incredulously.

"Because you were leaving anyway, because, I'm guessing that was your backup that torched a city block using enough fireworks to celebrate our Nation's birth?"

My mind was racing. *I did this all for her and she would destroy me.* I had saved a bad person from a bad person. I was the U.S. sending troops and money into a foreign land to help the warring factions 'see the light', and thus just nurtured more hate for the U.S., while training and arming those who wanted us dead in the first place. *Is this why everyone hated America? Because we loved too much?!?! How could I have been so naïve? Birds of a feather truly did flock together.* I managed to shake loose from my ever-constricting esophagus, "My team is worried about you... and me. And I'm worried about him."

She must have sensed my empathy, for it triggered her own, however deep it was buried inside of her, for she backed down an octave as a verbal reward for me assuming the submissive position in our newly formed dysfunctional relationship.

"Worried... Well that's good I guess. That means you're loved. And I'm at least liked by someone."

"Can we go then?" And with that question I had officially lost complete control of the situation. I was now acquiescing to my captive. She didn't just notice the newly formed holes in the armor, Gwen rammed acquisition and innuendo in with the speed of Bruce Lee firing fists.

"Go where? To your secret lair? Are you going to do to me what you did to Derek? How can I trust you? You haven't even told me your name, where you live, where we're going, or why you were there in the first place dressed to kill!" Her voice was too loud. If someone was within twenty yards, we were exposed and no one ever heard cops coming.

"You need to lower your voice," I whispered.

"Or what? You gonna hit me?"

Without even processing her remark to be hurt enough for the proper reply, I answered with a matter of factness that surprised even me, "I'll leave."

"You'll leave? Just get up and go?" Her voice rankled with sarcasm.

"This was supposed to be fun, and the fun has long since ended," I retorted with an empty heart.

"Fun? You were here for fun?" A hastily placed fake laugh escaped her diatribe, "You allowed events to spin out of control to the point of arson and assault, because it got in the way of a good old time?"

"Weren't you there to have fun? What happened to you?" I said it more of a question, in hopes of figuring out how I landed in my circumstance, but it had a devastating effect on Gwen that only a naked truth sheathed in an open-ended accusation could.

Her voice cracked, as tears cascaded over her cheeks, "I was..."

I noticed that off-in-the-distance stare of despair, and my heart stepped in front of my fear, "I'm sorry. I know what he tried to do to you. No one could ever deserve that. Especially a good girl. I have a sister... I got mad. I knew I had to stop him. I didn't plan on any of this, just like you didn't."

And with those startling revelations, Gwen began to weep and weep hard. We were now kneeling within the protection of the ancient holly bush, but her cries would travel on a night where the air was thick and the ears were cupped.

I did the only thing I knew had ever worked on me, what my dad, mom, or sister would do. I awkwardly made two steps with my knees and hugged her tight. She cried harder now, which I expected, for that was my M.O. I always cried more when one of my parents hugged me, as if they knew just how to squeeze the pain out. After some of the initial force of her pain left, I performed the ritual of kissing her on her forehead. For whatever reason, this always felt the best. It signaled the end to the bad spirits and allowed me to raise my head, and no matter the sin, no matter the outlook, I could smile one day again. I pressed my lips to Gwen's forehead more softly then my parents would have mine, since I didn't want Gwen to think I was trying to sucker her into sucking face. *It worked!* She looked at me, tears still streaming from her red-coated eyes—a hint of a smile touched her lips. Then she kissed me back, and not on my forehead!

Thankfully, my lips were wet enough from the sweat they had just received from her forehead, for my tongue was still buried deep within my mouth and could not be used to wet them anytime soon. I was so in awe of what was transpiring, I opened my mouth like a slack jaw yocal staring at a U.F.O., unintentionally signaling Gwen that I wanted to deep throat.

My mouth became a hanger for her tongue as it transformed in to the *Millennium Falcon*, slipping in before the Federation could register her call sign at port.   I went to push her off, but my boner made first land, punching Gwen in the stomach. *Why would my penis want to protect me from her? Lights! My penis was warning me of car lights!* I spun out of her grasp and took a mortal wound to the face. A branch in my right eye. I dropped. Gwen dropped next to me. As I thrashed in pain, she laid sprawled next to me trying in vain to stop me from rustling the bush. Finally, before the slowing lights arrived, Gwen leapt on top of me.

"Stop moving. They're here..." Her whisper trailed off as she took in the scene.

A cop car was outside and it had just turned on its spotlight no more than fifteen feet up from us where it shined its light under the car in the driveway of the neighbor. *We're caught!* My Grandfather would say, we were in left field without a glove. Our situation was even more dire than I could have thought possible, for my boner was more erect than ever before, clearly yelling in its proprietary silent language to run like the dickens! How my brain was able to process the situation, mitigate the massive pain impulses exploding from my eye socket, and come up with a quick tactic to possibly prolong our freedom, was astonishing, considering the majority of my brain's blood and oxygen was being bogarted by my boner.

I frantically whispered, "I'm going on top."
"What?"

"Switch." And with that, we flipped. I had my hands over her shoulders, palms out, her legs were out slightly to allow mine to be in the middle. Her arms at her sides. "I'm in black. Less chance of them seeing us."

"Brilliant," she whispered with a huge smile. I could see that smile now, because I was two inches from her face and the cop's spotlight was now upon us. Her stare went from happy to horrified when the light illuminated my face. *Was I that ugly, or did she finally notice I was that young??? Had she finally noticed the stiff arm emanating from my pants?*

"Your eye!" And with that, another droplet of blood splashed on her cheek. Surely before the lights illuminated the carnage, she assumed the drops were sweat, but now the truth was literally in her face and she was traumatized. Not only was I the worst kisser she'd ever kissed, but I was such a bad experience, that she most likely would never kiss another guy again. Making out with a Cyclops in the dirt while hiding from the law isn't something a woman brags about to her family at a holiday family function. No, it was safe to say that the only person Gwen would ever share this moment with would be her shrink.

Surprisingly, she took both hands and gently cupped my head. Taking her hand, she gingerly prodded the region near my eyelid. I couldn't tell exactly where at the time, for the area was in such pain and trauma that I barely felt her hand, if not for the light, I wouldn't even know the touch was true. As the powerful searchlight illuminated us both like an A bomb's radiation, a pool of serenity gently whisked away my fears. We remained motionless, locked as one. I was so enthralled with Gwen that I didn't want the cop car to leave, for I knew once it did, so would its searchlight and the most beautiful vision I'd ever beheld, would fade to black and forever be no more than a fleeting memory. The cop car began to creep along slowly at first and then the lights went on and the engine roared as the copper slammed the pedal to the metal. Clearly there were other sightings of refugees.

"You may need to go to the hospital."

"I can't."

"Yes, you can."

"You know I can't."

Resigned to the truth, "Well, we need to get you patched up at least, or you'll become infected and a real Cyclops by morning."

I was a monster now, and she was just being kind to the wild creature that had saved her life. "I'm going to be in so much trouble." My other eye had begun to water and I felt my nose begin to stuff. A look of sadness swept Gwen's face, and she wiped my cheeks like my father did not too long ago.

Before I could snort and wipe my nose, mucous dripped to her lip. "Sorry!" I flipped myself off of her and began to feverishly wipe my face, doing my best to avoid the wound. "I'm fine. Just a little blood and snot." I looked to her to show my shame and was met with a smile that vanquished all my pain and misery. I couldn't help but smile back, despite the horrific circumstances that brought us to this moment. "I'm not sure how we'll move now. I'm limited in my abilities and you don't know the terrain. Add the patrols, which minuses the roads, and what we're looking at is a mad dash."

"How far?"

"We're going to have to sprint to the end of La Rue. Last house on the left."

"The one with the giant fence?"

"Yes."

"You're rich?"

"No…" *I wasn't. My friend was. He had lots of money and two good eyes. She was going to end our relationship, faster than I ended Derek.*

"Your house is really nice."

"I don't live there. My friend does."

"Well, he's got a real nice house and I bet his parents got all the medical supplies we'll need to take care of that nasty scratch."

"You call this a scratch!? I expounded with visceral incredulity.

"You scratched your cornea."

"How would you know?"

"How??? … Oh yeah, I've been staring into your eyes for half the night."

"Someone's coming," I whispered.

"Where?" She whispered back as she scanned the foliage.

I hadn't heard anyone, but I couldn't tell her that Swissy had clearly sensed something, for he jerked up right at the end of Gwen's conjecture to alert us to the unforeseen danger.

"I have a sixth sense…" I reluctantly responded, not wanting to showcase my not so hidden talent.

Without a hint of sarcasm Gwen proclaimed, "That's awesome."

"I can also kind of communicate with animals via telepathy…"

"Really?"

"I don't like to talk about it…" I bashfully replied.

"Oh... well, do you think you could ask a raccoon in the nearby vicinity if the coast is clear?"

I half smiled, "It doesn't work that way."

"You okay to run?" Gwen asked as she jockeyed for a better vantage point within the thick canopy.

"I run from a lot of things. How about you? You're the one that had to beat that bastard off of you."

Though I couldn't see her features, her silhouette stiffened as her warm gaze glazed over. "I'm fine." The uncomfortable silence was broken by distant sirens, and I didn't want to waste more time debating the inevitable.

"The fire department will be here shortly, along with more cops. Let's rock." Grabbing a branch above my head without looking away from the road's edge, I pulled myself to a squatted stance, extended my hand and assisted Gwen to her feet. "As soon as we get outside, run down the street. If we see headlights, we dive for the nearest bush. If we're pursued, we make a dash for Whitman Court."

"No."

"Why?" I asked helplessly.

"I live there."

Taking a moment to crunch the key points of data, my brain fired a revised plan B, "OK, then south to Lover's Lane."

"You're a helpless romantic aren't you?"

"No," I balked breathlessly.

If light were love, Gwen's smile would be my soul's distress signal...

Chapter 13
The Final Leg

We walked slowly and silently out of the bush and crouched near the white picket fence.

"Once we get to the high bush line, run to it, but don't try to run through it. It's a meat grinder in there and by the time you exit the other side, your face will make mine look good."

"I think you're good looking." And with that she kissed me on the cheek before I could pull away. "I would have kissed you on your pouty lips, but they're currently covered in blood and snot," she added.

I wiped them feverishly, but knew any future attempt to kiss me would be thwarted by Swissy, which was diligently protecting my personal space once again. Though the awkwardness of it sticking out like a turd in a punch bowl had caused me to miss out on many a brilliant line over the course of the evening, Swissy had, for the most part, performed quite admirably throughout the night in a myriad of capacities. It alerted me to danger, buffeted me from the impact of nasty falls, and shielded me from unwarranted advances from my captive. A real honest-to-goodness appendage that performed multiple tasks, once again validated its well-deserved nickname.

But for all the multitasking my Swissy had taken the initiative on throughout the evening, the advances from Gwen, though unwarranted, were certainly not unwanted. Matter of fact, I was perplexed at my penis' overprotective posturing with regard to her mere presence. *What was it so worried about? I was actually finding myself quite smitten with Gwen. Could I one day love a woman my penis despised, or vice versa? That seemed silly...*

A simple question from Gwen snapped me back to reality, "On three?"

I nodded my head and began the countdown, "One, two, three!"

And with that we ran. I ran faster than I ever had before. All bragging aside, I was quite the runner—fastest kid in the grade on a good day. Of course, that was surely missed on my damsel in distress who was pulling away from me like a rocket stage in deep space. The gap was increasing by the stride and soon more than my ego would be in jeopardy, for if we were too far away to communicate, I may not be able to warn her of a car coming from our backside. Just as alarming, if the distance between us increased and we had to duck for cover, we'd surely be separated, possibly for good. I lit the afterburners with hopes of closing the gap. Gwen turned halfway to check on me, or to look off into a yard for something, and slowed her pace by a tick. I caught up considerably and we matched stride for stride.

She was a gazelle! In the open lamp light of the telephone poles I could see her elongated gallop was only made possible by her impossibly perfect soccer legs. *Or is it Track & Field...* She was an athlete my father would be proud to call his daughter. Her legs were shaped by finely-tuned muscle, covered in silky sun-soaked skin. The same width as mine, but nearly twice as long, made her stride graceful and her height, which was only three inches taller than me, seem majestic. *She was taller than me... We could never get married. I would look like a fool, especially on our wedding day if she decided to wear heels. Focus!* I staggered to avoid tripping over my own feet mid-stride.

Our pace quickened as we hit the last bend in the road that contained a gradual turn and decline over an eighty-foot spance, which acted as the demilitarized zone between Upper and Lower La Rue. It also meant we were rapidly approaching the main entrance to Wilder's Woods on our right, which I did not take into account when I hatched the getaway plan. As we descended upon the checkpoint, it dawned on me that there was most likely a cop car parked in waiting, with its headlights ready to beam on anything that crossed its path. Two kids running at this time of night were definitely chase-worthy, especially since the freak chasing the girl, who looked to have just been mud wrestling, was donning a ninja costume.

"Left! Duck!" My exasperated plea barely made it to my ears, between pants. I swung my arm and missed. I swung again and hit her left arm as it was coming back for another pump. She turned with a startled look in mid-stride as I applied the air brakes and ran for a huge patch of pachysandra off to our left where I dove head first, making sure to protect my face with both arms. Landing in the fetal position, I stayed motionless until Gwen slammed in behind me. *Were we spotted?*

I caught enough breath to speak coherently, "Switch."

"What?" She panted back.

"Switch the spoon."

Her light-colored shirt was to the back of the road and if we didn't want to be seen by yet another passing patrol car, I needed to once again make my dull black stealth suit our last line of defense. She rolled over me without another word and resumed the spoon position. We were rolled tight now as I covered her with my left arm as much as possible, while my right arm acted as her impromptu pillow. She breathed hard, and now that I held her in my arms, I could feel her entire body move with each deep inhale and exhale. I flexed and constricted my body around her like a tourniquet, denying even the night's air of her form. I was the beach and her breathing was the waves. *The pounding surf forever changes the sand, for the sand lives and dies for the land...*

Gwen asked between visceral breaths, "You see something?"

I exhaled a quick, "No."

"Then why did we stop? You hurt?"

"No."

"Well?"

"Ten feet down, to the right. That's the entrance to Wilder's Woods."

"So?"

"So, there's most likely a cop car in that entrance waiting for the criminal to return to the scene of the crime."

"Oh, that's right; you're a fugitive. I keep forgetting."

"I'm a hero."

"They'll make songs about your heroism in cell block C, where you'll be for the next ten years."

I paused. I hadn't started putting real world numbers next to my dastardly deeds as of yet. And now that she mentioned a block of time, I couldn't help but feel she was being optimistic.

My lack of response triggered her reply, "I'm just kidding, Silly."

"Oh."

"Quick, cover me good," she frantically whispered.

As I covered her like a blanket, our bodies and souls coalesced. I knew there had to be more to her command for concealment, for the pachysandra patch was also home to several low growing ornamental evergreen bushes, making it next to impossible for anyone to have seen us, unless they had also witnessed our arrival. Of course, no one had...

"You hear something?" I asked after what seemed an eternity.

"No."

"Then why did you have me wrap you tighter?"

"I was cold."

"What?"

"Aren't you my hero? Would you have me freeze to death after all of this?"

I couldn't help but smile and since my lips were already nestled against the nape of her neck, I found myself gently kiss it.

"Who can't help themselves now?"

I froze in mid-puck.

"I guess you owe me for kissing you without permission."

"I was simply checking your body temperature."

"With your lips?"

"I forget to stock my utility belt with a thermometer."

Gwen shook as she tried desperately to keep her hearty laugh inside. *I was witty! I said something cool! She laughed. I had kissed a girl and she let me and then laughed at my joke! Of course she laughed at my witty jokes and yearned for my touch, I saved her life by kicking the crap out of her assailant. Holy shit. She's my girl!*

"You mentioned you were freezing. Just trying to make sure you get home safely." With that, she stopped laughing and moving.

"What?" *Did she see someone?*

"We've got to go." She started to push up.

I held her down, "Hold a sec. Let me check to see if the coast is clear." I slowly pulled my arm and leg off of her. Last, I regrettably removed my face from her neck and craned my head back towards the entrance to The Woods. *Nothing...* I rolled two revolutions away from Gwen towards the road and stopped for a better look up and down La Rue. We were on the corner, just above the entrance. Though my vantage point was pretty good, the fact that a street lamp was more or less above me exposed me, while hiding everything beyond thirty-feet in shadows. There could still be a cop car less than fifty-feet away in the entrance, and he would be able to see us get up and run. *What to do...* The siren coming up the road, forced my hand.

I rolled back to the spoon position against Gwen's back, "Fire department."

"Which way?"

I craned my neck once again towards the road to adjust my plane of reference, "West Neck Road." And with that, the cop's lights turned on. I froze. Using zero air or mouth movement, I whispered like the dead, "Cop."

Gwen said nothing to her credit. Nor did she move a muscle for that matter. I didn't even move my head back to hide my eyes. The lights were pointed less than five feet in front of us. The cop car pulled out towards lower La Rue and stopped in the middle of the street. He was now twenty feet past us. His strobe lights went on, clearly using them to alert the oncoming firetruck of his location.

Then, without warning, the cop car lunged backwards forty feet in a blink of an eye, stopping parallel with us in the patch.

If he looked to his left right now for anything, we were close enough to be seen by the red and blue strobe lights. All sense of time suspended as we awaited our fate. I knew once that firetruck came, he would either lead it to the blaze or set up his position again and allow them to go about their business. If he followed them, we were in the clear, for the home stretch was four lawns away. If he decided to resume his sentry position, we were in a world of hurt. Either way, I felt as if the firemen were coming to rescue me. By the time the fire department lights got close, the sirens went dead and were replaced by the rumble of the big diesel and airbrakes. If anyone even glanced in our direction we were goners, for the lights were so bright from the newly arrived firetruck that the cop lights seemed to dim from a bad battery. *How did La Rue inexplicably turn in to the Aurora Borealis?* Loud inaudible voices carried between the firetrucks. More loud chatter emanated from the cop's CB, referencing a code 415. Some more talk from the firetruck continued until a firefighter got out and walked to the door of the cop car. They could have been talking sports for all I knew.

Whispering frustrations I couldn't help but voice, "Come on! You have multiple fires in the woods. Bodies strewn all over the place and enough alcohol and drugs to throw a sweet sixteen!"

"Easy... They're taking their time, which means it's no big deal in there."

"How would you know?"

"My oldest brother just past his police test and he's going to be a Suffolk County cop."

"Congrats," I replied with zero emotion. And not because I intended a sarcastic deadpan delivery to showcase my indifference to her family's success, but rather, I was simply immediately preoccupied with trying to figure out her age by using her older brother as a first clue. *Could she learn to drive before she dumped me? She had to be a teenager if her brother was old enough to be a Suffolk County cop. Hopefully she was Irish, for only Irish families had more than five kids, which gave us an outside chance that she was ten years his younger. Of course, the Irish also had kids born in the same year referred to as Irish twins, which could blow up my math quicker than Kring blew up the woods. How many brothers did she have? Would they all beat the crap out of me at once while my hands were tied behind my back with Gwen's bra? Maybe she had a younger—*

"They're moving!" Gwen whispered excitedly.

The cop engine was first, followed quickly by the loud, powerful diesel of the firetruck. I didn't dare turn my head to follow them down the path, for I heard the gravel, which signaled the use of the Wilder's Woods Road and the last thing I wanted was a bored firefighter standing on the rear bumper, spotting me in the lamp light. *10-9-8-7-6-5-4-3-2-1...*

"Coast is clear," I said matter of factly.

"What now?" Gwen's voice was low, but she also had ditched the whisper, most likely on my cue.

"We're going to get up and go full steam ahead."

"Are you sure?"

"Yes. Why?"

"Last time I went full steam ahead Captain, I left you in the dust." Without even seeing her face, for we were still in the spoon position, I knew the smile was ear to ear, and I couldn't help but be infected.

I gave her a quick tickle just to see if she was human and she responded by jerking her leg like a dog.

"Stop!"

"Shhhhhhhh..."

"Stop tickling me and I will!"

"OK!" I whispered.

"I'm really ticklish."

"Thanks for the head's up."

"Are you ready, or do you need a head start?"

Wow, she was good. She definitely had multiple older brothers, which meant Derek would need to get in line for his much warranted payback. I decided on a little guilt trip to lock her back up.

"Actually, I thought you should go first, in case a cop comes."

"How would that help?"

"You know where we're going. I could act as the decoy and have them follow me deep in The Woods, or towards Lover's Lane—afford you the time you need to get your bra and get home."

"Shut up."

"Wasn't the answer I was looking—"

"But shut up nonetheless."

"Roger that."

"You ready?"

"Yes."

With that, I regrettably pulled my body from hers, got up and as she turned over, I extended my hand to offer assistance. She took it, while simultaneously placing her feet at the tips of mine for leverage, springing up an inch from my face. She quickly glanced at my eye, before gently cupping my ears, and kissing me softly on the ravaged area. Her sultry stare switched to steel as she took my hand and walked me around the bush that we had laid against, all the while scanning the road, the path into Wilder's and most likely any windows lit or dark. I followed in a trance only to be woken by a distant dog bark.

Snapping from my sappiness, I squeezed Gwen's hand, "Ready?"

"Ready," she exhaled.

"Go."

And with that Gwen bolted, but this time, she did not let go of my hand. We ran as fast as we could holding hands, right down the center of the road, using the yellow line as our guide. *Beyond exhilarating!* It felt like a victory lap at full speed. With each stride, the pain from my injuries diminished, until they all but vanished as we approached the tree line. At ten feet away we slowed to a brisk walk and despite being emotionally and physically drained, I felt oddly revitalized, and in somewhat better shape than just an hour earlier. At three feet from the bush line, I pulled my flashlight from the holster and turned it on, momentarily taking leave of Gwen's warm embrace.

When I touched the first branch of the bush, I turned to Gwen, "Follow me."

I held every branch I could, while Gwen held her hands out in front to block any errant swingbacks of escaping foliage. The last leg of our journey was quick and painless. Within seconds we were standing in the sanctity of Kring's barricaded backyard. No one could possibly see us now, not even by chopper... *Unless of course they were using infrared... We'd better get inside sooner than later and pretend we were asleep.*

"We're here."

"Doesn't look like anyone's home..." Gwen half-questioned.

"If Kring is up there, he'd want it to look that way for sure."

"How do we get in?"

"There's a hidden trap door in the center of the floor, which we'll access after we climb the base for ten feet."

A cavalier nod signaled Gwen's acquiescing to our ascension, and without further ado, we began to quickly scale the trunk and found ourselves nestled in the bosom of the tree's base, directly underneath the treehouse's floor. I gave the secret knock, which comprised of three knocks, followed by a pause, then two knocks and then a final pause, finalized by a single knock. Nothing. My breath stopped, eyes widened, and something clamped down hard on my heart. I unconsciously grabbed at my shirt as if it had begun to attack me by tightening around my throat, in hopes of trying to strangle me. I slipped and began to fall, while Gwen did her best to stop me and we both fell back against a big branch, but luckily not to the ground.

"What's wrong?"

"Kr..." Was all I could say. I was panicked; I was frozen. *My best friend is dead. I left him behind. He went there for me and I left him. I killed my best friend... I hadn't even thought of him since we'd left. So caught up in my own survival and my pathetic dream of falling in love with an older woman that I completely forgot about my brother-in-arms. I thought I was in trouble for everything I did in Wilder's tonight? How about what I didn't do? Help my buddy... How would I explain to his parents, my parents, his brother, the police, my complete and utter negligence and abandonment of my best bud? I was a piece of crap, no better than Derek. I deserved to walk the remainder of my life alone and God-willing, my limp would return and my eye would not, giving people an easy target to make fun of, as they rightfully should...*

With that, the trap door swung open and Kring's head extended out like a turtle's, with red lamplight in the background making him seem more golem than human.

"What took you so long?"

"You're such a dick!"

"What?"

"I thought you were dead!"

"You were wrong once a—" Kring's smirk and bravado left him faster than my horrible scenarios of his demise, when he finally noticed the human underneath me. I saw Kring staring at what was exposed of Gwen and to Gwen's credit, there wasn't much, considering she basically put herself between me and the ground, not even knowing whether a branch would assist in breaking our fall. The tree's middle earthen shape had saved our lives!

"She's cool," I announced.

"She's a girl."

Quite a statement... After we all let the bombshell of Gwen's sex drop and settle, Gwen perked up somewhat. "Can you please get off of me? I can hardly breathe."

Holy crap, I'm killing her! She could have a branch lodged in her ribcage for all I know. I shot my hand towards Kring. "Grab my hand!"

Chapter 14
Rendezvous

To Kring's credit, he took hold of my hand, and took care of everything else he had to do in order to get me off of Gwen and the two of us into the fort with minimal drama. Once inside the fort, the red light illuminated everything well enough to take stock of what rations we had left. Though the soda and snacks were a welcome site, the extra firepower was something I wanted to disappear ASAP.

"Is that my bra?"

Oh, thank God... And with that I turned and saw Gwen staring at the wall with her brow furrowed and head tilted. I followed her amazed gaze to the wall, where her bra was suspended by two Chinese throwing stars and illuminated by not one, not two, but three candles. Kring's shrine just made an uncomfortable situation unbearable. Of course, no shrine would be complete without the creep factor, and to that, Kring had found an old poster of the movie *Jaws*. The giant great white shark preparing to lunge out of the water at an unsuspecting bodacious bodied swimmer, looked to actually be going for the bra, since Kring had draped the bra over the swimmer... *Oh my God!*

"Peaches?" Kring thumbed in the direction of the bra.

"Peaches?" Gwen and I asked in stunned unison.

"Wait, you named my bra?"

Kring's smile vaporized as the brevity of the situation finally hit home. "More of a secret code word..."

"Peaches?" Gwen asked again to apparently assist her in processing the last answer.

"Yeah…" Kring looked off to the wall, as if a cheat sheet for bullshit was hanging above the fourth candle.

"Why peaches?"

"You know…"

"No. No I don't. Please explain."

"Because, you know…"

"No idea," Gwen reiterated.

"The bra's cups… They could theoretically hold peaches and…"

"Theoretically," Gwen responded, with her head bobbing slightly as if she was actually weighing the scientific merits of Kring's babblings.

Looking to Kring and back to me several times before incredulously asking, "Are you saying my breasts are the size of peaches?"

"No," I quickly blurted.

At the same time, Kring clarified my horror with "Theoretically."

"No," I added again to quash his ridiculous theories.

"Are you saying then they're tasty like peaches?"

"No!" I said with conviction.

As Kring surely only accidently blurted, "Yes." And then quickly added, "No idea…"

"Do you guys like the taste of peaches?"

"No," I said, *but did.*

Kring was more honest, possibly out of pure ignorance of the reference, "Yes."

"No," I corrected him.

Believing he was catching on to my less than subtle hints, Kring offered a shaky, "Depends on the season..."

Kring's last comment on the seasonality of ripe peaches was not lost on any of us. Gwen squinted at him with a quizzical smirk, while the circumference of my wide-eyed glare was only surpassed by my mouth's gaping hole.

"He didn't mean it that way," was all I could finally mutter.

"What way?"

Retake the conversation dammit!

"What your bra holds other than your..." pointing at her breasts as if they would say their names to assist me in my diatribe.

"My peaches?"

"Whatever you call them, that's your business. Our business is getting you home safely with your bra."

Gwen lifted the bra to inspect it and then sniffed it curiously, while maintaining her gaze upon us. "Did you wash my bra?"

"Yes," Kring stated matter of factly.

"You what?" I blurted.

"Yeah so? Isn't that what you're supposed to do with dirty clothes?"

"But why..." I couldn't comprehend him at times, nor the speed and diligence that he worked. *His father would be so proud if he could see him now.*

"No, it's fine. Thank you," Gwen said with complete sincerity.

"See? Who's the fool now?" Kring said with a smirk.

"Relax," I rolled my eyes and hoped for an end to the most uncomfortable conversation I'd ever been a part of.

Gwen paused from smelling her bra and squinted her eyes as she took in Kring for the first time. Tilting her head, "You look familiar."

"Never saw you before."

"Are you sure?"

"Complete blank."

"Did I babysit you?"

"Impossible."

"Wait—are your parents' friends with the McMasters on Cranberry Drive?"

"Maybe."

"That's how I know you! Your family was at their Fourth of July party!" Excitedly patting her shirt at the shoulder, "I was the babysitter!"

"I wasn't being babysat, so I wouldn't remember your temporary employment."

Gwen, sensing his embarrassment, helped him through the memory to a better ending.

"Of course I wasn't babysitting you, but I did play a game with you."

The blaring fact that she was Simon in *Simon Says* and that Kring was a willing participant, didn't help too much, but it did give him a desperate out to be more conversational and less standoffish.

"Oh yeah, I remember now. My brother was afraid to play, because he suffers from socialization anxiety syndrome, so I played to assist him with assimilation."

"You're a good man," I quickly interjected.

"It was the mature thing to do," Kring remarked as he stuck his chest out slightly.

"How old are you guys?"

"I'm 9 and he's 10," Kring graciously answered as he pointed back to me with his thumb.

"Teen," I tried desperately to add without any success.

Gwen stared off into the distance with a beet red face, while her memory movie vividly played back all the kissing scenes in IMAX format of herself and a child she could have babysat. Her voice heightened and sounded noticeably alarmed, "Ten? Really? Wow! You're tall for ten."

"I'll be eleven soon."

"Yeah, like in twelve months," Kring chimed.

"Shut up fool." My snap was harder and louder than warranted, making me appear even less mature than my stunted age would garner.

"How old are you?" Kring asked.

Staring at me for the first time in what seemed forever, "Thirteen."

"Are you in high school?" Kring asked.

"Eighth."

"Those kids you were with. Were they in the Junior High, or High School?" Kring's calmness was surprising and snapped Gwen out of her daze.

Looking at Kring, "Some go to Finley, some to the high school."

"What about the guy we took out?"

"Derek's in twelfth, but how..."

"He's talking about someone else," I interjected.

"What?" Gwen and Kring asked simultaneously.

Ringing my hands out like wet rags and the truth of my actions, "We ran into resistance before we made it to you."

"Resistance?"

"It was unfortunate..." I added with as much empathy as I could muster.

"Unfortunate? Who are you guys?"

"We're friends of the forest." Kring's answer was so far creepier than even he intended it to be that he momentarily paused and inwardly reflected. Gwen seemed momentarily horrified, but to her credit, rebounded quickly with some much needed levity.

"Like Smokey the Bear?"

"Yeah... But unlike Smokey, we have no qualms starting a fire, to save the forest," Kring replied with mischief in his long stare to nowhere.

Knowing I needed to get a handle on our situation, I decided to get down to brass tacks immediately before Kring willingly recited our Shark Club Oath. "What happened to you after you launched the missile barrage?"

"I executed the plan to perfection."

"Walk me through it."

"What's to walk?"

"Humor me."

Looking to Gwen and then me, Kring half closed his eyes and breathed long and loud via his nostrils.

"Fine. I gave you your ten minutes and then I launched the full complement of ordinance. Gave our boy Henry a little reminder on who's who."

"Henry?" Gwen and I asked simultaneously.

Looking to Gwen, Kring asked, "You know him?"

"Yes. Do you?"

"We're intimately familiar with each other now."

"My God, Kring. What did you do?" I gasped.

Gwen seemed rattled, "Wait, when did you meet Henry? Was he the other guy you 'took out'?" air quoting for maximum sarcasm.

"Kring!" I pleaded.

"Relax, I just shored up our relationship."

"What's he talking about?" Gwen demanded of me.

"Henry pissed on him."

"What?"

Seething, Kring spat the words as if they tasted like the very piss that pissed him off in the first place, "I should have chopped his dick off."

"What did you do?" I asked.

"I got him to tell me his full name and address." With a quick smirk for his memory, "Sniveling bitch is a Bay Boy. Rode his bike all the way here."

"Henry's a good guy," Gwen said softly to no one.

"Outside of pissing on people?" Kring retaliated with righteous rage.

"It doesn't sound like Henry."

Kring was amped. His voice was beginning to raise, as Gwen began to question the play-by-play. "You want to know what Henry sounded like when I was working him over?"

"Enough! Gwen, I was there. Right there... Regardless if he did it on purpose, Henry pissed on him. All over him..."

With red, wet eyes, Kring looked off into the distance, hurt and ashamed.

"I'm sorry..." Gwen sounded and looked truly sorry. "It's Derek. He has that effect on everyone."

"Yeah... that Derek is an evil guy from what I've heard," Kring said absently.

"Yeah... well, we had a run in with him," I said.

"Yeah... how'd that go?" Kring scanned my facial features, with his chin and brow raised high.

I closed my eyes and exhaled, "The target was neutralized."

"Sounds like a successful mission. Other than the fact you brought back one of their gang members to our secret hideout and gave her our real names! Are you literally retarded?"

"She was in danger."

"Of what?"

"Derek," Gwen shot in.

Kring looked to her and then steadied his gaze upon me, "True?"

"True," I replied.

His voice lowered and his tone diminished, "What happened?"

"It all happened so quickly. I was on the ground a couple of feet from the base camp... Derek was... Derek's an evil bastard and Gwen needed me. I did what needed doing and then you lit the jungle and we needed to get out of the heat."

"That's it?"

"Change of plans."

"Change of plans?"

"Change of plans."

Kring looked at Gwen and then me again. "Fine. What now?"

"We get Gwen home. Get back here and go to bed before the choppers bask this bitch in infrared."

"I saw cop cars and a firetruck."

"We almost got caught twice."

"How did you get here?"

"We ran down the road..."

"You what?"

"We ran," Gwen interjected.

"What if you two were followed?"

"Do you see anyone?" Gwen retorted annoyed.

"No Gwen, I don't. But if you were followed by someone who didn't want you to see him, why would I?"

"Oh shit..." In my hysteria, I focused all my energies on not being caught by the cops, neighbors, or a passing motorist, completely forgetting about Derek's crew.

Kring was right! If one of Derek's cronies were hiding in the bushes from the law like we were, they could have easily seen us run by, and even tracked us to the high bush line. Even if they didn't see us make a beeline for Kring's, they'd have a general vicinity nonetheless.

"Oh shit? That's all you got? We could have five guys pouring gas around the trunk of this tree right now and we wouldn't know until her precious bra is burnt to a crisp!"

"It's my fault," Gwen interjected.

"That means nothing to me."

With a defiant finger raised, "You took my bra."

Kring rolled his eyes, but said nothing, for he hadn't a response worth voicing.

I tried to terminate the tension with talk, "They'll know who we are soon enough."

"How?" Kring shot me a glance.

"How not? Who else would do this? Kids from another town? They'd eventually come by here. Question us, question others. Someone would talk."

"They had no idea what we looked like, or how old we were. You can't think they're looking for two kids?"

"Bishop would rat us out."

"Who?" Gwen asked.

"Bishop Culver. He lives on the border-"

Gwen interrupted me, "I know Bishop. He was a no show tonight. Derek hurt his brother and they had a falling out."

"When?" Kring asked quickly.

"Last weekend."

"What happened?" Kring prodded.

"Derek was making fun of his weight and then gave him a wedgy. Bishop and Derek almost fought. Their relationship has been steadily deteriorating ever since."

"How do you know so much?" Kring inquired skeptically.

Gwen noticed and acknowledged his tone with a stiff back and chin when she responded. "I've been busy being a foolish little girl."

"You hang with some really bad people. Why should we give you the benefit of the doubt?"

"I can vouch for her," I proudly proclaimed.

"I wouldn't give me the time of day," Gwen dejectedly denounced herself, as she stared at her feet instead of me.

"Don't say that!"

But before I could tell her why, she told me why not. "I'm damaged goods. Kring's right."

"Kring?" I looked to him with all of Gwen's hurt and my love.

"Hey, don't look at me. I'm just trying to figure out what's what."

"The kid's got good instincts. You should be wary. Trouble follows me like a loyal dog." Gwen's self-pity was on full display, but Kring wasn't window shopping.

"If that's the case, you two are perfect for each other."

Gwen looked at me with eyes wide and cheeks blood red.

Kring looked at Gwen, then me, then Gwen again, finally settling his furrowed brow upon me. "So... Where's the next stop on the crazy train?"

"Whitman Court."

"Whitman Court?"

"Whitman Court," Gwen added for clarification.

"You live on the next block?"

"Yup."

"Do you know his sister?" pointing to me with his head.

"Who's your sister?"

I knew she'd know the name and was actually surprised that she hadn't been to my house before. "Libra?"

"Libra Sidoruk?"

"Yup..."

"No way!"

"Yup."

Realizing an uncomfortable situation just became unbearable, "Oh... we're friends with the same people and we've even played against each other in soccer."

"You go to school with her? Kring asked.

"No. I go to private school. St. Pats?"

"I went there for a year back in the day," Kring cordially commented.

"Oh... cool," Gwen was lost again in her new fear—fear of being discovered as a cradle robber.

We were a motley crew, with Kring being an arsonist, me a violent criminal and Gwen a pedophile. *Who were we scared of? You'd think it would be the opposite. If you listed our crimes without showing our faces, I bet the average person would assume we all had unkempt beards and scars. I would have an eye patch soon enough...*

"I'm surprised we've never bumped into you playing in Wilder's," Kring said.

"I haven't played in some time..." Gwen trailed off, knowing it could be perceived as an elitist remark.

"We ride our bikes there," I said to shatter the deafening silence.

"And keep the peace," Kring added.

"I see..."

Desperately trying to change the subject to something that didn't make me want to jump out the window, "Roy was hurt by Derek last week, but didn't let on to us when we met yesterday."

"Clearly, he was ashamed," Kring surmised.

"That's sad," Gwen added.

"Maybe Bishop will cover for us?" I reasoned aloud.

"Maybe not," Kring said.

"Why wouldn't he help you?" Gwen asked.

"Because he's a fat bastard and helping himself is all he cares to address, whether that's in The Woods or at the buffet line," Kring aggregately answered.

"You don't think he would be grateful for your deeds?" Gwen asked surprised.

"Bishop cares about ruling those Woods and getting all the food, beer, cigarettes and porn he can get his fat fingers on. If that means protecting us, he will. If that means ratting us, he will," Kring hotly hammered home.

"What about Roy?" I asked.

"What about him? He's weak, afraid and dumber than your dog. Besides, you gonna bet the farm on a pig?"

"He's got a point," Gwen acknowledged.

Kring seemed surprised she would take his side and looked to clarify her stance, "So, you agree we're screwed?"

"I don't know what you are, but I know I owe you guys my life... So to me, you're both heroes," Gwen sincerely said.

Kring looked astonished at her revelation and nodded his head absently in agreement with her assessment, while adding, "We are that..."

"We're going to get Gwen home and figure this out in the morning. I don't think we were followed. No one ran to the front. Those kids booked for home, which clearly isn't this way."

"That's for sure," Gwen added.

"By the way, remind me to do something about your face before we get some shut eye, or you may wake with only one."

"Is it that bad?!?!" I absently touched the area.

"You look like you stopped a bullet with your eyeball."

Reaching out for my face, Gwen exclaimed, "He does not!"

Kring looked at her hand warmly caressing my cheek and then did a double take of both us, before resting his knowing gaze on Gwen, "Don't worry, we'll take good care of him."

Gwen quickly lowered her hand and resumed her analysis of the floor boards.

Kring's eyebrow raised to me, "Ah... we should get moving then."

"Wait. I need to change."

"What?" Kring and I asked Gwen in unison.

"My bra. I need to change it."

"Why?" I asked.

"The one I'm currently wearing is an old one. It's not even mine. One of my girlfriends left it over my house well over a year ago. It was stuffed in the back of my drawer."

"So?" I questioned.

"If my parents are up when I get home, I better be wearing my bra and not holding it."

"Good point," Kring added before I could question further.

"Where do you want to change?" I asked looking to Kring.

"If you guys could be so kind and turn your backs, I'll do it right now."

"No problem," Kring spun on his heels like a palace guard during the raising of the flag ceremony.

I shook my head and turned. Some jostling signaled Gwen taking off her shirt and a hint of a popping noise alerted me to the unfastening of a tightly bound hook.

"Oh, that feels so good."

I struggled not to turn around to ask of what.

"That bra was soooo tight! I think it was Cindy's training bra. She'd laugh her ass off if she knew I was wearing it!"

I had no idea what to say, but Kring was chock full of suggestions and questions.

"So, you going to toss that bra?"

"Pardon?"

"The training bra. You need to throw it out?"

"I guess."

"I'd better dispose of that, if you're not going to take it with you. Evidence leads to questions."

"Oh right. Good point," Gwen added without a hint of sarcasm.

"Trel, could you help me?"

"With?"

"My bra."

"I'm turned the other way..."

"I'm decent enough for you to turn around."
Kring began to spin like a dreidel.

"Just Trel!"

"Fine," Kring lamented.

Gwen asking me to assist her in putting on her bra while Kring had to stare at the *Jaws* poster, was the equivalent of Kring and I standing at attention within the International Space Station, awaiting word from the President on who would be able to go on the mission's first and only spacewalk, only to have the President inform Kring that not only couldn't he go outside, but he wasn't even allowed to watch me suit up, let alone peek out a porthole to see me moonwalk to Thriller.

Though I felt the pain of my comrade in arms, it was a distant pain, like a thorn in an off- used finger. Besides, I had real concerns, such as my real world physical pain that could hamper my ability to successfully complete the coveted mission directive. The throbbing pain emanating from my chest, shortness of breath, coupled with muscle after muscle, locking up limb by limb made me wonder if one could contract frostbite in the dead of summer. It wasn't until I looked down at my hands that were slow to respond to the order of wiping the sweat from my brow, did I notice the root of the issue... Swissy. Literally loyal to a fault, Swissy had drained my body of already preciously low blood reserves, by hastily erecting itself into a battering ram, in a last ditch effort to protect me from the unknown of Gwen.

My only hope would be that I wouldn't drop dead two-feet from my dream after the harrowing journey I was subjected to today. The irony wasn't lost on me; as I slowly pivoted with a sheepish grin and hands in pockets, like a professor looking back upon his class to see if his point had been made after purposely droning on for two hours, just a day before spring break. "How may I be of assistance?"

Shirtless, Gwen stood stoically with her hands behind her back. The red lamp light accentuating her every curve and toned muscle. Her high, chiseled cheek bones, surely pronounced from the shadows they cast under the strange glow of painted cellophane wrapping made her otherworldly.

Her smile broad and inviting, "I can't get these straps to buckle. Can you get them on?" And with that she winked at me and turned around.

The muscle atrophy caused me to drag my feet as I walked and with my hands now raised straight at the shoulders, I resembled the undead, instead of someone more alive than ever in their life. She half turned her head, allowing her hair to fall over her shoulder.

"I'm not sure how many of these you've taken off, but putting one on should be a snap—just the two clips."

My hands were trembling and were clammier than a thief's exchanging a bag of sand for an ancient artifact. I approached Gwen and clumsily grabbed at both straps. Gwen sensed my hands and grabbed them, pulling me close, while allowing her straps to fall to the side. Taking my hands under hers, she wrapped them around her mid-waist and I stumbled into her back. She was sweaty, sticky and smelled of fresh earth. My lips went to her upper back and she tasted like a kielbasa. I knew at that moment I'd marry a farmer's daughter.

I inhaled deeply, as if she smelled of sunshine and my mom's spaghetti sauce. My eyes closed to savor the flavor, for I knew there wouldn't be seconds. Gwen slowly began to raise my hands and I neither helped, nor hindered her movement of me, any more or less than a stuffed animal would. Her stomach was all muscle, but her breasts were so... *Her breasts!!! I was touching breasts!!!* I froze like a cube. *It must be colder in here then I thought, for her nipples are as hard as diamonds. The poor girl allows me to touch the untouchable while she's freezing to death and all I do to repay her is ram her in the ass with a spear!* Luckily for us both, her long legs made her ass several inches above Swissy's vector, and thus it docked between her thighs with no one being the wiser. Gwen slowly let my hands down to her hips, where I rested them as she pulled up her bra straps and gently brushed my knuckles with them.

"Just grab the ends and you'll see the two small latches."

I did what she said without a word or breath.

"Now just clip, and we're good."

I did what she said without a word or breath.

"Thank you for being such a gentleman. Now if you'll turn around, I can put on my shirt." And before I could figure out what to do about the fact that my boner had locked us together like Legos, Gwen spun, kissed me and donned her shirt in one fluid motion. I stood hands to the side, boner to the front. She glanced down at it and then to me, a broad smile lighting her gorgeous face.

"You guys can turn around now."

I of course was already at attention, but Kring was to my side as Gwen tossed the training bra our way. Kring leapt in front of me, snatching the bra out of mid-air, like a desperate, drunken bachelor snatches the garter belt from the bride, during the too painful to watch "who gets married next" competition.

Gwen, saving me from the embarrassment of my newly formed appendage, allowed me to take a quick seat as Kring marched his prize back to the altar and affixed it to the wall as he spoke of our next steps.

"Gwen, I'm going to give you my Darth Vader cape."

"Oh, don't be silly, I wasn't going to keep the bra. You enjoy..."

"Thank you, I will... But we're in a tree, not under one, so this isn't a present exchange. The cape is black. It will help hide you on our impromptu jaunt to your yard. I'd say we could cover you in black makeup and clothing, but that would be problematic once you've arrived at your destination."

"Oh...," looking to me, Gwen actually seemed quite impressed.

Shrugging my shoulders, "He's good."

"The only other thing I'd add is this duct tape around the pink reflectors on the side of your sneakers. A headlight hits that and we're toast."

Looking down, Gwen seemed shocked that she hadn't noticed her glaring security breach.

"Can't see all the sites when you're speeding?" I offered.

Kring tossed her the tape and she caught it, quickly going about her business without hesitating.

"Don't overtape, for you'll have to rip that off quickly once you arrive."

"Got it," Gwen acknowledged, as she noticeably changed her pattern on the fly.

The rest of the setup was standard fare for a trip that would be quick and easy. Cross the street, up the Brady's backyard, hop a fence that Gwen said was already bent at the knee and we'd be home free. She lived technically two yards away from me. I was stunned I had never met her, and as we walked across the street and down the Brady's driveway, the realization that I would most likely never see Gwen again, hit home hard.

The feelings were so overwhelming that they replaced another powerful emotion—fear, which was spawned by the very real and grave possibility of bumping into the Hammond's dog, who was most likely still out and about and pissed as hell. Therefore, our pace was quick but controlled, as we walked the Brady's driveway, dismissing the odds of Mr. Brady taking a second bag of trash out for the night as improbable at best. The Brady's backyard was concealed on all sides by a high thick wall of forsythia, which afforded us excellent concealment on the final leg of our journey.

As we approached the far hedge line, Gwen slowed her pace, "I'm right on the other side."

My cheeks were flushed and I felt a sick heat emanating from my ears and nose.

"You want us to escort you to the fence?" I pensively posed.

"No. Better I go the last leg alone in case my father is up, or worse, one of my older brothers is walking in."

"Oh..."

"Yeah, the last thing you need to do is answer questions about us."

"About us..."

Gwen turned, gave me a huge hug and kissed me on the cheek and turned to Kring. "Thank you for everything. Saving my bra and my life." And with that she gave him a quick peck on the cheek.

"It's what we do," Kring responded with a cavalier air that was at odds with his youthful age and stature.

Turning back to me as she backed up with her outstretched hand still touching mine, "See you around."

As she walked through the bushes with the grace of a wood nymph, I knew I was in love. She had disappeared for some time before Kring spoke.

"Did you see that?" Kring asked excitedly.

"What?" I ask absently.

"What? She almost chomped my dick off!"

"What?"

"She lunged at me like I was the last grain of rice from a UN food drop."

"Watch your mouth..."

"Watch mine? Were you just listening? She—"

"You're treading shallow waters my friend."

"You're pathetic."

"Excuse me?"

"You fell in love in what, twenty minutes? Thirty at most."

"Seemed like a lifetime..."

"I hate to break it to you, but the only time difference that matters, is the time between your births."

"I know... I know..." And with that admission, my shoulders slumped, knowing my love had left forever, along with my second wind of the night. I needed a bed, before I crashed on the Brady's lawn.

"If you're done painting the picture, it's time we get home."

"What?" *How long had I been standing there?*

"We need to roll Bro. Tomorrow is gonna make today look like yesterday."

"Right." And with that, I walked back to reality.

Chapter 15
The Morning After

The next morning, I awoke on a massive couch in Kring's room that was brought up from the downstairs when his parents remodeled the den. Laying spread eagle on the ultra-comfy, cream-white Italian leather couch, I took stock of the immense size and scope of Kring's room, as well as my mental, emotional, and physical condition. I hadn't dreamt the entire night, which was odd, since I dreamt so much that the doctors had told my parents that one day I would most likely need to go on medication in order to sleep. I knew my eye was better, but not anywhere near fully healed, for it hurt to open, but was eventually soothed somewhat by continuous blinking. I was cautiously optimistic it looked as good as it felt, for I didn't feel like answering a million questions once I got home. The eye was, of course, the only thing that felt better from the night before.

Luckily, the stuff I knew wasn't going to look good, because of how bad it felt, could easily be covered up until it healed. The worst of it was the right side of my rib cage, which throbbed as soon as I used my elbow to prop myself up. Once I adjusted myself, the ribs began to feel oddly tight and my breath labored. My left wrist felt weak and numb, as if I'd slept on it, but lacked the tingling sensation signaling the new, unrestricted blood flow. Flexing my hand by opening and closing it, I looked over to Kring sleeping like a baby. I of course knew him too well to believe that, so I asked him a rhetorical question.

"You up?"

"Hours."

"Hours?"

"Since dawn."

"Couldn't sleep?"

"I could."

"Why'd you wake?"

"Check for evidence around the fort and in this room in case the cops come."

"You really think they'll find us this quick?"

"No idea. What I do know, is that they won't find anything to incriminate us on my property."

"What did you do with the clothes?"

"They're hidden with everything else, deep within the basement."

"Why won't they find it there?"

"Not a chance. It's behind the wall safe my dad has hidden behind the oil burner. He doesn't even know I know, that it's there. And what's more? I set up a false wall behind his stuff to hide my stuff."

"His stuff hides your stuff..."

Arms now crossed, cradling his massive pride, "Not only does his stuff hide my stuff, it protects it."

"How so?" I asked the rhetorical question as cannon fodder for his ego's onslaught.

"He not only stacks a huge amount of money in there, but also his hand gun, which I may add is technically illegal and my mom's pot to boot, which is more than technically illegal. Once the cops see that. Boom! It's all about them and let's face it, what would you really hide behind that? A nuclear weapon?"

"Brilliant," I had to admit.

"Yes..."

"You cleared the shrine you set up to Gwen's breasts?"

"Of course."

"You got the extra ammo-"

Cutting me off mid-sentence, "You wanna do a quality control walkthrough? Get off your lazy ass and do one."

"Settle down, Sally. I'm still waking up."

"You slept like a baby. I'm surprised."

"Why?"

"Why? I thought between falling in love and committing a violent crime you would have a lot to contemplate."

"I didn't fall in love."

"No? OK."

"Why would you even say that? I mean—"

Kring cut me off like a teacher scolding a brat, "Shhhhhh!! You hear that?"

"Hear..."

"That!"

"Yeah. That's an engine."

"Cops."

"What?"

Kring threw his covers to the side and crab-walked over to the window, craning his neck over the sill and then quickly dropping to the prone position.

"Cop car in the driveway."

"Shit!"

Kring's hands were now covering his head as he rocked back and forth on the ground, occasionally pressing his lips against the carpet, while deeply exhaling through his nose. "We're screwed! I'm so dead. My dad is going to kill me."

I did my best to comfort him to no avail, "Hey, it's our word against theirs."

"What are you babbling about? We taped one and beat the other."

"It was self-defense. Remember?"

"What about shooting off ten pounds of TNT and almost burning down The Woods?"

"Preventative medicine?"

"This is no time for jokes," Kring snapped.

"I know, I'm sorry," I conceded contritely.

"What are we going to do?"

"Keep your voice down, first off. Second, if it goes down, I'll take responsibility for everything," I declared.

"You?"

"Yes."

"I'm gonna claim ignorance to the fact that you used my house as a base of operations for multiple missions?"

"Well... yeah, you're screwed too, but I can take the majority of the blame and make you look like a little scared kid, who went along with my crazy idea, because you wanted to be accepted in—"

"Shut up," Kring snapped.

"Right," I replied.

"What now?" Kring asked.

"Do you think you can look outside and see what the cop is doing?" I wondered aloud.

"Christian!" An old broken voice screeched from the bones of the home.

"Oh crap!" Kring yelped.

"Christiannn!" The old wheeze of a woman nearing the end of a very long life cycle was unmistakable. Miss Mary's voice sounded like the Grim Reaper kept her alive just to torment other old people.

"Christiannn! Come downstairs please, and bring your friend."

"OK. What do we say?" I asked.

"We shouldn't admit to anything until we speak to my dad's attorney."

"What right is that? The fifth?" I asked.

"What?" Kring asked as if he was annoyed that he couldn't hear me over the cat calls from the coffin.

"The Constitution. I know one of the rights allows you freedom of speech and I think five allows you to keep quiet."

"Whatever you do, don't exercise three." And with that, Kring got up and walked to the door, cracking it an inch.

"Be down in a minute Miss Mary!"

"What's three?" I asked longingly.

Turning he closed the door and rested his back against it. "Three is your right to be a retard. Look, we went over this last night."

"Yeah, but that was our story," I countered.

"Yeah, and it's still our story," Kring contended.

"That we hung out here all night and played in your room?"

"Exactly."

"You're nuts!"

"Christiaannnn!" The voice grew louder and began to crack.

"Just a second! He answered with bane in his breath, then turned to me and said matter of factly, "Act surprised when you see the cop."

"OK." And with that I got up to face the music.

We stumbled and bumbled down the stairs to portray two kids that were woken well before cartoons signaled the arrival of a Sunday morning. In the foyer, near the stairs were two cops. I slipped taking them in and almost knocked Kring down with me. The cops scanned us with their unreadable facial features.

"Boys, this is Officer McNally and Officer Kelly. They would like to ask you some questions."

We both nodded.

"Good morning," Officer McNally said.

We both nodded.

"You say 'good morning' back," Miss Mary reprimanded us.

"Good morning," Kring and I responded.

Officer McNally looked over to his partner and then back to us. "You boys hear, or see anything last night that seemed out of the ordinary?"

"No—" I began to say when Kring spoke up.

"I saw lights last night. Something woke me and I saw lights, but I don't know what time it was."

"What kind of lights?"

"I thought it was a fire truck."

"Anything else?"

Before Kring answered, he looked to the railing, then shook his head, "I went back to bed officer."

Officer Kelly who'd been staring at me, while Office McNally stared at Kring asked me, "What happened to your eye?"

I touched my cheek as if forgetting it was there, "I caught it on a branch outside."

"Outside where?"

"In the backyard. Is it bad?"

Looking to his partner, "You'll live."

Officer McNally, shook his head and looked out a window, "Thank you boys for your help. If you hear of anything, we would appreciate your help."

"What happened?" Kring asked.

Office McNally looked to Officer Kelly and then Miss Mary. "Some really bad kids, did some really bad things in the woods last night and we need to find out who they are before they do something that bad again."

Miss Mary piped in, "They exploded fireworks and almost burned down an entire forest. One of the kids almost died!"

We both looked shocked at the last statement and the effect wasn't lost on the cops.

Kelly added, "We found two boys. One's still in the hospital, while the other..." Looking back at his partner, "the other may need more long term assistance."

McNally added, "Do either of you boys know Derek Fisher or Henry Carpenter?"

We both shook our heads with a residing, no.

McNally added, "Good, because they're high school kids and one of them is a real bad seed, so you shouldn't know them."

Kelly added, "And that's why the Carpenter kid found himself in a mess no doubt. Wrong time, wrong place, wrong people. Now things may never be right for him."

"Yes Sir," I offered as acknowledgement to his painfully obvious statement.

Boring down on me, McNally pointed, his finger less than a hand from my chest, "You ever go into the woods?"

"Yes Sir."

"Why?"

"We've always ridden our bikes there."

"That's private property. You know trespassing is against the law?"

"No Sir."

"No Sir what?"

I didn't understand the question, nor his annoyance at my simple and innocent answer.

Sensing my cluelessness, "Do you know it's private property?"

"Yes Sir."

"So you know you're breaking the law?"

"No Sir."

"How's that?"

"We thought Mrs. Wilder didn't mind us there. She used to drive by us riding and would wave. Honest!" I began to get nervous. *Did they know what I did in The Woods last night and couldn't prove it and were now going to get me on a technicality, like convicting Al Capone of tax evasion?*

Kelly applied a warm hand to McNally's shoulder, "I'm sure you did kid. Been a long night for everyone."

Shaking his head, McNally added, "Yeah, well, if the old lady sees no issue in your riding there, just do it before sunset and if you see anything, you tell your parents right away."

"Yes Sir!" We bellowed like hardened marines on morning parade lines.

"They're good boys," Miss Mary proudly stated as she put her bony arms over our shoulders.

Looking at my eye one more time, Office Kelly reminded me to keep it wet and clean and with that they bid Miss Mary a good day and walked back to their squad car.

"You boys want breakfast?"

"Yes," we eagerly replied.

"We'll be upstairs," Kring added. We hustled up the stairs to his room and Kring slammed the door behind us.

"You think they're on to us?" I asked nervously.

"No."

"Just like that?"

"Like what?"

"You seem so sure we're getting off scot free," I challenged.

"I never said we're in the clear. But I'm pretty sure we're not going to jail before breakfast."

"You see how he grilled me?" I rallied.

"You crumbled," Kring corrected, as he strolled to his bed, jumped on and fit like a ball in a mitt.

"I was awesome!" I declared.

"You were less than spectacular, to be kind."

"I was good enough, I guess..." I muttered as I peeked out the linen-draped window.

"What now?" Kring vexed.

"I gather we sit and wait... And hope we're not in juvy by the morrow," I said absently.

"Juvy?" Kring questioned nervously.

"Jail for kids," I remarked, still peering through the window.

"I can't do jail!" Kring cried.

"I'm not sure it matters what you're up for."

"You better get your 'A' game on! You're talking like a loser!" Kring barked.

"Why do we even need a game plan?"

"Pardon? Your eye infection spread to your brain?"

"Seriously, what's there to do?"

"What's there to do? How about locking down this neighborhood before the enemy storms the gates?" Kring admonished.

"I thought you were talking about the law..." I replied.

"The law? They're our last concern now. It's apparent the kid we gave the tape job to isn't talking, because he's planning on acting as our judge, jury and executioner."

"You think he knows who we are?" I asked.

"No idea. We went over this. Unless he's a total idiot, he'll start riding around and asking questions, or if he's halfway intelligent, he'll start with Bishop and Roy. He probably thinks they're responsible for it in the first place and will most likely corner pork chop somewhere in The Woods, where he'll spill his guts faster than he filled them."

"We were just talking to Roy about taking back The Woods..."

"That's right!" Kring exclaimed. "And if Bishop wants to get back in the groups' good graces, he'll happily sell us out."

"Wow... we're sitting ducks," I acknowledged.

"Damn right we are! We need to figure this out ASAP. What're we gonna do? Wait here for certain death, or deal some death ourselves?"

"We deal in death now?" I questioned. "You're a dealer?" I asked as I finally turned to make eye contact, only to find Kring still sprawled on his bed with his hands cradling the back of his head, as if he were chilling surfside.

"No, I'm a broker," Kring corrected.

"A broker?" I asked.

"I'm a broker like my father and his father before him," Kring explained.

"A broker?"

"Yes. A broker."

"Not a dealer?"

"Exactly."

"What's the difference?" I had to ask.

"A dealer sells you what you want, a broker sells you what he's got."

"Oh...well... I hope you got some backup in your bag, Broker, because I'm not sure what the heck you and me are going to do. We're just two little kids. Our enemy is bigger, badder and outnumbers us three to one."

Kring sprang from his bed and punched his fist to his palm, "We need to galvanize this street and have the others stand with us!"

"Galvanize who? Jim? Kurt? Bishop? The Floyd Brothers? We started this club to spy on them, because they were plotting against us."

Kring began to pace, "My enemy's enemy is my ally."

I rolled my eyes and exhaled, "You're Jimming right now."

Stopping his pacing, Kring regarded me with utter disdain, "This has nothing to do with Jim's fetish for using obscure references to belittle your already battered self-worth."

"What's a fetish?"

"It's one of the oldest military doctrines of all time."

"Had no idea. I thought it had to do with a wardrobe."

"What? Not a fetish, you imbecile! I was referring to the proverb, *my enemy's enemy, is my ally.*"

"Fair enough, Rommel."

"Rommel?" Kring asked.

I broke eye contact with Kring and once again peered out the window, "He was supposedly some military genius Jim was babbling about."

"How about you quit your babbling and impress me with a plan."

I ducked my head slightly to avoid being seen by a bird, "Well, who do we have to work with?"

"Jim, Kurt, Franky, Freddy, Bishop, Roy... The kids from Upper La Rue?"

Looking back to Kring, "Upper's out. I don't know half of them well enough to trust them and the other half are on vacation."

"What about Brady and Sean?" Kring asked.

Shaking my head, "Brady's away at some creative camp, remember?"

"Right..."

I thought a little harder, "Sean may be able to help us."

Kring stepped closer to me, "You think we can trust him? He may feel like he's got to tell an adult." I checked the window latch before acknowledging his point. "Kurt's out I guess," Kring mused.

"Yeah... I think he's got a crush on Derek."

"Speaking of crushing Derek, what do you think he looks like now?"

I looked from the window ledge to my hands, pausing to reflect on my dastardly deed, "Like the crap I'm going to take after I eat the nasty porridge old Miss Mary is gonna make us eat."

Kring smiled, "You know, my parents think she's a great cook. My mom actually has her cook for the week sometimes."

"I'm sorry..."

"Well?" Kring begged.

Turning to Kring, "Well, we have you, me, Roy, Franky, Freddy, Jim, and Bishop," I surmised.

We went over who and what we had at our disposal from the various ages of our group, to who could fight and who'd flee. In the end, Franky was our rook, knight, horse, and castle, for he was a human muscle who placed in States for wrestling, three grades above his own. After it was acknowledged that he would be left with a five on one scenario every time we played out the battle, the consensus was that we were most definitely screwed.

"We're screwed," Kring stated matter of factly.

I pressed my arms to either side of the window sill and let out a sigh, "I can't do this anymore."

"You're tapping out now?"

I looked up, feeling the blood drain to the back of my throat, "Not for good. I just need to take a break and clear my head."

"How long do you need to compose yourself?" Kring quipped.

"This is useless! Can't you see? You and me planning for a war without an army is as silly as The Alien Club having a secretary without a phone."

Feeling my fatigue, Kring dialed it down, "Fair enough, but you're not bailing until you help me eat that spooge that's currently peeling the paint off the kitchen walls."

"How do you fuck oats up?"

Chapter 16
Everything Comes Full Circle

We ate in silence as Miss Mary preached proper fireworks safety and social grace. Her impromptu seminar on illegal fireworks turned into a short history lesson on her family's exploits into an illegal moonshine operation and her temporary marriage to her second cousin in order to get the title to her uncle's '48 Ford, so she could drive from her personal hell in the Mississippi bayou.

After eating, I took my hobo bag, hugged Kring and walked out the door. The sun was bright, but I could feel the storm clouds a brewing. Deep in thought, I walked mindlessly across the Kreagan's front yard. Normally I wouldn't walk on their beautifully maintained front lawn, due to the respect for Mr. Kreagan's professionally landscaped efforts, but today I was lost in thought and a social faux pas here and there was more than acceptable for a ten year old facing twenty to life.

"Hey! What are you doing?" I snapped from my daze and looked for the angered voice—*Jim...*

"Get off the lawn before you make it look like yours."

I raised my hand as if a stranger had asked me to stop blocking the sun at the beach, "Sorry." And with that I began to angle myself towards the street with a quickened step.

"Hold up, Trespasser!" Jim bellowed from his front stoop as he stormed in my direction.

I was so close to home! Twenty yards at best, and I was on my side of the disputed property line.

"You're trespassing!"

"Sorry. I'm getting off now."

"Too late!"

I turned, half-expecting a karate chop, but Jim simply walked in front of me and extended his arm, pressing his outstretched palm in to my chest. I stopped and exhaled, not even looking up to see his disdain for my vagrancy.

Three and half years my senior, Jim wasn't much taller and suffered from the same lackluster physique as I, though his form had dark skin and fabulously thick black hair, which served him well in masking his massive head. As his older brother Sean looked 100% like his Irish father, Jim was a spitting image of his 100% Italian mother, with the addition of handsome hazel eyes that if he'd learn to use them correctly, could get him into more trouble with the ladies than his million mile per hour mouth could get him out of.

His fly-off-the-handle hot headedness and loose lips came from her as well, and had landed us in more verbal sparring matches than I cared to remember. Though Jim lacked the speed and dexterity of a true fighter, he'd developed a thick skin both physically and emotionally from the almost bi-monthly beat downs from Sean that rivaled those in professional wrestling. Though barely a better student than a fighter, Jim had a photographic memory, and applied his spare time to higher learning. An oddly uncomfortable and out of place scholar, Jim was well-versed in history, economics and politics and would quote famous people and historically obscure events to win arguments in games such as Flashlight Tag and Kill the Man with the Ball.

I knew today would be no different, so I decided to acquiesce to his authority in hopes of culling the confrontation. "I said I was sorry."

"So?"

"So, can you please let me go?"

"I don't have to. It's my yard."

"I know. I apologize for intruding. I'll be leaving now." I began to walk around his outstretched hand, but Jim sidestepped my efforts and reapplied the pressure of his palm.

"What's up?"

"What's up? How about your tenure as a free man."

I felt my heart skip a beat and my legs grow weak. Fortunately for me, I had still not looked up, so Jim could not read my terror like headline news.

"Oh... you have nothing to say to that?" Jim pried.

"To what?"

"To the fact that your little secret isn't a secret after all."

What did he know and how? "What secret?"

"Come on! Don't try to play me!"

"I'm really tired Jim."

"I can see that. You look like something the cat dragged in."

"That's being kind. I looked in a mirror this morning and almost ran."

Jim seemed to pause at the self-deprecation. "Yeah... well, I know why you look like you do," Jim conceded.

"Yeah... how's that?"

"Because after the cops and firemen drove by, I waited outside on my front steps to see more of them, but the real show started when the lights went out."

He'd seen. What exactly he saw, I wasn't sure, but he definitely saw something and I needed to know what.

"And what did you see?"

"Don't play stupid with me. I saw you!"

"Fine."

"Fine? That's it?"

"That's it."

"You know if I tell on you, you're going to be in huge trouble."

"Yeah... but I can't stop you from telling on me, so I'm screwed. Besides, I'm in bigger trouble than you can imagine right now, so getting a grownup involved might not be a bad idea."

"You think that now, but wait until you're grounded."

I couldn't help but laugh like a madman left to the Gospel on a street corner in Manhattan. "Grounded? I'm ground chop meat! Toast! Grounded? I won't be around long enough to give my parents the pleasure of a prolonged punishment."

"You gonna run away?"

Jim's last statement hit home harder than I could have anticipated, because until he said it, I didn't really envision myself going through with the unspeakable. Running away and winding up like all those kids on the back of the milk cartons. Would I be just a picture on my parents' piano that they would hold when times were tough and ask it why I didn't feel all the love they thought they were giving?

"Maybe... I really haven't given my escape plan much thought, though I've briefly entertained running away as a viable option."

Looking somewhat confused, "Do you know what I know?"

"No."

"I saw you run down the street with a girl, hop into Chris'

bushes, and then twenty- minutes later, reemerge with her and I'm gathering Chris, but you had draped a cape on the girl."

"Sounds about right."

"You better tell me why."

"Why?"

"Because I'll tell on you if you don't."

"But won't you just tell on me regardless? Isn't that your thing? You hold information over people's heads and use it against them to either punish them, or empower yourself, or both?"

"I do nothing of the sort."

"What are you doing right now?"

"This is different."

"Why?"

"Because whatever you're involved in has the cops involved and I'm scared for my family. I'm acting in the best interest of the neighborhood."

"So your actions right now are not just valid, they're righteous."

"I'm this neighborhood's Templar Knight."

"Is that more powerful than a Palatine?"

"It's from *The Bible*, not Dungeon and Dragons—you twit!"

"Easy. Watch your Templar, I think it's rising."

"You think this is a joke? Let's go and tell your mom together. Think she'll giggle?"

"Please leave me alone."

"What are you going to do if I tell her right now?"

He had me beat soundly and we both knew it. Why couldn't he just finish me, like the wolves finished the deer in the Mutual of Omaha nature documentaries that aired every Sunday morning.

They at least respected the process and made sure that none of the deer was wasted. But that wasn't Jim's style. Jim lusted for one's agony.

He wanted to see me emotionally bleed out on his lawn, so I gave him the show he'd paid to see. "I'm a dead man walking! Happy?!?! If you're seen standing next to me when the wrong guy rides by, you're dead too, so I'd do yourself a favor and walk back in your house and close your door!" I felt the heat in my cheeks rise a degree for each word my tightened throat managed to squeeze out, as Jim analyzed me, clearly enjoying the suffering firsthand.

With little conviction Jim uttered, "Well I'm sure you're getting whatever you deserve."

"Yeah? Do you know what I did to deserve this? Do you know what's going to happen to me? Because I don't!" As I pleaded answers, Jim became blurry. The warm embrace of a tear on my cheek signaled that I was about to cry.

"You going to cry, baby?"

I answered with a sob and dropped my head again, weeping uncontrollably. After what seemed like an eternity, Jim removed his palm from my chest.

"Hey..." Jim's arm moved to my arm. "Hey, I didn't say I was going to definitely tell your mom. I was just saying what if..."

I couldn't stop crying and the fact that Jim thought that my mom knowing was actually something that was making me cry, made me realize just how much trouble I truly was in, and that in turn, made me cry even harder.

Jim put his other hand on my other shoulder, "Hey. It's going to be OK. I wasn't going to tell anyone. I was just screwing with you. I'd be in trouble if my parents found out that I was up and out that late at night anyway."

I continued to weep and found myself in Jim's embrace.

From a front window, Mrs. Kreagan's loud Italian voice shook me to the core, "What's going on out there?"

"Nothing Mom!"

"Is that Trel?"

"Yes! It's fine."

"What's wrong?!"

"Nothing!"

"Is he hurt?!"

"He hurt his eye; he'll be fine."

Jim pushed me back and lifted my head with one of his hands, "Just go with it. OK?"

I shook my head.

"I'll get him some ice! Let's go." We started walking to the backyard along our property line. "You can't go home like this; you look like shit."

Between sobs, "I feel even worse."

"If we bump into one of your parents, let me do the talking."

"Kay."

"You and I were playing in your tree in the front yard and you poked your eye on a branch."

"Kay."

"We're going to into the clubhouse. We'll be safe in seconds."

"Kay."

Jim led me like an old lady across a busy road. "Who's got you so spooked?"

"You don't want to know."

We made it to the door to Jim's garage that led to his garage's attic loft.

Putting his arm over my shoulder, he ushered me inside while he scanned the yards for eyes, "We made it. Let's get you situated."

We climbed the stairs and entered the main room where an old couch and some antique chairs littered the floor. Mrs. Kreagan was an interior decorator so she used the loft as a misfit Toyland for furniture and fixtures.

"Sit there. I got a can of soda somewhere... Oh here!"

He cracked it and handed it to me, "That's got caffeine in it, so watch your consumption."

"Kay." As I sipped, I stopped crying, which later in life I learned was an old technique people who fired people learned. Give a crying employee a glass of water to stop them from crying and give them their severance check to get them walking.

"Talk to me. I can help."

"You can't."

"I can try."

"I don't want to get you involved. They'll kill you too."

"Kill me? Someone's trying to kill you?"

"Yes."

"Who?"

"They're from the other side..."

"The other side of what?"

"The other side of The Woods."

Jim was silent for a moment. "Who?"

"Don't know all their names. Derek is one."

"Derek... How do you know Derek?"

Jim knew Derek?

"Why is Derek going to kill you?"

"Because I almost killed him."

"How?"

"Mashed his face like potatoes."

"Impossible!"

"Why's that impossible?"

"What? When? Where?"

"In The Woods last night. You gonna rat me out?"

Jim was silent again, obviously weighing his options. "No... I won't say a word."

"Why should I believe you?"

"Because I hate Derek."

"Wait. You know him?"

"Yeah..."

"How?"

"He... he hurt me."

"When?"

"It's not relevant."

"It is to me!"

"Why?"

"Why? I'm spilling the beans here!"

"So?"

"So? So how about some of that French stuff you're always quoting?

"Carpe Diem?"

"The squid sang."

"Quid pro quo?"

"Yeah! Some of that."

A tight smile and Jim seemed to eat something. Then he shook his head as to give his mouth permission to speak, "It's Latin, not French, but point taken."

"Well? Some squid please."

Looking off to the cobwebbed window, "I tried to join his club. The club in The Woods..."

"He rejected your application? That's it?!?!"

Jim stopped me with a raised hand and closed eyes, "He made me haze for membership and then purposely made me fail, for he was never going to allow me to join."

"What's haze mean?"

"He made me do things in front of a bunch of older kids— other members. If I did what they asked, I could become a member."

"That's stupid."

Instantly angered, "The coolest fraternities in the best colleges make you haze!"

"What did they make you do?"

Shaking his head, as if still in disbelief, "He made me expose myself to all the guys and then play with it a little..."

"What!?!? You beat off in front of other guys?"

"I didn't beat off! I just had to touch it... Or so I thought..." Jim's voice sounded hurt.

"Did they all watch?"

"Yes... Then Derek told me to turn around and when I did... When I did... he jabbed me with his cigarette."

"Oh Jim..." was all I could respond with.

"I jumped back and fell, because my shorts were around my ankles." Tears streamed down his face, eyes bulging as they struggled to keep the flood waters from breaking line. "That's when they all began to laugh at me and I realized it was all a joke."

"Oh my God..."

"They started throwing stuff at me. Cigarette butts, beer cans..." Jim's voice trembled as he looked at the wall, as if a big screen TV hung there, playing the scene in hi-def. "They made me run from the camp with my shorts down, and when I fell again, one of the boys kicked me. When I tried to get up, he kicked me again, causing me to fall yet again. He followed me for what seemed to be an eternity, as the rest laughed, egging him on to kick me even harder." Snot poured from Jim's nose, "I left my bike behind. They stole it... Or sold it... Or whatever... I told my dad I lost it at Robin's Stationery." He began to sob uncontrollably. "He was so mad." Jim covered his face with both hands, "He beat me and my mom did nothing!"

I found myself holding Jim as he went limp in my arms. Convulsing now, Jim couldn't gain enough control to finish a sentence, "I'm... so... so... ashamed!" The words cut his cries.

"Do you know his name?"

Jim cried hard, "Who?"

"The one that kicked you when you were down."

"Does it matter?!?"

"Yes."

"Why?"

"We need to make him a priority."

"A what?"

"A high value target."

"We can't do anything! You said it yourself! They're going to kill you."

"I know. But I'm gonna take some of them down with me."

Jim's shakes seemed to lessen and he released himself from my hug. He stumbled awkwardly to the sofa and collapsed. "You're not going to die. We're in this together."

"We got Kring too."

"Kring's a kid."

"He's more of an asset than you can imagine."

"What do you mean?"

"He rained the pain last night..."

"Yeah, how hard?"

"Like a monsoon..."

"What's his take?"

"He doesn't know what to do either."

"Who's the girl, or can't you trust me?"

"Gwen."

"Gwen? Gwen Chandler?"

"I couldn't say."

"Her last name is top secret? Come on!"

"I don't know her last name."

"Well, I know there's an older girl who lives on Whitman Court, and her name is Gwen Chandler."

"That's her then."

"What she's doing with you?"

"I have no idea."

"Does she know what you did to Derek?"

"Yes."

"What if she tells on you?"

"She won't."

"How could you possibly know what she will and won't do? She's a girl."

"She's my girl."

"Yours? Please..."

"I guess that's stupid..."

"Dumbest thing you've said in quite some time."

"And I've said some really stupid things as of late."

A hint of a smile, "You have..."

I surmised, "Well, let's just say that she owes me."

"And you think she'll make good?" Jim wondered aloud.

"I'm betting my life on it," I said matter of factly.

"Can she help us?" Jim asked.

"Gwen?" I responded.

"Yes."

"How?" I asked.

"I don't know," Jim sounded annoyed, deep in thought again.

"I think we're on our own on this one. I spoke to Kring at length on this very subject all morning until I couldn't take it anymore and decided to go home and take a breather. Now I'm here." And with that I walked over to the big old recliner next to the couch Jim was sprawled on and sank deep.

Noticing I had finally sat, Jim said, "That's a great chair. I'll let you have it."

"Thanks," I replied, "But I don't have anywhere to put it. My room is the size of a walk-in closet."

"That's being kind."

"Thanks."

"I meant you can have it here when you come back to the club."

"Come back to the Alien Club?" I asked skeptically.

"Hell yes, come back! You can have your pick of the litter," Jim boasted with outstretched hands, as he lovingly admired the eclectic collection of forgotten furniture.

"Tempting, but I'll pass," I regretfully replied.

"Why? You're too good for my club now? You're a big wig at the Shark Club?"

"How...?"

"What? How do I know you have a secret club, whose main directive is to spy on my club?"

"Well, yes," I replied, much to my chagrin.

"You'd like to know, wouldn't you? It's eating you alive right now I bet," Jim spat.

Did I even tell Kring the name? "Actually, it's not. I'm more curious than anything. How would you say it... more of an academic exercise," I decided.

"So you're not dying to know?" Jim's right brow raised in question.

"I'm dying to know how I'm going to get out of this mess I got myself in. Who knew what about what silly club I could care less about, isn't at the forefront of my worry list," I said more abrasively than I intended.

"Fine, I won't tell you then," Jim added defiantly.

"Could it help us forge a plan of action against the Dragon if I knew how you knew?" I asked.

"Maybe. Maybe not," Jim's hands weighing the possibilities in the air like a scale.

"Look. I don't care about the Alien Club anymore—whether I came up with the idea, or you. Whether I'm an officer of it, or just a foot soldier. To be frank, I don't much care about the Shark Club either, for they were in essence the same club in the end, just two guys talking shit," I clarified for Jim.

"The Alien Club was more than the Shark Club could ever hope to be," Jim added with disdain in his voice.

"Actually, I wanted the Shark Club to be everything this club wasn't, and I wanted it to be nothing like the Alien Club," I proudly proclaimed.

"That makes no sense," Jim said.

"You wouldn't understand..." I responded.

"I would, if it made sense."

"What's the Alien Club in the end? You and me. What's the Shark Club in the end? Kring and me. Change out this beat up old attic for his beat up old treehouse and it's the same thing, minus the paperwork, drama, and deceit."

"What deceit? There wasn't any drama either!" Jim snapped.

"We started a club. Whose idea it was is irrelevant. We started it. Then we spent countless hours drafting a code of conduct, rules, a hierarchy, and then went and recruited people to fill those positions," I listed.

"You need the proper foundation in any governmental body—" I cut Jim off with a hand in the air.

"Great point. But here's the problem with that: we were just two kids wanting to have fun. We created bullshit and everyone who came here knew it. We had no one. No one really was a real member. They just came here to hangout when they were bored and eat the free food you and I stole from our houses," I said.

"That's what you think."

"They used us Jim! Don't you get it? They were never loyal members of the club. We were a bar, giving away free drinks and as soon as we began to charge, the loyal patrons moved to the next free spot," I exclaimed.

"The Woods aren't free. I can serve notice to that!" Jim retorted.

"Free they're not, but apparently The Woods are fun and our club wasn't," I answered.

"So, now what?" Jim asked exhausted from his recent cry and the weight of reality.

"Well, do you know where the others stand? Kring and I had no idea. Gwen said Bishop had a falling out with Derek, because of Roy, but now that Derek is out of the picture, we weren't sure if Bishop would try to reassert himself in the club."

"I think if I talk to Bishop, he's on our side," Jim said.

"You're going to talk with Bishop? I thought you guys were on the outs big time?" I asked.

"Yeah... but I was the one guy who stood up for his brother when Derek gave Roy the wedgy and Bishop knows that. Once I tell him what happened to me..." Jim's voice trailed off as he looked off into the distance.

"You're OK with telling someone about this?" I asked.

"No. But it appears I have no choice. He's got to know what those bastards did to me, before he exposes Roy to it a second time."

"You're right. What about the Floyd's?" I asked.

"They'll do what they're told," Jim responded absently.

"They've been playing both sides of the fence," I opined.

"Yes, but I'll talk to Bishop about that and set them straight," Jim replied.

"What about your brother?"

"What about him?"

"We could really use the firepower."

Rejecting my idea as folly, "Not a chance."

"What if you told him—"

But Jim cut me off, "He can never know what happened to me!"

"Relax Bro... I'm sorry," I softly said.

"He can't know..." A single tear jogged his right cheek.

"OK. May I ask why?"

"Because he'll just make fun of me and use it against me later. Hang it over my head!" Jim seemed to be watching the future unfold before his eyes as his rant grew in intensity.

"Hang what over your head?" An exasperated voice barked from the bottom of the stairs. And with that, heavy feet pounded the old wooden planks that comprised the barn style staircase.

"Oh shit," Jim's hands already covering his eyes.

Sean's head popped out of the opening in the floor to where the stairs ascended. "Who's going to hold what over who?" Looking to me then Jim, then to me, and back to Jim, he asked casually, "You crying pussy boy?"

"No," Jim weakly replied.

"No? Because you look like you've been bawling. And don't try shielding your eye; I know when you've cried. You've done it enough," Sean said as he dramatically rolled his eyes and shook his head.

"Leave us alone!" Jim demanded.

"Or what? You going to cry some more?" Sean mockingly questioned.

"Sean, please..." I didn't know what to say.

Sean looked at me again, but this time as if it were the first time he noticed me.

"What happened to you? Your eye's in pretty bad condition and you look like you've been crying as well... Wait, did you two have a lover's quarrel?" Smiling and holding his hands to his heart.

"Fuck you!" Jim raged.

"Testy aren't we? So, let me guess... you're out of KY Jelly and no one wants to catch?" Sean was smiling bright in the window's broken light.

"We've had a rough week," I replied.

"Rough?" Raising an eyebrow, Sean seemed a little more serious.

"Yeah..." I looked at Jim, but said no more.

Sean sensed something and changed his tune, "Listen, Mom was worried about Trel and told me to find out what happened. I was about to go over your house when I heard Jim screaming."

"I wasn't screaming!" Jim screamed.

Sean raised his outstretched open palms, "Relax Bro."

"I can't relax. I'm mad," Jim responded.

"I can see that," looking to me. "Is he mad, because of your eye?"

I didn't really know how to answer Sean, but knew that Jim and Sean needed to talk and not with me. "I think Jim can answer that better than me." And with that, I got up and walked to the windowsill and stared out the window.

"What's up Bro?" Sean asked Jim.

"None of your business," Jim responded.

"You're my brother; you're my business," Sean stated.

"You'll just make fun of me and use it against me later," Jim replied.

"I'm hurt you would say that!" Sean replied.

"Hurt? You hurt me all the time. You mentally and physically hurt me daily and you're surprised I would think you would do that again?" Jim's face was fire-engine red, veins popping from his neck.

"Whoa. Hold on partner," Sean patted his outstretched hands in the air to signal a slowing of the conversation.

"You gonna beat me again in front of Trel? Show him what a big man you are?" Jim asked.

"Why would I do that?"

"Isn't that the modus operandi of this family? Dad beats you, like he did this morning, and then you'll find a reason to beat me at some point today?" Jim spat in utter disgust.

Then Jim finds a reason to start a fight with me.... of course! That makes perfect sense! How did I never put two and two together until now! What a fool I've been.

"What are you talking about?" Looking to Jim and then shooting me a glance.

"Don't worry about Trel. Everyone in the neighborhood knows Dad beats you like a drum."

Sean looked in my direction with his mouth half-open and words half-swallowed.

"It's true," is all I said without making eye contact.

"That's ridiculous!" Sean retorted.

"Is it? He beat you this morning. Why? Was he hungover? It's Saturday, so he wasn't going to work for a couple of days, so it wasn't the stress," Jim air-quoted in dramatic fashion to mock his own statement. "Was it the weather?"

Sean stood silently—no longer looking at Jim, but at the ground. His outstretched hands were now held together in front of his belly, thumbs rotating for position.

"They may trade Jackson..."

"They're what?" Jim and I both asked.

"The radio... The radio said Reggie Jackson was on the trading block."

"So?" Jim asked disgustedly.

"So, he got mad I guess..."

"Dad beat you because of a baseball trade?"

"He said it was because I lost his wrench, but we both know I never borrowed it."

"You OK?" Jim asked with great sincerity.

"Yeah... He didn't go off. Just a couple of punches." He took his hand and moved it gingerly to his left ribcage. "A little sore here. But in his defense, I don't think he knew he was going to land this one, and immediately stopped after he saw me buckle."

"I'm sorry..." Jim whispered.

"You're sorry? Imagine how sorry you'll be when I'm off to college next year and you've got the only ass left to kick," Sean remarked half-jokingly.

"I'll run away before he does that to me," Jim said with steel in his voice.

"I wouldn't blame you," Sean said with zero sarcasm.

"Why don't you run away?" I asked without thinking.

"I can't, because I have a little brother at home whose ass can't yet take a pounding." Smiling at Jim, he then looked to me, "You got to tell your buddy here, to eat more of Mom's pasta, so he gains a couple of pounds in the rump. More cushion for the pushing."

Jim began to tear more and a quick sob left his throat. "They beat me up in The Woods, but worse, they humiliated me and stole my bike."

"I thought your bike was stolen at Robin's Stationery?" Sean asked.

"I lied."

"Why?" Sean asked.

"I was embarrassed. No, I was ashamed," Jim corrected himself.

"Who beat you up?" Sean asked.

"Some guys that go to Jr. High and a couple that go to the high school."

"How many were there?" Sean asked.

"Six."

"Give me names."

"Derek..."

"Derek Fisher?"

"Yes."

"That piece of fucking shit! He's a dead man. Who else? And tell me everything," Sean demanded.

"You promise you won't say a word to Mom or Dad?" Jim asked.

"I promise," Sean put his hand to his heart.

"You promise never to use any of this information against me ever?" Jim asked.

"Do you think I'm a monster?" Sean asked incredulously.

"Answer me!" Jim snapped back.

"Why would I use it against you, you're my bro," Sean sounded hurt.

"Promise me."

Sean, walked to where Jim sat and knelt before him, putting his hands on Jim's knees. "I promise I will never, ever, say a word of this to anyone, nor will I ever use it against you. As the Lord is my witness—and Trel as well."

Jim looked up to me and I nodded my head to signal my approval of his recount. Jim began to talk and didn't stop for a good half hour. When he finished with his beating from his father and how it hurt even more than usual because of the pre-existing injuries and the emotional torcher he had already endured, as well as the shame he felt for not being honest, the effects to Sean were visibly noticeable. Tears streamed down his now crimson-colored face and his eyes remained closed. When Jim finally ended, Sean hugged him and whispered that he loved him in his ear.

Still on his knees he looked to me, and then back to Jim, "We're going to brawl with these bitches. I'm going to beat Derek so hard that his momma ain't going to recognize him when I'm done."

"Trel already took care of that," Jim said.

"Pardon?" Sean asked shocked.

"I sent him to the hospital. The cops casing the neighborhood are looking for me."

"What?" Sean, still on his knees, was in a state of shock, and my breaking news didn't help him regain his composure.

"Don't worry; they have no idea it's me." As the vivid memory of me introducing myself to Derek played out, "I think they're looking for someone much older," I added, which somewhat settled my tattered nerves.

"How?" Sean asked, still trying to process the fact that I sent a kid like Derek to the hospital.

"You really don't want the particulars to this one. Safe to say, he got his come-up-in's in spades. Derek will never be the same..." I then added, "Nor will I, for that matter."

Sean was now looking at me as if we were meeting for the first time in a dark alley, "Okay... and did you take care of anyone else, or did Derek quench your thirst?"

"We worked his buddy Henry over, but in the end, we just scared him."

"Who's we?" Sean began to look in the shaded corners of the room.

"Not important, because he won't be any help to us when it's go time," I answered.

"Why?" Sean reluctantly asked.

"He's fine," I assured him. "He's just too young to fight," I continued.

"Christian?" Sean guessed aloud.

"The very one," I replied.

"Christian is involved in this mess?" Sean seemed both perplexed and disgusted.

"It's unfortunate, but we can shield him from anything further if we plan it out right," I answered.

"First of all, you're too young to be involved," pointing to me, Sean seemed angry.

"Jim, how could you let Trel and Christian fight your battles?!?! They're fucking children!" Sean was outraged.

"I didn't!" Jim snapped back with scorn.

"No? They did this on their own?" Sean's sarcasm was thick.

"Actually, we did just that," I said. "But to be fair, we didn't head out last night looking to hurt anyone."

"Well, that's good," Sean said.

"So what's your plan? Jim and I have talked about it and Kring and I did as well. Jim believes we have Bishop, Franky, Freddy and I guess to a much lesser extent, Roy. Clearly Roy and I will be liabilities, but I can occupy a couple of fists while you guys do the damage and get some much needed rest." I spelled it out like I was drafting a backyard football play on my palm.

"You're not fighting anyone Trel," Sean stated sternly.

"But..." I tried to correct him, but Sean cut me off.

"No buts! If your parents, or worse, my parents, ever found out I took you to a brawl, I'd be a dead man."

"But..." But before I could finish my retort, Sean cut me off again.

"And if you think my dad beat me badly this morning, imagine how hard he'd beat me, if God forbid, something bad happened to you in that brawl—" Sean looked off into the distance, clearly living his fears in real time.

"I can send word," I shot out before Sean could silence me.

"What word?" Sean asked.

"Word of the brawl. You're going to need the other side to show, in order to kick its collective ass. Right? Someone's got to get the word out, or you'll be swinging at air." My reasoning sound, I waited for him to accept.

"Are you sure no one suspects you're involved with Derek and Henry?"

"Absolutely not," I assured him.

"Where you going to go?" Sean asked with skepticism.

Looking at Jim with silence in my eyes, "I have a trusted ally that will assist me in my efforts."

"Fine, but don't let me hear you got yourself into trouble. Your job is to get in, get the word out, and get out. Understood?"

"Yes."

Jim asked his brother while trying to push his heart back out of his throat, "When and where is it going down?"

"Wilder's Woods. Tomorrow morning."

"Tomorrow?" We both blurted in response.

"Yeah, tomorrow. What works for you guys? Can you pencil it in on your calendars for this month, or are you booked through Labor Day?" Sean sarcastically asked.

"Besides, I'm going out tonight and I can ask around. Maybe figure out who's going to show from the other side."

"You can't tell anyone!" Jim shouted.

"Relax Bro... I promised you I wouldn't say a word, and I won't. I just want to figure out who's loyal to who and what that means for us come the morning."

"OK, fine. What's my role?" Jim asked.

"Your role is to rally the troops. Get all your boys, because we're going to need them," Sean responded shaking his head, as if he still couldn't believe he'd agreed to not involving his friends.

"I'm on it," Jim said.

Sean looked at me and then swung his pointed hand back and forth between Jim and I, "Remember, we need as many people as we can to be there on our side by 9am."

"When's the fight?" I asked.

"10am," Sean replied.

"Why the hour? Are we going to practice?" Jim asked inquisitively

"Practice?" Sean looked at him, as if it was the stupidest question ever asked.

"You've never been to a brawl have you?"

"No," Jim answered embarrassed.

Shaking his head again with his eyes half-closed, "A brawl is a numbers game. The more guys you have, the better your chances are. If you swing enough, you'll eventually knock one of the bigger guys down, and then the numbers really change. Once the other side shits the bed and begins the retreat, that's when the bloodshed begins."

"Oh..." was all Jim could say in response.

"We need numbers right off the bat, because this fight goes down at 9:05. We're not waiting for them to amass an army. We're going to start as soon as they have more than three people show, because from what you're letting me on to believe, we have five people, at most on our side."

"You, me, Bishop, Franky, and Freddy..." Jim listed reluctantly.

"Fat Fuck Freddy? He couldn't fight his way out of a paper bag. What about Kurt?"

"Kurt's crazy and we're not on talking terms," Jim responded.

"Well, here's some advice: you better start talking and get real chummy quick, because if I go down and you're left with nothing but your charm, you won't be talking to anyone for six months, because your jaw will be wired closed for healing purposes."

Six months... Was that how long Derek would be walking around with a wired mouth? Part of me felt like he got off easy for what he attempted to do to Gwen; the other part felt disgusted with myself for thinking I was the person to determine his sentence.

"10am, Wilder's Woods," I said to break up the silence that preceded Sean's scenario.

"10am, Wilder's Woods," Sean repeated my statement.

"9am us," Jim added.

"9am us," Sean repeated.

"Eat and rest well, Gentlemen." And with that, Sean got up and walked to the stairs. Before he descended the rickety flight, he turned, "Tomorrow is going to be the biggest test of your lives. Nothing you've ever experienced will prepare you for it. It will test you on every level. Any failure, at any level, whether that be mental, emotional or physical, could leave not only you dead in the water, but everyone else. You're not only fighting for your life, but for those around you. Trust, loyalty... You can never turn your back on your boy and run. If you do, you'll never stop running from yourself." And with that, Sean assaulted the staircase on his way to the kitchen for a much delayed breakfast.

The room was silent, with neither of us looking up. Birds that had made the attic home returned to nest, for they had thought the place once again abandoned, when I finally broke the silence, "What if we're outnumbered?"

"So be it," Jim answered with a cavalier tone, not accustomed to someone currently shitting his pants.

"So be it?" I replied. "What if we show up tomorrow and we're outnumbered 3 to 1? What then? What if Sean gets sucker-punched right off the bat and we're down to just us?"

"It will be, what it will be," Jim said.

"That's it? No plan? No nothing? You're confident that we'll survive this tomorrow?"

"Forget the numbers. The odds of victory are rarely in the favor of the more numerous," Jim said slyly.

"It's the people with less that win?" I asked with sarcasm in my tone.

"It's the advantages and/or perceived advantages that win battles, not the numerical superiority, but rather the superior intellect," Jim said as if reading from a history textbook.

"You gonna whip out my father's chess set when it's go time?" I asked.

"No... but war is chess nonetheless. Look at the pieces next time you play. Pawns, knights, castles—war is a calculated exchange of resources to reach an end goal."

"I get the big picture thing as much as the next guy, but I got to tell you Jim, I'm worried... The natives will be more than just restless, they'll be out to make a sacrifice to their Gods," I said with true fear in my voice.

"Did you know Christopher Columbus once made the moon disappear?"

"Sorry?" I asked for clarification.

"Christopher Columbus, the great explorer. The one who discovered America, or at least the one we're taught discovered it."

"I know who he is. I'm a quarter Italian," I replied slightly offended that Jim would even question both my pride in heritage and my fifth grade education.

"Did you know he wasn't actually looking for America, but in fact, a faster ocean trade route to Asia?"

"Yes," I confirmed the obvious with rolling eyes.

"Did you also know he didn't in fact land on America, but an Island in the Gulf of Mexico, called Hispaniola, which is now home to not one, but two nations?" Jim was now standing before me, voice calm.

"Yeah, I knew that. He thought the original people—"

"Indigenous people," Jim cut in.

"Yeah, the same thing," I replied absently.

"Not really, but please, continue," Jim corrected yet again.

Realizing where this was going and any attempt of me trying to recite a vague recollection of a fifth grade history lesson to an eighth grade history nerd was a non-starter. So I acquiesced to his far greater and more detailed knowledge, in order to facilitate his BS story about something that related to nothing, so I added with disinterest.

"Anyway, it gets a little hazy after the fact that he was in the wrong place, but America is America, because he stepped up to the plate."

"Yes... well, he not only found himself in the wrong place, but found himself, along with his entire crew, starving to death in what is now Jamaica."

"Fascinating."

"That's not the half of it."

"I didn't think so..."

Jim, ignoring my sarcasm, transformed the attic into a grand lecture hall, "At the beginning of their tenure as marooned explorers, they begged and bullied the local tribes for food. Once all the resources were close to exhaustion, the locals finally refused to offer additional aid. Columbus and his crew were dynamos when it came to sailing and debauchery, but farming wasn't their forte, so they were up Shit's Creek without a paddle. On the verge of death by either starvation or by an attack from their now hostile hosts, Columbus had an epiphany when he was reviewing some of his astronomical charts made by the brilliant, Portuguese mathematician, Abraham Zacuto. You see, other than assisting sailors locate latitude, the charts predicted both solar and lunar eclipses."

"And?" I interrupted with a dramatic yawn.

"And, Zacuto had predicted a lunar eclipse on February 28th 1504. Columbus, knowing he knew something his enemy did not, took advantage of it by telling the tribal elders that he was in fact a god, and that he would turn off the moon if they didn't feed his men. They, of course, didn't believe him until the very moment the moon disappeared. Once it vanished, they begged like dogs at the table for him to return their beloved moon. Columbus quickly agreed to their terms of surrender, portraying the benevolent leader, for he knew his window of opportunity was rapidly dwindling. Moments later and precisely on schedule, the moon returned and his men never went hungry again."

"As always, your impromptu history lessons are both timely and interesting," I said with as much sarcasm as my tired bones could muster. "But what does this have to do with tomorrow?"

"We've got to block the moon," Jim said.

"Block the moon?" I repeated. "In the middle of the day?"

"Not literally, figuratively," Jim answered with contempt for my inability to grasp his metaphor.

I knew I wasn't catching on anytime soon, so I just stared at him like he had a piece of pizza hanging from his forehead until he decided to finish his tired analogy.

"We need to make our enemies believe we're greater than we are—bestow upon them crippling fear of our potential fury. Back them in to a corner and then make them think we're gods!"

"How in God's name are we pulling that off?"

Shrugging his shoulders, "That's a good question... We've got the day to be brilliant."

Chapter 17
Wonder Twins' Powers, Activate

Leaving Jim's garage attic, I felt torn between the two me's—the one me was going to die tomorrow in a storm of punches and kicks, while the other me was going to see Gwen within the hour. My heart raced with anticipation. I yearned for a reason to see her, for I knew I couldn't just show up at her window and assault it with pebbles until she acknowledged my existence, and this situation gave me a real world reason to rendezvous.

But with any rendezvous, the real reason behind this one would be top secret and thus the blood from my heart pumped throughout my body like a torrent spring river, threatening to drown the newly hatched butterflies fluttering in my stomach. *How would I get to her? Was she even home if I got past her older brothers and, oh yeah, her parents? Did she have a killer attack dog to boot? What if she wasn't even home?* She was a triathlete, which meant there was a high probability she was at a sporting event today, even in the dead of summer.

If she wasn't home, I'd have to bike into enemy territory and look for an enemy I couldn't recognize. That seemed like folly. No, getting to Gwen seemed the only sensible path, regardless of where that path would lead. Regardless of when and where I saw her, I needed to clean myself up first with a shower and fresh underwear.

Upon entering the back door of my house, I switched to Mountain Lion Mode. This sultry, controlled stalking stride, assisted me in maneuvering around the various obstacles that a house presented itself, quickly and quietly, while maintaining a predator's persona. I got to the bathroom I shared with my sister relatively quickly and quietly, not even waking the dog from the couch it wasn't supposed to be sleeping on. I slipped through the partially opened bathroom door and began to close it in one fluid motion, when a foot blocked its closing.

"Ow! You're crushing my foot!" Libra wailed.

I yanked back the door and violently raised a finger to my mouth, making the angry librarian call, "Ssshhhhhhh!!"

"Don't sshhhh me Little Brother!"

I looked over her shoulder as best I could, but her height thwarted my visual check of the hallway. "What do you want?" I strained.

"I want to use the bathroom," Libra responded as if it were the dumbest question ever asked.

"But I'm about to use it," I said.

"You were about to use it, but you're not, because I'm using it," Libra corrected me.

"But you weren't using it!"

"Yes I was," she retorted.

"You were in your bedroom," I pointed out.

"I went to get something," she explained.

"The light was out. What were you getting, a flashlight?" I snapped.

"I turned off the light to save money. Unlike you, I care about how hard Dad works."

The fact was that Libra had big hair and the amount of electric used to dry her hair on a normal school day, not counting twice a day on the weekends, was costing my dad three hours of salary every time she turned the setting to high heat.

"Please! Go use the other bathroom. I need to shower," I pleaded.

"You're showering? You don't shower. Are we going somewhere? I'm not going anywhere. Did Mom tell you where we're going? Crap! I'm going to the movies tonight with everyone! Mom! Mom!"

I gave her another angry librarian, "Sssshhhhh!!"

"Don't shhhh me!"

"We're not going anywhere!" I yelled in a whisper.

"Why are you whispering?" Libra asked.

"Dad's been working extra-long hours and he needs his rest. He's napping and you're waking him up."

"Dad's at the store right now," Libra said with a raised eyebrow and awareness.

"Oh, is that right? Well, Mom's most likely concentrating on something..."

Libra cut me off, "Concentrating on something? You mean like cracking a safe, or operating on the President?"

"I mean don't bother her with your nonsense. We're not going anywhere and I'm going to take a shower, so please remove your GIANT foot, so I can close the door and begin."

"Why are you showering?"

"I just am."

"You don't just shower."

"Yes I do."

"No you don't."

"I smell. I've been playing for days. I shower once a week and this is it. If I miss it, I won't shower for another week. It's like taking the trash to the curb; it happens once a week and if you don't do it, you miss it."

"Trash goes out twice a week."

"You get the point," I added annoyed.

"I get that you're up to something," Libra said as she stood with one foot in the door's path and arms crossed.

"You wouldn't understand..." I said sadly.

"I wouldn't understand that you're in love?" Libra's tone exuded mock.

How did she know? For the love that is all Holy, by the Creator's light, has He allowed those who would trespass against me, to do so in complete secrecy?!?

Apparently reading my quickly scanning eyes, Libra decided to squash any thoughts I had on a global conspiracy with a far simpler explanation. "You're a stinky boy. You refuse to shower for weddings, birthday parties, even Aunt Hilda's funeral. You're only going to shower if you believe it will help you with something. The only thing a clean boy has over a stinky one, is a fighter's chance with a girl," Libra's smile confirmed her brilliant deductive reasoning.

"I... I'm showering... Does it matter why?" I asked more timidly than I intended.

"Yes. Yes, it does Little Brother." Smiling more now with her arched eyebrow, "For I need to know and approve of all your love interests."

"Who said anything about love? I'm just showering for her..." *Oh crap, I opened the door.*

"Who is she? And don't tell me you don't know, or I'm telling Mom right now!"

"Quiet! Lower your voice... please?" I lowered mine as I went from demand to favor.

"Fine. But you better tell me her name right now," Libra demanded.

"You have to promise not to say anything," I pleaded.

"Tell me," she reiterated.

"Promise me," I replied, finally exuding some backbone to my tone.

"Tell me," raising her voice.

"Promise me!" I proclaimed.

Libra finally acquiesced, "Fine. I promise."

"Promise what?" I demanded for clarification's sake, since Libra was tricky, and I needed verbal confirmation that she was promising to meet my demands to a T.

"I promise not to tell anyone the name of the person you're so deeply in love with that you're planning on scraping away a summer's worth of dirt and grime in hopes of her not noticing that you're a little weak, pathetic, freckled face boy," Libra pronounced.

And with every jab, I came closer to being knocked out. She was right. As hurtful as her tirade was, it was true. I was in fact a little, pathetic, freckled face boy. She'd forgotten to mention a couple of other negatives that would surely make me the most ineligible bachelor in America, i.e. violent criminal and failed politician were at the top of the list. My head sank with each appropriate blow and my hand left the door and fell to my side when I added my crimes to her short list of inadequacies.

Clearing my throat, "You're right..." was all I could answer with.

"Of course I'm right. Libra knows all!" Libra bellowed with dramatic flair.

Still not looking up, "Gwen Chandler."

"Gwen Chandler?" Libra thought out loud. "Wait! Gwen from Whitman Court?" She asked for clarification.

"Yes," I confirmed.

"Gwendoline Chandler?" She asked herself with sass in her tone.

"I think it's just Gwen," I replied.

"No, it's Gwendoline. You're in love with Gwendoline!"

"Quiet!" I snapped.

"Why would I be quiet when proclaiming the love my brother art thou has for thou dearest Gwendoline of Whitman Court?"

"Shut up!" I demanded.

"Silence love? I have not the heart to stifle another's." Libra grabbed her heart and smiled at the ceiling. "I too am in love therefore! I too celebrate your love with the enthralling Lady Gwendoline!"

"Please! You promised!" I pleaded.

"I promised not to tell anyone her name," she countered.

"You're doing so right now! You're telling the world! Keep your voice down!" I violently whispered.

"But what I didn't promise was, not telling people you were in love," she smiled widely and looked me over from head to toe, noticing my eye for the first time, her eyes widened. "What happened to your eye?"

"Oh nothing. Just playing with Kring in the bushes," I responded in my best casual conversational tone.

"Were you playing with Chris in the bushes... Or Gwen!" *How... How could she read my mind? What did she know?* I panicked and grabbed her by the shirt.

"Back off!" I screamed.

"Get your stinky hands off of me!" Libra yelled while trying to contain her laughter.

"Leave me alone!" I yelled.

"You leave me alone! Your hands are on me! I'm just standing here!" She countered as the laughs poured between words.

"I hate you!" I exclaimed.

Libra finally freed herself of my tired grasp, "That's because all the love your little heart can hold, is earmarked for the Lady Gwendoline of Whitman Court, and thus your poor sister will go throughout life with no love at all," she feigned a whimper and squeegeed an imaginary tear on her cheek.

"I don't care how big my heart grows, there will be no room for you!" And with that I felt the first tear form on my right eye. I quickly wiped it in hopes of Libra not seeing, but that was like hoping to wipe blood from a cut, so a shark wouldn't smell it.

"Is that a tear I see shed?" Libra mocked sincerity.

"No," I replied.

"No? Are you sure, my Prince, that a tear did not take leave of your eye?"

"Yeah," but as I confirmed the non-tear event, another followed from the left.

"And that? Is that yet another, my Dearest Brother?"

I wiped it, but now I was shoveling sand against the tide, for both eyes began to sprout leaks like an old ship hitting shore.

"Leave me," I trembled.

"Leave you? In your time of need? Who would I be, if I were to leave you now?" Libra opined.

"You'd be my older sister for once," my voice trembled.

Libra began to say something, but stopped. Her smile dissipated. "For once?"

"Yeah... for once..." my throat constricted with each vowel.

Libra exhaled, "OK, Little Brother. You win this one. But only under three conditions."

"Three?" I asked mortified.

"Three," Libra confirmed.

"That's ridiculous!" I hissed.

"That's the deal kid. Or, I could tell Mom you're sneaking around the house taking covert showers, because you're in love with Gwen. And then of course I'll need to confirm your relationship with Gwen... And then there are so many other people and places I'll need to cross-check and vet to hopefully make sense of this torrid love affair..." Looking at me with one eye and her head tilted up and to the left.

"Fine!" I agreed.

"Fabulous. Shake," Libra extended her hand to make her victory official.

I reluctantly extended mine and limped across the finish line.

"One, how do you know Gwen?"

"I met her yesterday."

"I didn't ask you when you met her, I asked how."

"Relax, I'm getting there," I responded in kind. "We met in The Woods. She was with a bunch of guys who I didn't know, so I didn't want to stick around. They were older, like her, so I left as quickly as possible."

"What were you doing in The Woods?" Libra asked, most likely not aware that this constituted her second question.

"I was spying on them." Libra's brow furrowed. "Chris and I have a new spy club. That's what we do... spy."

"Did you see what happened?" Libra's voice became stone.

"See what?" I asked innocently.

"See what happened in The Woods last night?" Libra reiterated.

"I saw some stuff. I'm not sure what you're referring to."

"I'm referring to two boys getting the crap beat out of them by a group of loons."

"What?" I asked stunned.

"You were spying on them and didn't notice The Woods being blown apart while a gang of commandos stormed their campsite and beat the crap out of half the party?" Libra asked sarcastically.

"That must of happened after I left..." I slowly said.

"Must of... So what are you hiding? How did you fall in love with the fair lady Gwendoline? You were just spying on the group, saw her from afar, and now you're in love? You want me to believe that nonsense?" Libra grew madder with every word and her voice signaled the same.

"Keep your voice down. You promised," I pleaded.

"And you promised to tell me the truth," Libra retorted.

"What do you want to know? I love her and she most likely doesn't know I exist. Happy?"

"OK... so you saw her last night in The Woods from afar, saw her incredible beauty, and vowed to one day visit her and profess your love? Does that sum it up?"

"Pretty much," I said while fighting a smirk.

"That makes sense. And is that where you hurt your eye?" Libra asked nonchalantly.

"Yeah, poked it with a branch. It was dark."

"That must hurt."

"It's alright. Don't even notice it's there half the time," I said smoothly.

"You can see alright?" Libra asked with some genuine concern.

"Yeah. Thanks," I replied somewhat taken by her change in tact.

"That's good... What are you planning on doing when you go to see Gwen?" Libra asked with genuine curiosity.

"I'm not sure," I said, for I wasn't.

"How are you planning asking her to come outside? Are you going to do something romantic like toss a pebble at her window, or are you just going to man up and knock on her door and ask if she can come outside?"

"I don't know. I was hoping to wait around until she just came outside," I said.

"Hide in the bushes and make sure the coast is clear isn't a bad option..." Libra weighed in.

"You think it wouldn't come across as shady? I don't want to freak her out," I said excitedly.

"She may be somewhat freaked out especially if you take into consideration, you're not supposed to know where she lives," Libra finished her thought with crossing her arms and staring in to my eyes.

"What?" I asked.

"How do you know where she lives?"

"What?" I asked again, even quicker than the first time.

"How – Do – You – Know – Where – She – lives?" Libra made each word a sentence. She had lured me to this point. She was the craftiest sister in all the land, and I once again fell for her diversion.

"You already asked your three questions. Conversation is officially over." And with that I attempted to close the bathroom door, but much to my chagrin, Libra had silently maneuvered her way into the bathroom during her interrogation.

"Our deal was that you answer my three questions truthfully, Little Brother, and you have clearly misled me, if not full out lied to me."

"How can you say that?" I asked hurt.

"There's no way you could know where she lives and you know it. Admit it!"

"She lives on the next block," I responded in my best innocent and emotionally hurt voice. "I've seen her a thousand times over the years going to and from school. She's babysat Chris. Hasn't she been here for a birthday party???" *I was good. How did I possess such mastery of BS? Maybe I did have what it took to be a real spy... What did James Bond have over me? Looks? Gadgets? An expense account? I was only ten... I bet he didn't have my game at ten.*

"You're lying to me," Libra said, snapping me out of my happy thoughts. "And I'm going to call up Gwen right now and ask her how she knows you." And with that, Libra turned and began to walk out of the bathroom.

I panicked and jumped on her back, wrapping my arms around her head and shoulder, like a frightened chimp attacking its master during a three-ring circus finale.

Libra braced herself on her bedroom doorframe with one arm, abruptly halting our decent. *She was strong...* She was maybe the best athlete in her entire school, including the guys! Along with softball, basketball and lacrosse, Libra played soccer for the high school from time to time when their roster was thin, which was obviously a big deal for someone in junior high. What's more, during the fall, she not only played soccer for the school, but also rostered for two additional Division One travel teams, just to keep herself in game shape. If emasculating boys was her hobby, her secret passion must have been Brazilian Jujitsu, for she was able to reposition her body within in a belated breath well enough that she no longer needed her arm as a support, while at the same time, snatching my right arm with her left hand. With her now free right hand, she grabbed my left hand, which was wrapped around her face and began to pry it loose.

I knew if I held tight, I would do major damage to her face and those scratch lines would be all the proof Libra would need to launch a full parental investigation into my whereabouts the night before and my subsequent plans for the upcoming day. Therefore, I had no choice but to release and jump from the wild bull before she tossed me into the stands. As I dismounted, Libra spun and struck my flailing body with a perfectly time body blow. The force was so powerful that it altered my trajectory, causing my crumpled form to land face first on the bathroom counter. An electric jolt of pain shot through my temple, as an errant ceiling light flickered due to the room shaking from the mini-quake.

I knew I had to get to my feet quickly in hopes of defending myself, but something was very wrong with me, for though I could feel the ice cold bathroom tiles, I couldn't feel my face, which was laying upon them. I saw Libra turn and stare at me, her face donning the same unreadable expression she used during family game night. To add to my hysteria, I had momentarily forgotten how to get up.

My arms would help... Of course, my arms! Push up! I was on my left side, thus my left arm should have acted as the jack, but it wasn't responding. Libra was going to kick me in either the face or the stomach, both of which would be fatal blows and I wasn't too confident in my current defensive capabilities, since my upper extremities weren't responding to even the most basic of commands. Being I couldn't physically protect myself, I desperately tried to think of something to say in hopes of keeping her at bay until I could get back on my feet and continue the fight. My normal wit was escaping me, most likely jumping out the window when Libra blocked the door. More concerning was my inability to articulate a basic conversation. I knew what I wanted to say, but making my mouth's motors move to my mind's commands was escaping me for some apparent reason.

"Trel. Trel? Trel!!" *Libra sounded panicked on that last Trel... Is she hoping I'll get up before Mom comes, so she can finished me with a legitimate KO? Does she really think I'd get back up, just so she could knock me down again? I'm your brother, not a Weeble Wobble.* Besides, I needed to conserve my ass for later, for I had an entire woods that would be teeing off on it. The greedy bitch was thinking about herself once again, and that got me angry. I felt my face flush with blood, the warm sensation felt amazing against the cool tiles and suddenly found myself quite content with laying there for the remainder of the day. *Dogs did in fact have the life.*

"Trel! Answer me!"

Bitch, if I could answer you, I'd tell you to go fuck yourself. So guess what... It's better I just take the high road and lay low.

Libra bent down and put her face next to mine, "Trel? Trel, can you hear me?"

Of course I can hear you. My sister couldn't stop being mean for a second. Unreal! Mocking me while I'm on the floor in what must be obvious pain. Furthermore, why is she yelling at me from two inches away? Did I fall on my ear? I can hear her just fine, so I'm guessing I have nothing to worry about on the deaf front, but I may have a major issue in the looks department, for if she's looking at me and wondering if I've lost my hearing, I might have lost some of my head. Gwen is definitely never going to kiss me again now that I'm a hideous beast. I might as well look like this on the outside, for everyone is surely gonna know sooner than later that I'm this ugly on the inside. Fittingly, a perfect look for a guy serving twenty to life. All I need now is a tattoo of my mom and a motorcycle and I can pledge the Hell's Angels.

"Trel..."

Libra sounds scared? It must be a ruse.

"Trel? Please say something."

Fine....

"I'm gonna get mom! OK?" Libra's voice trembled.

Don't get Mom you idiot! I'm fine.

Libra took off, yelling for mom. *What was she thinking?* I needed to get to my feet before my mom came, along with an onslaught of questions, for she would surely notice my eye if she were to check my head wound. I needed to rise. At least get to my knees. *My hand!* I could feel it. As crazy as it seemed, blinking seemed to pump blood through my arm. *Blink Bitch, Blink.* I continued a cadence of hard, crisp blinks, as if I had an errant eyelash trapped under each lid, using my tear duct system to extract them. *It's working!* My arms began to fill with blood and the accompanying tingling sensations that signaled the blood and oxygen's return boosted my demoralized moral.

I propped myself up and surveyed the tile floor once again to see if there was blood. Nothing. I wasn't bleeding, which was an excellent sign for a speedy recovery. I heard commotion in the background and the slamming of a screen door. Heavy foot falls forewarned of a mom on the move. I grabbed the top of the counter and began to pull myself up. I took my other free hand and grabbed the tub and got to my knees with relative ease. The room spun a little and the lights flickered for some reason, but I was stable enough to drop my hands.

My mom was in front of me within seconds, "Trel! Oh my God!"

She looked to be worse for the wear. Not an athlete by today's standards, the run from somewhere in the yard must have been a chaotic romp, for her breath was heavy, her hair a mess and her face was flushed with blood and sweat. She needed to hold onto the door to stop herself from falling. *Where did she come from, the next town?* Once she stabilized herself against the doorframe, she knelt in front of me.

"Are you OK? Speak to me!"

I was going to say something, but Libra cut me off, as usual, "He can't talk. He's retarded. I'm so sorry."

"Shut up Libra!" My mom yelled, half turning to my sister who seemed to genuinely believe I had lost more than my strength and balance in the fall.

"Trel. Can you understand me?" My mom asked in vain.

"Yes," I said and with that my mother held my cheeks and wept.

Cupping her mouth, "Thank you Lord! Thank you!" My mother cried to the ceiling.

Libra sank to her knees and put her hands over her head.

What had she told Mom? I better double down and bet it all... "Libra and I were playing. I fell."

"Playing?" Mom asked as she looked back to Libra for confirmation.

Libra looked at me in stunned silence.

"Libra! Were you playing?" My mom asked with heat.

"Yeah..." Libra shuddered as she looked at me with great worry in her eyes.

My mom turned to me again and moved my head to the side and gently touched my temple. "It's already swollen! You need ice. Libra! Get him a bag of ice." Libra sprung to her feet and bolted to the kitchen. "Your eye looks like it got walloped as well. That was one heck of a crash. Honey, you cannot play so rough. You're gonna kill yourself one day."

"Sorry Mommy," I said with sincerity.

Her smile warmed the room as always, and when she bent over and kissed me on the cheek, I felt the throbbing pain subside.

"How was Christian's last night? Did you guys stay up all night?" Mom asked with a twinkle in her eyes.

"Yes," I said and smiled. The smiling hurt, which meant the shot to the chops was worse than I had originally assessed.

Libra was back with a sandwich bag filled with ice.

"Thank you," Mom said to Libra without turning around. She held the ice up to my face and the cool rush momentarily exasperated the pain from a dull throbbing to an electric jolt that touched the back of my cranium.

"Do you think you can get up?" My mom asked.

"Yes," I said.

"Libra, get behind him and make sure he doesn't fall backward."

"OK," Libra responded.

I put my hands back on the countertop and tub and began to rise. Libra lifted me as well, and truth be told, applied enough force to get me up without me having to use my arms. When I stood, my legs felt like they were made from Jello and my vision had become blurry. I began to blink again in hopes of pumping blood to my eye muscles.

"Keep holding!" My mother barked.

"I am!" Libra snapped back.

"I'm fine," I assured them.

"You're going to the couch or your bed. Which is it?" My mom asked.

"He should go to the..."

"Quiet!" My mom cut Libra off.

"Can I sit on the back patio?" I asked.

"Of course you can, Sweetie," my mom replied.

"I got him," Libra confirmed before she was asked.

"Are you sure?" My mom questioned.

"Yes. I got it. He's in good hands," Libra answered annoyed.

"Walk slowly."

"Yes Mom," Libra and I said in unison.

"If you feel woozy, Libra will stop."

"Yes Mom," Libra and I said in unison.

We walked slowly to the outside with my mom in front of me walking backwards and Libra behind me holding me loosely at the hips. I was more than fine by the time we reached the back door and wanted the whole show to end before I sat down, but knew the next question before it was asked.

"What can I get you to drink Sweetie?"

"Iced tea would be great," I answered.

"Be right back. Libra you got him on the chair?"

"Yes, Mom," Libra said.

As Libra lowered me she said under her breath, "I'm fine, no need to get me anything."

In my Mom's haste she clearly had forgotten Libra and it hadn't gone unnoticed.

"You had me worried, Little Brother." Libra said as she looked at the side of my face.

"How bad is it?" I asked.

"You look like a monster," she said as a warm smile creeped across her chin.

"So, I came out unscathed?" I replied.

Libra's laugh was loud and true. "Yes! You're the same, but just a little uglier," she confirmed with a broad smile that accentuated her handsome facial features.

"Sweet. I was worried there for a moment."

"Nothing to worry about," she replied.

"Good, because I was worried Gwen was going to toss when she saw me," I said with all seriousness.

Libra looked deeply into my eyes and then to the side of my face once again, before looking back to acknowledge my mother hustling out the door with my drink order.

"Here you go Sweetie. More sugar than you probably should have, but maybe your body needs the added nutrients."

Libra concentrated on an object in the far corner of the yard, while she held her tongue.

"Libra, will you tend to your brother while I finish up in the garden?"

"But of course, Mother," Libra mockingly replied in her poorly executed English accent.

"You're lucky he's still alive." And with that, Mom walked to her garden in the one corner of the yard where the sun poked through.

Turning to me after watching mom depart, Libra appeared peeved, "You're lucky you're alive. I would have brought you back from the dead and killed you again."

"Get in line," I said.

"Get in line to kill you?" Libra asked.

"Yeah," I confirmed.

"Let's get one thing straight. If anyone gets to kill you, it's me. Anyone else staking a claim on my kill, deals with me. Understood?"

"Yes."

"So, can you tell me why you want to talk with Gwen?"

"You don't want to know. Just know that I have to."

"Do you want to?"

"Yes. In the worst way, but it doesn't change the fact that I have to regardless of whether I want to," I surmised.

"Sounds serious," Libra said with a hint of humor.

"It's serious as a heart attack," I confirmed.

"How we going to do this?"

"We?" I asked stunned.

"We," Libra confirmed.

"We're not talking to Gwen; I am," I corrected her with absolute resolve.

"I don't care how you dice the salad, we're gonna eat it together. Mom's not letting you off this property without me. That's a conclusion that I'm sure you can come to, even in your depleted mental state."

"Well, you can't be there when I speak to her. You'll ruin it all."

"I don't have to speak at all. I can simply sprinkle rose petals before you as you walk up to her front door and announce your arrival like in one of your fantasy adventure books. Does Gwen read those?"

"I don't know what she reads," I snapped.

"You must have a lot in common to be so in love. Does she like to pick her nose?"

"Shut up!" I spat.

"Don't get so upset, I was just kidding. If she's gonna be my sister-in-law, I'm gonna need to know all about her. Our bonding is almost as important as yours," Libra said with smiling eyes.

"She won't marry me... I'm a smelly little boy, who looks like a freak show now. What would an older amazing girl want with me?"

Libra snapped back, "What? You're not smelly! You're stinky and you're certainly not ugly. You're quite handsome."

"No I'm not," I said as I crossed my arms.

Libra was sitting and she moved in close, putting her hands on my crossed arms.

"All my friends say you're the cutest brother out of all of the little brothers."

"You're lying to me," I said sadly.

"Trust me. Gwen thinks you're cute. She might have a hard time seeing your cuteness today, because it's hidden behind a watermelon sized wound, but I'm sure once you pour on the charm—"

"Shut up!" I cut her off.

"So, what's the plan?"

"I don't know," I responded somewhat absentee.

"Well, what were you going to do before you had to take me along?" Libra asked.

"I was going to wait outside until she came outside," I said.

"Where were you going to wait?"

"In the bushes."

"So, you were going to wait in the bushes and then just jump out of them when she walked by, or make a bird call to alert her of your position?"

I looked at Libra with as much anger as my tired eyes could shoot.

"If you decide on that approach, I wouldn't wear that scary ninja outfit you wore to Christian's last night." A huge smile exploded on Libra's face.

My eyes went from hate to shock, and she saw it, and let out a massive laugh.

"Oh Little Brother! You're the best! Does Gwen know you dress up like a ninja and spy on people?"

"Yes," I curtly retorted.

Libra's eyes showed confusion as they closed halfway and crossed, "Wait, she knows you're a nerd and you think she'll still speak to you?"

"Yes," I confirmed.

"Interesting..." Libra put a finger to her face to let me know she was thinking.

"How about I get Gwen outside to speak with you?"

"How?"

"I'll call her up," Libra said.

Wait, that's brilliant! If she could only follow the plan and not deviate to something over the top complicated and stupid.

"How would you call her...." I began to think out loud.

"I would pick up the phone and call her and then speak to her when she answered the phone," Libra's tone mocking me with each word.

"I got that. Thanks. But what will you say?"

"I'll say, my brother wants to speak to you. Come outside and speak with him."

"Oh..." *It did seem quite simple.*

"I could add that he wants to ask you to marry him, so wear something magical that the two of you will remember for all eternity."

"Quiet fool!" I snapped.

"I'll walk you across the street and be in the distance. I won't listen to what you guys have to say," Libra assured me.

"You promise?" I asked.

"I promise," Libra said.

"Call her. Let's do it," I said.

"How about I'll call her while you're in the shower?" Libra said as she sniffed the air and flinched.

"I smell that bad?" I asked.

"You smell worse than you look and you look like something you flush, not wash." And with that Libra got up and walked to the backdoor. Before she went in, she yelled to my mom in the backyard, "I'm going in now! The prince is taking his refreshments on the back patio and I'm drawing him a bath, for he must be presentable, if we are to bring him before his loyal subjects!"

"He's not allowed to go anywhere!" Mom yelled.

"Relax! I'll escort the Prince personally and attend to all his wishes and health!"

"You're both nuts!" My mom yelled and then went back to her gardening.

Libra looked over to me and gave me the thumbs up, "I'll pick out proper attire for your tryst, my Lord."

I smiled, despite my best efforts to make a scowl. "Thanks."

Chapter 18
The Face that Launched a Thousand Ships

After I got out of the shower, which seemed like an eternity, I went into my bedroom to find a very well laid out set of clothing. Libra had even gone through the painstaking process of finding the one pair of tighy-whities that did not have at least one bacon strip on them. She was really setting me up for success, versus the usual failure and it boosted my confidence that today's meeting would go well on several fronts. I got dressed quickly and opened the door, finding Libra on the other side waiting with arms crossed.

"A word, my Prince?" Libra's tone said it was a command, not a question.

"Of course, come in," I held the door open, and after she walked past me I scanned the hallway for followers, before I closed and locked it. Libra was facing the windows with her arms still crossed, clearly contemplating what her next statement would be.

I gave her no time, "What did she say?"

"She'll meet us in the Brady's backyard, next to the bushes that separate their properties."

"Excellent job, Sis!"

"She asked about you."

"Oh?"

"She seemed very concerned."

"What did you tell her?" I asked nervously.

"I told her your eye and cheek were worse for wear and that it could take weeks before you'd be the same."

"Why did you tell her about my cheek?"

"Because she's gonna see it and she should think you got that last night, along with whatever happened to your eye."

"But that's not what happened," I contended.

Libra turned to me, "But that's what you want her to believe."

"Why?" I asked.

"Guilt," Libra said.

"Why would I want her to feel that?" I asked.

"Because, you're in a relationship now. It's par for the course."

"I'll never lie to her. I love her!" I proudly proclaimed.

"You what?"

"You heard me. I love her."

"What did she do to you?" Libra was upon me in one stride and rested her hands on my arms.

I shook them off, stepping back a pace, "She made me grow."

"Grow? You're taller? You're wiser? Did she make you grow in your pants?"

"I'm wiser, that's for sure. And... yes, she makes me pitch a tent if you're writing a book."

It was Libra's turn to step back. She put her hands to her face, covering her mouth and what looked to be a giant open-mouth smile. Face now red and eyes wide, Libra quickly scanned my package and then looked me dead to rights. "Did she touch your penis?"

"Shut up!"

"Did she?"

"That's none of your business!"

"Yes it is, and if you don't tell me, I'll meet that private school hussy in Brady's backyard and beat her so hard, the only sports she'll ever play again will be in the Special Olympics." Libra looked mad for some reason and one hundred percent serious.

"I touched her with it."

"You what?"

"Not on purpose!"

"You touched her with your penis by accident?"

"Yes," I said in all seriousness. "We were laying on the ground and I rolled over and it was... straight. I didn't know until it was too late."

"That's it?" Libra said once again shielding her mouth with both hands.

"There was another time where she went to kiss me but it was really straight and she couldn't get close unless..."

"She what?" Libra stumbled back until she fell on to my bed.

"You promised to not say anything to her, or anyone else. Sister swear!"

"Gwendoline Chandler tried to kiss you?"

"More than once," I added, quite smitten with the memories.

"More than once?" Libra tried to confirm my outlandish statement by repeating it, but it was clear her mind could not wrap itself around the visual.

"More than once," I said with pride.

"What happened?"

"Well, Swissy protected me more often than not..."

Libra crashed to the floor screaming and laughing uncontrollably. "No! Oh my God, I'm going to piss my pants!"

"Why?"

"Swissy? Please don't!" Libra could not breathe due to her deep laughs and had to space her words in order not to hyperventilate, "Is – Swissy – the – name – of – your – penis?" Libra violently contorted her body while rolling on the ground.

"Yes."

"Your penis protected you from the girl you're in love with?"

"It didn't know any better. It's always got my back."

Libra curled up on the floor and looked to be having a seizure. Convulsing between cackles, she finally raised her head and looked at me. Tears streamed her cheeks as she slowly got to her feet. *Why had she been crying?*

"Oh Little Brother. I love you! I simply love you! Your penis was shrewd, for private school girls can be dangerous. If your penis does that again, run."

"Are you serious? What if it does it during our meeting today? I need to say, what I need to say! Besides, I think my penis is overreacting."

Libra fell to the ground again and began to shake uncontrollably.

"Are you OK?" I asked somewhat concerned.

Between bellowing laughs Libra gave me a thumbs up.

"Well, we better get moving, Sis; just thinking about meeting Gwen got my penis nervous."

Libra shook harder and now was wrapped in a tight ball. "Stop—" she managed to squeal, "Please! Please stop!"

"Stop what?" I asked.

"Stop talking about your penis," she begged.

"Fine."

After what seemed like an eternity, Libra managed to get herself off the ground and wipe a face full of tears onto my white cotton bedsheet, where her heavy mascara made zebra stripes that would remain forever.

"And whatever you do, don't bring up your penis issues with her. She won't understand."

"OK." *Sounded like good advice...*

"Shall we, my Prince? Your bride awaits." And with that Libra opened the door for me and we hastened our pace to make our rendezvous.

Walking to the backyard Libra was full of advice on what to say and what not to say. I made sure she understood that I had no intentions of divulging to Gwen my true feelings, for I understood and appreciated the age gap, and how uncomfortable it had to be for Gwen. Libra just shook her head anytime a potential romantic interest could be a possibility, as if I was telling her I kissed an alien while holding a kite in a lightning storm.

As we crested the hill to the backyard's plateau, I saw Gwen anxiously awaiting my arrival along the hedge line. It was a good 100-feet to the line, but I could make out every detail of her beauty as if we stood close enough to kiss. Being my mind was busy processing her many features, I hadn't partitioned enough processing power to work my legs and other secondary motor reflexes, causing me to trip over my own feet. I did not fall to the ground, just stumbled forward awkwardly for a couple of steps.

"Easy Prince," Libra said softly from behind.

"I got this."

"Yes you do."

Without turning, I said, "I'm going the rest alone."

"Ok Brother. But remember, I'm here if you need me."

"Always." And with that, I walked to Gwen like a man on a mission.

As I approached, Gwen waved once to my sister and then immediately put her hands in front of her and held them tight. If I could make out her toes, I'd say they were wrestling each other. When I got to within twenty paces, Gwen could apparently make out my new facial feature, because she gasped and put her hands to her mouth. I kept walking towards her, even though I wanted to run in shame. I wouldn't have gotten far, because once Gwen regained her composure, she ran to me even faster than she ran the night before.

"Oh my God!" Gwen stopped short of me and extended her hands to firmly hold my shoulders. "What did they do to you? I'm so sorry!" Gwen screamed. She grasped her mouth again and began to cry uncontrollably.

Penis be damned! I took a hold of Gwen and held her tight. "It's alright. I'm fine. Looks worse than it is. Leebs thinks I'll be back to my creepy self in two weeks."

Gwen's cries went from hard jerking cries to deep sobs. Gwen was taller, and thus her crying on my shoulder was somewhat awkward. As I picked her head up she looked off into the distance to my sister.

"I'm sorry!" she yelled.

"No need to apologize," I reassured her.

"Your sister is going to kill me, and rightfully so."

"She'll do nothing of the sort," I said.

"I would, if you were my brother. I'd kill me right here, right now!"

"Well, Leebs is the best sister in town and she's promised not to kill you, or tell anyone what happened."

"What does she think about everything?"

"Everything?" I asked.

"What did you tell her?" Gwen asked.

"Not much actually."

"Does she know about Derek?"

"No."

"No?"

"No."

Gwen's voice raised, "Why not?"

"Why? I'm not sure... Didn't you want me to keep it a secret?"

"Your life could be in danger!" And with that Gwen pushed me aside and stalked to Libra. I fell in line behind Gwen, trying without success to grab her arm to slow her advance. Libra waited with arms crossed and head tilted. "I'm sorry!" Gwen shouted to Libra before she arrived.

Libra said nothing until Gwen stood two feet from her.

"Sorry for what?" Libra asked as if she had no idea who Gwen was before meeting her in the backyard.

"I'm a complete idiot! I fucked up. Forgive me. I don't expect you to, but hear me out."

"Sure," Libra said slowly.

"Your brother didn't tell you how we met, apparently."

"No. It's all a big secret. Care to fill me in?"

"He saved my life last night."

Libra looked at me, then to Gwen, then to me, and then to Gwen.

"Explain yourself."

"You heard what happened in The Woods last night with Derek Fisher?"

"Derek Fisher?" Libra asked incredulously, as she turned to me, "What the fuck were you doing anywhere near Derek Fisher?"

"He saved me from him!" Gwen interjected.

"When did you think I was talking to you?" Libra asked with an edge.

Gwen looked to the ground, avoiding eye contact to showcase her submissiveness.

"What were you doing in The Woods with Derek Fucking Fisher?" Libra asked.

"I already told you I was spying on him with Kring," I said.

"You never mentioned Derek Fisher!" Libra scolded.

"We had heard there were bad kids in The Woods making trouble and we wanted to find out who they were and to see if we could get them out of there."

"Are you crazy?" Libra yelled.

"Apparently, yes. I've been replaying the whole night in my head—what led us to what we did and what we did while we were there, and I've come to the conclusion that I am, in fact, most likely insane."

Libra looked at me, not speaking for a moment. She looked at Gwen, "You hang out with that scumbag?"

"Not normally..."

"Private school girls are fucking freaks. Does Derek have an issue with Trel now because of your lovers' tiff?"

"Well, I'm not sure if he knows who your brother is."

Looking to me, "Because you were donning your ninja outfit?"

"Yes," I confirmed.

"Where's Derek now? I'll make sure he knows what fucking time it is."

I cleared my throat, "He's in the hospital."

"Why?"

"I swung for the fences."

"You what?"

"Swung like Daddy taught us?"

"Like Daddy taught us?"

"I don't understand; you don't know about any of this?" Gwen asked befuddled. "Everyone in town is talking about this. My phone has been ringing off the hook. The cops came, Derek's in the hospital, and Henry is in some protective custody-slash-psych ward being evaluated."

Libra cut her off, "Wait, Henry? Henry who?"

"Henry Carpenter," Gwen said.

"What happened to him?" Libra asked.

Gwen turned to me, looking for my answer, but I couldn't speak, so she did. "He was in the wrong place at the wrong time... just like me... just like your brother and his friend."

"I can't believe you got poor little Christian involved in this!" Libra yelled in horror.

"It all happened too fast and we had no idea any of this—"

Libra cut me off, "Do you have any idea who Derek Fisher is? He's an evil bastard. Scum of the earth. A Satan worshiper! Do you understand? He worships the Devil. His friends are murderers and thieves!"

"I don't know if that's true," Gwen interjected.

"Did I ask you for your opinion?" Libra demanded from Gwen.

"Sorry," is all Gwen could muster before she stared at the ground once again.

"Don't speak to her like that," I said with heat.

"Pardon?" Libra asked surprised.

"You heard me. Don't speak to her like that. She didn't do anything wrong. She didn't ask for me; I asked for all of this."

"You had no idea what you were asking for. You're a little kid! She on the other hand is..."

"Is what?" I demanded. "An adult? Libra, we're all kids. Derek is an evil bastard and he was going to do evil things to Gwen. I did what I had to do in order to stop him from doing those things. If I didn't do those things, would you want me as your brother?"

Libra looked at me as if it were the first time we met. She looked at Gwen.

"He was going to rape me," Gwen whispered. "I was so scared," Tears streamed down her face. "I thought it was all over when your brother came out of nowhere and knocked Derek's head off. The Woods exploded, and your brother took me to safety and then home."

Libra didn't say anything for a bit. "My phone privileges were taken away for a week because of my fight with Karen White, so I haven't been updated on the latest current events. Everything I've heard has been from mom this morning."

"Your brother is a hero," Gwen said looking fondly upon me as a warm smile redirected the tears to the sides of her cheeks. "He's right out of a movie."

"Like James Bond... a fighter and a lover?" Libra drawled as she adjusted her crossed arms and cold stare towards Gwen.

Gwen's face turned fire engine red, "I didn't know how old he was. I swear! I had no idea... At least the first time..." she said sounding confused.

"The first time? You jumped my brother's bones more than once?"

"It wasn't like that!" I snapped.

"I'll warn you one last time about private school girls, and then you're on your own," Libra halfheartedly jabbed.

"I know there's no excuse for what I've done. I would kill me if I were you," Gwen stated.

"Luckily for you, I promised my brother that I wouldn't say or do anything, or you would be in fact dead right now."

"Libra!" I warned.

"Relax Bro. Your lady is safe, as are her dirty little secrets," Libra assured us both.

We all remained silent for a moment before I spoke, "There's going to be a brawl in The Woods tomorrow."

"What?!?!?" Gwen and Libra shouted simultaneously.

"Sean is going to lead the kids from Lower La Rue to fight Derek's crew."

"What?!?!" Gwen and Libra shouted simultaneously.

"Tomorrow morning. Sean wants Derek's side to show at 10am. We'll be waiting for them at 9am to get a jump on the crowd. It's a numbers game."

"You're not..." Gwen and Libra started to say at the same exact time and then stopped as they looked at each other in shock.

"I know, I know. I'm not to be anywhere near there, but I will—" I put up a hand before they could object. "I'm not planning on fighting, but I need to be there even if it's in emotional support."

"You'll be nowhere near it," Libra said

"No choice, Leebs. Man's got to do, what a man...

"You're not a man! You're my little brother!" She shot.

"True, but tomorrow I need to be The Man. This is all going down in part because of me, and I'm not walking away from my friends," I said matter of factly.

"Sean is an asshole!" Libra snapped.

"Don't hate Sean; he's more adamant of my absence to the show than you are."

"He shouldn't have even let you know it was going to take place."

"He had no choice." I said.

"Why?" Libra asked.

"Because I'm the messenger," I replied.

"The messenger?" Libra asked.

"I'm to tell Gwen that there's going to be a brawl tomorrow and she needs to tell Derek's crew to show up at 10am." I looked to Gwen.

Gwen seemed slightly saddened by my news, and frowned at the ground.

"And of course I was more than just slightly excited to take the assignment, since it meant I had a reason to see Gwen."

Gwen's head shot to me with a big smile on her face. Libra made an exaggerated puking noise and Gwen once again stared at the ground, only to quickly shoot up a sexy sideways smile and wink, before refocusing on the grass' growth.

"I'm going to be sick. And not just by your creepy love affair, but more so by the fact that you have a satanic cult wanting to kill you." Libra was clearly beside herself.

"I'm sorry..." Gwen went to say more, but Libra cut her off yet again.

"I get it, you're sorry for exposing my brother to your psycho freak show and making him fall in love with you. Point taken."

Gwen looked at me shocked, as if Libra just said I hated her.

"I never said that!" I yelled hurt.

"Right. Gwen, who you telling about this?" Libra asked annoyed.

"I can... I can tell everyone I guess."

"Everyone is going to know. That's a given. But you're aware who Derek Fisher really is, outside of just an asshole?"

"Kind of..." Gwen seemed to cringe every time my sister addressed her.

"He's one of the most evil people you'll ever meet, and he has friends, if you can call them that, who are just as evil. They'll be there! They'll be there in droves and these guys don't just want to hit someone, they want to kill someone."

"Sean's pretty bad ass..." I began to say, but Libra would have none of it.

"Shut up! You don't get it Little Brother! Do you?! Many of the guys showing up in those woods tomorrow are going to be ex-convicts—guys who went to jail, not after school detention or juvy, but jail! And some served sentences for crimes you can't imagine are even committed, forget all the crimes they got away with... Guys who are on drugs and have nothing left to lose. Older guys. I'm not talking seniors in the high school, I'm talking twenty something year old hardened criminals looking to hurt someone without concerning themselves with the consequences."

Gwen covered her mouth once more and let out a weep.

"That's right, Gwendoline Chandler! You hang with the worst people on the fucking planet and now my little brother's life is in jeopardy!"

"Stop!" I yelled. Libra did. I looked to reassure Gwen with a gentle hand to the side of her arm, "Gwen, you need to do your best on this and know I have no ill will towards you. I was there last night and know the truth."

"I'm so—" Gwen began, but I wouldn't let her finish.

"I made my bed, I'll lie in it now," I reassured her.

Libra looked to me with angry eyes, only to quickly break contact, due to the kindness in mine.

"I've got to go," Libra said.

"Where you going?" I asked.

"I've got to make some calls."

"You promised not to say anything."

"I promised not to tell everyone that my brother fell in love, not turn my back on him and let him get himself killed."

"Who are you going to tell?" Gwen asked.

"Have no fear—I won't use your name, but people must know that I need support. I'll let them think he tried to rape me if it means getting the football team there," Libra stated.

"You can use my name. Tell them it was me. I'm not ashamed," Gwen's face now was up, chin high as she stared back at my sister with defiance.

"Good. You have to stand up to these kind of people. Your brothers—are you going to tell them what happened? They'll find out eventually you know," Libra asked with skepticism in her voice.

"I'm telling anyone who'll listen. I'll be damned if anyone's gonna hurt m..." Gwen trailed off, eyes open as if she was about to choke on a poorly sipped soda can.

"Your man?" Shaking her head with her eyes half closed, "I'm gonna be sick," Libra finished.

Gwen stared at the ground once again.

"I'll meet you back at the front of Brady's garage in one minute, Romeo." And with that, Libra stalked off without a formal parting with Gwen.

After Libra was thirty paces from us, Gwen whispered "She loves you... and hates me."

"She'll warm up eventually. It took her ten years to tell me she loved me."

Gwen exhaled, "I can't believe you're ten."

"My age has been a tough pill to swallow as of late for me as well," I added.

"I wish we could be something more than just neighbors, but..." Gwen winced as if the embarrassment was physical pain.

"But the age difference is too great for you?" I asked rhetorically.

"I'm afraid so," Gwen admitted.

"I'm OK with that. I know it's got to be hard on you. No one would let you off the hook for it," I agreed.

"I feel so torn," Gwen admitted.

"I feel a lot myself," I said somewhat more sheepishly than I intended.

"Oh yeah?" Gwen's smile came back. Touching my chest, "Are you sure you're ten? Could your parents have messed up on the birth certificate? Maybe you're adopted?"

"I wish that to be true on more fronts than one, but no," I looked up at her with one eye squinted even though the sun was blocked by the towering maples. "I'm ten and in love."

Gwen kissed me gently on the lips, and stepped back suddenly before I could grab her. "Farewell Trel." And with that she turned and ran for home.

Chapter 19
Time to Rise, Shine, and Walk the Line

I woke early and tired. I wasn't in my normal fetal position with a pillow tucked between my legs, but rather I laid on my back, board straight against the mattress, like a cadaver in a classroom. I hadn't slept much, for my mind raced through various test tracks to determine today's winner. When I did sleep, the dreams were powerful, vivid affairs and more often than not, ended poorly for me. My only saving grace was that I got to bed early enough, which meant my body was at least somewhat rested.

The day since leaving Gwen was oddly mundane, split between my room and backyard, either playing by myself, or assisting my father from time to time with various tasks to upkeep the property. Surprisingly, I didn't hear from Kring, Jim, or any of the neighborhood boys for that matter, nor did I see any boys I didn't recognize on the street when I had to walk out front to help my dad. An uneventful day was what I probably needed anyway, for today was going to be anything but. I did have one constant interaction throughout the day and it was now staring me in the face with a look of great concern—Libra.

Libra was throughout the day, like she was now, less than two-feet away from my grill every chance she got.

"Did you sleep?" she asked.

"I'm gathering that's a rhetorical question, considering you were staring at me all night," I replied with a long yawn.

"When I came in and checked, you were restless, but sleeping for the most part," she said.

"I feel like I fought all night. I'm exhausted," I whined.

"You've been through a lot. Your body and mind are in shock. It's natural," Libra assessed.

"What time is it?" I asked.

"7:30am," she replied.

"7:30? I've got to get moving!"

"Relax. You've got time to eat, go to the bathroom, get dressed and still have time to meet up with Christian and whomever else."

"You think I can get out of here without Mom and Dad being the wiser?" I asked.

"I got you covered on that. I'll tell them that you're biking with me, while I jog to the school and do sprints. They'll be so tickled pink you and I are spending time together that they shouldn't question a thing."

"Brilliant!" I added.

"You sure you want to go through with this?" Libra asked longingly.

"We both know I have no choice," I replied reluctantly.

"If anyone comes close to you, I'll kill them," Libra spat.

"I know. But please allow the situation to unfold on its own. I can't have you laying waste to The Woods because a bird chirped," I surmised.

"Fair enough. Can I at least threaten Gwen when this is all over?" Libra asked with a smile.

"Don't lay a hand on her," I demanded.

"I would never harm the picturesque beauty of the fair lady Gwendoline, but I got to tell you, it's eating me alive inside that she cradle-robbed my brother," Libra answered.

"For the last time, I was a willing participant," I argued.

"It still disgusts me," Libra scolded.

"Besides, look on the bright side, I'm a changed man and you and me will be closer because of it forever."

"If you think hooking up with that hussy has given you a window into my soul, you're more retarded than I thought, and possibly still feeling the effects of your clumsy, drama queen spill in the bathroom," Libra opined with heat.

"On the contrary, my good sister. Now that I know I have an outside chance with a super-hot girl your age, I'll be much nicer to you, since all your friends are super-hot as well," I said with a shit eatin' grin.

Libra smiled, shook her head and looked out the window. "Oh Trelly... you're so helpless."

"Speaking of super-hot friends, what's Ven up to these days?" I asked sheepishly.

"Ven? You mean Vanessa? As in Vanessa Grath?" Libra asked for confirmation.

"That's the one. What's she doing?"

"She's currently doing the QB of the high school varsity team. Get your head back in the game Little Brother. Shit's about to get real. Focus up." And with that Libra got up from her chair that she'd propped against my bed sometime throughout the night and walked to the door. Turning back, "Get dressed, get fed, and get focused, understood?"

"You're talking to me like Dad talks to you before a big game," I said half-joking.

"Exactly Little Brother. We're going to prepare like this is the biggest game of our lives. We're teammates now and this is a must win," Libra's voice was ice.

"But I thought you said yesterday that this wasn't a game?" I questioned with a slight tremble in my voice.

"This is going to be a battle, no doubt. But it will be a test, no different than a championship game. The victor will have to showcase mental and physical toughness, as well as remain steadfast in their will and conviction," Libra sternly stated as if she was giving a pregame speech to her teammates before the State finals.

"I'm ready," I said with little conviction.

"Good. Step one, get out of bed," Libra said.

"Got it," I said back to reassure her.

"Don't get it, do it. Do it now," Libra said slowly and concisely.

I threw the blankets to the side and pivoted myself to the side of the bed and then stood. In trying to spring from the bed to show my sister "what time it was", the painful reminder came crashing in on just how epic my journey from two day's prior had been. "Your muscles are surely feeling it this morning. I can see how you rose. They're fatigued. It's natural. You need water. You need to get water on your face, you need to change into clothes. The ones we discussed. You need to eat something healthy and light. Make sure you take a banana with you as well. You need to hop on your bike and ride up and down the block at a nice relaxed pace until I come outside. Warm up, man up."

"OK," was all I could say in response.

Looking down the hallway, then back to my feet, she added, "Remember, no retreat, no surrender."

"No retreat, no surrender," I confirmed.

Looking lovingly to my bruised face and ego, "I love you Little Brother." And with that she was gone.

"Shit..." I muttered to myself as I scanned the room for the appropriate gear. Libra was very specific in what I was to wear. Even if it was going to be hot today, I needed to wear jeans and my steel tipped hiking shoes. A dark t-shirt with the widest neck hole possible and my BMX riding gloves. And under no circumstances a second layer, especially if it had a hood. Libra explained in depth how a hood could be pulled over my head and used to blind me as my assailant, or worse, multiple assailants, held it like a leash while they pummeled me to death—how the biggest mistake anyone ever made in a fight was how they dressed for it, because they could lose the fight before the first punch was even thrown. Dress for success she said, and Libra knew from experience.

Libra could brawl with the best of them. She was the only white girl in our school to ever successfully fight a black girl. And not just a onetime fluke mind you, but twice. What's more? Normally, if a white kid in our school were to gather enough courage up to fight a black kid, they would inevitably be attacked sooner than later by an angry mob of black kids in the main lunch room to serve as a warning to the other white kids that resistance was futile. Of course none of his white friends would intervene on his behalf during the ten on one ass- whooping, and thus, the kid would be pummeled by every member of the 'hood until the teachers arrived. Libra, on the other hand, was never accosted by the roving gangs after her cat fights, for most of the girls that would have led the posse either knew Libra from sports, or as a child from the YMCA after school and summer programs. Regardless of who knew her from where, everyone knew Libra wouldn't wait for the teachers in the fetal position, weeping against the lockers, and that at least the first wave of weaved wigs had a legitimate shot at being knocked out. And truth be told, even in the 'hood', gold fronts weren't cheap.

I walked into the bathroom, took a leak, soaked my head under the bathtub faucet, brushed my hair back quickly, walked back to my room, and quickly got dressed. Not only did I tie my laces extra tight, but I triple knotted them as well, as per Libra's detailed instructions. A quick glance in my full length door mirror showed me someone I didn't want to ever meet, let alone become, and I quickly opened the door before I had to make formal greetings. I walked briskly to the kitchen for some much needed chow, where an empty bowl and spoon awaited me on the table next to a wide array of cereals to choose from. A glass of orange juice was waiting for me in my mother's hand.

"Sounds like today will be fun and exciting!" Mom said in her super cheery morning tone.

"Excited can't touch the surface on how I'm feeling," I replied sarcastically.

"Hey, you don't sound like a guy who's about to hang-out with his super cool and super popular sister all day! You know who she can introduce you to at the track?"

"No, I know... It should be awesome," I replied with slightly more enthusiasm.

"Your sis says you're not to eat too much, because you can't have a full belly when you're performing strenuous activities. So I've put out a fine selection of cereals for you to choose from." My mom's glow in the morning kitchen was always infectious, even in the most darkest of times, for which today had certainly qualified.

"Thanks Mom. You're the best."

"You're the best, Baby."

I picked my selection, poured them out, and began to eat. I was famished. My body and brain clearly needed the nourishment, and with today's journey still ahead of me, I gladly filled my belly to the brim.

"Hey there Partner, don't eat too much. Libra doesn't want you doubled over due to a full stomach. Coach's orders."

"Every time my mother brought up today's events in complete ignorant bliss, I felt a knife of deceit stab me in the throat. I deserved it, for my mother was fueling me to fight, completely unaware of her role in my crimes. And I knew she'd rather choke to death on that cereal than feed it to me, if she knew it was assisting me in hurting someone.

"You're right. I'd better get warming up on the bike before Libra comes out and starts barking orders."

"By the way, Mister. New rules in the Sidoruk household as of this morning. No biking up at Wilder's Woods. No nothing up there for that matter until further notice."

"Why?" I asked too fast.

"Well, there's been some really bad things happening up there as of late and I don't want you anywhere near it," Mom said with great concern.

"Like what?" I asked.

"Like boys getting in to trouble. Bad boys, doing bad things." Mom stared at me all too knowingly.

"What kind of bad things, Momma?" I asked in my most innocent of voices.

"Like hurting each other and the woods."

"Sounds scary," I said.

"Rumor has it there's a satanic cult in the woods as well, and it could be related to that horrific murder in Smithtown over the spring. Parents are going to hold a meeting on it this Wednesday at the Donaldson's to discuss what we can do."

Adults? Discussing the happenings in The Woods? They'll ruin everything! I've really destroyed The Woods for good. Fighting over a piece of land that the tide was about to take out was what this amounted to. We were shoveling sand against the tide and there was a full moon tide coming in three days and the beach was never going to look the same. Better to burn out than fade away.

"You got it Mom. Maybe I'll do one last ride through it this morning before I go with Libra to the track. Should be alright in the daylight."

"Well, maybe one last ride. But don't go in alone. Are you talking with Jim again? Mrs. Kreagan said you guys had another issue. Do I need to address something with her?"

"No, we made up. Matter of fact, maybe I'll ask him to escort me and Christian into The Woods. Heck, I'll have the whole neighborhood watch my back if it makes you happy," I said, feeling disgusted with myself as I finished a lie that could implicate my own mother should the shit hit the fan. *Surely she'd take the guilt to the grave and I knew it as I said it. How low could I sink, before I drowned in my own filth?* Suddenly I felt sick to my stomach and the light breakfast felt like a bowling ball. I rose from my seat, hands holding me steady on the kitchen table's top. "I'd better get moving. Libra's in playoff mode."

"She sure is. I haven't seen her this amped in quite some time. She loves you dearly you know," my mother's voice rising slightly to emphasize the question of her love in my own soul, but I knew Libra's love was true.

"I know," I said with conviction. "Leebs love me, that's for sure. I'm just not sure if that love is justified."

"Don't you ever say that!" My mom erupted as if I said I was the one running the cult in The Woods.

I jumped back in shock of her tone, and she noticed how startled I was. Deciding to dial back her zeal, "She loves you, because you're the best brother God could have given her. She just sometimes has trouble expressing it, but she always knows it." My mother winked at me and turned to the counter to busy herself with cleaning a spotless counter.

"Thanks," I picked up my bowl and glass and began to walk towards the sink.

"Don't bother cleaning up, Honey. I got it," Mother said without looking up.

I deposited the items in the sink and walked over and hugged her from behind. "Thanks Mommy, you're the best mom ever."

She held tight to my hands, raised her head and exhaled deeply. "Promise you'll be smart in the woods."

"What?" I blurted.

"Promise me," she repeated.

"Promise that I'll be smart?"

"Yes. I know you'll go there and I know there's trouble there.

I need to know you'll be smart when you're there. Promise me you'll be smart," she said again, this time with more conviction.

"I will Momma. I'll be smart about it." I kissed her on the back and pulled my arms from her grasp. She reluctantly let me go, *maybe more symbolic than I knew at the time.* I walked out the front door with purpose and jumped the three steps that comprised my front stoop in one fluid motion, sticking the landing like a cat on a fence post. I surveyed the front yard, quiet except for the cicadas and the occasional bird chirp, a warm weak breeze blew in over the tree tops. It was a day reserved for weddings and funerals. I wasn't getting married to Gwen any time soon, so the picturesque scene was oddly ominous.

"Fixed the crank shaft."

I turned abruptly to my left. My father stood holding my bike up by the handle bars. How long had he been watching me? "You look good. Strong," my dad offered a tight smile as he flexed his free arm at the bicep.

I looked myself over and back to him, "Thanks, Dad. I needed the bike in optimal condition for today's excursion."

"I heard you're going with your sister to the track and meeting the athletes," my dad looked me over again approvingly.

"Yeah, I'm just going to ride around while she sprints a marathon and cools down on the blocking sled."

"She practices like she plays. You should take a valuable lesson from her on how she lives her life."

"We're different people Dad."

"I'm not saying you need to be your sister, or even live your life like her. I'm saying you can take lessons on life from her.

There's a difference."

"What's the difference?" I asked sadly.

My father closed his eyes to assist him in a deep breath before he continued, "You... You're you. Be you. Swing for the fences."

"I'm not playing ball today."

"Forget playing games, I'm talking about life and to a lesser extent, death. Whatever it is. Swing for the fences. Whether it be games, work, school, girls, fights... Whatever it is. Swing as if you'll never strike, or ground out. Forget the fans, the other team, the gravity of the situation... be in the moment and take it."

"OK," was all I could answer back on such heavy and unexpected advice. *What did he know? What did he suspect?* My father was literally brilliant and at times appeared all knowing. Walter Sidoruk was the textbook definition of "Old School", born in the Great Depression, raised in a tough neighborhood in Brooklyn, where his father beat him like an egg every time a dog barked, Walter knew pain and preservation. Him simply standing before me in middle class suburbia with a house, an important job, and all his teeth, real or fake, was a testament to his fortitude.

He edged the bike closer to me, "Take your bike and get ready." I walked up and grabbed the handle bar and began to pull it away without looking up, but his hand held fast, the bike moved not an inch. "I said take the bike," my father leveled.

"I'm trying," I said without looking up.

"You're trying?" he said surprised.

"Yes. But you're not letting go," I pulled again, as I said it, this time with a little more force.

"Take it like you own it. Like you're taking a pitch with the game on the line."

"What?"

"Swing boy. Swing for the fences." Looking down I could see his grip tighten on the handle bar, muscles within muscles restricted over his chiseled forearm. I, in turn, took both hands, doubling down on the bars on either side of his hand and gripped down until I could see the whites of my knuckles. I looked up to see if he had even noticed me getting ready, only to see his eyes were on fire, as if he were watching a volcano erupt at its base. I stared into his eyes, as he slowly nodded his chin. I yanked with every fiber of my being. Violently pivoting my body in a reverse baseball swing caused the bike and the attached parent to lurch forward. My father, clearly not anticipating the sheer magnitude of torque a sub 100-pound human could generate, was not properly balanced for a counter weight and lunged clumsily forward to his knees as his glasses flew off his face to the pebble covered driveway. Using his free hand, he tried in vain to grab the glasses before they skidded across the stones and thus had to use the hand that previously held the bike to stop himself from hitting the driveway face first.

The instant loss of a counter weight made the bike feel like a surprisingly empty cardboard box in my hands and it flew over my right shoulder as I stumbled backwards to the ground. As I fell, I calculated the arc of the throw and knew my life would soon end after the bike had landed, for the bike flew true and hit my father's car's hood, bouncing once before smashing in to the windshield. A massive spider's web instantly formed before my fall was complete. By the time my head hit the pebbles I knew the day and my life was going to make the windshield look good. I craned my neck to get one last look at my father before his shoe crushed my head like a grape in hopes of pleading for my life. But to my surprise, he was still on his knees with his one arm holding him up as he searched for his glasses. Quickly finding them, he hastily put them on after a quick clean from his sweat soaked t-shirt. He then pushed himself up as he reviewed the damage, resting on the back on his knees as if he was staring at the surf after swinging across the sound. While gazing upon the damage, obviously debating on whether to kill me here or somewhere more private, my mom flew out the door to settle his internal debate.

"Walter?!?!" She yelled. "Trel!!! What the fuck!!!" She ran and slid to me like I was first base. "What have you done to my son you fucking bastard! I'll kill you before the cops get here!" Her fist pumped tight and forbidding.

My father did not answer, but stayed fixated on the windshield and the costly damage to the hood. "I adjusted his bike and swing," and with that he smiled broadly.

"You what?" my mom exasperatedly asked.

"Car's a piece of shit. Kid's a keeper." And with that he pushed himself up more gingerly than his voice would lead to believe, his knees were pocked full of pebbles and dripping heavy with blood, which he apparently didn't notice.

"You're bleeding Walter," my mom said surprised.

"Luckily I'm wearing shorts," he said. Walking over to the car, he gently removed the bike from the windshield and propped it up with the kickstand, inspecting it one last time. I was propped on my side by my good arm, and my mother still knelt by my side, clearly unsure of whether my father had lost his mind. "Bike looks no less for the wear." Turning to me, "Go ahead, give it a spin." I got up without taking my mother's outstretched hand and walked over to the bike, made quick eye contact with my dad, and hopped on.

Tightening my hands on the bars, I commented on the setup, "Seats a good height." I looked to my mom who still knelt on the driveway. "Love you guys. Thanks Dad." And with the informal farewell, I began to pedal with the force of nature.

I was biking up and down the street effortlessly when Kring approached on his bike, looking as if he'd seen a ghost, "Holy shit! Did they attack you guys last night?"

"What are you talking about?" I asked.

"Your dad's car! It's destroyed!" Kring proclaimed excitedly.

"Oh no, my dad and me did that."

"You who?"

"My dad wanted to get me pumped up for the day," I said absently.

"Your whole family is nuts. I'm sorry."

"It's cool," I said with a smile.

"What's the plan?"

"The plan? Oh that's right, we haven't spoken in quite some time, have we?"

"Seems like ages. I've been on lockdown," Kring admitted.

"We're going to war," I said with cavalier flair.

"We're going where?" Kring asked befuddled.

"War. We're going to war."

"When, where, who, how?" Kring's question cadence quickened with each word.

"In fifteen minutes or so. Wilder's Woods. I'm not sure who will be there outside of Jim, Sean, Leebs and myself."

"What?!?!?" Kring yelled.

"You heard me."

"How did this all go to crap? I leave you to your own devices for twenty four hours and you completely fuck us into a hole! I'm not surprised."

"What hole?"

"What hole? Libra knows about this? Libra! Your sister knows what happened up there and now she's our last line of defense against an enemy we're 100% oblivious to?" Kring summed up with disgust.

"Well, 100% is a slight exaggeration. We've seen at least six of them and I've also found out that the majority of them are in fact devil worshipers and ex-convicts."

"Pardon?"

"Yeah, so Derek ran a cult, and that cult happened to worship the devil of all things... Silly right? And apparently that's a big thing with criminals and drug addicts. Hell. Go figure..."

"Are you fucking with me right now?"

"I wish. Anyway, we're supposed to get there early so we can get a jump on them, because we're thinking we'll be short on numbers."

"When were you going to tell me what the deal was?"

"I was told not to include you, because of your age."

"My age? You're old enough to go to war?"

"Well, I don't have much of a choice, but even though I'm going, I'm still forbidden to fight."

"Why you going then?"

"Moral support?" I questioned.

"Moral support... What happened to your face?"

"I got into a fight with Leebs."

"When?"

"Yesterday."

"Your sister know everything?"

"Yes."

"Including what I did?"

"To some extent, but trust me, she's focused squarely on me."

"Does she know the guys we have beef with?"

"Yes. She's the one that told me about Derek being a devil worshiper."

"You said Sean and Jim are fighting too? Do they know what they're getting into?" Kring asked.

"Yes. Turns out Derek's got more enemies than just us. Jim had a beef with him and now Sean does as well."

"Chance we'll have some backup?"

"Good chance actually. Jim was going to do his best to galvanize the block, Leebs was going to recruit from the high school and Gwen was going to ask anyone she knew."

Clearly confused at the pace of developments, Kring shot out. "You spoke to Gwen? When?!?"

"Yesterday."

"Where?"

"In Brady's backyard."

"How?"

"Leebs set it up?"

"Libra knows about Gwen?"

"Yes."

"Does she know what Derek tried to do to Gwen?"

"Yes."

"Does she know you're in love with Gwen?"

"Yes," I said somewhat surprisingly easily.

"Does she know Gwen is... Holy crap! How could you not tell me all this? How could you leave me in the dark?!?!" Kring was frothing at the mouth as he spat distaste and distrust.

"I'm sorry. I was trying to protect you..."

Kring cut me off, "It's not your call! Not your right! This is my fight, just as much as it's yours!"

"You're right... I screwed up," I admitted all too easily.

"You're damn right, I'm right!" Kring clarified.

"So, what now? I can't let you come. And I swore to not tell you. Which means I've already broken the first promise by telling you..."

Cutting me short again, "Like Hell you can't. I don't answer to you! You're not my daddy!" Kring snapped.

"No I'm not."

"But your dad would never forgive your best friend if he allowed you to walk in harm's way," Libra said from behind.

Kring and I jumped as we darted looks to the side. We hadn't even noticed her approach. *Wow, I really needed to get my head in the game, or I'd lose it soon enough.*

"Don't sneak up on us like that Leebs!" I yelled a whisper.

"Sneak up? How about I just walked down the middle of the street?" Libra said as she turned and swept her hand to show us the wide berth she was afforded in her approach. "Christian. You can't come and it's not a debate. You're too young."

"But it's not fair! I'm a big piece of this pie! None of this would have gone down if it weren't for me. I deserve to be there!" Kring pleaded.

"I don't doubt that. But now's not the time to be thinking of yourself. Things are about to get serious. People are going to get hurt, possibly go to the hospital or worse, die."

"Then why let your brother fight?" Kring asked.

"He's not going to fight. He's going to run once this goes down. I'm fighting in his place."

"You're fighting guys?"

"Sure, why not? Personally, I'd rather fight two white guys from the suburbs at the same time, regardless of how bad they are, than one Sister from the hood any day of the week."

"I never said I'd run," I said somewhat embarrassed for Kring to hear my imposed escape plans.

"At least you'll be there," Kring shot back.

"No time to debate, looks like we've got company," Libra said as she looked down the road. Jim and Sean were walking up the street with the Floyd brothers on either side. A quick scan of the landscape made the approach of Bishop and Roy Culver from their lawn easily enough to spot.

"We'll have reinforcements in The Woods," Libra added.

"How many?" I asked.

"Well, I told the football and lacrosse teams what the deal was."

"What about the soccer and baseball teams?" I inquired.

"It's a fight, not a function."

"Dad played baseball," I replied somewhat defensively.

Dismissing my blabber, Libra couldn't contain her disdain, "Hopefully your girl spread the word with as much zeal as she spreads everything else."

"That's cheap," I snapped.

"Sorry, but after this is all over, she's gonna answer for what she did to you."

"She didn't do anything to me for the last time!"

"Kissing a child is child molestation, and I don't care how beautiful, or rich you are."

"Wait, Gwen kissed you! What?!?!" When the fuck…"

"Oh, you didn't hear?" Libra asked Kring mocking shock.

"Libra, you promised!"

"Hold on Bro-ham. I had no idea you didn't tell your best friend you made out with one of the prettiest girls in town, who's also by the way, old enough to be your babysitter."

"You made out with Gwen? When?!?"

"We kissed. That's it. We didn't suck face."

"When? I demand answers!" Kring was hot.

"Some that night and then yesterday she kissed me when we met."

"Are you fucking with me again? Is this all a joke? Is there really a fight in The Woods about to take place? Am I being punked?"

"Nope. Your best friend is a freak stud. He landed Gwendoline Chandler, private school aristocrat, part-time model, and full time ho-bag."

"She models?" Kring asked completely shocked.

"Part time," Libra quickly added. "And she has the nerve to

model teen athletic wear, even though she couldn't make my travel team. Can you believe that shit?" Libra said shaking her head.

"No," Kring said shaking his head. "I literally cannot believe any of this, including what I've seen firsthand. Forget about the stuff you're making up."

"She models?" I asked if it was the only thing I heard the entire morning.

"Oh yeah. You're the bomb Little Brother. You'll be legend someday."

"I will?" I said surprisingly.

"The sad part, is that's it's all downhill from here. There aren't many Gwendoline Chandlers walking the earth, and out of that handful, none of the others are going to be giving you the time of day." My face looked obviously more hurt than I probably knew it to be and therefore Libra added, "At least for the foreseeable future. I'm sure when you're old enough to kiss a girl, you'll do so." Resting her hand on my shoulder and smiling warmly at my busted face, "I'll even help you get a girl of the appropriate age."

"Thanks for the pep-talk Leebs. Kring, let's take a bike ride and chat a quick sec, before I got to go."

Kring looked at me, then to Libra, then to the parties arriving. "Fine."

We biked up the short hill that separated Upper and Lower La Rue and spoke while we pedaled. Kring was first... "I cannot believe you're about to turn your back on us. We started this together and we need to finish it together."

"You're right."

"I'm right? Then what you're doing is wrong."

"You're right."

"You keep saying that, which makes you a complete dick."

"True. But hear me out."

"I'm not hearing your babbling nonsense. I'm pissed."

I stopped pedaling, stopping on the side of the road, "Listen! There's no time to relive all my fuckups over the last seventy-two hours, nor yours for that matter. But what we can do, is make sure we don't fuck up any further."

Kring had stopped a little in front of me, but did not turn to face me, "Go on..."

"Ride like the wind to your house. Grab the remainder of your fireworks and setup shop a good, healthy distance from anywhere. I imagine this will go down west of the pass in the big clearing."

"A little south of their camp," Kring thoughtfully added.

"Exactly. Wait there. You'll have to move quickly, because you'll have to don full day camo, have a full weapons load and be in position before even we're setup at 9am. That gives you fifteen minutes."

"That's insane!"

"So is wanting to be there in the first place."

"True."

"You only have to promise me three things," I said knowingly.

"What?" Kring asked begrudgingly as he maneuvered his bike around to face me.

"You're not to launch Rocket One until it's an all-out slug fest."

"Fair enough. What else?"

"You're to get the hell out of there as soon as you light the fuse." I held up a finger to make my point and to ensure there would be no counterpoint.

"Fine. And the third?" Kring asked reluctantly.

"You run and tell our parents."

"Our parents?"

"Yes. Tell them to call the police and that our lives are in grave danger."

"We'll be dead if I tell."

"We'll be dead if you don't. Promise me, or the deal's off."

"Promise."

"Godspeed," I said to Kring's back as he bolted on his bike. I biked back to the small crowd at the base of the hill next to the entrance of Wilder's Woods.

Sean looked to me, "Christian shot by without so much as a hello. Is he cool?"

"He's good," I assured the troops.

I nodded to the rest. I could sense the excitement. Sharp smells of sweat and fear tainted the warm wind's pine-laden fragrance. War's smell was more than the gun's powder and the blood's iron, it was the collective smells, which saturated the sense and soiled the soul.

"For Christ's sake, did they do that to you?" Franky asked.

I looked to Libra and smiled, "No. Sibling rivalry."

"Gee whiz Libra, save some for the Satan worshippers," Bishop barked half-jokingly.

"Got to toughen him up," Libra said as she looked me over once again.

"What brings you to our... Impromptu football game?" Jim said to Libra with absolutely zero believability.

"Save it, Kreagan. I know what went down. I'm here on my brother's behalf and talking about what needs to be done is a waste of time."

"Libra, no one here doubts your uncanny abilities in the world of mixed martial arts, but this is a guy thing," Franky said in order to reason.

"Thanks Franky, you're a true gentleman, as always. Make sure you watch my back when I'm kicking someone's balls across the forest," Libra winked at me as she high-fived Franky.

The rest of the guys remained perfectly still, outside of several hands slowly moving towards the fronts of zippers. Two cars slowly approached from the south, filled with big heads.

"Holy shit! They're early and we're outnumbered," Bishop blurted.

"Relax, that's my boys," Libra said annoyed.

"Your boys? That's Chad Lassen and... Is that Todd McShey?" Sean asked bewildered.

"Those are them." Libra said with a smile.

The first car pulled up. Two in the front, three in the back. Massive hulks of flesh. The car held the first string Varsity offensive line.

"Hey there Beautiful," the driver said.

"Hey Chaddy," Libra's smile was warm, as if she was greeting him in an outdoor arboretum.

The passenger and left guard for the Huntington Blue Devils, Todd McShey leaned over, "Where we parking? I got to take a leak!"

"Get off me you animal!" Chad barked.

"Sorry. Where?"

"Right over there. And tell your boys to be quick about it. We need to get in The Woods, before someone spots us," Libra conveyed curtly.

"You got it my Lady!" Chad said as he motivated his '73 Impala to the curb. They were quickly followed by a beat up old Cadillac Brougham that was stuffed with enough humans to make a circus clown envious. The looks on the remaining faces were far more dire than Chad or Todd would have led us to believe the situation to be, which added visual stress lines to my comrades' already creased craniums. The boys got out quickly and kept their collective heads on pivots, surveying the surrounding landscape as they approached our group.

Sean was the first to speak, "Had no idea the offense would show?"

"That's odd, because it's usually the defense that doesn't show come game time," Todd tallied.

Sean took his hand wholeheartedly, "I'll let that go, considering the circumstances." Handshakes went around and I received more than my fair share of looks, as did Roy.

Libra addressed the situation before it spiraled out of control, "Derek tried to kill my brother and he's got to be here, and that's that."

One of the other guys from the second car spoke up, "Just keep him back. No need for him to get in the middle of this."

"Point taken. Shall we?" Libra offered as she gracefully swept her arm to the entrance of The Woods.

It was the first time I noticed the weapons. Brass knuckles were already on two of the boys and one held a small, thin bat, while another twirled a tire-iron like a baton. Something with a metal handle wrapped in weathered duct tape protruded from another boy's belt line and then everything started moving too quickly to process. We were walking briskly for The Woods in order to avoid detection, and thus the time for talk had ended. In total, we numbered twenty. Twelve hired guns and the nucleus of Lower La Rue. Jim walked by as I took in the empty stares.

"Where's Kurt?" I inquired.

"Kurt? Oh, he's at some religious function, or something to that nature."

"He knows?" I asked.

"No. I didn't get to him yesterday, just his mother. I asked if he could go fishing this morning and she said he'd be at some religious thingy majigy. Sounded like bullshit."

"Oh..." was all I could respond with before Jim moved up to talk to Bishop in hushed tones.

I looked in my sister's direction to say something that would tame the wild butterflies banging against the walls of my stomach, but she seemed to be taking joy in her stroll with Todd and Chad. Roy walked up to my right, clearly as nervous as I, "You ready?"

"I guess..."

"I'm scared," Roy admitted under his breath.

"Me too," I answered honestly.

"We could leave you know, and no one would say jack," Roy reasoned.

"I'm sure they wouldn't, but my sister is here now, on my behalf might I add, and from what I've heard, your brother is here on your behalf as well, so I don't think turning tail is really an option."

"I guess you're right. Still it's an option," Roy announced again.

"But not really. Not for me at least. Besides, we're not supposed to throw."

"What are we supposed to do then? Cheer?" Roy asked incredulously.

"Well, we do have half the football team here. Maybe we could make some pompoms out of pricker bushes."

"You seem to be handling this well," Roy stated somewhat annoyed.

"Truth be told, I'm a complete mess. But me running isn't going to help boost morale. Better give the troops something to fight for. I leave and so does their reason to fight."

"Don't lie to yourself. Those guys are here for your sister," Roy chided.

"No doubt. But I'm their lie. All good stories need one," I answered.

"You're a lie?" Roy asked.

"Sure. Admitting you got your ass kicked, or seriously hurt another person on behalf of a piece of ass makes you look like a fool at best. But give someone a noble fight and men will travel half the globe to kill another's God."

"You're quite the philosopher these days."

"I think it was Pluto that said it," I remarked.

"You take your lessons on life from a fucking dog?" Roy asked stunned.

"Not the cartoon character—the philosopher Pluto," I responded half annoyed.

"There's a guy named after a dog and you're taking advice from him?"

"I think he was named after the planet..." I said absently.

"There's a planet named after Pluto?"

"What? I'm not sure who said it. It doesn't much matter. We're here."

Chapter 20
Out Manned and Outmaneuvered

We had walked to the center clearing and guys were spreading out a couple of feet from each other. I had no idea the proper fighting circumference needed, nor the proper fighting stance for that matter, so I took position behind and off to the side of my sister who stood between Chad and Todd. Sean walked along the perimeter speaking privately with each man, most likely giving last minute pep talks and tactics. Jim looked lost and quickly glanced at the other boys in an effort to better understand what to do as well. Some of the older boys air-boxed while one or two high fived each other and/or bumped chests to apparently signify game readiness. Libra stood for the most part motionless. Arms down and fists clenched. Todd and Chad whispered in her ears from each side occasionally. Most likely sweet nothings that varied to their final bill on the war effort, to what they would do during the war to justify the steep cost. Libra looked like a tightly wound spring ready to unload on either of the two meatloafs standing next to her if the enemy feared to show.

But show they did. Within seconds, The Woods were alive. Where birds chirped and chipmunks frolicked, now boots stomped and boys cackled. And not just boys, for as the figures moved from behind the trees, young men with angry expressions appeared. More often than not, the man had a three-day old shave that needed attending to and tattoos of strange events woven down his finely chiseled arms. As the men came closer, scars of battles, most likely more serious than the current, came to view on their faces. One wore an eye patch with a skull and cross bones. Some smiled, most of which were missing teeth.

Our mercenaries, though big for boys, were in fact just that, boys. The average age was sixteen, and outside of the offensive line and Sean, not many were bigger than Bishop. No doubt feared in the hallways of high school, but not in the hallways of the state penitentiary. Not only were we out manned physically, but numerically as well. We were twenty strong, but the enemy had closer to thirty. If you took my sister, Roy, and myself out of the mix, we were looking at almost 2:1 odds. Not good, considering most of the enemy soldiers appeared to be carrying weapons, except for maybe two or three. Out manned and out gunned, my breakfast was trying to find a backdoor faster than I.

I was behind the line by a couple of feet, but when the enemy walked towards us, I couldn't help but notice our entire line step back a pace and assume a defensive position. So much for our grandiose plans of outnumbering and bull rushing an unsuspecting army of weak drug addicts and wannabe punk rockers. We were in a fight every person on our side knew couldn't be won and another step back from our side confirmed my worst fears. We were about to turn tail and run like bitches. Not a word was spoken, but I could feel the screams of terror inside each person, with only Libra's body language cloaking dread.

"Shit," was all I heard from Sean under his breath.

And as I heard the silent cries of fear from our side, so in turn did the other side. Hardened criminals are like any other animal. A good criminal can weed through the crowds and find the weakest link, just like a pride of lions can locate the wounded calf in a herd of gazelles. We were the prey and they were the predators, meaning Roy and I were the first likely targets. I could easily enough outrun my portly pal, but would one trophy be enough for this group? Likely not. Sean would probably take the brunt, for he had to show some honor for his family's namesake. Though no one yet knew of what had happened to his brother, sooner or later word would leak out, and he'd be shunned for running and leaving others to take the beating for his family. As for my chances of survival, I couldn't leave Libra's side, for she had committed twelve strangers to my cause, and in doing so, thirteen years of hard fought street cred.

As if she could hear my thoughts, Libra turned with red rimmed eyes, "As soon as this starts, you're to run. Run home and get Dad."

With that, the first voice from the other side sized us up and struck us down, "Looks like we're fighting the football team!"

And then the chorus of taunts commenced, "Is that number 87 there? You're a big boy 87! You offense or defense boy?"

No one answered.

"You gonna sack me 87?"

"Look at the two big boys next to the bitch! You gonna block for her? Who's blocking me?"

With every jab to our side, the other side moved another foot closer. I heard commotion to my left and saw one of our guys stumble back and trip over a log.

"Hey, you OK little man? Don't die before I get there!" Laughter ensued and the men advanced at almost a leisurely pace.

The one who had called my sister a bitch walked ahead of the others. He was as stacked as my father—6' 6", 220 and less than 8%

body fat. He was even bald like my dad, but he was much younger and most likely shaved his head to showcase his tattoo that looked like a demon of sorts stabbing itself with a large sword that was aflame. He donned a tight white tank top that was half tucked into his painted on, dirty jeans that were covered at the bottom by impossibly large, black boots. His arms were the size of my legs and nothing was going to stop him from killing us all.

"Hey Bitch, come to see the show? Maybe we can turn this into a dinner and a movie?" Todd and the other useless fuck next to him did nothing but touch Libra's arms, as if his vicious verbal assaults would somehow be lessened by their emotional support.

"You hurt my brother!" Libra screamed as she bolted for the man. Todd and his pussy bitch of a friend grabbed at Libra as if she was a dog escaping from a screen door towards an unsuspecting postal worker, but did not pursue once she cleared their outstretched arms. The chiseled and tattooed man's facial expression went from stunned to smug, as the opportunity to degrade a woman in front of her fearful friends presented itself to him with little to no effort.

I began to run after Libra as fast as my decimated body would allow on instinct alone, lacking both a game plan and the ability to actualize anything remotely worth executing. My masquerade of manliness was muted by Libra's shape shifting speed. Three times faster than I'd ever be, in addition to having the jump on me, Libra was upon the giant before I left the starting gate. Libra closed the distance at such an unfathomable speed that the giant barely had enough time to stick his chin out for her to hit.

At four feet away Libra sprang into the air and at 5' 7" had almost a full foot to leap vertically before she was eye level with the bastard. The fact that when her fist connected with his face, she was a good foot above him, showcased her Amazonian athletic abilities. The hit was true, with the immediate damage of the impact as self-evident as the rights afforded a U.S. citizen under the Constitution. Libra punched like my father, and at that moment, I realized she was the only person on our side to have fought a man of the giant's girth, for she had in fact fought my father. She hadn't won the war by a long shot, but she was successful in their latest battle. My father hadn't hit us since his last fight with Libra in the spring.

He had beaten her for getting loud with my mom, after lying about going out with her friends. Unlike prior altercations, Libra wouldn't back down and when my father came into her room for her formal punishment, she refused to take it lying down. He hurt her bad to make a point. Real bad... We had to take her out of school and tell people that my dad took us away on a surprise work vacation. We didn't go far, just New Jersey, and we didn't stay at a resort, just a cheap motel on the side of the highway. My mom took us to plenty of places and took plenty of pictures, but they were always of my sister's left side, for her right looked like mine did now. The punch was thus for two men. One for the bastard that stood before her now and one for the bastard currently standing in her kitchen. The power used in the swing was equal to that of two punches as well. Each powerful enough to crush a man's face, ere go the sound that her fist made when it connected with the tattooed man's jaw.

Stumbling back several feet, the man looked drunk and somewhat disinterested in my sister and the entire scene, for he momentarily gazed off into the distance towards the Culvers' backyard and began to blink heavily, as if he were desperately trying to remember why he'd called her over in the first place. Libra's inertia had carried her several feet past the giant, where she stuck the landing like an Olympic gymnast and immediately spun to face her dazed foe. Setting her legs, bent at the knees, shoulder width apart, loaded her frame for maximum torque within the short delivery window. Without hesitation, Libra stepped back a foot and screamed, "DIE!"

Libra's legs were granite. The same length as Gwen's, but twice as thick. She'd once scored a goal, filling in as a goalie from her own goal. So when she lined up and kicked what looked like an eighty-five yard field goal attempt into the crotch of the tattooed man, the ending was all too predictable. The jeans were tight. Ball tight. And thus there was nowhere for the man's balls to go, but up. And up they went, for before he fell, I could swear I saw them hit the insides of his cheeks. Dropping like a dead branch in a windstorm, the tattooed man fell to the ground cupping what was left of his sack. Libra stepped back a couple of feet, no one else moved. The man shook as if he had a high fever, his eyes rolled back white, as if he was possessed. He moved one of his hands off his package to put up in a vain attempt to block my sister's next lethal shot and it was blood red... As were his jeans... The simultaneous yelp of fifty males is something I will never forget.

Libra surveyed the battlefield, vehemently voicing violence, "You're a bunch of child abusers and rapists! I'm a girl, come get some!"

Some of the men looked at each other, and more than one turned and walked. Most likely because they were in fact one, or both, and the reality of the situation meant the possibility of another arrest and a long hard block of time in the slammer. Still, others didn't waiver and began to advance. I was to my sister's side by the time the first group arrived. I heard movement along both lines.

"Ahhhhh!" A war scream deeper than a Viking King's erupted from the west. Huge men running not around trees, but through and over smaller ones, rapidly approached with long golden manes, attached to neckless tree trunks. Each slab of cement used appendages larger than my torso for motivation, with the largest closing in on seven feet and three hundred pounds. The largest of the three Thors, reached the first relatively large male in seconds, slamming him with a straight arm. Before the crumpled remains of the man hit the ground, he'd done a 540 in mid-air, landing sideways. Clearly incapacitated before the ground's impact, the life-size action figure had paid him no further heed and had already finished his second man off with a flying leg kick, before the first had hit the ground.

The line of drug addicts, thieves, and rapists had jumped back several feet and began to regroup, much to their dismay, as the second and third Thors arrived, looking to show up their big brother. The smallest, if you could call him that, dwarfed the largest of our group by three inches and twenty-five pounds. Gwen's brothers were something out of a Hitler youth propaganda film. Tall, huge, handsome, with stone set jawlines and hair thicker than a vault. All three were either in college playing Division One something, or highly recruited to do so. Blue eyes pierced the enemy lines looking for someone dumb enough to advance. Gwen followed seconds later, red faced, but not out of breath by a long shot.

Libra looked to her, "Bout time... Sis."

A couple of men whipped out their crudely crafted weapons and began to advance on her brothers in numbers.

"Derek tried to rape me!" Gwen yelled as she advanced to everyone's surprise. "Who among you are rapists?" She ran before her brothers. "Show yourselves!" she demanded. Her brothers, noticing the lethal weapons, got into defensive stances and surrounded Gwen, while the rest of our line wavered.

Sean, sensing something, moved up with a couple of our guys fanning out to either side, while Bishop quickly closed the gap on an angry man, as they both went through the prefight ceremony of air-boxing and juking. Sean and a man who seemed a little drunk began to dance, when Jim approached me with his fists pumped and arms bent like a boxer from the '30s. Looking ahead, a smile pierced his stoic stance, "Remember. Block the moon, be a God." And with that Jim called out his opponent. "Hey Kevin! Where you at bitch?! Kevin you faggot bitch! Everyone! Stop what you're doing!"

Since no one was technically in the middle of an actual fight, all eyes centered on Jim as he spun in circles demanding everyone's attention and Kevin's presence like a gladiator goading a slave on the floor of an arena.

"Kevin, you pussy bitch! Where you hiding?!?!" Kevin, momentarily confused, half ran to Jim, looking around for the hidden trap that Jim had surely laid.

A voice from behind Kevin cackled, "Hey, it's the cry baby with the ash hole for an asshole!" Laughter ensued. Kevin looked around to his party and raised his hands. "Looks like he liked it more than he let on. Back for more?" He asked Jim for all to hear.

"I'm here to settle this for everyone. Your friends are pussies, as are you. They're tough when they outnumber people, but let's face it, one on one you're all a bunch of bitches. I shouldn't have trouble with just you."

Kevin couldn't help but smile and shake his head. "You're nuts, but super." Looking to Sean for clarification, "Your brother gonna cheap shot me as I pummel you to death?"

Sean stared at Kevin and then looked to Jim. "I'll respect the challenge. My brother can fight his own battles."

"Oh yeah, is that why you're here? Because he's fighting his own battle?"

"You needed six guys the last time you had your way with him. Shows me he's got more than a chance," Sean said with more optimism than what was clearly warranted.

"Let's do it, Kreagan. This is going to hurt," Kevin said as he stalked to Jim with fists by his side.

"On one condition!" Jim yelled as he backed up slightly.

"A condition? Who is this asshole?"

"Don't you mean ash hole?" Someone yelled from the background, with subsequent laughter erupting from the inside joke.

"OK ash hole, what's your condition?"

"This fight decides who owns The Woods! Loser leaves for good!" Jim's voice was strong and righteous.

Kevin looked to his left and right, and then raised his hands in question, "Is that acceptable?" Some guys shook their heads, while others just raised their hands, or shrugged their shoulders in indifference. "You're gonna die. You know that right?" Kevin admonished almost not believing his good fortune of killing two birds with one stone.

"I'm not only going to kick your ass, I'm gonna literally kick the crap out of your ass!" Jim spat.

Jim's bold prediction was met with overzealous laughter from Kevin's friends.

"You're going to kick the crap out of me?" Kevin said somewhat stunned as he touched his chest.

"That's exactly what I said!"

"Actually, you said it like someone who's never kicked the crap out of anyone."

And with that Kevin quickly closed the distance to Jim and rocked Jim with a massive right hook, squared up perfectly on the side of Jim's giant block head. Jim never had a chance to stop the lightning strike from Kevin, for Jim had the coordination of someone in an infomercial and a head so large that it emasculated hot air balloons. But unlike a hot air balloon, Jim's head was anything but empty, or light for that matter. Instead of being filled with hot air, Jim's head was packed to the brim with heavy brain and bone. His nickname in our backyard sporting events was ROG, short for the Rock of Gibraltar, because he would inevitably have at least one bad play a day, due to the enormous size and weight of his head. This play though would end horribly for the opposition, for though Kevin was tough as nails, his fist wasn't made of concrete and when it hit Jim's concrete head, it shattered like porcelain. Jim of course didn't leave the exchange unscathed. He stumbled back several feet and partially fell, gaining a precarious foothold, by grasping a low hanging branch from a nearby tree. Kevin reeled in pain, but saw his opportunity to finish Jim plain as day, as Jim slowly blinked, apparently fixated on a nearby gopher hole. He also knew from years of scrapping that he was now down a hand and though it was surely enough to still best Jim, he wouldn't be able to defend himself if things went south after finishing him. Reluctantly releasing his hand, Kevin stalked to Jim and teed off with his left, connecting with Jim's head before Jim could even stand fully upright from the last wallop. This punch, like the last one, hit true on the side of Jim's head. The results were the same for both parties. Jim stumbled back, this time hitting the ground and rolling to his side, while Kevin buckled over in pain. Both his hands were now not just broken, but shattered. Jim momentarily got to his feet, but looked lost as he staggered through the forest thicket, like an old man stumbling through an isle of Toy's R Us on Black Friday with a Christmas list written out in Crayola by his five-year old grandson.

Eventually falling face first in the dirt, Jim struggled to his knees and addressed his foe, "What's wrong Bitch? You look like you're trying to pull down your pants! You want me to help you?"

Jim tried to spring from his kneeling position and almost fell again as he shook the cobwebs from his noggin. But got up he did, and as he advanced on his wounded opponent, Jim began to strut. "Let me help." Jim landed a massive open palmed slap to Kevin's jaw, jolting Kevin back. "Hey, where you going? Turn around." Jim took and landed an open handed windmill swing that caught Kevin squarely on the chops. Kevin spun sideways, but surprisingly stayed on his feet, like a puppet yanked by an angry master. Pausing briefly to admire his work, Jim got back to business and closed the distance between them, standing strong behind him. "Here you go Honey. Daddy's home!" And with that Jim yanked Kevin's pants to his ankles, sprang back to his feet and violently pushed Kevin at the shoulders, who quickly fell to the ground on his knees, with his back to Jim.

"Hey, looks like you're ready for me!" Jim looked up, triumphantly bellowing, as he measured the crowd's reaction like a gladiator panning to his adoring fans. "Hey, remember, payback's a bitch!" Turning slightly in my direction, Jim spoke softly, "Looks like it's time for a lunar eclipse."

Turning back to his sacrificial lamb, Jim took a step back, set his feet and punted his foot clear up Kevin's ass. A sharp snapping noise, similar to dry wood being split in the dead of winter emanated from Kevin's asshole, signaling the transformation from crack to crevasse. The haunting noise, accompanied by a high-pitched scream from Kevin, reverberated throughout the forest, triggering a flock of birds to explode from the canopy, and migrate south. The devastation was painfully obvious, as shit sprayed everywhere within a ten-foot blast pattern. Jim was covered head to toe in shit, as was all the surrounding vegetation. A second chorus of yelps erupted from the collective, as one didn't need a doctorate in proctology to know that Kevin's anus would never be the same. Kevin laid face down in the dirt crying without the help of breath. He was crippled for life and couldn't even turn around to defend himself from further insult and injury.

"What's that Kevin?" Jim yelled, holding his hand to his ear as if he was truly trying to hear Kevin's silent pleas. "You're attracted to me and that's why you wanted to see my ass in the first place? You now want me to do what?" Jim looked to Kevin's friends, "Your boy wants me to shove something up his ass? My dick is earmarked for the ladies, so I guess I'll use a branch! What do you think? You're friends with him; what do you think he'll like best?" The woods grew quiet.

Sean was upon Jim in short order. "It's over."

"Nothing's over! They scarred me for life! They tried to rape a girl and pissed on Chris! They're fucking animals!"

"I'm telling you it's over! Walk away. Now."

Jim looked at Sean, "But..." Tears were forming on his face.

"I came here to ensure your revenge, and you got it in spades."

"But they scarred me..."

"Trust me, Kevin will never be the same... Nor anyone that saw what just happened for that matter. I think he needs an ambulance."

"What?" Jim asked.

"I think he's bleeding worse than the guy that Libra robbed of his privates." Motioning his head to the man who remained still on the ground shaking slowly.

"My God...What have I done???" Jim sullenly said, as he snapped from his momentary psychosis, looking to the ground searching for something he'd never find.

"You heard the man!" Sean said loud and proud. "This settles matters and unless the remaining bunch of bitches wants to go to hospital with these two, I suggest you walk!" No one moved. Everyone was planted like statues, for whoever moved first was more often than not, on the losing end of a prolonged retreat and beating.

Then the fireworks erupted and mayhem began. Kring unloaded a salvo of bottle rockets tied together, carrying an ordinance of three M-80's. The resulting explosions along the enemy line was immediate and violent. Everyone ran holding their ears, and/or covering their eyes. Grown men screeched like little girls as they blindly bounced into trees and each other, botching a hasty withdrawal, while heavy smells of metal and burnt hair caused me to frantically check my person. The rockets continued to rain, following their retreat, perfectly timed and spaced to maximize both mental and physical duress. The enemy was gone in seconds, leaving only the two slain warriors to await the authorities.

"Shit, we got to split!" Someone yelled.

And with that, kids shot off left and right, many of whom were not even heading towards the cars. Sean looked to Jim, Libra and me, "Let's move!"

"My house!" Bishop yelled. My parents aren't home!" We all took off after Bishop through The Woods. I turned to locate Gwen before I left, but her brothers were high-tailing it out of The Woods with Gwen being pulled in tow as if she was the President and them her Secret Service.

Libra grabbed me by the arm, "Move!" I ran like the wind!

As we approached Bishop's, Kring fell in next to me stride for stride, "Enjoy the show?"

"A little over the top, but I won't ask for a refund," I managed to shoot between breaths.

"Move!" Libra yelled from behind, clearly annoyed at the fact that she had to run at half speed.

We all made it to Bishop's and ran behind his house, where we found the basement door partially opened. All the kids piled in like ants in a hole come high noon, while slamming the door shut, Bishop took a head count.

"We got everyone?" Sean demanded.

"Who's not here?" Freddy asked.

"Shut up!" Franky said.

"You OK?" Sean asked Jim.

With massive twin purple gourds protruding from either side of Jim's already huge head and sporting a peculiarly perplexing perpetual smile, Jim resembled a kind, jovial alien race from Star Trek.

"I'm fine. Never felt better," Jim answered seemingly in good spirits despite the obvious physical trauma.

"How about you Leebs?" I asked.

"I'm good."

"Holy crap Libra! You crushed his nuts!" Bishop barked.

"Who the fuck were those guys with that girl?" Roy asked.

"Gwen's brothers," I said.

"I knew I knew that girl!" Franky announced.

"She's hot!" Freddy chimed in.

"Yeah, I think I'm gonna ask her out when the dust settles," Franky proclaimed.

"You? Wait in line," Bishop boasted.

Sean looked to me, "Dream on. She's taken. Besides, we got a lot more pressing problems and they need to be addressed ASAP."

"Such as?" Jim asked.

"Such as the two guys that are lying in pools of their own urine and blood that we left in The Woods. The cops will be there soon, thanks to Mr. Grucci over there," pointing to Kring. "What were you doing there? You weren't supposed to even know it was going down. Who blew that?" Looking to me.

"It was me," I confirmed. "I blew it. I had no choice but to tell him."

"What's done is done," Libra stated. "Besides, Christian's diversion allowed both parties to separate in the end without any additional casualties."

The room grew quiet, for all knew what she said was true.

"Fine. But that still leaves us with two bodies," Sean looked around for answers to his observations.

"That actually leaves us four bodies now, if you include what happened a couple of days back," I said somewhat sheepishly. "They'll connect the bodies and the fireworks and the shit's gonna hit the fan," I continued.

"What the fuck are we going to do?" Franky asked aloud. "We look like the villains."

"Relax Franky," Sean snapped. "We don't look like villains. We look like scared kids. Three out of the four guys in those Woods are real villains, serving time behind bars."

Bishop chimed in, "I have no idea who the big bald guy is... or should I say was... now that he's a chick. But Derek and Kevin are both on probation, and will most likely go to jail for an extended period of time if they're connected to this."

"We need to get to the authorities before they get to us!" Freddy sprayed.

"You need to shut the fuck up and let the people with brains think," Franky spat as he backhanded Freddy upside the head. Freddy rubbed his head and sniffled quickly to hold back a quick cry.

"Enough Franky," Sean said. "We're all in this together."

"Everything we've done is in self-defense," Kring stated. The room grew quiet. "Henry peed on me, Derek tried to rape Gwen, that bald guy was going to hit Libra, and Kevin broke his own hands on Jim's head," Kring looked around the room.

"And you had enough T&T to invade Mexico on whose behalf?" Jim asked Kring.

"On your behalf... Neighbor." Kring's level stare was more than Jim was willing to commit to.

"Point well taken... Neighbor," Jim finally agreed.

The basement door shook from a pounding fist and everyone jumped.

"Cops!" More than one person whispered.

The basement window curtains were smartly closed prior to Bishop and Roy leaving their house for the brawl, so we couldn't see outside and they couldn't see inside.

"Quiet!" Sean whispered.

Again the pounding commenced.

"Trel! I know you're in there! Open the door!" Gwen's voice screamed.

"Open the door!" I yelled to Bishop.

"Shit!" Bishop hesitated and then opened the door with a foot blocking a full swing.

"Let us in!" A man's voice boomed.

"Shit!" Someone said behind me.

"It's OK. They're my brothers! Quick!" Gwen pleaded.

Bishop opened the door and three large men burst through the door followed by Gwen. All three had to hunch over due to the low ceiling. The room became tight quarters and the smell of sweat and stale damp basement air was suffocating.

"Which one of you is Trel?" Gwen's largest brother looked between Sean and Bishop, then to Franky.

"Here," I said.

The man looked over me, settling on Jim, "You're Trel?"

"No, I'm Trel," I said louder.

"You're Trel?" Her younger brother said astonished.

"I am," I confirmed.

"You're Trel?" The second brother added for clarification.

"In the flesh," I said halfheartedly.

All three brothers looked to Gwen for clarification as something clearly wasn't adding up and I knew all too well, that it was the sum which wasn't greater than the whole.

"He's the one," Gwen said, face as red as ever.

"He saved your life? This child?" Gwen's middle brother asked.

"He did," Gwen confirmed.

"You're in love with…"

Gwen's older brother hit his younger brother before he could finish his statement. "Long day… Sorry you had to do what you had to do. You must be traumatized. Our family is forever grateful for what you've done and sacrificed," Gwen's oldest brother said with great sincerity and speed.

"Kring here was instrumental in the operation," I said pointing back with my thumb to my brother in arms.

"You?" Gwen's brother asked beside himself. "Who's the third musketeer, an infant?" Gwen's oldest brother shot him a cool glance, but couldn't bring himself to offer a rebuttal.

"This went sideways quick. We need to think quicker than we've previously acted in haste," Gwen's oldest brother said in a fatherly tone. "I saw a second man down. Who was he?"

"A jerk," Libra said.

Gwen's youngest brother looked to Libra. "Libra? What are you doing here? I thought that was you?"

"Trel's my Brother."

"Wow! That would be cool if you..." Gwen's youngest brother stopped himself halfway through his thought and looked to the ground with the same red face as Gwen displayed from time to time.

"Well, no doubt he was a jerk, but who's responsible for his current condition?" Gwen's oldest brother asked.

"I am," Libra said.

"You?"

"Me."

Looking around to his brothers and then to the rest of us, "Remind me never to come between you and your brother when you're hashing out a sibling rivalry." Focusing back on me, the oldest brother did a double-take and pointed to my face, "Did Derek do that, or her?"

Pointing to Libra with a thumb, while using my other hand to air circle my wound, "This is all Leebs. Derek never got a shot off."

All three brothers first thought it a joke, but when the statement hit home as true, serious looks of concern settled on everyone.

"Oh... Alright then..." Looking back to his sister, the gravity of his sister's claim that the boy she loved had a sister who wanted to kill her finally registered, "Any ideas?"

"I'm going to the police and you're taking me," Gwen said.

"We're all going to the police," I said. "We're all in this together," I added.

"He's right. We all made this bed. We all own it," Sean added.

"So why don't we just call the cops and have them come to us?" Freddy asked.

"Can we use your house?" Bishop asked, "Because if my dad comes home and finds the cops here, I'll be in worse shape than the guys we left in The Woods."

"We're going home right now and calling the cops from our house," Gwen said looking to her brothers.

The brothers looked at each and then nodded in acquiescence.

"Fair's, fair," Gwen's oldest brother said. "Time to face the music."

"What if the cops see us on our way to your house?" Jim asked.

"No matter. But they won't. We have an old path through The Woods from our house to here," Gwen's middle brother proudly proclaimed.

"What?" Kring asked. "There's no trail. I've combed these Woods for years. I know it like the back of my hand."

"It's most likely overgrown by now, but we followed it here and it was still good enough to spot by eye..." Gwen's brother smiled as he defended his old turf.

"You can see for yourself," Gwen's oldest brother offered.

The gang looked around to gauge the others' reactions, and eventually we all made for the exit. Once out the backdoor, we took a brisk jog to the tree line at the Culver's backyard, where an old spice trail lay just yards within... *It was like following a wild game path!* How we missed it all these years was quite hilarious to us all, but as we approached Whitman Court, the gravity of the situation began to weigh heavily on my mind.

Stopping at the edge of the tree line before Gwen's yard, her oldest brother turned and spoke. "I'm going in to talk to our parents with Steven. Gwen and Sturgis will take you around back. Sturgis, please make sure our guests have something to drink, and if someone needs to go to the bathroom, I cleaned the cabana this morning and stocked it with paper goods."

We followed the siblings around back as the two older boys made their way inside. Once in the backyard, I realized just how poor we were.

The backyard was lavish and manicured like the gardens of the arboretum my mother dragged the family to from time to time on the weekends to listen to music without words. Their outside furniture was nicer and surely more expensive than our inside furniture and their granite pool could bathe my entire family tree at once. The only person I even knew with a pool was Kring and you had to pee in his to heat it. This one had steam rising from the top, fed from a massive, elevated Jacuzzi. The yard was anchored by a small thatched house that had a bar outside and several lounge chairs and umbrellas adorning the pool's intricately laid stone patio.

"The bathroom is in there if anyone needs it. I know I went in my pants earlier," Sturgis half joked.

"Thank you," I said absently as I tried to absorb the riches.

Gwen walked to my side. "You thirsty?"

"Yes," I looked at her longingly, wishing she'd quench my thirst with a wet kiss. But it was not going to happen, and if the trek back was any indication of our future relationship, this was the last time I was going to see this home's backyard, unless I purchased a subscription to *Better Homes and Gardens*.

Chapter 21
A Brave New World

We waited in mostly silence until the brothers came out, accompanied by their father. He looked absolutely stunned, and his face, though stoic, was betrayed by worried eyes. He took us all in and then rushed to his daughter, hugging her tightly. Kissing her on the head, he let out a quick sniffle and weep. When he looked up, his eyes were red and tired.

"We're going to figure this out. The police are coming. None of you will be in trouble. I will personally speak with each of your parents and take care of what, if any, legal issues may arise." With that, he looked for us to acknowledge our understanding. We all nodded and he continued, "I'll call your parents one at a time and tell them to come here so I can speak with them face to face." Mr. Chandler slowly made eye contact with each and every one of us to gauge our current condition and once he was satisfied with what he saw, he went inside to make his calls. Everyone's parents came sooner than later, as did the police. Statements were given and tears were shed, as curses were cursed.

My mother cried hysterically for what seemed like an hour, before my father offered to kick my ass. "Walter! You ever touch him again and I'll cut your dick off while you're asleep!" which in hindsight wasn't the smartest thing to say in front of seven cops, but the point was made, and in the heat of the moment, the plain as day threat was quickly lost in the unfolding events. Gwen's father seemed to take most of it in stride, even when Mr. Culver showed up tanked and tried to take a swing at Gwen's middle brother, Steven, for no apparent reason. That too was brushed under the rug quickly and without a formal complaint.

The day dragged on for what seemed like an eternity, until Mr. Chandler said to the Sergeant, "If this goes any longer, I'll have to order lunch for our guests."

The Sergeant responded quickly and curtly, "Sorry Mr. Chandler, we're wrapping it now. I'll contact you with any further questions."

"Thank you Sergeant O'Hara, I'll make sure to mention your professionalism to Senator Moynihan and the Commissioner at next weekend's outing."

"Much appreciated as always, Mr. Chandler. Boys? We ready?" The officers all looked up and nodded. Minutes later the police were gone and everyone was walking to their cars. As we opened the door to our gold Aspen station wagon, Mr. Chandler came jogging up.

"Patty, I'm so, so, sorry about this."

"That's OK, Ken. My kids knew what they were getting into, or at least knew better."

"I'm mortified. I'm just..." Looking to my dad, "Walt, I know you must want to level me right now, but I just don't know what to say, other than you got good kids." Pointing to Libra, "Sounds like your daughter's foot lived up to the legend. Every goalie in the country heard his cry." Internally noting that his soccer story was being wasted on my parents' exhausted ears, he finished with a warm hand on my mother's shoulder, "I hope we can catch up at the next YMCA fundraiser and please let me know what I can do if you run into any issues."

"What's going to happen to those crazy bastards that now want to kill my kids?" my mother prodded.

"They're going to jail for a long time. I'll make sure they don't see the light of day. All three were already on double jeopardy as is, and are going up the River without a possibility for parole for years to come."

"What about this Henry kid who's friendly with your daughter? Sounds like he's a Bay boy and untouchable, like the rest of rich society," my mother's voice began to rise.

"He's in a safe place right now being evaluated. I'll speak to his parents in the morning or later today if possible, but you'll never have to worry about him. He's not a bad kid, just a dumb one."

"Let's go," my dad said with finality. We all piled in the car quickly and quietly.

"See you around, Ken," my father said as he started up the 'Gold Glove' as he so lovingly referred to it.

As we drove off, I saw Gwen looking from her bedroom window. She raised a hand and began to wave before she stopped and looked down. She couldn't say goodbye and neither could I. We never should have met in the first place, let alone fallen in love. Not a word was spoken on the quick drive home, for my parents needed to concentrate on driving without the use of forward visibility, meaning both their heads leaned out their respective windows like dogs. The silence continued once we walked inside. My parents ordered pizza that night and walked next door to speak with the Kreagans and Pelagattis about our options. I sat with my sister on the couch and watched a bad movie that we'd seen more than once.

"You miss her already. Don't lie," Libra said not waiting for an answer.

"Why would I lie to you? I started missing her when we got in the car."

"She's no good for you. She's a mess. She's rich. She's old and..."

"Please Leebs... let it go," I said softly.

"Fine. But... Fine. I'll let it go."

"You really crushed that guy's nuts," I said while remaining glued to the screen.

"I did."

"You think he'll go all the way now and become a woman?" I asked in all seriousness.

"I hope so," Libra said while trying to hide a huge smile.

"I'm sorry that Mom always treats me better than you."

Libra did not respond to my apology for what seemed like an eternity.

"It's not your fault you're so cute. Older women just can't get enough of you."

"You think Mom and Dad will forgive me for what happened?"

"You? Yes. Me? No," Libra surmised.

"You? What's there to forgive? You did what you had to do."

"As did you Little Brother."

"So we're good?"

"I think so."

"What about the rest of them? Sean, Jim, Roy and so forth..."

"I could give a shit what happens in their houses right about now."

"Leebs..."

"To answer your question, all's good in the neighborhood."

And with that, we watched the remainder of the terrible movie and fell asleep on the couch before my parents got back.

The next day it was business as usual and school started up a couple of weeks later. Libra went to her school, and I went to mine. I didn't bother bragging about what had transpired over summer recess, for none of my friends would ever believe the tale to be remotely true. Truth be told, I didn't care much to talk about what I did with the kids in my grade, for on returning, I felt older and wiser than my contemporaries, and somewhat disinterested in what seemed to matter to the average fifth grader.

I had lived, lied, loved, warred and sacrificed more than most adults could ever hope to. I had held true to my beliefs with steadfast resolve, spied deep behind enemy lines, ran from the cops, and broke the heart of a teen model and future runner up to Miss New York. I was a man trapped in a kid's body with the soul of an ancient shaolin Kung Fu master.

Oddly enough, school was surprisingly difficult for such a worldly, deep-thinking Renaissance man such as I, for every time the teacher droned on about a topic that bored me, and much of what was said, did, I thought of one thing—my first and only love, Gwendoline Merinda Chandler.

On the odd occurrence that I wasn't thinking of Gwen, I thought of my comrades in arms, for the Alien Club was more than a club, it was an accidental brotherhood. We had come together in Jim's garage attic to better understand ourselves and our environment. We were in essence aliens, and Wilder's was as much a Martian landscape as any planet in the Universe. With our spacecraft crashed, we feared sending a distress call to the mothership, and out of pure desperation, we banded together and faced our fears as one. In doing so, we forged a friendship that would transcend our future social-economic statuses, religious, and political beliefs, as well as the distance and time that would one day separate us all. And though I would go on to join various clubs later in life, I never again wielded a club in violence.

I will always be an alien, until I return to Heaven...

Thank you for reading my book!

I put my heart and soul in spinning the tale and would love nothing more than to write something worth your time in the near future.

PS
This is the section of the book where I'm to tell you more about myself, but to be frank, I'm a half finished, scratch & sniff book with more questions than answers.
Hopefully by the next book I'll have something worth writing about.
I will say this; I'm finally doing something I love for a living and I'm done living with regrets.

Made in the USA
San Bernardino, CA
24 February 2016